AROHA AND THE BILLIONAIRE BOSS

by

SERENITY WOODS

Copyright © 2024 Serenity Woods

All Rights Reserved

This book is a work of fiction. The names, characters, places, and incidents are products of the writer's imagination or have been used fictitiously. Any resemblance to persons, living or dead, actual events, locales or organizations is coincidental.

ISBN: 9798883504388

CONTENTS

Author's note on pronunciation 1
Chapter One 2
Chapter Two 12
Chapter Three 25
Chapter Four 33
Chapter Five 39
Chapter Six 48
Chapter Seven 57
Chapter Eight 67
Chapter Nine 77
Chapter Ten 89
Chapter Eleven 97
Chapter Twelve 106
Chapter Thirteen 116
Chapter Fourteen 125
Chapter Fifteen 134
Chapter Sixteen 144
Chapter Seventeen 153
Chapter Eighteen 163
Chapter Nineteen 173
Chapter Twenty 181
Chapter Twenty-One 189
Chapter Twenty-Two 198
Chapter Twenty-Three 203
Chapter Twenty-Four 216
Chapter Twenty-Five 224
Chapter Twenty-Six 237
Chapter Twenty-Seven 248
Chapter Twenty-Eight 258
Chapter Twenty-Nine 269
Chapter Thirty 281
Chapter Thirty-One 290
Chapter Thirty-Two 299
Chapter Thirty-Three 309
Chapter Thirty-Four 318
Chapter Thirty-Five 326

SERENITY WOODS

Chapter Thirty-Six	336
Chapter Thirty-Seven	345
Newsletter	353
About the Author	354

Author's note on pronunciation

In Māori, each syllable is given the same amount of emphasis. So Aroha is pronounced Ah-roh-ha (not like the Hawaiian Ah-LOH-ha!) Also, the R in her name is a consonant that doesn't exist in English. It's softly rolled, a bit like a soft D. If you'd like to learn how to say it, you can watch my good friend Maea (whose name rhymes with fire!) say it in a video on my Facebook page. She demonstrates how to say "I love you so much," - "Ka nui taku aroha ki a koe," and she begins with the word "Aroha", which means love.

Chapter One

Aroha

"All right," I say to my best friend, Gaby, "who are you trying to fix me up with this time?"

It's the twenty-first of December, and I'm on my lunch break, talking on the phone as I walk back through the streets of Christchurch to the beauty salon where I work. Gaby has just invited me to a festive trivia evening at a bar tonight. It sounds great—except I know she has an ulterior motive.

She protests, "Not at all, I swear. It's just that the trivia teams are in groups of ten, and we need one more to make up the numbers."

"Yeah, right." I know her better than that.

We met at high school and became firm friends, despite having vastly different backgrounds. My family is very normal—a Pākehā or white mum, a Māori dad, two younger siblings, and a huge extended family, none of whom has a spare dollar left at the end of the month.

Gaby's mum is a famous actor, and Gaby is super rich, as is her husband, Tyson. She's told me it's his company's do tonight, so the other people in the team are likely to be the four friends with whom he runs the firm. They're all wealthy and intimidating, even though she insists they're perfectly normal.

So which one is she planning to fix me up with? Two of them have partners. "Surely you're not hoping I'll get off with Alex?" Her brother is nice enough, but he's a little laconic for my tastes. I do like a smooth-talking man.

"No," she says, "he's invited the girl he's had his eye on for ages."

"She's got a Christmassy name, hasn't she? Holly? Ivy?"

"Yeah, Mistletoe. He calls her Missie. Anyway, she's coming."

"So it's Henry, then?" I name the other single man. He was married, but he separated from his wife last year. It's not the first time she's tried to bring us together. "I've already told you, he's a lovely guy, but he's not my type."

"He's tall, dark, handsome, and loaded," she says. "What's not to like?" Her voice turns sly. "Or is it that you're more interested in someone else…?"

My lips curve up. "No…"

She's talking about James Rutherford, and the annoying thing is that she's right, I do like him. I made the mistake of telling her after a few glasses of wine at her hen party. The first time I saw James years ago, I thought he was the most gorgeous guy I'd ever seen in real life, and I've had a crush on him ever since.

"I don't blame you," she says. "He is rather tasty. He's related to Ernest Rutherford, you know, the father of nuclear physics. Apparently, he's very generously endowed…"

"Ernest or James?"

She laughs. "James. I don't know about Ernest."

"Who told you that?"

"Cassie let it slip," she says, referring to his current girlfriend. "A few weeks ago, when she got drunk, she said his dick's so big his pants have a zip code."

I giggle. "Will she be there tonight?"

"Yeah," Gaby says. "But that relationship definitely has a 'best before' date on it."

It's not the first time she's said it, but I don't understand why Cassie would ditch a guy who's gorgeous, wealthy, and has a huge… appendage? And even if she did, a single James would be one of the most eligible bachelors in Christchurch, if not the whole of New Zealand. I don't know him well, but I know enough to understand he'd never be interested in me.

We've met socially a few times through Gaby and Tyson, but we lead very different lives. Before Cassie, he had a string of rich, beautiful girlfriends, the socialite types who wear designer clothes, drive Mercedes or BMWs, and have thousands of followers on Instagram. I'd never be able to compete with my charity shop clothes, my battered old Honda, and my twenty-four Insta followers.

"I don't need a boyfriend," I tell her.

"Aw, Aroha, come on. I can't remember the last time you went on a date. Please come out."

"You don't need me," I tell her. "I'm terrible at quizzes, you know that. My general knowledge is appalling."

"Oh rubbish, you're smart as."

"Gaby, the guys are all geniuses, and you're a teacher. I pull hairs out of people's legs for a living."

That makes her laugh. "You'll get back into childcare soon," she promises. "You're wasted in that beauty salon."

I sigh. I don't mind working in the salon, but I miss being with children.

"Come on," she says, "forget the guys. There'll be mulled wine, mince pies, and dancing after the quiz. It'll be fun!"

"Yeah, all right," I reply, because it does sound like fun, and I definitely need a bit more of that in my life.

"Six-thirty-ish for seven at The Pioneer," she says. "I'll see you then."

"Yeah, see ya." I end the call and pocket my phone. I'm only making up the numbers, but it should be a good laugh.

I arrive back at Radiance Salon and go inside. It's a small beauty spa on the outskirts of Christchurch. Although I like that it's only a seven-minute drive from my house, it's a bit out of the way and too isolated for walk-in traffic. I'm sure it was cutting edge when it first opened, but the rooms could do with a spruce up and some new equipment. It's often quiet in the afternoons, and I get a little bored when there's not much to do. But I set myself to sweeping the tiles and tidying the bottles of nail polish, glad to have a job, even if it's not the one of my dreams.

*

The spa is open until seven p.m., and sometimes I work late, but today I finish at five-thirty, and I head home to the house I share with three other girls. When I was first looking for my own place, my limited funds meant I could only afford a room in one of the less attractive suburbs. Everywhere I viewed was either the size of a postage stamp, had damp or mold or both, was located in a bad area, or all of them combined.

Vernham Crescent was a pleasant surprise—it's far from one of the most affluent parts of Christchurch, but I liked the way the road encircled the park with its children's playground and dog-walking area, and it seemed like a quiet, suburban neighborhood. The house and garden were well-tended, the room was clean and a decent size, and the other girls were friendly enough, so I was quick to snap it up.

I'm the first home, so I make myself some cheese on toast and take it into my room, having bites while I extract items of clothing out of the wardrobe and hold them up in front of the mirror. What should I wear? The guys have usually worn suits whenever I've seen them, but the trivia night is in a bar, so it's going to be super casual, right? Equally, I want to look good. Capri pants, then—my navy ones are old but they show off my bum, which I consider is my best asset. I settle on my raspberry-colored top that's both Christmassy and flattering to my light-brown skin.

I have a quick shower, put on my makeup, and I'm just doing my hair when my phone rings. I look at the screen, not surprised to see it's my mum, as she calls me most days.

"Hey, *Māmā*," I sing à la Frank Ocean, as I put the phone on speaker and continue to play with my hair, trying to decide whether to wear it up or down. "What's up? How's the Christmas cake coming along?" She's been feeding it brandy for the past few weeks. It's going to be so alcoholic that one slice will be guaranteed to put you over the limit.

"Aroha," she says, and something in her voice makes me put down my brush.

"What is it?" I ask, my heart instantly racing.

"Dad's just come home. He said... he said the plant's closing. He's been let go."

Despite the warm evening sunshine gold-plating the bed, cold filters through me. Dad has been a process worker at South Island Meats, a beef and lamb processing plant, for fifteen years. I love my father with all my heart, but he's unskilled, fifty-two years old, overweight, and not in the best of health. The likelihood of him finding another job is not good.

Finally, I find my voice. "You're kidding me? Four days before Christmas?"

"I'm sorry," Mum says, and she bursts into tears.

She's apologizing because she knows how badly this is going to impact me. Even now, she's thinking about everyone else. My heart goes out to her. She's had a hard life, and it doesn't look as if it's going to get any easier in the foreseeable future.

My brother, Rua, has autism with high support needs, so she has to look after him twenty-four-seven. She sometimes works as a cleaner in the evenings once Dad's home, but that only pays minimum wage. I also have a younger sister who's still at school— she helps out where she can with part-time jobs, but it's never enough.

I've contributed to the household bills ever since I gave Mum half of my babysitting money as a teen. I still transfer a third of what I earn into her account every fortnight after I get paid. But even though this room is cheap, after taking out the rest of my household bills, food, and petrol, it leaves me with a minuscule amount.

I lean my forehead on the window. Even if I gave her everything I have left over, it wouldn't be enough to pay their rent and bills. If Dad can't get a job I'm going to have to move back home. All of my earnings, together with their benefits, might just be enough to keep us all afloat.

I'm twenty-five, and it's the last thing I want to do. I like my independence, and it would be embarrassing to admit I live at home. But that's the last of my worries. Family comes first, and I'll always do anything I can to help.

"Try not to worry," I say. "We'll sort it out, one way or another. How about I come and see you tomorrow, and we'll all have a chat about it?"

"You're a good girl," Mum whispers. "I don't deserve you."

"You deserve a lot more than me, but unfortunately life is rarely fair." I sigh. "I'm sorry, I'd better go. I'm supposed to be going out tonight."

"Oh?" She brightens. "Anywhere nice?"

"Gaby invited me to a quiz night at the bar with Tyson and his friends. I wasn't keen on going in the first place, and I really don't feel like it now."

"Oh, Aroha, please go. You don't get out enough as it is. Don't let it spoil your evening."

I don't point out that it already has, or that I can't afford to spend valuable dollars on luxuries like alcohol. Instead, I say, "Okay. I'll tell you how it went tomorrow. *Ka kite anō.*" It means see you later.

"I love you, sweetheart," she says.

"Love you too, *Māmā.*" I end the call.

I sit on the edge of the bed, thinking about the people who are going to be at the bar tonight. I feel an ugly twist of envy. Gaby has always had money, even when we were at school. Tyson and the guys he works with are all loaded. James is, I think, possibly the wealthiest of them all, because his father is some kind of financial whiz—I'm pretty sure Gaby dropped the word billionaire into the conversation at some point. I can't even conceive of being that rich.

It's impossible not to wish for more than I have. I'd like a job I enjoy, in a pleasant working environment, where I wake up excited to go to work every day. I'd like my own place, a whole house or apartment to myself, I don't care how small, where I don't have to fight with others for the bathroom, label my food, or follow a duty roster for chores; where I can walk around naked if I want, and where everything is always exactly where I left it. And despite my protestations to Gaby, I wish I had a partner, too. A boyfriend who was crazy about me, who doted on me. Who put me before everything else in his life. And if he was great in the bedroom, well, that would be a bonus.

But, right now, more than anything else, I'd like not to have to worry about where the next dollar is coming from.

Imagine going into the supermarket and not having to mentally add up what you put in your trolley to make sure you don't go over your budget. Choosing a bottle of wine, or a new iron, or a kettle, without having to pick the cheapest. Let alone shopping in a boutique, Pretty Woman style, and buying whatever clothing you liked, or going into a jeweler and choosing a ring without asking the price first.

I don't resent people who've worked hard to earn their fortune, but it's so unfair that some are born into money and have never faced hardship. They've never had to return items in the supermarket because they don't have enough money to pay for everything, or lived on noodles for a week because they don't get paid until the end of the month. They've not had to watch their mother cry because she can't afford to buy her kids Christmas presents. And they've never felt the despair that comes with being poor, or the utter despondency of being in debt, and knowing you'll never, ever earn enough to claw your way out of the hole.

Gaby would want me to tell her what's happened, but I won't. She knows I'm not rich, but she has no idea, I think, just how little money I have. I couldn't bear her pity—I have some pride, and I've always been determined to cope on my own.

Right now, I want to curl up into a ball on my bed, pull my duvet over my head, and cry myself to sleep. But I've never given into self-pity yet, and I don't intend to start now. I count my blessings: I'm in good health, I have a job, a roof over my head, food in my belly, and a loving family. It's a lot more than many people have. I'm not going to succumb to envy. I'm going to get up, finish my hair, get dressed, go out, and have a great evening, because although these guys are rich, they're all kind, pleasant people. I'm going to try to forget about my woes tonight. And then tomorrow I'll sit down with a piece of paper and a pencil, and I'll have a think about what I can do going forward.

I can't fool myself completely—my fear is going to push through my bravado like a hernia throughout the evening, but I'll have to do my best to deal with it when it happens.

I settle on wearing my hair up and add a piece of silver tinsel fixed with a bobby pin to the center of the twist. It's nearly six-fifteen now, so I slip on my white mules with a small heel and grab my purse, phone, and keys. An Uber is a luxury I rarely indulge in, but screw it—it's too far to walk, and I'm going to have a drink tonight. I've scrimped and scraped all year, and after buying all the members of my family a small Christmas present, I have forty dollars left. I was going to save up for something nice to cheer up my bedroom, but if I'm not going to be able to stay here anymore, it doesn't matter anyway.

I call for an Uber, and in less than five minutes I'm heading toward the city center.

When I arrive, I stand outside the bar for a moment, doubt making my stomach churn. I should be able to afford two glasses of wine for myself. But will I be expected to pay for a round for everyone? I hadn't thought of that.

"Aroha!"

I turn, and my heart bangs on my ribs like a kettle drum at the sight of James Rutherford walking toward me with a smile. Oh wow. He's a tall guy, maybe six two, slender and muscular rather than big like his colleague, Henry, and damn does he look good today. The last few times I've seen him he's been in a suit, but today he's wearing tight black jeans, a dark-gray shirt hanging over the top with the sleeves rolled up a couple of times, and a pair of well-worn black Converses. His hair is fashionably cut and styled, and his eyes are obscured by a pair of aviator sunglasses that I'm sure are Cartier or Gucci or some other expensive brand rather than from the two-dollar shop, like mine are. As he walks up to me, though, he lifts them up onto his hair, revealing his attractive eyes. They're an unusual turquoise color, slightly more blue than green, fringed with dark lashes. His cheek and jaw bear a slight shadow—God knows how he keeps it at the exact length for designer stubble. Mmm. He's gorgeous.

"I didn't know you were coming," he says, and he leans forward and kisses my left cheek, then my right. His cologne infiltrates my senses, spicy and smoky. He's what my dad would call a pretty boy, but to me he oozes such masculinity that it makes my knees wobble.

"Gaby asked me at the last minute." I'm conscious that I sound breathless. I clear my throat. "Is Cassie coming?"

"Uh…" He glances over his shoulder. His gaze returns to mine, hardening. "We had an argument, and she's sulking. She's on the phone to a friend."

"Listing all your faults?" I tease.

His lips twist. "Probably. There are enough of them. Shall we go in?"

I hesitate, still debating whether I'm making the right decision.

"Everything all right?" he asks.

It's going to be embarrassing to ask him, but it'll be even more mortifying if I need to pay for a round and have to admit to everyone that I can't afford it.

"Um… I was just wondering, are we paying for our own drinks tonight? Only… um…" I tuck a strand of hair behind my ear. "It's nearly Christmas, and money's a little tight, and I'm not sure I can afford to pay for a round for everyone…" My face burns.

His eyebrows rise, as if he hadn't considered that anyone wouldn't be able to afford one round of drinks, but he wipes the look away quickly, well-brought up enough to know not to comment on it. "I've already paid for the whole evening," he says, "including food and drinks. You don't have to pay for anything."

"That's very generous!"

"Well, it wasn't me per se," he clarifies, "it's entertainment expenditure, tax deductible. So you can eat as many mince pies as you want." His lips quirk up. It's a polite way of saying I can drink as much as I like.

"Thank you. I could do with a glass of wine tonight," I add with feeling.

"Bad day?"

"You could say that."

He gives me an appraising look as if he's wondering whether to ask what's happened, but we don't know each other well enough, and he just says, "Shall we go in, then? Get stuck into the mulled wine?"

"Don't you want to wait for Cassie?"

He looks away, along the road, his smile fading. "I'm not sure if she's coming."

"Aw," I say.

His eyes are distant, and he looks thoughtful. I wonder what they argued about. It's a shame, so near Christmas, but then I know the pressure of the festive season puts added tension on relationships.

"Is she the one?" I ask, before I can vet the words.

His gaze comes back to me. "How does one know?" he replies, with some amusement.

"Does she make you happy?"

He opens his mouth to reply, then hesitates and closes it. His puzzled eyes meet mine, and our gazes lock. Oh man... I adore this guy, and I know my feelings must show in my eyes, but I can't tear them away. My pulse speeds up, and for a long moment I can't catch my breath.

"Hello."

The woman's voice comes from beside me, and I glance over to see Cassie standing there. Her gaze isn't friendly. She saw us staring at each other.

"Hey, Cassie. Nice to see you." I flash her a smile, conscious of the temperature dropping by ten degrees. "I'm going in to find Gaby." I slip away before either of them can say anything and go into the bar.

Jesus. That was a close escape.

The place is hot and heaving. Christmas music mingles with laughter and voices. Fairy lights flicker above the wooden bar and on the huge tree in the corner. The whole place smells of cinnamon, orange, wine, and the spicy scent of mince pies.

I spot Gaby standing with some of the others, and I push through the crowd to stand beside her. "Hey, you!"

She turns, her face lights up, and then she throws her arms around me. We've been best friends since we started high school, and she met her husband, Tyson, only a few years after that. I watched her fall in love, and then saw her heart break when Tyson ended up in a wheelchair after a car accident. I have to admit I assumed she'd break up with him after that, but she stuck by him, and after several years of physio, and thanks in no small part to the mobility aids his friends invented for him, Tyson can now walk, albeit a little stiffly.

"I'm so glad you came," she says. "Merry Christmas."

"Merry Christmas." I think briefly about my parents, and despair flutters in my stomach. But I ignore it, and I turn to say hi to the others, determined to enjoy myself tonight.

Chapter Two

James

"I wasn't sure if you were going to come," I say to Cassie.

She doesn't reply, and as we study each other, I'm conscious of the yawning chasm that's been growing between us.

I very rarely lose my temper, and even when I am pushed beyond my limits, it switches off in seconds like a boiling kettle. Cassie's like one of the geysers in Rotorua, constantly running at a high temperature, always ready to blow. I never know if she's about to take offense at some throwaway comment, and she erupts regularly, sending scalding water onto me.

I'm not angry with her anymore. I'm just tired of the argument. But fury still brims in her eyes.

For a moment, I think she's going to accuse me of having an affair with Aroha—she always assumes I'm sleeping with every woman I meet. But instead, she says, "You're not going to apologize?"

"No, because I don't have anything to apologize for."

"You never admit it when you're wrong," she snaps.

"Cass, I haven't lied to you at any point. I told you when we first started dating that I don't want kids. It's not my fault you assumed you could change me."

"All guys say that when they're young," she replies. "Everyone goes on to have children eventually."

"Not me."

"Not even if it's what I want?" She makes her voice a whisper, and her eyes are full of longing.

I know her well enough to understand she's trying to guilt me, but I can also see the hurt and confusion behind her fury. She thinks the reason I don't want the whole marriage and two-point-four kids thing is because I don't love her enough. It's not, although at that moment,

I realize I don't. But she's trying to use emotional blackmail to force me to change my mind, because she doesn't want to lose the prospect of marrying someone wealthy.

I feel a stab of guilt at the harshness of that. She does have feelings for me, I'm sure of it. But I know friends who've had similar problems with women who've only been after their money, and once that worm has wiggled its way into your brain, it's impossible to get it out again.

Cassie has many good points—she's beautiful and smart, and she's popular in real life and online—she works for a famous Kiwi fashion house, and she's well known in the industry, with over a hundred thousand followers on Insta. But she's also manipulative, spoiled, and spiteful. She's like a hedgehog, covered in prickles, and I'm tired of being constantly stabbed.

"Are you coming in or not?" I snap, and I turn and walk into the bar. She follows, and I don't know whether to be relieved or exasperated.

We go over to where the others are ordering drinks and say our hellos. Not wanting to sour the evening, I attempt to hold Cassie's hand, but she pulls hers away.

Alex spots it, and his eyes meet mine. "Drink?" he asks.

"God, yes."

His lips curve up a little. "Cassie, Chardonnay?"

"Please."

I join him at the bar. "A glass of Chardonnay, and a double of the Glenlivet, please," he asks the bartender, "with ice."

"Missie not here yet?" I ask him.

He shakes his head.

"She still coming?"

He hesitates, then gives a slight shrug. "Time will tell." A very Alex answer.

The bartender slides over the wine, and Alex takes it to Cassie, then comes back. "Everything all right?" he asks me.

"We had an argument on the way here."

"What have you done?"

I give a short laugh and accept the glass as the bartender pushes it over to me. "I told her I didn't want kids."

"Ah."

"Yeah."

"Do you not want them? Or do you not want them with her?"

I meet his gaze. I can't remember the last time we talked about something intimate like this. I've known Alex since I was eighteen, and he's a good friend, but we're guys, and guys don't talk about stuff. It's a well-known rule.

"A little from column A, a little from column B," I reply.

His lips curve up. The glib reply tells him I don't want to talk about it.

"Did you know that phrase came from Americanized Chinese restaurant menus?" he says. "Diners picked options from two groups, A and B."

"I thought it was from The Simpsons."

He laughs. "Yeah, that as well."

We walk back to the others, and we've just reached them when I spot Mistletoe Macbeth walking through the door. "Target spotted, eleven o'clock," I tell him.

"Eleven o'clock from where you're facing, or where I'm facing?" His joke trails off as he turns and sees her. She's wearing a white crossover dress with big red flowers that accentuates her hourglass figure. Alex stares at her, his eyes widening. He inhales deeply, puffs out his cheeks, then blows out the breath, which morphs into a laugh as he turns back and sees us all watching him.

Frowning a little, she walks up and says, "Hello."

"Hey." He kisses her cheek. I know him well enough to see the look of relief that passes quickly over his face. He doesn't show emotion very often. I think he's really keen on this girl. "Glad you came," he says. "Can I get you a drink?"

"Um, I'll have a glass of Sav, please."

He nods and walks over to the bar.

Juliette grins at her. "Hello."

Missie gives her a curious look. "What did Alex say when I walked up that made you all laugh?"

"He didn't say anything. This is what he did when he saw you." She copies what he did, widening her eyes in the same way.

Missie jaw drops in alarm. "Oh no. I'm showing too much boob!"

"No, sweetheart, I think you're showing exactly the right amount," Juliette says as we all chuckle. "Come on, let me introduce you to everyone. You know James, and this is his girlfriend, Cassie."

"Hey, James, and hello, Cassie, nice to meet you." Missie holds out her hand and gives her characteristic sunshine smile.

Cassie shakes her hand, then knocks back what's left in her glass. Jesus, she's drunk the whole lot in a few mouthfuls. "James," she says, holding the glass out.

"Alex is at the bar," I say, irritated by her rude manner and the fact that she's obviously decided to get drunk. She doesn't hold her alcohol well, and I'm not in the mood to be cleaning up behind her.

She meets my gaze, then saunters off to Alex.

"You two all right?" Juliette asks with concern.

"Nope." Already regretting coming, I huff a sigh and wave a hand, and she moves on.

Juliette introduces Missie to her partner, Cam, and to Gaby and Tyson. They chat for a bit, but my attention is drawn by Cassie, who has made her way back to my side. I know that look; she's going to sulk for the rest of the evening. My heart sinks, while my anger rises. I'm so tired of this.

The bar is busy, and a man knocks into me as he passes with a tray of drinks, causing me to take a step to the side. I bump shoulders with someone and discover it's Aroha. She stumbles, and I slide my free hand under her elbow to help her regain her balance.

"Sorry," I murmur.

"If you're trying to make me fall over, just wait until I've had a few more drinks," she jokes. She looks up at me, and for a moment, our gazes lock again the way they did outside, and neither of us can look away.

She's beautiful in a different way from Cassie, who's tall, busty, and blonde. Aroha is maybe five foot six at the most, and slender, with small, high breasts and slim hips. Her skin is an attractive light brown, and her hair is dark brown, while her eyes are hazel. She has a few freckles across her nose. I know she's a beautician, and her makeup is immaculate, her eyelids covered with a pretty bronze shimmer. Her lips are the same color as her raspberry top, just a few shades lighter, and she moistens them with the tip of her tongue as she sees me looking at them.

I've known her for five or six years, and the first time I met her, I thought how gorgeous she was. But she was dating someone else, and by the time I heard she was single, I was seeing someone. The timing just hasn't worked. But I like her, and I'm pretty sure she likes me, too.

Conscious that I'm still holding her arm, I say, "Sorry," again, lower my hand, and drag my gaze away from hers. I've been called a womanizer more than once in the past, but I would never cheat on a girl I was with. Whatever Cassie and I are going through, she deserves more than that.

Alex is leading the way over to our table, and the rest of us follow, carrying our drinks. Two benches face each other across a rectangular table. He slides along the bench to the end, and Missie sits next to him, followed by Juliette, with Cam squeezing on the end. Cassie slides across on the other side and I follow.

"After you," Henry says, and Aroha hesitates, then sits next to me. Henry lowers himself down, but the dude is six-three and built like a brick khazi, and Aroha has to squeeze up against me to avoid being crushed.

"I feel like the burger in a Quarter Pounder," she says as Henry and I sandwich her between us.

"I have been complimented on my buns," I reply, and she giggles.

Next to me, Cassie huffs a sigh. I turn slightly toward her and put my arm along the seat behind her. It rests on her hair, and she makes an annoyed sound in the back of her throat as she tugs it free.

"Sorry," I say, removing my arm, but she just throws me a glare, then takes out her phone.

Gaby and Tyson take the two chairs at the end of the table, and the trivia team is ready.

While the MC explains how the quiz is going to work, Alex murmurs quietly in Missie's ear. She scolds him, and he says, "James will remember all the rules. He always tells everyone what to do anyway."

"Someone has to," I say. "You lot are useless."

"You don't have to be so rude about it," Cassie replies sharply.

Her pissy attitude is really starting to annoy me, but I refuse to let it show. "I wasn't talking about you," I say as mildly as I can. "I was referring to these losers." I gesture at the rest of them.

She just lowers her gaze back to her phone, ignoring me. I grit my teeth. I can see that the others are embarrassed by our exchange, and I don't blame them. There's nothing worse than a couple bickering in front of people. At this rate, we're going to recreate the episode from *The Office* where Michael and Jan invite Pam and Jim to dinner.

A waiter arrives with a large bowl of mulled wine and a tray of small glasses, and Juliette and Missie ladle the wine into the glasses and pass them around. Cassie refuses, but I accept one, desperate to numb the irritation I'm feeling. It's incredibly sweet. The smell of the red wine with orange, cloves, cinnamon, and raisins immediately transports me back to Christmases when I was a teen, which doesn't help the uneasy feeling in my stomach.

"What do you think?" I ask Aroha as she puts down her glass after taking a sip.

"It's not really my thing," she murmurs, obviously not wanting to be rude.

"Nor mine." I raise a hand, attracting the gaze of the waiter, and he comes over. "Can I have a double Glenlivet on ice, please, and…" I look at Aroha. "Do you drink whisky?"

"Um… yes…"

"Make that two, please." I glance at Cassie. "Do you want anything else?" She shakes her head, not looking up from her phone, so I nod at the waiter, and he goes off to order.

"Thank you," Aroha says. "What a treat."

"No worries." There's no time to talk further because the MC has started.

It's a standard trivia quiz, with questions divided up into categories, and we progress through Geography, History, Sports, Music, and Food. The people I work with are good company, and as the alcohol flows and everyone relaxes, we bicker good-naturedly about the answers with much laughter. Despite Aroha's protestation that she's terrible at trivia, she throws herself into it, having a go and not caring if she misses the mark, and it's a lot of fun.

Cassie, however, refuses to join in at all. The others cast her glances occasionally, and Alex even tries to draw her in by asking her if she knows the answer to some of the questions, but she just says no and returns her gaze to her phone.

I'm annoyed and embarrassed, and when the MC announces a ten-minute break, I murmur to her, "Come on Cass, please don't sulk."

"Fuck off," she says, loud enough for everyone to hear. She picks up her purse and phone and says, "I want to get up, please."

"Cass…"

"Now," she snaps.

Henry stands, Aroha scoots along, and I follow. Cassie gets to her feet, then, without saying anything to the others, heads for the exit.

I stand with my hands on my hips for a moment, my stomach churning. More than anything, I want to sit back at the table, drink my whisky, and just be with my friends, without this constant cloud of misery hanging over my head.

But Cassie is my girlfriend, and I need to sort this, so I follow her out.

I catch up with her just as she goes through the door, and I slide a hand under her arm and pull her to one side. She snatches her arm away, turning to glare at me.

"Where are you going?" I ask crisply.

"Home." Her bottom lip trembles. "My home."

She's referring to the fact that I haven't yet asked her to move in with me. My jaw tightens. She has a point. We've been dating since March, so nearly nine months. She often stays over at my apartment in the city, and my wardrobe and bathroom are scattered with her things. But I haven't taken her to my house in West Melton. It's my space, and I know if I ask her there, it will involve a commitment I'm not prepared to make.

Unbidden, I think of Aroha's words, *Does she make you happy?*

It's such a simple concept, but I haven't thought about it like that before.

It's a stab in my gut, but the answer is no. I stayed with her to pacify my father, who has insisted that he'll write me out of his will if I don't settle down soon. I don't need the money for myself—Dad gave me a significant sum when I graduated from university, and I've more than doubled it with careful investments—but I know so many charities and causes that could benefit from the vast fortune. Still, it's not worth committing myself to an unhappy marriage for.

"Cass," I say with a heavy heart, "I think we need to accept that we're done."

Her eyes widen, and her jaw drops. "You're breaking up with me? Four days before Christmas?"

I'd forgotten the time of year. "What's the point in dragging it out until the New Year?" I ask, trying not to wince.

"Is it because of her?" She jabs her head toward the bar.

I blink. "Who?"

"Aroha!"

"Jesus. Of course not."

"You like her though."

"She's a friend. There's nothing between us." It's the truth, I tell myself, although I feel a twinge of guilt at the thought that I do find Aroha attractive.

"I thought you loved me." Her whisper ends with a hiccup.

"I don't," I say honestly. "Or not enough, anyway. And you don't love me either."

"I do."

"No, you don't." I open my mouth to accuse her of being disappointed because she's going to lose my money, but I close it again. I don't want this to turn nasty. "You know I'm right," I say more gently. "You don't trust me. We argue all the time. We're just making each other miserable. You deserve better than me."

She meets my eyes. Resignation settles over her like a mist, which tells me that deep down, she agrees with me.

"I do deserve better than you," she says eventually.

"I know."

"You're an arsehole."

"I know."

She glares at me. "Is there someone else?"

I shake my head, irritated. "There never was."

"You never cheated on me?"

"No."

She looks surprised. Jesus, she really thought I had. She's accused me often enough. Resentment burns inside me, killing off the remainder of any feelings I had for her. I would never cheat on a woman. If she didn't believe that, she never really knew me at all.

Her eyes shine with unshed tears. She knows how angry that's made me. "So this is it?"

"You deserve someone who'll give you everything you want. Marriage, kids. You can't make me into that person. It doesn't work like that."

She looks at the cars passing by. Then, without saying anything else, she turns and walks away.

I watch her until she turns the corner, then sigh. It's Longest Day, and the sun won't set until around nine, but it's low on the horizon, bathing the city in a warm orange glow. Christmas lights are springing to life in all the restaurants and bars, while people spill out onto the streets like beads from a broken necklace.

I feel a wave of relief at the thought that I'm free, followed quickly by a gut-wrenching twist of sadness. Cassie was my first long-term relationship. Before her, I'd kept things short and sweet with other girls, and I'm upset that it was a mistake to try something more serious.

I'm twenty-eight, heading toward thirty, and my father wants me to settle down and get married, but I don't see it in my future. Every woman I've met wants children. They might say they don't, to please you, but ultimately it seems nature takes over, and I don't want kids. Or, rather, I don't want to be a father. No, correction, I don't want to turn into *my* father. I'd rather stay single.

It'll mean he'll change his will, but for the first time I realize I'll be free of him. I'm never going to earn his approval, and now I can stop trying.

The thought should make me happy, but I feel depressed at Cassie's departure, even if I know it was the right thing to do. It's been a shit week, actually. I've spent most of my free time with my sister, who's having a tough time, and I'm absolutely shattered. The sunlight bounces off the cars' windows, the glare making my eyes sting. What should I do? Go home? I've had too much alcohol to drive back to the house. And in the apartment, surrounded by Cassie's things, I'll just stew in my misery, and it's never fun getting drunk on your own. I grit my teeth. I don't want to feel regretful and melancholic. They're inconvenient, unpleasant emotions. Turning, I go back into the bar and head over to our table.

"Stay where you are," I tell Henry and Aroha as they prepare to get up. I climb over the back of the bench and slide into the corner beside Aroha.

"All right?" Alex asks.

"Hunky dory." I knock back the whisky in one go, then blow out a long breath. "We broke up."

"James!" Juliette exclaims. "Oh my God, I'm so sorry."

"Are you okay?" Aroha's hazel eyes study me with pity.

I nod. "It's been coming for a while." I glance around the table. "Sorry, I didn't mean to bring the mood down. Would you rather I go?"

"Absolutely not," Alex states. "Time to drown your sorrows. Consolation whisky, anyone?"

Henry, Tyson, and Aroha nod, and Alex asks the waiter for doubles of Glenlivet on the rocks all round.

I assume the unpleasantness is over, but then Cam tells Juliette that he's leaving too to see his brother, and he walks out. Furious, Juliette refuses to follow him, then, clearly miserable, accepts the rest of Henry's whisky and downs it in one.

"Well, this is turning out to be quite the evening," Tyson states. He looks at his wife. "You want a divorce now or do you want to wait until the end of the day?"

Juliette snorts and I give him the finger, which makes everyone else laugh.

I have a big mouthful of whisky and let it sear down inside me. Maybe after a lot more of these, I'll start to feel better. Or to forget, anyway.

"These things happen," Aroha murmurs to me. "Maybe tomorrow when she's calmed down, she'll decide she wants to try again."

"*I* broke up with *her*," I tell her firmly. "She didn't argue. We've been heading toward it for a while. So no, I don't think that's going to happen."

She's quiet for a moment. Then she says, "You want to borrow my hanky?"

I give a short laugh and look at her. "I'm good, thanks."

She smiles. "It's her loss."

"Maybe. She called me an arsehole. She's probably right."

She tries not to laugh, and fails. "Here's a joke for you. What does a blonde do with her arsehole in the morning?"

My lips curve up. "I don't know."

"She packs his lunch and sends him to work."

I grin. "Yeah, that's about right."

The MC announces the second half of the quiz is about to start. Aroha holds up her whisky glass. "To singlehood."

I tap mine to it. "Yeah. To singlehood." I feel a touch of sadness, but it's overwhelmed by relief. I don't have to pander to Cassie anymore. To dance around her moods, to worry why she hasn't texted or phoned, to constantly wonder what I've done wrong. It's liberating, and even though I know the sadness will come back later, as I knock back the whisky I tell myself I'm glad I ended it, and it's only going to lead to better things.

At first I assume everyone's going to feel awkward because of what's happened, but we order a couple of platters of breads, dips, and hot savory nibbles, and the atmosphere seems to improve without Cassie's glowering and Cam's barbed comments.

We answer questions on Science, Art and Literature, and Kiwiana—items and icons from New Zealand's heritage. Gradually, my frustration and resentment fades away, erased by the good company and the alcohol. I know I'm drinking a lot, but I don't care. I keep the mulled wine and whiskies coming, encouraging Aroha to finish hers each time. I can't imagine not being able to afford a single round of drinks, and she insinuated that she'd had a hard day, too, so I make sure she always has a full glass waiting.

I've met her a few times in the past, but we've never exchanged more than a few sentences. It's nice, therefore, to spend some time getting to know her. She's surprisingly funny. After a few drinks, she begins to tease me, and it's impossible not to flirt back.

Luckily, nobody notices because they're all three sheets to the wind, too. "I've got an idea," Juliette states during one of the breaks, slurring her speech just a little. "You all have to tell me a joke to cheer me up."

Everyone groans, but agrees to do it.

"Alex?" she says. "You first."

"Do you like my shirt?" he asks Missie. "It's made out of boyfriend material."

Juliette giggles. "Not bad. Missie?"

"Um… My partner asked to play doctor, so I kept him waiting outside the room for an hour."

That makes us all laugh.

"Aroha?" Juliette prompts.

"Relationships are a lot like algebra," Aroha says. "You look at your X and wonder Y."

My lips twist. "Yeah."

She elbows me. "I wasn't referring to you."

"No, it's okay. I don't mind being the butt of everyone's humor."

"Well, you did say Cassie called you an arsehole."

Everyone laughs, and I meet Aroha's eyes again, and a tingle runs down my spine at her mischievous smile. Feeling naughty, and holding her gaze, I say, "Hey, let me wipe your seat for you." I pick up a serviette and wipe my face, then grin.

"James!" she scolds as everyone whoops. "You wicked man."

"It was a joke!" I protest. I wink at her and stretch out my arm along the back of the seat. It's not around her… but she takes the hint and moves an inch closer to me. Mmm, that's nice. She's warm, and I can smell her perfume, something exotic, like jasmine on a warm summer night. She's so easy after the prickly Cassie, like aloe vera for my soul.

"Henry?" Juliette asks. "Come on, you haven't given me a joke yet."

He studies her, his lips curving up, and gradually an attractive blush blooms in her cheeks. "What's orange and sounds like a parrot?"

She blinks. "Huh?"

"A carrot."

She stares at him for a second, then dissolves into peals of laughter. "I thought you were going to tell me a rude joke," she manages to get out between giggles.

"Why?" he says, amused, his eyes warm. "I'm a gentleman."

"I know, that's what made it so funny!" Her laughter is so contagious that eventually we all start chuckling.

The bar delivers a plate of mince pies to each table, and we all take one. Aroha is just about to take a bite of hers when she suddenly sneezes, sending a shower of icing sugar in my direction.

I cough and dust it off as she looks at me with mortification and says, "Oh my God..."

"I should put you over my knee for that," I tell her, giving her an amused look, and she blushes scarlet. She likes me, I can tell. She's giving me all the signs—twirling a strand of her hair, laughing at my jokes, leaning against me...

James, I warn myself silently. We've both had a lot to drink, and I'm severely on the rebound. The last thing I should do is flirt with someone new. But she's so gorgeous, and she's staring at me with that look in her eyes. What's a guy to do?

Alex has gone off to the Gents, and when someone bangs into Gaby's chair for the umpteenth time, she makes an exasperated noise, gets up, and slips in beside Juliette. This means that when Alex returns, there's no space for him to sit.

Unperturbed, he tells Missie to stand up, climbs over the back of the seat, and slides in behind her.

She laughs. "Where am I going to—"

In answer, he pulls her onto his lap, and she squeals, but turns and puts an arm around his neck. He'd never normally do anything like that in public, so I know the Christmas spirit is affecting him too.

"Jesus, how many whiskies have you had?" I ask, amused.

He just smirks and murmurs something in Missie's ear, making her laugh.

My smile fades. They look so happy. Were Cassie and I ever that happy? I'm not sure now.

Aroha leans closer to me and murmurs, "I went into a sex shop last week."

My eyebrows shoot up. "Pardon?"

"I said to the guy behind the desk, how much is that big red vibrator? He said, 'Ma'am, the fire extinguisher isn't for sale.'" I chuckle. She smiles and says, "That's better. You looked very sad."

"Well, a vibrator joke is guaranteed to put a smile on my face."

She gives an impish grin. "Somehow, I knew it would." She winks at me.

It's only now that I'm beginning to realize how miserable I've been. I'd forgotten what fun it is to flirt with a girl, and the pleasure of having her flirt back. Nothing is going to come of this, but it lifts my heart, which is a special gift so close to Christmas, when otherwise I'd be sitting at home, stewing in gloom. I'm really glad I stayed.

Our table comes second in the quiz, which is a miracle considering how much alcohol we've imbibed, and then the dancing begins. We sit and chat for a few songs, but then Justin Bieber's *Mistletoe* starts up, and Alex says, "Everyone up." We all groan, but he says, "I want to dance and I'm not making Missie climb over everyone—up!"

Tyson leads Gaby onto the dance floor. Alex heads off with Missie. Henry and Juliette face each other, and then without saying anything, he takes her hand and leads her there.

It's just me and Aroha left. We're still sitting together on the bench, with her almost tucked under my arm.

We study each other, our lips curving up. I feel reckless and impulsive. Fuck it. I'm not hiding anything. She knows I came here with Cassie, and she saw what happened. It's Christmas, and she's alone. It's polite, right?

"Want to dance?" I ask.

"Definitely," she says, her vehemence making me laugh. She scoots along, I follow her out, and together, we head to the dance floor. When we get there, I turn her into my arms, take her right hand in my left, rest my right on her hip, and we start to move.

Chapter Three

Aroha

Ooh, I'm more than a little tipsy. I rarely drink this much, but after Mum's announcement today and the fact that the drinks were free, I threw all caution to the wind. I like whisky, and I rarely get to drink an expensive one like the Glenlivet, especially in a bar where I'm sure it's over fifteen dollars a shot, and James was ordering doubles.

Luckily, I'm not bad at holding my drink, and at the moment I just feel warm and mellow and happy. I'm dancing with a gorgeous guy, and I'm pleased that he's lost the haunted look he had when he came back into the bar. I first met Cassie at Gaby's wedding back in March, so he's been with her a while. I don't know the circumstances around why they broke up, but even though a relationship ends because it's already souring, it's still painful to go through, and I'm sure he's hurting inside.

He took my hand as we walked onto the dance floor, so he's holding me formally with his other hand on my hip. But we're only a couple of inches apart, and I can feel the heat of his body through his shirt. I can see his Adam's apple, and the hollow at the base of his throat. God, he smells good.

We don't speak for a while, but I can hear him humming along to the song. I'm not sure if, when it ends, he'll lead me back to the table. Maybe he'll even head off home. I need to make the most of the time I have with him. How often do you get to dance with a guy who's young, rich, and gorgeous? I feel like Cinderella at the ball. I mean, he's not going to give me a glass slipper or anything, and even if he did, it wouldn't fit, but for a girl with only forty dollars in her account—actually, thirty-one dollars after the Uber—it's fun to dream.

I don't know that much about him. Gaby's told me a little over the years. He's the son of an Australian investment banker, someone who's into hedge funds or asset management or something about which I know precisely zero. He's a computer engineer and also knows a lot about finance, and he runs a company with Alex, Tyson, and Henry. And he's had a lot of girlfriends. That doesn't surprise me. He's gorgeous and wealthy, a combination that's certain to make him a babe magnet.

He drives a beautiful silver Porsche 718 Spyder RS, which I know cost him three hundred and fifteen thousand dollars, because I looked it up. He wears an Omega watch. Gaby said he lives in some mansion on an estate in West Melton about half an hour from the city center that has a pool, a tennis court, and its own botanical gardens, but during the week he stays in an apartment in the city. And he's dancing with me. I'm not a gold digger, but Jesus, I'm only human. What girl wouldn't be wowed by a man like this?

I'm a little intimidated, to be honest. He's only three years older than me, but he's so far out of my league that it's almost laughable. My excitement dulls a little. He's dancing with me because he's being polite. He didn't want to leave the only single woman sitting at a table on her own.

But we have flirted since Cassie left. I remember his words, *Let me wipe your seat for you*, the glint in his eye and his mischievous smile as he brushed the serviette over his face, and the way he put his arm almost around me, encouraging me to move up against him. He finds me attractive, I know he does.

The song changes to *Last Christmas*. We didn't speak throughout the previous song, and I wonder whether he was thinking about Cassie the whole time. I glance up at him, expecting his gaze to be off in the distance, and wait for him to say thank you and move back.

Instead, I find him watching me, with no sign of letting me go. He doesn't look away as our eyes meet, but instead sings along to the lyrics, telling me that this year he's given his heart to someone special.

"You have a nice voice," I say, because I want to say something, and I can't think of anything else.

"Thank you," he murmurs, the deep, rich tone giving me the shivers.

Beside us, I can see Alex and Missie laughing, and across the floor, Juliette and Henry are talking as they turn to the music. But I feel tongue-tied, as if I'm dancing with a movie star.

Basically, I'm not used to being with guys like this. The few boyfriends I've had have been quiet and sensible, because the gorgeous, wild boys only go for the gorgeous, wild girls. I'm neither gorgeous nor wild, and I'm not reckless or impulsive. Usually, I'm organized and in control—it's no surprise that I'm a Virgo. On a journey, I'll plan the route and know where the best places are to stop. I like things color coded and in alphabetical order. I never spend more than I have, and I rarely overindulge with food or drink.

But tonight, I do feel reckless, and yes, maybe a little wild. Where has living within the rules ever gotten me? I'm twenty-five, and I haven't done anything—I haven't traveled, or taken drugs, never had a one-night stand, or done anything spontaneous. I feel as if I've lived within a cage, and for once, I want someone to unlock it and throw open the door.

The music changes to Mariah Carey's *All I Want For Christmas is You*, and he grins. "Come on. Show me what you've got."

Ooh, he can really dance. As he realizes that I'm not terrible on my feet, he picks up the pace, spinning me away from him before drawing me back into his arms. Whoa, I'm glad I'm not wearing high heels like Missie—I'd be off them in seconds. But he's careful to keep me tight against him most of the time as we move to the music. Our hips wind together, and we dance to the whole song, until it changes again to another slow one, Judy Garland's *Have Yourself a Merry Little Christmas*.

Once again, he pulls me close, smiling. "Do you want to sit down?" he asks.

"No. Um… unless you do?"

He shakes his head. Thrilled, I give into the impulse I've had since we went onto the dance floor, and I brush the short hair on the back of his nape with my thumb. In response, he flares his hand at the base of my spine and pulls me the last fraction of inch toward him, so our bodies are flush.

"You can dance," I tell him, a tad breathless.

"Well, we were hardly doing the Samba, but after the amount of whisky we've had, I'm just glad I didn't tread on your toes."

I giggle. "Not at all. You were great."

"Never give a sword to a man who can't dance. Or so Confucius says."

"I have to say you handle your weapon exceptionally well."

That makes him laugh. He has beautiful, straight white teeth and a dazzling smile, and my comment makes him look at me with renewed attention.

Mmm, things are getting interesting.

I look around, at the couples swaying to the music, the lights twinkling on the Christmas tree, and the glitter in the air that's floating down from the balloons in the net above us. Some of it's on James's hair, making it sparkle in the fairy lights.

I'm tired of being practical and dull. I'll never look like a model, or be extroverted enough to draw the eye of someone like this permanently, but right here, right now, he's dancing with me, and I know I'm not imagining the heat between us.

"It's probably the whisky talking," I tell him bravely. "But they do say dance is a vertical expression of a horizontal thought."

He smiles. Wow, his eyes are exceptional, a beautiful deep turquoise, like a tropical sea.

"Do they now?" he murmurs, his gaze sliding to my lips.

I let them curve up, then moisten them with the tip of my tongue. "They do. And I can understand why, dancing with you."

His gaze comes back to mine. Mmm, I like being this close to him. If I were to lift up a little onto my tiptoes, I'd be able to kiss his jaw. I don't, but I could. He's pressed against me all the way down. I can even feel his wallet in the pocket of his jeans. At least, I think it's his wallet.

Without meaning to, I give a short laugh, and he looks down at me. "What?"

I think about what Gaby said about him being generously endowed, and I bite my bottom lip. "Nothing."

"Come on, spill the beans."

"Just something Gaby said."

"About what?"

I shake my head.

"Aroha…" His deep voice scolds me. "Tell me what you laughed at."

I move my hips against his. "Is that your wallet in your pocket, or are you pleased to see me?"

His eyes flare, as if someone's turned up his desire like the flame of a Bunsen burner, and now it's burning white-hot.

"You want to get out of here?" he murmurs against my ear.

I nod eagerly.

"Come on, then." Keeping hold of my right hand, he leads the way across the bar.

My heart is hammering. Jesus, am I really going to do this? Some of my friends use Tinder for one-night stands, but I've never done it. I'm under no illusions, though. That's what this will be, if we go back to his place. This isn't the beginning of a beautiful friendship. It's lust, pure and simple.

He pushes the door open, and we go outside. It's cooler out here, but still warm. The street is busy, the restaurants and bars heaving with people coming and going from Christmas parties. Fairy lights are visible through most of the windows, and they also twinkle in the trees. There's magic in the air.

James leads me across the road, stopping outside a closed bank, where it's quieter. He turns to face me, and brings me up close to him.

He cups my face in his big, warm hands, and strokes my cheeks with his thumbs. "You're incredibly beautiful," he murmurs.

It's the nicest thing a man has ever said to me, and I blink a few times, unused to such an effusive compliment. "Thank you."

"Are you always so polite? Or are you on Santa's naughty list?" He gives a wicked smile.

"Me? I'm a good girl." I can't keep the touch of wistfulness out of my voice.

He lifts an eyebrow. "But you don't want to be?"

I look at his mouth, gather my courage, and give a small shake of my head. Oh my God, I can't believe I'm doing this.

His gaze drops to my lips. "We'll have to see what we can do about that."

I shiver.

"Can I kiss you?" he asks.

I nod.

He tilts his head a little to the side, then lowers his lips.

I hold my breath as he presses his lips to mine once, twice, and a longer third time. Then he lifts his head and gives me an amused look. "Don't forget to breathe."

I exhale in a rush. "Sorry."

"It's okay." He tucks a strand of hair behind my ear. "Are you sure you want to do this? We've both had a lot to drink, and I know you said you had a bad day. I don't want you to do something you'll regret in the morning."

"I'd never regret being with you," I tell him.

He smiles, but I can sense his hesitation. Oh jeez, I think he's having second thoughts.

Before my nerves get the better of me, I lift my arms around his neck, slide a hand into his hair, and pull his lips down to mine. Opening my mouth, I touch my tongue to his lip. He groans, deep in his throat, and strokes his tongue against mine.

Ooh, yes, that's lit the touch paper—fireworks go off between us, and the temperature rises by about thirty degrees. He pushes me up against the wall, deepening the kiss as he presses his body to mine. I've got sparklers in my eyes, rockets going off in my brain, and a big Catherine wheel spinning in my stomach. What's it going to feel like to go to bed with him?

He kisses me for ages, still cupping my face, delving his tongue into my mouth. When he finally lifts his head, I'm breathless and dizzy, filled with an ache deep inside.

"The Clarence is just around the corner," he says, his voice husky with desire. "I can see if they have a room available, if you like?"

"Yes, please," I say, and he grins, grabs my hand, and walks off briskly, pulling me with him.

"So polite," he teases, striding out. "We'll definitely have to do something about that."

I laugh with sheer exuberance, half-jogging to keep up with him. I'm so excited, I can barely breathe. I glance up at him as we walk, my heart thundering at the thought that this gorgeous guy is interested in me. He winks at me, then, as we turn the corner, leads me across Cathedral Square. I barely glance at the half-built Cathedral that was damaged so badly in the earthquake in 2011. Instead, my gaze is drawn by the newly built Clarence Hotel, whose windows glow in the darkness, drawing your eye toward it.

I've honestly never stayed in a hotel. When I visit family in Kaikoura or Timaru, I stay with them, often kipping on the sofa or even the floor. I look up with wide eyes as he leads me through the automatic doors at the entrance, and we find ourselves in the lobby.

It's quiet and elegant, with a polished wooden floor, a curved reception desk, subtle uplighting, and ferns in stylish pots. A man is sitting behind the desk. James goes up to him and says, "Hey, Vic."

"Hello, Mr. Rutherford," Vic says. "Looking for a room?"

"Please, have you got anything?"

"There's nobody in the penthouse tonight."

"Sounds great." James hands over his credit card without batting an eyelid.

Jesus, the penthouse? I try not to look shocked as he scribbles his signature on the form, and Vic hands him a keycard. I feel a little embarrassed. Does James bring girls back here a lot? I wonder whether Vic will look down his nose at me, but he just smiles and goes back to his computer, and James continues on toward the elevators. It's that easy. Wow.

He presses the button and the doors open, we go inside, and I watch him swipe his card. There are twenty-four buttons on the pad, and he presses number twenty-four. The doors close, and the elevator begins to rise.

He turns to me and moves me up against the mirrored wall, then tucks a knuckle under my chin and lifts it so I'm looking at him.

"You sure about this?" he asks.

I nod. "Are you?"

He tilts his head, his eyes turning sultry. "Yeah. I'm not going to ask every five minutes, though, because there's nothing sexy about that. You want me to stop at any time, you just tell me, okay?"

"Okay." One-night stand etiquette, I guess. I'm half-tempted to admit to him that I've never had one, but I don't want to come across as foolish or immature, and I don't want him to stop.

In the back of my mind, an image flashes, and emotions whip through me—terror, shame, guilt. But the alcohol lets me push it all away. Just because it happened before doesn't mean it's going to happen now. James is lovely, and I'm not going to pass up the chance to sleep with him out of fear.

He leans on the wall, above my head, and nuzzles my ear. "You smell amazing," he murmurs. I shiver, and he groans. "Jesus, every time you do that, it drives me crazy."

I drive *him* crazy?

He crushes his lips to mine, and I moan, which makes him press up against me. Ooh, he has an erection, and Gaby wasn't wrong—even through his jeans I can feel it, long and hard against my tummy. I lift my arms around his neck, meeting each thrust of his tongue with one of my own, and by the time the elevator stops and the doors open, we're both out of breath and panting.

He takes my hand, and I follow him out and along the corridor. It's empty, with only two doors, one on my left, and one on the right, further along. He leads me to the right one, swipes the card, and opens the door.

I go inside, but there's no time to stop and look around because even before the door has swung completely shut, he backs me up against the wall, and his mouth is on mine again.

"Aroha," he says with a groan, and the sound of my name on his tongue makes me dizzy with desire.

I'm not stupid; the alcohol has really kicked in, and I know I'm drunk—possibly the most drunk I've ever been, almost—almost—enough to completely wipe away the heavy feeling of despair that's been growing since my phone call with my mum. I can still feel it, as if I've eaten a dozen stones, one after the other, and they're sitting in my stomach, weighing me down. But the alcohol makes me not care.

The city was nearly destroyed twelve years ago in a horrendous earthquake. Many people died. But I'm alive. All that matters is right here, right now. I don't care about tomorrow. There's only James, and his hot mouth, and his hard body, and his strong hands.

We're both consenting adults. Both single, now he's broken up with Cassie. So what does it matter? Carpe diem, right?

Chapter Four

Aroha

He slides his hands under my butt and picks me up, and I wrap my legs around his waist, still kissing him as he carries me through the apartment. We bump into the sofa, then the doorway, and we both laugh.

I glimpse a leather sofa, abstract art on the walls, a gleaming kitchen, and a fantastic view of the city, and then he's going through the door to a separate bedroom.

Stopping in front of the bed, he lowers my feet to the floor. I toe off my shoes, and he does the same, and then we're kissing again, hungrily, as if our lives depended on it. God, I've never wanted a man so much. I want to devour him. I want him to devour me. I want him inside me—I want him to fuck me more than I've ever wanted anything in my entire life.

He unbuttons his shirt, and I toss my purse on the chair, then tear off my top. He takes off his jeans, and I put my phone on the bedside table, then slide down my pants and kick them away. He kisses me again as he undoes my bra, and I feel a brief flare of nerves as he draws the straps down my arms, but the look in his eyes as he drinks his fill wipes away any nerves.

"Look at you," he murmurs, "Jesus, you're so fucking beautiful."

I laugh and fall back onto the bed, and he grins and climbs on top of me, lowering down so he can kiss me again. He's only wearing his boxers, and wow, the man is built like a god. All his muscles are tight and toned, from his bulging biceps to his defined abs and pecs. Ooh, his skin is hot against mine, and now there's hardly any clothing between us I can feel his erection, still thick and hard as he presses against me.

He lifts his head, and his turquoise eyes are blazing. "What do you want, Aroha?" His voice is husky with desire. He kisses up my jaw, runs his tongue around my ear, and sucks the lobe. "How do you like it, baby girl?" He kisses back to my mouth, then touches his lips to my nose. "Sweet and tender?"

I dig my nails into his back. Ignore the memories hovering like ghosts at the edges of my mind. "I want you to fuck me into next week," I say, without reservation.

His eyes widen, and a look of pure delight crosses his face. "Ha!" He chuckles. "I knew you belonged on the naughty list."

"I didn't, until I met you."

He studies my face, and for a moment I think he's not sure how he feels about that. Then he gives an almost imperceptible shrug.

"First things first," he murmurs. "Lie back and spread those gorgeous legs for me. I want to taste you."

I think I might have fainted if I hadn't been lying down. My heart pounds as he kisses down my neck to my breasts. He kisses across them, then stops to admire a nipple before tracing his tongue around the edge. I shiver, and he groans, then covers the nipple with his mouth and sucks.

Ooohhh… everything clenches deep inside, and I give a heartfelt moan.

He gives a sexy growl. "Jesus, you're killing me here." He swaps to the other nipple briefly and sucks that, too, then moves between my legs and kisses down my belly. When he reaches my knickers, he hooks his fingers in the elastic and pulls them to one side.

"Ah, baby…" He brushes up my thighs, then gently parts me with both hands. "You're so fucking smooth."

I close my eyes, relieved I waxed only a couple of days ago, and try to relax.

He inhales. "You smell amazing."

Oh thank God I had a shower before I came out.

Resting his hand on my mound, he strokes his thumb down into my folds, then back up again, presumably spreading my moisture across my skin. Then he licks slowly from my entrance all the way up to my clit, and my head explodes.

Okay, not literally, but it might as well have. My brain has turned to mush. My head's spinning. I've lost the power of speech. I can only lie there and groan as he proceeds to arouse me using his lips, tongue, and fingers. He licks and sucks my clit, then slides his thumb down and teases my entrance.

I tense a little, unable to help it, but he doesn't stop. He waits for me to relax, then eases his thumb inside, a little at a time, continuing to lick and stroke, and the intense feeling inside me builds.

"James," I whisper, sliding a hand into his hair.

He lifts his head, continuing to arouse my clit with a finger. "Are you going to come for me, sweetheart?"

The muscles deep inside me start to tighten. "Oh God, yes…"

"Good girl, come on then, I want to hear you scream my name."

Jeez, I'm not going to do that. I hardly know the guy. I bite my lip, but then he covers my clit with his mouth and sucks, and that does it—my muscles clench so powerfully that it makes me cry out, "Oh my God, James!" and then I tighten with six or seven hard pulses before I collapse back onto the pillows, sated and exhausted.

He kisses up my body, then falls onto the bed beside me. "Mmm," he murmurs. "Merry Christmas."

I laugh and push up onto an elbow, and the room spins. Whoa, I'm so drunk. What a terrific evening.

"Your turn, big boy," I tell him, kissing his chest. I'm going to enjoy this.

Lifting up, I kiss across his pecs, admiring his broad shoulders, his muscular chest. I kiss his flat nipples, then press my lips down his sternum to his tight, flat belly. The scatter of hair on his chest leads to an intriguing line of hair that disappears below the elastic of his boxers like an arrow pointing to the most fascinating part of him. Inhaling, and enjoying the intoxicating scent of his cologne, I kiss down over the silky fabric…

And then I stop. He no longer has an erection.

Okay, it's not that weird—I suppose it took me about ten minutes to come, and men aren't robots—maybe he just needs a few minutes to get interested again. But he's young and sexy, and I would've thought having his tongue buried inside me might have been enough to keep him hard for a while.

Surprised, I lift up and look at him.

His eyes are closed. His lips are parted a fraction.

"James?"

He emits a light snore.

I sit back on my heels and stare at him. Fucking hell, he's asleep.

Well, that's a first. I've had guys fall asleep minutes after having sex. I've never had one doze off in the middle.

I guess it's not shocking. I'm pretty wasted, and he has drunk more than me. But even so, I'm a little hurt. Clearly, my performance wasn't interesting enough to make him stay conscious. Hell, I didn't even get a chance to begin my performance!

Should I wake him? That seems pointless. I don't know if it's just the alcohol or if the stress of his breakup or whatever else has been happening in his day has got to him, but I can't imagine he's going to be able to shake it off without having a good night's sleep.

Should I just go, then?

I look around the room with fuzzy eyes. I'd have to find my way downstairs, call for an Uber, and stay awake long enough to get home, if I can remember where home is. Without throwing up as the car went over every bump. Jesus, I really shouldn't have drunk so much. I'm such an idiot.

I'll stay, just for a while. Get a bit of sleep. And work out what to do and say in the morning. He's hardly going to blame me for being inebriated and coming onto him when he was just as bad. It was a mistake, born out of alcohol and misery on both our parts.

I fold the other half of the duvet over him, then go into the bathroom and pee. I'm too ashamed to look at myself in the mirror, and stumble out again, trying not to knock into the table on the way.

Opening the wardrobe doors, I discover a blanket tucked in the corner. Taking it, and collecting my phone from the bedside table, I go into the living room to the sofa, collapse onto it, and pull the blanket over me.

At least I got an orgasm out of it. I think about how I clenched around his fingers and cried out his name, groan, and pull the blanket over my head.

Within minutes, I fall asleep.

*

When I wake, daylight is streaming across the room, thick and golden as butter.

I blink, moisten my lips, and then push myself up to a sitting position.

I still have the blanket over me, but someone has also covered me with the duvet. My clothes rest on one of the armchairs, neatly folded. On the table is a glass of water, two Panadol, and a note.

With a shaking hand, I pick the note up. It says:

Sorry, I had to shoot off. Didn't want to wake you. Feel free to order whatever you want from room service and put it on the bill, which I've settled. You don't have to check out until eleven. Thanks for a great evening, James.

I read it again, and a third time. Then I put it down.

Heat creeps up my neck and into my face. So this is what it's like to have a one-night stand. I feel ashamed and humiliated. To leave without even waking me! Obviously he's too embarrassed to face me.

It occurs to me then—maybe he doesn't remember falling asleep before we got down to anything. He might not recall anything about last night—I know some people when they drink a lot can't recall a thing. He might not realize we didn't actually go all the way.

Well, Aroha, this is what you get for drinking a Pacific-sized amount of whisky and going back to an almost-stranger's hotel room. I was lucky not to have put myself in danger. He could have done anything to me, and I wouldn't have been able to stop him.

I sulk. I should have been so lucky.

At least I got an orgasm out of it. He didn't even get that. Serves him right. I'm glad we didn't have sex. He doesn't deserve to experience my superb lovemaking skills after treating me like this.

Then tears prick my eyes. The thing is, I really liked him, and I have since the moment I met him. I was so looking forward to this. And I was stupid enough to think that maybe, when we woke up, he might even want to see me again.

But then I remember that he broke up with his girlfriend only last night. He was hurting, and drowning his sorrows, and I practically threw myself at him. What man in his right mind would say no to free sex? But maybe at some point he had second thoughts. Their argument could have just been a bad row. He might have decided to call her, in the hope of giving things another try.

I sink my hands into my hair. What was I doing, going back to his room just hours after I saw him break up with her? Of *course* he was on the rebound. I'm such a fool. I've just embarrassed myself, and made things really awkward, because he's Gaby's friend, and in a few days' time we're all going to Damon's wedding, so I'm bound to bump into him there.

Well, I'll have to lift my chin, pin a smile on my face, and make a joke of it. It's not all my fault. He could have said no. He could have refused to flirt with me, or dance with me, or kiss me as if his life depended on it. He had plenty of chances to tell me it was a bad idea.

I glare at the note. *Feel free to order whatever you want from room service and put it on the bill.* Fucking cheek. Just because he has money. I should order two of everything on the menu. Get a bottle of champagne, a massage, and have all my clothes cleaned. Steal as much as I can and make him pay for it. Serve him right.

I don't, of course. I pick up my clothes and, pulling the blanket around me, I take them into the bathroom. I wince at my smudged makeup and wild hair. Using the hotel's complimentary toiletries, I do my best with my makeup. I use their free comb to scrape my hair off my face and wrestle it into a ponytail. Then I pull on the clothes I took off so hastily last night.

When I'm done, I lean on the basin and close my eyes. It's impossible to forget the way he held me tightly as we danced. The heat in his eyes. His groan as I shivered and he said, *Every time you do that, it drives me crazy.*

The way he murmured, *Lie back, baby girl. And spread those gorgeous legs for me. I want to taste you.*

Ah, jeez. But hey, it was only oral sex. It's not rocket science. He wasn't *that* good.

Tears squeeze through my lashes, and I press my fingers to my lips. No, I'm not going to cry over him. I'm going to learn from this very bad mistake. No more trying to escape my problems by drinking to excess. Today I need to see my parents and work out what we're going to do.

I go out of the bathroom, collect my purse from the chair, and slip on my shoes. I fold up the blanket and put it back in the wardrobe, then replace the duvet on the bed.

Finally, I glance around the apartment. My first—and no doubt my last—time in a penthouse. It's a beautiful, luxurious place. Imagine having enough money to rent somewhere like this as well as having your own mansion. Being so wealthy that you never have to worry about paying a bill again.

Turning away, I walk through the living room to the front door, slip out, and let it close behind me.

Chapter Five

December 27th

James

"Glass of champagne, Mr. Rutherford?"

I look up from my phone at Andrea, the flight attendant. "No, thank you. I'll have a coffee once we've taken off."

She nods and returns to her area.

I'm on The Orion, our company plane, about to fly to Wellington for Damon's wedding. The plane seats eight passengers, four chairs on one side of the aisle, four on the other, in pairs of two facing each other across two tables.

I'm sitting on one side by the window, opposite Henry, who's also by the window. Across the aisle, Juliette sits opposite Gaby and Tyson. Cam is apparently visiting family and won't be joining her. Juliette and Henry haven't spoken since they took their seats. Yet another fallout from the trivia night, I'm guessing.

Gaby gives me an amused look. "Not drinking, James?"

"It's a bit early for me." It is only eleven a.m., but that's not the reason. Normally I'd have indulged in a drink on the flight. The truth is that, despite it being Christmas, I haven't touched a drop of alcohol for six days, and I don't plan to for the foreseeable future, either.

"Something to do with what happened on the trivia night?" Gaby asks. "Aroha won't tell me."

That surprises me. I know she and Gaby are best friends, and I'd assumed Aroha would reveal what occurred in my hotel room in gleeful detail.

Well, I'm certainly not going to reveal it. "Let's just say whisky and I aren't on speaking terms at the moment."

Tyson, sitting beside her, snorts. "I know what you mean. I don't remember my head touching the pillow that night."

I watch Henry glance at Juliette. She looks out of the window, not meeting his gaze.

I blow out a breath. "What are we waiting for?" Alex and Missie are flying up in his helicopter, so we're all here.

"The last passenger," Juliette says. "Here she is."

I look across at the doorway, and my heart shudders to a stop as Aroha appears. Oh fuck. I didn't even know she was going to the wedding, let alone traveling on the plane.

I left before she woke up on the twenty-second, and I've been in Lyttelton for the past few days, so we haven't spoken since that night. It's my fault. I'm the one who left, so I'm the one who should have contacted her. I've been distracted, though, tied up with my sister's ongoing drama. I meant to call Aroha, or text at least, but didn't get around to it. I might have over the next few days, but, well, it's too late now.

She glances around the cabin and sees me. From her lack of surprise, she guessed I'd be here. I smile, but she's already turned her gaze to Andrea, who's gone over to welcome her aboard.

I glare at Gaby and mouth, *You could have told me!* She just grins. I look back at Aroha warily. Wow, she looks stunning. She's wearing long, cream, wide-leg pants and a white blouse. Her dark hair is pinned up in an elegant twist, and as usual her makeup is expertly applied with neutral shades. I think she's wearing false eyelashes, because her eyes are huge and dark. She looks classy and gorgeous.

She walks up the aisle and stops by the tables, and everyone calls out hello. Juliette's bag is resting on the seat beside her, and she's busy studying her phone. Aroha hesitates, and I can see she's wondering whether it's polite to ask Juliette to move the bag when there are two free seats on the other side. She blows out a breath, then says to Henry, "Mind if I sit here?"

"Of course not," he says with a smile.

She slides in next to him. "Sorry if I held everyone up," she announces. "There were roadworks in Aranui."

It's a cheaper suburb in the city, and I remember her concern at whether she'd be able to afford a round of drinks at the bar. Clearly, money is tight for her. But then it is for most people, I remind myself. It's easy to forget that when you're wealthy.

"Would you like some champagne, ma'am?" Andrea asks her.

Aroha flushes. "Um, no, thank you."

"A soft drink?"

"No, I'm fine, thanks."

Andrea nods. "Can you fasten your seat belt?"

I watch Aroha investigate the two sides of the belt, glance at Henry's, then clip hers together. Andrea shows her how to tighten it.

"I'm just going to give a brief safety talk," Andrea says.

She proceeds to run through the emergency procedures. Aroha watches her as if it's the most fascinating thing she's ever seen. I would have said hello, but she hasn't looked at or spoken to me yet.

When Andrea finishes, she goes over to her own seat and buckles herself in. The plane trundles across to the main runway, and the engines roar, ready for takeoff. Aroha looks out of the window, watching as the wheels leave the ground. Soon, we're up in the clouds, heading for Wellington.

She's now busy looking at her phone. Henry glances at her, then his eyes meet mine, and he pulls an 'Oh, so you're in the doghouse, too?' expression.

My lips twist, and I look out of the window.

After a few minutes, the seat belt light goes off, and Andrea rises and comes over to ask if anyone would like a hot drink. Most of us request tea or coffee, and she goes off to make them.

"Excuse me," Henry says to Aroha, "do you mind if I get up?"

"Um…" She studies her belt. He gestures to his own and shows her how to lift the tab to undo it. She does the same and rises, and he scoots over the seats and heads for the bathroom. She sits back down, makes herself comfortable, and looks at her phone.

Then, without lifting her head, she looks up and meets my eyes.

"Hello," I say softly.

"Hey."

We study each other for a moment.

I take a deep breath. "I just wanted to say—"

I stop as she shakes her head. "Don't worry about it," she says.

I frown. "But—"

"James," she says. "I'd rather just forget it ever happened." She drops her gaze back to her phone.

Across from us, out of the corner of my eye I see Gaby glance at her briefly before looking at me.

I keep my gaze on Aroha. I don't know what to say. She's giving me the cold shoulder, and I thoroughly deserve it. I just hope it doesn't spoil the atmosphere. There's nothing worse than two people being frosty at a gathering, and I already nearly ruined the office party by breaking up with Cassie in the middle of it.

Well, it's my fault she's upset. It's up to me to fix it.

"Is it your first time on The Orion?" I ask.

For a moment, she doesn't say anything. Then she finally lifts her head and gives me a small smile. "It's my first time on a plane, full stop."

My eyebrows rise. "You've never flown before?"

She shakes her head, leaning back as Andrea places her coffee before her.

"Wow." I fly several times a week: to Wellington, Auckland, or Dunedin, abroad to Europe and the States, and several times a year to Sydney, where my father lives. I've been doing so for years. I'm stunned to think this is her first flight.

"It's a lovely plane," she says, looking around. "Not bad for a first timer."

I sip my coffee. "No, you don't normally get served champagne in cattle class."

She gives me a wry look. "When have you ever flown cattle class?"

"As a teenager. My dad was a big believer in teaching his kids the value of money, and when I did my OE, he made me fly economy and backpack around Europe."

"Slumming it," she says, in a tone that suggests she's thinking *Jesus, this guy's a knob*. Of course, if she hasn't flown, she hasn't traveled either.

Henry comes back, and she gets up to let him in, then slides back into her seat. "I guess you've flown all around the world," she continues saying to me, fastening her belt again. To be fair, she doesn't sound resentful.

I nod. "I'm Kia Kaha's international liaison, so if any business needs doing abroad, they send me."

"I can see you as a sales rep," she replies. "You could sell Christmas to turkeys."

Henry coughs into his tea, and Gaby giggles.

I meet Aroha's beautiful hazel eyes. She lifts an eyebrow, challenging me to dispute that. I have a choice now—take offense, or make a joke and let it slide.

Her lips curve up a little. I was with Cassie so long I'd forgotten that not every woman is spiteful. She's teasing me.

"I could sell sand at the beach," I reply.

Her smile broadens. "Fire to the devil?"

"Salt to a slug," I say, and she laughs. Yeah, that's better.

Andrea brings over plates of chocolate biscuits and mini muffins and leaves them on the tables. Aroha looks at me and Henry. We both gesture for her to choose first. She blushes, then examines the options. My gaze lingers on the curve of her Cupid bow, and the way she's sucking her plump bottom lip. I can remember how soft her mouth was. The way she moaned when I teased her tongue with mine.

I glance at Henry. He smirks. Surreptitiously, I give him the finger, and he stifles a laugh.

Aroha chooses a chocolate muffin, and Henry and I dive in. Gaby starts talking about what's happening over the next few days, and Aroha listens, chipping in with questions.

Well, it looks as if I might have diverted that crisis. She might not have forgiven me, but if we can get through the next few days without an unpleasant atmosphere, I'll be relieved.

The rest of the flight is uneventful. I have some work to do, and so I get out my laptop and spend thirty minutes finishing off a report.

"James," Gaby scolds after a while, "I hope you're not going to be working while Damon and Belle are exchanging their vows."

"I just want to get this finished," I reply. "I haven't had much chance to work over the past few days."

"Oh, of course," she says, "you've been with Maddie, haven't you? His twin sister," she says to Aroha as she glances at her.

Her eyebrows rise. "You have a twin?"

I nod. "I spent Christmas with her."

"How's she doing?" Gaby asks.

I shrug. When Aroha looks at me, I say, "Maddie's got a four-month-old baby. She's suffering from postnatal depression. Maddie, I mean."

Her brow creases. "Oh, I'm sorry."

"I imagine those first few months are tough anyway," Gaby says, "what with being sore and exhausted, let alone if you have depression."

"It's been very tough on her."

"What's your niece's name?" Aroha asks.

"Leia."

"As in the princess from Star Wars? With the cinnamon bun hair?"

"She was General of the Resistance," I remind her. "She was far more than a mere princess."

"What a shame she wasn't born on May the Fourth."

The reference to Star Wars Day makes me laugh. "Maddie swears that when she starts Leia on solid food, she's going to tell her to 'use the forks.'" It's a joke from The Simpsons.

Aroha grins. "So are you training her to be a Jedi?"

"I have been known to flash my lightsaber around at parties."

She giggles, and Gaby rolls her eyes. "Are you two going to flirt like this all week?"

I give her a wry look. "I'm just glad she's not sticking pins in a voodoo doll of me."

"I only do that at night," Aroha states, and I give a short laugh.

The seatbelt light comes on, and Andrea comes over to collect the plates and cups, then check that we're all ready for landing. She returns to her seat, and I look out of the window, seeing the city nestled between the Cook Strait and the Remutaka Range.

As I settle back into my seat for the landing, I glance at Aroha, and catch her eye. Her lips curve up a little, and I give her a genuine smile. At least she's talking to me. I can't expect more than that.

The plane lands, and Aroha lets out a long breath she must have been holding. "You okay?" I ask her.

She nods, her cheeks flushed. "I was a bit nervous about the taking off and landing. I'm glad we got there in one piece."

"Where are you staying?" I ask. "At the Magnolia?"

Most of the wedding will be held at Damon's parents' place, but even though the property is huge, they obviously have a limited number of bedrooms, so Damon has booked a couple of floors in the closest hotel.

Aroha nods, and Gaby says, "I think we all are, apart from Alex and Missie." Alex is Damon's best man, so it makes sense that he's up at the house. "It's a bit early to check in, though, so the van is taking us up to the house for lunch, and then we can call in to the hotel afterward to change ready for the hen party and stag night tonight."

Sure enough, a minivan is waiting to collect us, and once all our luggage has been put in the back, the van threads through the busy Wellington streets. Brooklyn Heights is a mansion, really, perched high on a hill and divided into several levels, with a huge pool and three apartments at the base that belong to Saxon, Kip, and Damon.

We exit the minivan, and I put on my sunglasses as we all walk down to the top terrace. It's a beautiful summer day, bright and hot. I'd been looking forward to the wedding, as I know it's going to be a spectacle, with several hundred guests. Breaking up with Cassie, the mix up with Aroha, and then all the worry about Maddie, had dimmed my enthusiasm a little, but I feel better now I've seen Aroha and hopefully smoothed things over.

The terrace is busy with guests and waiters in black suits, handing out glasses of champagne. I refuse and take orange juice instead.

"Not drinking?" Aroha asks from beside me.

"No." I watch her take the orange juice, too. "You neither?"

She shakes her head, and we exchange a mutual wry smile. "I might have a glass or two at the hen party," she says, "but I've learned my lesson. Bad things happen when you overdo the alcohol."

I study her mouth. She has an unusual Cupid's bow, pointed rather than curved, and a bottom lip that is soft and kissable. "It wasn't all bad, as I recall."

"Can you remember any of it?" she asks, a tad tartly.

I open my mouth to reply, but Damon interrupts us to say hello, and the moment's lost. He takes us all over to a table overlooking the beautiful view of Wellington and the harbor beyond. Here are the crowd I know from Auckland, as well as Damon's brothers and their wives.

Not long afterward, we hear the sound of a helicopter landing on the pad behind the car park, and then five minutes later Alex and Missie join us on the terrace. There's another round of introductions, hugs, and kisses.

Alex looks the happiest I've ever seen him, practically glowing with pleasure as he introduces his girl to his friends. I'm pleased for him—he's been single a long time, and I know he's been interested in Missie since she first came to the office back in March.

She's currently shaking hands with Saxon, who's teasing her, "You seem like a nice girl. So why are you with this miserable old fart, then?"

His wife scolds him, but Alex just says, "He's got a point."

Missie gives him a mischievous look. "Because he's really, really good in the sack."

There's a moment of stunned silence, and then everyone bursts out laughing.

"That's the first time I think I've ever seen you speechless," Saxon says. "I like her already."

"Thank you for that," Alex says to Missie, looking amused.

"See, why can't you say nice things like that about me?" Huxley, one of my friends from Auckland, says to his wife.

"I would, if you didn't fall asleep during sex," she retorts. Huxley winces and proceeds to try and explain that he'd been up half the night looking after their baby.

"You're lucky," Aroha says. "Not everyone has an excuse as good as that."

Everyone looks puzzled. I wince, because I know what's coming.

"James!" Juliette declares. "Please tell me she's not talking about you!"

Henry and Alex see me wincing and laugh, and Tyson says, "Jesus, bro. Seriously?"

"Thank you," I say to Aroha. "Go on then. Clearly the world needs to know what an idiot I am." I glare at her, annoyed that she's mentioned it in front of everyone.

Her cheeks redden, though, and as our eyes meet, she drops her gaze. I think she spoke without thinking, and she obviously realizes she's embarrassed me.

Ah, it was my fault. I'm not going to blame her. She's right to mock me for it.

"I'd had a lot to drink," I say, "and it was very late. I took her home, promised her the best sex of her life, then fell asleep before I could get her knickers off. It wasn't my greatest moment."

Everyone laughs, including Aroha. Missie grins, then changes the subject, and the conversation moves on.

I wait for a moment, listening to everyone talking, but I'm standing in the sun, and it's searingly hot, so I wander away and move into the shade. I lean on the barrier, looking out at the view.

After a while, I glance across at Aroha, surprised to see her watching me. Our gazes lock the same way they did that night at the bar. She doesn't smile, though, and neither do I. I can't tell if it's guilt that she's feeling, or resentment. Maybe both. I guess I deserve the latter, but it does disappoint me. I really like her, and I had the chance to get to know her better, and I fucked it up. I'm angry at myself, and embarrassed at my idiocy.

My phone buzzes in my pocket, and I take it out and check the screen. It's a text from Maddie, replying to one I sent earlier, asking her how she was feeling today. *Four out of ten*, the text says. *Not one of my better days.*

I sigh and text back, *You know where I am if you need to talk. Give Leia a hug from me.*

What's the temperature like? she asks. She means with Aroha. When we were young, Maddie and I used to argue all the time, but after Mum died and we found ourselves adrift on an emotional raft together, we grew closer and more supportive of each other. Over Christmas, I admitted what happened on the night of the twenty-first, and I told her that Aroha was on the plane while we were in the minivan.

Sub-zero, I reply, somewhat dramatically. *She hates me.*

Aw, I'm sure she doesn't.

She does, and that's fair enough.

James, even though you like to cast yourself in the role, you're not the devil.

I give a short laugh. *I'm sure she would contest that.*

Sweetie, give yourself a break. Try to put it behind you and move on. Maybe there'll be another single girl there who'll be able to distract you.

Yeah, I reply, thinking that's the last thing I need. *Speak to you later.* I send it and pocket my phone.

The truth is that I don't want anyone else. Even though I'm glad it's done, I'm still heartsore over Cassie, and I feel wretched over what happened with Aroha. Both of them are better off without me.

Chapter Six

Aroha

I glance over at James, leaning on the barrier looking out at the view, and feel a sharp stab of guilt. I shouldn't have said that in front of all his friends. I wanted him to feel bad, but as soon as I saw the hurt on his face, I wished I hadn't said it. Ultimately, all he did was fall asleep—it's not like he harmed me in any way.

I should go over and apologize. But even as I get to my feet, Damon's fiancée, Belle, says, "Girls, come on, I want to show you my dress," and Gaby catches my hand, and there's no time to talk to him before I'm walking up to the house with the others.

We ooh and aah at Belle's beautiful gown and talk for a while before we eventually make our way back to the terrace. Lunch is being served, and I look around for James, but can't find him. Eventually I ask Tyson where he is.

"He caught an Uber to the hotel," he informs me. "He said he was tired and wanted a rest before the activities this afternoon."

It's the day of Belle's hen party and Damon's stag party. Neither of them wanted to go to clubs or have strippers, so the girls are having a beauty spa followed by a movie, and the guys are going to play a game of paintball and then have a party around the pool before we all meet up later for music and dancing.

Disappointed that I won't get to apologize to James, I help myself to some lunch, then join the others while we eat. I feel tired and irritable and out of sorts. It's been a horrible few days. Mum and Dad have tried to put on false jollity, but Christmas has fallen flat for me, and it's been hard to summon the enthusiasm to open presents you shouldn't have bought and food you shouldn't have paid for when you know you're going to be broke for the foreseeable future.

Once my siblings went to bed, Mum, Dad, and I talked for ages about how we're going to dig ourselves out of this hole. Dad promised he'll find himself another job, even if it's just cleaning floors, and Mum said she'll work every evening after he comes home. In the end, though, that's not going to be enough to pay the bills. I told them I would move back home, and that I'm going to give them all of my wages.

They both got upset at that. I know they feel bad for putting this pressure on me. But it's what families do, right? You support each other when times are bad. You put them before yourself.

So I gave notice to the other girls in the house, and because one of them had a friend who was looking for a room I was able to move out yesterday. Depressed and low, I didn't really feel in the mood for a wedding, but in the end I thought that the least I can do is escape my situation for a few days, travel up on a private plane, stay in a hotel that's been paid for, and eat the food that's been cooked for me.

Now, though, I wish I'd been stronger and refused to go. Seeing James on the plane was hard, and I upset him with my comment about him falling asleep, and now we're tiptoeing around each other as if we're surrounded by landmines that might go off at any moment.

But I'm here, and there's no point in shutting myself away. I need to enjoy this wonderful opportunity to eat and drink and dance, because it won't be long before I'm back in my old life, with all the struggles that entails.

After lunch, I go with the others back to the hotel, check in, and go up to my room. I don't know where James is—I assume he's on the same floor as everyone else, unless he checked himself into a suite.

My room is apparently a standard one with a king-size bed, a small kitchenette, a sofa and a TV, and a separate bathroom, but it feels luxurious to me. I make the most of the bath, soaking in it for over an hour, as I don't have one at home, and then take my time to get ready for the hen party. Damon's mum is apparently putting on some kind of beauty spa, but later there's going to be music and dancing. I opt for a loose summer dress that's easily removable for the various beauty treatments, but I take a bag with me that contains my jeans and my favorite black-and-white top for the evening, and a pair of silver sandals with a small heel that I don't get to wear very often.

At 2:45, I wander down to the lobby to join Gaby, Juliette, and some of the others, and climb aboard the minivan, ready to head back to Brooklyn Heights. Behind us is another minivan that's going to take the guys into the city for their paintball game. I turn in my seat just in time to see James climbing aboard. He's wearing a pair of cargo pants and a long-sleeved tee, but he still manages to look wealthy and sophisticated.

I turn back as he disappears into the van, feeling a tad miserable. I wish I'd had a chance to talk to him.

"Aw," Gaby says, reaching over to hold my hand. "Come on, sweetie. Don't let him get you down."

"I feel bad," I murmur as the van pulls away.

She snorts. "It's his fault for dozing off when he has the most gorgeous girl in the city in his bed."

"Don't start feeling sorry for him," Juliette says. "He deserves everything he gets."

I smile, but I still wish things were better between us. Oh well. Maybe later I'll get to smooth things out.

It turns out to be a fun afternoon. Damon's mum, Mae, has turned the whole of the top terrace into a beauty spa, bringing in a dozen beauticians to pamper all the women Belle has invited to her hen party. It's nice to be on the other side of the table. I have a hot-stone massage, which is heavenly, and bits and pieces waxed, and then a manicure and pedicure. The beds are grouped so we're all able to chat, music's playing, and they're serving champagne and cocktails, so it's a very merry atmosphere.

I'd promised myself I wouldn't drink too much after the debacle on the twenty-first, but it's hard not to imbibe when you're surrounded by so much lovely food and drink. I limit myself, though, and make sure to have a glass of water or orange juice in between each cocktail, so by the time we retire to the movie room to watch *Mamma Mia!*, I'm just relaxed enough for my problems to take a back seat.

The food is delicious, and we have great fun singing to all the songs. Afterward, we sit outside for a while as the sun goes down, chatting and laughing, until finally Gaby announces it's time for some special entertainment, and we all head to the lower terrace, where several rows of seats have been laid out.

It turns out to be Alex who comes onto the stage and entertains us with a comedy routine, which I did not expect, especially when he announces he'll take off a piece of clothing if he can't make us laugh. But it's what happens afterward that really makes my jaw drop.

As he finishes his routine, music starts and lights flash around the stage, and the rest of the guys come out. They're all wearing black suits and white shirts, and they stand in a line as Paua of One's *I Scream* rings out, and Damon begins singing into the mic.

Oh my God, James is there, looking absolutely devastating. Man, that dude knows how to wear a suit. My jaw drops, along with everyone else's in the audience. I know he can dance because he spun me around the floor on the night of the Christmas party, but now he really shows his moves as the sexy lyrics of the song make me melt.

"Take it, take it, take it inside,
Gonna take what I give you, gonna open wide…"

James is looking at me as he sings that! Or am I imagining it?

"Gonna melt on my tongue, gonna taste so sweet,
Girl I'm coming for you, are you coming for me?"

It's impossible not to think of the way he went down on me in that hotel room, and how he made me cry out his name as I came. My face flames, but luckily it's dark and nobody's looking at me.

And now… oh my God… they're all starting to unbutton their jackets, and while they sing they toss them into the audience, then proceed to take off their waistcoats and shirts. Once they're naked from the waist up, as the guitarist goes into a break, as one, they all jump down, walk up to their partners, and pull them to their feet.

The music's too loud for me to hear, but I see Juliette inhale as Henry goes up to her and holds out his hand. And then I have eyes for nobody except James, as he appears before me.

"Come on, Aroha," he says, raising his voice above the music and holding out his hand. "Water under the bridge, right?"

He's moving his hips from side to side, bare-chested and gorgeous, his eyes alight with mischief. Even if I was still annoyed with him, I'd find it hard to resist him right now. Holding out my hand, I let him pull me to my feet. He slides an arm around my waist and pulls me up close to him, and I lift my arms around his neck as we begin to dance.

My heart hammers as we move to the music. Ohhh… he's so sexy, and we move so well together. 'Dance is a vertical expression of a horizontal thought' could never be more true than right now, as he sings the lyrics in my ear, "Ice cream, you scream, scream for me!"

"Aaaaah!" I yell, pretending to scream, and he laughs and spins me around, catching me before I can fall over.

Ah fuck, what's the point in holding onto grudges? It's just a bit of fun, and it doesn't mean anything. I play up to it, winding my hips against his, and he pins me to him, matching every move I make. Ooh, that's hot, and when he finally releases me so he can join the others on the stage again, I feel a pang of disappointment.

But it's only temporary. They finish their dance, and we all clap, and then immediately the DJ starts playing Nine Inch Nails' *Closer*, another steamy song. The guys all don their shirts and jump back down to us, and everyone starts dancing again.

As James murmurs the lyrics in my ear, heat floods my body, and I have to stifle a groan. This guy… he's driving me crazy. The lights flash around us, and it's hot, and I feel as if I'm going to melt.

The music changes without a pause, and for a moment I think he's going to stick with me. But then Alex announces it's time to change partners, and James smiles and turns to Juliette, and that's the last time I see him for a while.

I knew it didn't mean anything though, right? It was just a bit of fun. I dance with Henry, and Alex, and Damon and his brothers, and in the end I'm having such a fantastic time that I stop thinking about it. It's a wonderful evening, and when it finally winds up around two a.m., I head back to the minivans with Gaby and the others, tired and longing for bed.

James is in the other van, and when we get to the hotel, he takes another elevator up to our floor. I've just reached my room when I turn and see him coming out, laughing at something Henry has said, and I watch as he strolls down the other end of the corridor and lets himself into a room.

I go into my own, let the door close behind me, head into the bedroom, and flop onto the bed. Why am I disappointed? It's obvious nothing's going to happen between us. And I wouldn't want it to, anyway. What happened before was a mistake, and we both know it. It's best we stay friends, and at least now we've got over that little blip, and there's a more pleasant atmosphere.

Still, I sigh, thinking about how he murmured in my ear what he wanted to do to me like an animal, and it's a long, long time before I finally get to sleep.

*

The next day, it's the wedding rehearsal.

In the morning, I have a light breakfast sent up, then visit the hotel's gym. I don't get much of a chance to use one because I can't afford it, so I use the treadmill and the exercise bike, then visit the pool and have a swim. Afterward, I spend the morning in my room, just enjoying the peace and quiet. I have lunch sent up and eat it while watching TV. Then I take my time getting ready, and finally join the others in the lobby at two-thirty, ready to go to the church for the rehearsal.

James is there, but he keeps his distance, and although we exchange a smile, we don't talk.

We go to the church, which is a lovely, old, non-denominational building, which I like, and the wedding organizer runs through the ceremony. Afterward we go back to Brooklyn Heights. Dinner is a sit-down affair, and I sit with Gaby, Tyson, Juliette, and some of the guys from Auckland, while James and Henry are at another table.

Speeches follow the meal, and then finally it's time for music and dancing.

It's a glorious day, and I'm so pleased the weather is good for Damon and Belle. The setting sun floods the terrace with golden light, and everyone seems to be having fun.

I dance with the girls for a while, and then the music changes to a slow song. To my surprise, Alex comes up to me and asks if I'd like to dance, and I let him take my hand and turn me into his arms, and we move slowly to the music. I've known him longer than James, since I first met Gaby at high school. Like James, he's three years older than me, and he appears reticent and serious, but it's relatively superficial, and he has a very dry sense of humor. I still find him a little intimidating, though, just like I do James and their other friends. Maybe it's because they're all wealthy businessmen, despite their young age, and I'm just... me.

"Are you enjoying yourself?" he asks.

"I'm having a great time," I say honestly. "I'm really glad I came." Out of the corner of my eye, I see James dancing with Juliette. He looks so handsome in a smart navy suit with a light-pink shirt. All the young, single women here have their eye on him, and I'm not surprised.

I look back at Alex and find him watching me with a smile. "Shut up," I say.

"Why don't you just tell him how you feel?" he asks.

"He's not interested in me, Alex."

"What makes you say that?"

"He fell asleep on me! And he doesn't care enough to apologize to me for it."

Alex gives me an amused look. "It's not that he doesn't care."

I frown. "What do you mean?"

"Aroha… He's liked you for years, and he finally gets a chance to get intimate with you, and he blows it like a champion. He's *mortified*."

My eyebrows rise. "Really? He told you that?"

"He doesn't have to. I know him well enough. He's finding this whole wedding excruciating."

My jaw sags. "Because of me?"

"Of course, because of you. He likes you a lot, and now he's ruined your friendship as well as embarrassing himself. He's really upset."

I glance across at him and inhale as I see him watching me over Juliette's shoulder. He quickly looks away, but not before I see the sadness on his face.

"It's up to you," Alex says, "and I understand why you said what you said. I've no doubt he deserved it. But he's one of the good guys. It might be worth cutting him some slack."

I look back at Alex and smile. "Are you turning into a matchmaker now you're almost an old married man?"

"I've been dating Missie for a week."

"Aw, come on. I can see how happy you are." I grin. "Alex is in *luuurv*."

"Yeah, all right," he says good-naturedly.

I laugh and let him spin me around, and it's not long before the song ends.

Alex goes back to Missie. I think about what Alex said and debate whether to talk to James, but I can't see him now. I need to visit the bathroom, so I decide I'll do that first, and then I'll hunt him down and, if nothing else, apologize for what I said in front of his friends, and hopefully clear a few things up.

I go up to the house and find the bathroom. I'm just washing my hands when I feel my phone buzz in my purse where it's hanging on my hip. Taking it out, I see the name Patsy on the screen. It's my boss from the beauty salon. Smiling, I answer the call.

"Hey, Patsy."

"Hello, Aroha."

"Happy New Year."

"Ah… yes. Same to you. Um, Aroha, do you have a minute?"

"Yes, of course. Is everything all right?"

"Not really. I'm so sorry to do this to you, but Alan and I have been discussing the business, and… well… we've been making a loss for a while, and I don't think that's going to change anytime soon. So we're going to have to let you go."

I'm having trouble breathing. I'm losing my job? Now?

"Please take this as your official two weeks' notice. As you know, we're closed until the fourteenth of January anyway, so you can take that time to find alternative employment. Redundancy pay is usually a week's pay for every year worked. You've only been with us six months, but we'll still give you a week's pay as compensation. It's the best we can do. I'm so sorry to do this to you, especially at this time of year."

I'm in shock, and bitterly disappointed. But I was the last to join, and therefore no doubt the first they're letting go.

"We might even have to close eventually," Patsy says. "It's hard at the moment. Everyone's struggling."

She lives in a three-bedroom house in Avonside, and she drives a brand-new Rover. Her kids have ballet lessons and violin lessons, and her husband bought her a huge diamond solitaire for their tenth wedding anniversary. I don't think she quite understands what it means to be struggling. But what's the point in telling her that?

"Well, thank you for letting me know," I say, doing my best not to let my panic filter through.

"Thank you for your hard work, Aroha. I'm happy to provide a glowing reference for you."

"I appreciate that."

"You're a lovely, hardworking girl. I'm sure you'll find another position soon."

"Goodbye." I end the call.

I slide the phone into my purse, then stare at my reflection.

First my father, and now me. Dad's going to be like a deer in the headlights. Mum's going to cry.

Oh dear God. What am I going to do?

Chapter Seven

James

"Have you seen Aroha anywhere?" I ask Damon's mother, Mae.

"I just saw her going into the house," she replies with a smile. "Probably visiting the bathroom."

"Thank you." I leave her to her guests and head up to the house.

It's the perfect opportunity to get Aroha on her own. I've just finished dancing with Missie, who told me in no uncertain terms that I'm an idiot for not apologizing to Aroha for leaving early the morning after the trivia night. I had my reasons at the time, but she was right—I should have woken Aroha to explain. With her gently prompting that an apology might go some way to putting things right between us, I'm determined to seek Aroha out and at least try.

I go into the house and find the nearest bathroom. The door's shut, so I cross to the window and look out at the view of the terrace and the city beneath it. The evening seems to be going well. I can only hope the wedding tomorrow is as much of a success as the rehearsal.

It's funny to think of Damon getting married. He's not the first of our group of friends, of course—Henry married Shaz a few years ago, and Tyson and Gaby got hitched earlier this year. The guys I see occasionally in Auckland are all married, as are Damon's twin brothers. Even Alex—Oscar the Grouch—has found himself a girl. Both Saxon and Huxley already have babies, and no doubt more will be on the way very soon.

I feel like a guy standing outside a pizza parlor, declaring that he doesn't like pizza. Other people are confused, and insist that if only you try it, you're sure to like it. They don't seem to understand when you tell them you say you don't mind who eats it around you, but you've decided it's just not for you. Why do people always want you to eat what they're eating?

The door opens behind me, and I take a deep breath, turn, and smile at Aroha as she comes out. She looks gorgeous today in a long summer dress, and her hair is loose for once, and looks like satin where it tumbles down her back.

"Hey," I say, "can I talk to you?"

She glares at me. "Now?"

Jeez, she's still mad at me. "Come on," I say gently, "I just want five minutes."

I hold out my hand, intending to lead her into the library I know is just along the corridor. She ignores it, though, and strides past me into the room, where she stands in the middle, arms crossed and shoulders hunched.

"What do you want?" she snaps.

I take a deep breath. "I want to apologize for leaving early the other morning. It was rude and unforgivable, and I really am sorry. In my defense—"

"James," she says, "I'm really not interested."

She's not making this easy. "Come on," I say, "let me explain…"

"Why should I?" she demands. She's breathing fast, and she looks distressed. "You flirt with me all evening, dance with me, stick your tongue down my throat, invite me back to your hotel room, and then you fall asleep on me? You embarrassed and humiliated me, James. And I'm really not in the mood to forgive you right now."

I study her for a moment. She looks a mixture of furious and upset. I lift an eyebrow. "I didn't fall asleep right away, from what I recall."

Her eyes widen. "You remember what happened?"

"Of course I remember," I say, amused. "I was tired and exhausted, not comatose. I'm not going to forget something like that." I can still remember the taste of her, the way she slid her hand into my hair, and how she moaned my name as she came. I've dreamed about it every night since.

But I frown as her chest heaves with indignation. "I really am sorry, and I'd like us to stay friends."

"Well, I don't. I hate you, and I never want to see you again."

I stare at her, shocked at her vehemence.

She presses her fingers to her mouth. Then, to my surprise, she bursts into tears.

"Hey. It's okay." She's talked to me several times since we met on the plane, and she even danced with me, so I was sure she'd gotten over any anger she felt. I have a feeling there's something else going on here. "Come and sit down."

I take her hand, relieved when she doesn't snatch it away, and lead her over to the sofa. She drops onto it and covers her face with her hands. I lower down beside her, concerned that she's so upset.

"It's okay," I murmur. Normally, I wouldn't touch a girl who was upset like this, but I know Aroha, and I'm concerned. I rest a hand on her back and rub gently, ready to remove it if she stiffens. But she doesn't. To my surprise, she turns and rests her forehead on my shoulder.

Touched and pleased, I bring my arms up around her, then think maybe that's not the best idea. But it's just the way I am—I'm a hugger. Luckily, she melts against me, so I give her a big cuddle as she cries.

"Sorry," she manages to get out in between sobs.

"It's all right. There's nobody here." I hold her tightly, leaning back against the sofa, and she curls up against me. "Just let it all out."

She cries for a while, and I stroke her back and murmur not to worry and that everything will be all right.

Eventually, her sobs quieten down, and she sniffles and snuffles. I take my pocket square out and hand it to her, and she wipes under her eyes and blows her nose.

"I'm so sorry," she says again when she can eventually talk. "I didn't mean what I said. I don't hate you."

"I'm glad. I hope we can stay friends."

"Me too."

Relieved, I kiss the top of her head. "Now, what's really the matter?"

All the air leaves her lungs in a rush. "I just had some bad news."

"Oh no. What's happened?"

"It's a long story."

"I'm not going anywhere."

She sighs and doesn't say anything.

"Come on," I prompt, giving her shoulders a squeeze. "A problem halved and all that."

"You can't help, James."

"You don't know that. Come on. Tell me."

She sighs again. "On the trivia night, I found out that my dad had lost his job. He's a process worker at South Island Meats."

"Ah, jeez, I heard they were laying off staff."

"He's been there for fifteen years. He's fifty-two and unskilled. He's going to find it hard to get another job."

"Yeah, it's not easy at that age. What does your mum do?"

"She has to look after my brother most of the time. He's twelve. He has autism with high support needs."

"Oh." I wasn't aware of that.

"He receives funding to go to a specialist school twice a week, but he doesn't like it there, and he gets upset when he has to go. Mum often keeps him at home anyway, even though I tell her she needs time without him. But he's happier there, playing with his robots. She does clean in the evenings sometimes."

"Do you have other siblings?"

"One sister. She's seventeen and still at school, but she has part-time jobs to help out. I give Mum a third of what I earn, but it's not much—the salon only pays minimum wage."

Jesus. I had no idea. "So they're struggling to pay the bills?"

"Yes, and that was before I got tonight's news."

My heart sinks. "What happened?"

"My boss rang to say she's letting me go. So now I don't have a job either. I've had to move back home because I can't pay my rent. And now we'll have no money coming into the house." She leans forward and covers her face with her hands, then sinks them into her hair. "What a fucking mess."

"I'm so sorry." Words are no use in this situation, though. "Aroha, let me help."

"You've already given me your handkerchief," she jokes.

"I'm serious. You know I'm wealthy. Let me help you out."

She sits up, stiffening. "That's very kind, but no thank you. I don't want charity."

"It's not charity."

"Of course it is."

"Then call it a loan."

"No, thank you. We've gotten this far without having to borrow, and I don't want to start now."

Frustration flares inside me. "Honey, you can't sit there and cry your eyes out, then tell me you won't accept help. What about Gaby? She's your best friend. She'd gladly do something."

"No."

"Does she know about your father?"

"Yes. But I don't want help."

I frown. I do understand, but it seems crazy that we all have money, and she's struggling. "How about Alex? He'd hate to know you're suffering."

"No," she says again, sharply.

"Please, let me do something."

"All I need is a job, and I'll start looking as soon as we get back." She blows out a breath. "Well, as soon as everywhere opens. Why did this have to happen right at New Year?"

"What will you do?"

"I'm not sure. There are usually vacancies for cleaners. I guess I'll have to start there, at least until I can find something better." She sees the look on my face. "I'm not too proud to clean. It's a good, honest way to make money."

"I know, but..." An idea comes to me then. "Don't do that. Come and work for me."

Her eyebrows lift. "What do you mean?"

"I'm working on a project at the moment—a presentation I've got to give in Sydney in January. I'm the keynote speaker at the Assistive Technology Conference."

Her eyes widen. "Wow."

"I'm giving a talk about our exoskeleton and other devices we've invented. Well, technically Tyson and I are doing it, but he's a chicken and he hates public speaking, and there are going to be, like, five hundred people there, so I'll probably be doing most of the talking."

"What a shock."

I give her a wry look. "I have to put the multimedia presentation together, and I was thinking about getting some help. Most of our staff is on vacation until the fourteenth."

She blinks, then says, "Sorry, but I don't know much about computers."

"I'm also producing a folder for everyone. You can use a printer, right?"

She looks doubtful.

"It's easy," I say. "And you can make coffee?"

"Yeah..."

"Come and work for me for a couple of weeks as my assistant. Help me set up the presentation. Make me coffee and boss me around."

"I can do that."

I smile. "There you go."

But she frowns. "Don't you have a PA or an assistant?"

"No. Alex doesn't like the 'every manager has his own PA' dynamic. He says it leads to territorialism, and he's probably right. We have a team of assistants and secretaries we can call on, but like I said, they're all on vacation."

It's not strictly true—a couple of them were due to come in and help me, but I can easily give them some more paid leave. I'm sure they won't argue.

She hesitates. "I don't know…"

"It's got to be better than cleaning. Come on, just until you find something better. I'll pay you ten grand, how's that?"

She looks startled. "Christ, that's about ten weeks' work at minimum wage."

"Oh, well, it should help then?"

"James, you can't pay me ten thousand dollars to use a printer. Alex would have a fit."

"I can tell you with complete surety that he wouldn't, he'd want to help too, and anyway he's not my boss."

"I thought he was in charge."

"We're both directors, the same as Tyson and Henry. Alex is the bossiest, that's all."

"I find that hard to believe."

"If you're going to be my assistant, you won't be able to talk to me like that. You'll have to be a good girl." I smirk.

"If I'm going to be your assistant, you won't want to get sued for sexual harassment," she points out sarcastically.

I wince. Actually, she's right. If she works for me, I'll have to behave myself or Alex will have my guts for garters.

Her expression softens. "Do you really mean it?"

"Of course. I told you, I want to help, and this way we both get something out of it."

"Okay. When are you back in the office?"

"The four of us will be in on the third."

"I'll start then."

"Are you sure? You don't have to."

"I don't have anything else to do."

I nod. "Okay."

"I'll talk to Alex about wages. You should pay me for the number of hours I work."

"*I'll* talk to Alex." I give her a direct look.

She meets my gaze for a moment. Then she says, somewhat meekly, "Okay."

"And now, back to our original conversation. Again, I want to apologize for what happened on the night of the party. I'm not trying to make excuses, but I want to explain so you understand it was nothing to do with you. I'd had a bad few days—I'd been staying with my sister because she'd been under the weather. I think I told you she has postnatal depression."

"Yes, you did mention it."

"Maddie has been struggling with breastfeeding. She's had lactation consultants, but it just isn't working for her. The healthcare professionals, her nanny, and even other mothers at the clinic kept saying she had to persevere, implying if she put Leia on the bottle, she'd somehow be letting her and the baby down."

Aroha nods slowly. "Formula shaming. I've seen that happen with healthcare professionals and other mums."

"It's crazy—as if going through the process of having a baby isn't hard enough. She has mastitis, plus apparently postnatal depression can decrease milk supply. She knows breast is best and all that, but when I went to see her, she was just bawling her eyes out, and she was so unhappy. She told the nanny that she wanted to put Leia on the bottle, and the nanny just kept saying if she persevered, she'd get through it. But Maddie had had enough. She fired the nanny, which was fair enough, but then she felt guilty and upset about it. I told her that nobody has the right to tell you what to do with your own child, and I went out and bought all the kit—bottles, sterilizing stuff, and formula. She started Leia on the bottle straight away, and she immediately felt better."

Aroha hesitates. "Do you mind me asking, is she married?"

I grit my teeth. "No. The father was a guy she dated a few times. He disappeared and didn't even know she was pregnant. He's a lowlife who I detest with every bone in my body."

"I'm so sorry."

I huff a sigh. "It's done. Anyway, he's not on the scene. She used to live in Auckland and moved back here six months ago, and she hasn't made any close friends. Our father lives in Australia. My mum was a Kiwi and brought us back to New Zealand, to Christchurch, when she split up with my dad. She died when we were twenty-two, from breast cancer."

"Oh James, I'm so sorry, I didn't know. No wonder you're close with Maddie, especially with her being your twin."

"Yeah, and now she only has me. Her housekeeper quit just before Christmas too, so she's been struggling to do the washing and keep the house clean on top of not feeling well." He gives me an embarrassed look. "I know most women are in the same situation, but Maddie is… delicate is the wrong word, but you know what I mean. She struggles. She says she doesn't want another nanny but I'm going to try to talk her into it. Anyway, I'd been with her for a couple of days, trying to give her moral support, and help out around the house while she looked after Leia. I got back here and went to work in the afternoon, and then went around Cassie's, and she was snotty with me because it was her birthday on the twentieth and I didn't spend it with her—I was with Maddie."

"Ah, jeez."

"We'd been having problems anyway, and… well, I won't go into that. But she was unhappy, and then it just blew up that evening. I was angry and pissed off, because even though I knew it was over, we'd been dating a while, and it still made me sad."

"Of course it did."

"But I didn't want to go home because it's no fun drinking alone, so I thought I'd stay with my friends. And I started on the whisky, and then you were there, being all fun and gorgeous, and you don't know how wonderful that was after spending so long with Cassie, who'd been prickly and unhappy for ages. And then we danced, and we were flirting, and I knew if I asked you back to my room you'd say yes. And I thought why shouldn't I? We were both grownups. I was single. I had no intention of getting back with Cassie. And I'd always liked you. So I did, I took you back to my room, and I went down on you, which was fantastic, I have to say, and then I lay back on the bed, and… I don't know what happened. I was so tired, and mentally and physically exhausted, and I'd drunk too much, and I felt happy because I'd given you an orgasm, and I felt kinda sated even though I hadn't… you know… and, well, I just fell asleep. I didn't mean to. And it was nothing to do with you."

AROHA AND THE BILLIONAIRE BOSS

She's staring at me, and her makeup is slightly smudged from where she was crying, but her eyes are huge, and a fascinating mixture of green and brown, and beautiful.

"My phone woke me up," I tell her. "It was five a.m., and it was Maddie again. She was crying. She didn't feel well, and she couldn't get Leia to sleep. She was exhausted. I told her that I had to go into the office, but that I'd be there in the afternoon. I remembered then that I had a Zoom call with a guy from the UK at eight a.m., and I needed to do some preparation for it. So I got up, and I found you on the sofa."

I study her face, my lips curving up at the memory. "You looked gorgeous, and you were sound asleep, so I thought I'd leave you to it. I admit, I was distracted. I wasn't really thinking straight. I scribbled a note—I can't even remember what it said—and headed out. I worked all morning, briefly made an appearance at the staff office party at lunch, then drove over to Maddie's again, and I stayed with her until I came to the wedding."

I take Aroha's hand in mine. "I'm so sorry. I shouldn't have taken you to the hotel after breaking up with Cassie. I was using you, and that was unfair. And I should have contacted you and apologized for leaving you without waking you. I admit that after the first day, I was embarrassed and couldn't think what to say. I'm ashamed of myself, though. Will you forgive me?"

She wipes under her eyes. "Of course I forgive you. I'm sorry, too, for embarrassing you in front of your friends. I shouldn't have said that."

"It's all right, I deserved it."

We look into each other's eyes and smile.

"Bit of a shit Christmas really, isn't it?" I say, and she gives a short laugh.

"Yeah. I'm sorry about Maddie. I've seen how new mums can struggle even when they have a partner, so it must be hard for her being alone."

"I do my best. I was with her at the birth."

"Really?"

"Yeah. We've always been close, and she was frightened, so I told her I'd be there when the baby was born. It was pretty amazing."

"That was good of you, James. Not every man would have done that."

I think of how jealous Cassie was of Maddie, and how much she hated that I went over to see her so often. It's refreshing to have someone understand how important our relationship is. "I've helped her as much as I can, but she's struggling. I'm trying to get her to move in with me, as it would be so much easier than having to drive over to Lyttelton all the time." I sigh. "Anyway, that's my sorry story."

"I'm glad you told me."

"And I'm glad we can still be friends. And now work colleagues!"

"I really appreciate that," she says. "I can't tell you how much."

"It's the least I can do. Now, come on, shall we get back to the party? Hopefully you'll be able to enjoy it a bit more now you know you have a job for a few weeks, anyway."

Chapter Eight

Aroha

The party is in full swing when we return to the terrace. James smiles and touches my upper arm in an affectionate gesture before leaving me with the girls and walking over to where Damon is talking to Saxon at the bar. I watch him go, my stomach a washing machine of conflicting emotions.

"You okay?" It's Missie, with Alex in tow, both of whom are looking at me with concern.

"Yes, fine." I tuck a strand of my hair behind my ear. "I was just talking to James. He… um… apologized for the other night."

"Good man," Alex says.

I blow out a breath. "Um… Alex, he told me he'd talk to you about this, but I wanted to mention something."

Missie smiles. "I'm just going to get a drink. I'll be back in a minute." She walks away to the makeshift bar they've erected to one side.

Alex gives me a querying look.

"Can I tell you something in confidence?" I ask.

"Of course."

"I found out last week that my father's being made redundant."

Alex's eyebrows rise. "Where does your dad work?"

"South Island Meats."

"Ah, I heard about the layoffs. I'm sorry to hear that."

"That's not the worst bit—tonight I discovered the beauty salon where I work has also closed."

His brow furrows. "Jesus. I'm so sorry."

"I… um… was a bit upset when I bumped into James, and I told him about it. And he's offered me a temporary job helping him prepare for his keynote speech in Sydney until I can find something else."

He nods. "That's a good idea."

"It was very kind of him, but the thing is that I'm not an office worker—I don't know the first thing about computers."

"I'm sure he took that into account."

It's a very Alex thing to say. "But he's offered me a ridiculous amount of money, and I just wanted to say to you that I don't expect you to pay it. I'm only worth minimum wage."

He fixes me with an Alex stare. "Well, first of all, minimum wage isn't a representation of a person's worth—it was created to ensure that workers are paid at least that amount for their time."

I flush, aware I'm being told off. "I know, but—"

"And just because you haven't worked with computers before doesn't mean you don't have other skills. You're calm, reliable, smart, and efficient, and you have common sense, which is more than a lot of people have."

My face fills with heat. "I wasn't fishing for compliments."

"I wasn't giving one. I was stating a fact, and, knowing James, he's also well aware of how valuable you are. Kia Kaha is precious to him, and he wouldn't have offered you a job if you couldn't help in some way, no matter how guilty he felt over what he'd done. Also, I'm not his boss. Whatever agreement he makes with you is his business."

"Maybe, but he said he's going to pay me ten thousand dollars. That's, like, ten weeks' work at minimum wage."

Alex doesn't bat an eyelid. "You know he's Head of Finance at Kia Kaha, right?"

"Oh. I thought he was a computer engineer."

"He is. He's a smart arse. He has two degrees."

"Really?"

"He majored in computer science with me, and then he took an online degree in economics and finance in the evenings because he wanted to help out more with the finances at the company. He got an A+ in his finals and was apparently top of his cohort, even while working ten-hour days."

"Wow."

"He has the smartest financial brain of any guy I've met. So I'm sure he knows what minimum wage is, and whether we can afford what he's offered."

My blush deepens at his gentle reprimand. "Okay."

"He can even count to twenty without taking his shoes off."

I nudge him with my elbow. "All right."

He dips his head to look at me. "Don't worry about it. He genuinely needs help for the presentation, so it's not entirely altruistic. You'll be doing him a favor."

I know he's being kind, but I appreciate his attempts to reassure me. "Thank you."

"I'm glad he apologized," he says.

"I said sorry, too."

He smiles. "Good girl."

Oh God, these guys. I clear my throat. "He told me about Maddie."

He frowns. "Yeah. I worry about her. She's vulnerable, and she leans on him a lot."

"Did you ever meet Leia's father?"

"No, but James said he was a—" He blinks, catching himself. He hardly ever swears.

"C U Next Tuesday?" I offer.

His lips curve up. "Yeah."

"What was he like?"

"The polar opposite of guys like me. He majored in Exercise and Sports Science at Otago. He would have been one of those students who wore shorts all year round and put traffic cones on the top of statues."

"You wouldn't have done that?"

"God, no, we were far too nerdy for that. We were vampires and never saw sunlight. We might have invented a computer program that calculated the angle needed to climb safely up said statue." He chuckles.

"Did James get on with him?"

"Oh, one hundred percent no. It was the first and only time James has ever gotten into a fight."

My eyebrows shoot up. "Really?"

"Yeah, it was just before Maddie found out she was pregnant. James arrived at her house and said Blue was there, banging on the door."

"Blue?" It's a strange name.

"He's a redhead and Australian. The Aussies sometimes call redheads Blue."

"I didn't know that."

"Maddie had told him to get lost, but he wouldn't leave her alone. He was drunk, I think. He was yelling and broke a window or something, then when James tried to manhandle him off the property, Blue punched him."

"Shit. What did James do?"

"Gave him a right hook and knocked him flat, then rang the police, who came and took him away. I don't think Blue did time for it, but he hasn't been back since."

"Wow. I can't imagine James being violent."

He smiles as Missie comes back over with her drink. "We all become Neanderthals when the women we love are threatened."

I sigh. "It must be nice to have someone to look after you like that."

"Aw," Missie says, "you'll find someone soon, I'm sure." Pointedly, she looks over at James while she sips her drink.

"Not while you're working together," Alex states. "That's one policy I do put my foot down on at Kia Kaha."

"Ooh," Missie says, "I love it when you do that."

He looks down at her and murmurs something in her ear, and she giggles.

I roll my eyes. "I need a drink." I walk off, smiling, leaving the two of them to start dancing together.

I try to forget about my worries for the rest of the evening. Panicking won't help, and I don't get to go to parties like this very often. So I reassure myself that at least I have some money coming in over the next few weeks, and spend the evening dancing with the girls and occasionally with the guys.

And, of course, working at Kia Kaha means I'll get to spend some time with James. I can't deny I'm looking forward to that. Even though I still think he should have woken me before he left that morning, his story touched my heart, and Alex's confirmation that James's sister leans on him means a lot. I've seen many new mums struggle, so I know how hard it can be, and just because someone can afford a nanny doesn't mean they don't find the process of having a newborn hard, as Maddie has proven. I feel for her, and I'm glad she has her brother to help her.

I have a great time, and it's around two a.m. when Gaby comes over and says, "A group of us are taking the minivan back to the hotel now. Do you want to come?"

I nod, tired and more than ready for bed. All around us, people are starting to head back to cars and taxis. I say goodnight to Damon and give Belle a big hug, and wish her luck for her big day tomorrow. Then I follow Gaby and Tyson to the minivan and climb on board.

At the last minute, James bounds up the steps and swings into the seat beside me. "Wow," he says as the van driver closes the doors, "I only just made that."

I smile at him. "Have you had a good evening?"

"Yeah." He smiles back. "It got much better after our conversation."

"I'm glad. What time are you going to the Heights tomorrow? You're a groomsman, right?"

"Yeah. I'm heading over to Damon's apartment at midday with Henry and Tyson. We'll get dressed there. What are you up to in the morning?"

"I'm going to do what I did today—go to the gym, have a swim, and then just chill out in my room."

"Good," he says. "Get some rest. I'm going to work you hard."

I open my mouth to reply, but nothing comes out as his words conjure up images of exactly what working me hard might entail.

"Aroha," he scolds, eyes gleaming. "You've got a dirty mind."

"You said it."

"I was talking about using the printer."

"Yeah, right."

"You'd better not let Alex hear you flirting. He's got a bee in his bonnet about sexual harassment at work."

"I've already had the talking to. I told him you were employing me, and he said it's one policy he puts his foot down for."

He chuckles. "That sounds like him."

"He was singing your praises."

"Oh?"

"I didn't know you were Head of Finance. Or that you had two degrees."

He shrugs. "I like studying. I'm doing an MA at the moment."

"Wow. You're a glutton for punishment."

"I like broadening my mind."

"You're quite smart really, aren't you?"

"In some ways. In others, not so much." He laughs and turns to answer a question from Tyson, and before long we're pulling up at the hotel. We all tumble out, and as we're all on the same floor, we squeeze into the elevator and ride up together.

When the doors open again, we spill out, and everyone says goodnight and starts heading for their rooms.

"Goodnight," James says. "I hope you sleep well."

"I'll sleep better than I was going to because of you," I tell him honestly.

His lips curve up—he likes that. "I'll see you tomorrow at the church?"

"Yeah. See you tomorrow."

We smile at each other, then head off in opposite directions.

By the time I reach my door, he's already opened his and gone inside, and it closes behind him.

*

Next day, the wedding goes like a dream. The weather stays fine all day and all evening, which means the photos are full of sunshine, and the plans to have dinner outdoors can go ahead.

I don't get to talk to James much, but that's fine—we bump into each other from time to time. I see him in the church, helping people to find a seat, his natural charm winning over old aunts and uncles alike. Back at the house, I watch him helping Alex, the best man, to get everything organized so that Damon's day goes as smoothly as possible.

We do have a dance later on, and we chat about the day and say how much we've enjoyed it. I try not to flirt, though. Alex's warning is in the back of my mind, and I intend to honor it.

At the end of the day, I go back to the hotel with Gaby and Tyson, but James stays behind, so I don't get to see him again until the following morning, when we all board The Orion at ten to go back to Christchurch. This time, James sits next to me, and we chat while we drink our coffee, looking out of the window occasionally at the Southern Alps beneath us.

"What are you doing for New Year's Eve?" I ask.

"Seeing Maddie," he says. "I can't leave her on her own."

"Of course not. I'm sure she'll appreciate you being there." He gives me a strange look, and I say, "What?"

He shakes his head. "I spent too long with Cassie, that's all."

"She didn't like you seeing Maddie?"

"No. She was very jealous. But then she was jealous of any woman I had contact with, family or not. She accused me of having an affair at least six times over the course of the year."

"Wow. So much for trusting your partner."

"Yeah, and I never gave her anything coming close to a reason to accuse me. I'd never cheat on a girl." He sounds indignant.

"You're quite the gentleman deep down, aren't you?"

He meets my eyes, and his turn sultry. "Most of the time."

Ooh, I promised myself I wouldn't flirt. He doesn't make it easy, though. "Naughty boy," I scold.

He blows out a breath and looks away. "So… you're coming into the office on the third?"

I hide a smile. "Yes, I'll be there. What time do you start?"

"I'm usually in by seven thirty, but you're welcome to start at nine."

"I can be there for eight if you like?"

He smiles. "Sounds great."

We continue to chat until the plane lands, and then I call for an Uber.

"You going back to your place?" James asks, "or to your parents?"

"To my parents. I've given up my room to someone else."

His brow furrows, but he just says, "Well I hope it all goes well. I'll see you soon."

"Yes, okay."

We look at each other for a moment, while around us the others gather their cases and start heading across the tarmac. Today he's wearing jeans and an All Blacks rugby top, and the summer breeze is ruffling his hair. He hasn't shaved this morning, and he has a hint of stubble on his jaw. He's incredibly good looking. I'd have said he was far too handsome and wealthy and powerful to be interested in someone like me, but there's definitely a smidgeon of interest in his eyes.

He glances over at the others. I follow his gaze, expecting them to be watching us, but they're all walking away, and he looks back at me.

"Happy New Year," he says.

"Happy New Year," I whisper, heart thumping as he moves closer to me. Oh shit, he's going to kiss me. What do I do? I should say no. Tell him it's an imposition. Scold him for assuming I'd want to kiss him back.

I don't, though. Funny, that. I just forget to breathe as he bends his head and touches his lips to mine.

It's an innocent kiss, the kind two friends might have when wishing each other well, just a press of lips, no tongues. But the feel of his lips against mine is like touching a lit match to a fuse. It shoots from my mouth all the way through me, firing all my nerve endings, making all the hairs on my body stand on end, while my nipples tighten in my bra. Ooh, it's been a long while since a simple kiss has done that.

I wait for him to move back, but he doesn't. He holds the kiss, just a fraction longer than he should before he lifts his head.

I glare at him, and his lips curve up. "What?" he asks. "You haven't started working for me yet."

"No, but somewhere Alex's head is exploding."

"He's not my boss."

"Don't tell me he doesn't scare you."

That makes him laugh. He picks up his case and hands me mine. "Come on. The Ubers will be waiting."

We cross the tarmac into the airport, then head out of the front doors to the waiting cars.

"See you on Wednesday," he says.

"Yeah, see you." I cross to my Uber, put the case in the boot, and get in. Within seconds, we're heading away, into the busy traffic.

I press my fingers to my mouth, remembering how it felt when he kissed me. It didn't mean anything. He was literally just saying goodbye.

But I can remember the subtle heat in his eyes, and the way he lingered, just a fraction too long for friends. I'm going to have to be very careful over the next few weeks, or I'm going to end up in serious trouble.

*

Wednesday 3rd January

I arrive at the Kia Kaha building just before eight, park my car out the front, and make my way around to the side entrance. James texted me yesterday to say that, as the office isn't officially open, they keep the doors locked, and to let him know when I arrive, so I message him to say I'm here. Just a minute later, I see him striding across the lobby.

The last few times I've seen him here, he was wearing a suit. I wasn't sure if I'd be expected to wear office attire, so I'm in a short-sleeved white top, a black skirt, and the neutral-color sandals I wear with everything. But today he's wearing cargo shorts, a gray tee, and Converses. He's clean shaven, but he looks tired.

He smiles as he unlocks the door and opens it, though, and says, "Hey."

"Morning." I go inside, and he locks the door behind me. "Happy New Year."

"Happy New Year." He leans forward and kisses me on the cheek, leaving behind the faint scent of his cologne. My heart lifts. It's only been a few days since the wedding, but I've been busy trying to work things out with Mum and Dad, and it's been a tough time. Seeing James again gives me a buzz I hadn't expected. "How are you doing?" he asks as we walk through the lobby.

"I'm okay, thank you."

"Good. You've been to Kia Kaha before, right?"

"Not for a while." It's a beautiful building that looks as if it's been built around the landscape, with natural wood, lots of plants, and glass walls that make it feel light and airy.

"The bathrooms are over there. Emergency exits there and there. If you have to go out, just let one of us know and we'll lock up behind you."

"Okay."

"We're in the boardroom." He gestures along the glass-walled corridor. Ahead of me, I can see Alex, Henry, and Tyson sitting at the long wooden table in the center of the large room, laptops before them, chatting as they choose Danish pastries from a box.

"How are Maddie and Leia?" I ask.

He runs a hand through his hair. "Leia's fine. Maddie's… struggling. She's still got mastitis, and she's feeling rough."

"Is she on antibiotics?"

"Yes, and painkillers. She's stopped breastfeeding now, and Leia's doing well on the bottle, but I guess the body continues to produce milk for a while."

"Yes, I think it can take weeks or even months to dry up."

"I hope it doesn't take that long for her. She's really unhappy at the moment. I promised her I'd go and see her this weekend."

"Did you talk to her about her coming to live with you?"

He nods. "She says she doesn't want to cramp my style."

"Well," I tease, "I'm sure you have a revolving door on the front of your house, so…"

He gives me a wry look, but the worry lines still mar his forehead. He's really concerned about her. I know what that's like. I hope she feels better soon.

Chapter Nine

James

Ahead of us, the sliding glass doors to the boardroom open, and the guys look over as we go inside.

"Hey, Aroha," Henry says, and the other two echo his greeting.

"Morning, guys." Aroha smiles at them all, then bends to greet Alex's dog, Zelda, as she runs up. "Happy New Year."

"Great that you're joining us," Tyson says. "We really need some help."

"I'm looking forward to getting stuck in," she says. She looks to her right. "What a great view." Another pair of sliding doors that are currently open lead onto a private terrace with stone steps down to the Avon. Willow trees trail their fingers in the water, while ducks paddle slowly upstream.

"It's not a bad place to work," I reply. I gesture to the table against the right-hand glass wall. "Help yourself to coffee anytime you want, and pastries are on the table. Morning tea will be around ten—we normally have some muffins delivered. Lunch at one—again, it'll be delivered, just club sandwiches and stuff."

"Okay. Would any of you like a coffee?"

I finish off the last mouthful of mine and hold the mug out to her. "Yes please, that would be great."

"I wasn't talking to you," she says.

I lift an eyebrow as the others laugh. "Is this what I'm going to have to deal with while you're here?"

She presses her lips together and takes the mug. "Just teasing." She walks over to the coffee table. She's wearing a white blouse, a black pencil skirt, and high-heeled sandals. Her toenails are painted cherry red. God help me.

As she bends forward to pick up a fresh mug for herself, her tight skirt reveals her shapely butt. I try not to groan. She was put on this earth to torture me.

I inhale and look away quickly, discover Alex watching me, and blow the breath out. His lips curve up. I've already had the 'we don't bang the secretaries' speech. I give him a sarcastic look and take my seat.

"We're just talking about the presentation," Tyson says to Aroha, "and clearing up what we want it to look like."

"I'll be working on handouts, right?" she asks, changing mugs to make my coffee.

"That's the plan," I reply. "We're assuming there'll be three hundred and fifty attendees. It's probably going to be nearer three hundred, but I'd rather over- than underestimate."

She brings our coffees, and I take mine. "Thanks." I beckon with my head for her to follow me to the table on the other side of the room.

I gesture to a large pile of white cardboard folders with the Kia Kaha logo that haven't yet been folded. "These arrived from the printer last week. They need to be folded into shape. Each one is going to have about a dozen items inside. So far we've only got a couple finished." I show her the documents that are ready. "The pamphlets need to be folded in thirds with the logo on the top." I fold one to show her, and she nods. Then I indicate the three piles of double-sided A4 sheets that list the products we've designed and their specifications. "These need to be collated, one of each, and stapled in the corner." I do one to show her. "That should keep you busy for a while."

"Okay, thank you. I'll get started." She pulls up a chair by the table and sits.

I go back to my seat. "Right. Where were we?"

"Case studies," Tyson says. "You want to start with me?"

"You think that looks too much like an ego-wank?" I ask. "Talking about ourselves and how great we are?"

Henry shakes his head. "I think we should go personal. Play on their emotions. One of our friends was in an accident and was told he'd never walk again. But we were all determined to help, and look at him now."

"Like Lazarus," Tyson says. "I could lie on the floor, and then you could demonstrate how you made me get up and walk."

We all laugh, and Aroha chuckles as she begins shaping the folders.

"Henry's right," I say. "We should always focus on the personal."

"On helping people walk again?" Henry says.

"Yeah, but not just that. It's a good time to reiterate that the aim isn't always to get people on their feet, because that's not always possible. It's about setting realistic goals and working with the patient. We're about giving people more independence, and handing them back some control over their own lives. Something small to others might be a huge improvement to another person."

Aroha glances at me, and I'm sure she's thinking about her brother. I meet her gaze and smile, and she returns it before she goes back to the folders.

An idea occurs to me then. It's not the time to discuss it, so I jot a note down on my phone. I'll think about it later, maybe have a chat to Henry.

"So you introduce me," Tyson's saying, "then I'll talk about the patient's involvement, dedication, and commitment."

"I think so, yeah, how much of your recovery is in your own hands."

"I'll draft that part and read it to you this afternoon," Tyson states.

"What then?" Henry asks. "How many cases do you want to highlight?"

"I think three will be enough," I say. "We should include a woman and then a child so we can talk about THOR."

"Alison Fletcher?" Henry suggests. "She made an excellent recovery."

"That's true," Alex says. "But I was thinking of Marama Bell. Although she's still in a wheelchair, she's regained a lot of motor function after her stroke, and she's very vocal about how we've helped. I'm sure she'd be glad to do a five-minute video or something."

"Good idea," I say. "And I'm guessing you think we use Finn for the spotlight on THOR?" Missie's boy was in a car accident and was also told he wouldn't walk again. Alex was determined to prove the doctors wrong, and Finn can now walk with a cane, and looks likely to regain a high proportion of his mobility.

"If that's okay with you guys," Alex says, and we all nod. "He'll be happy to do whatever we need," he continues.

"Can you draft those two case studies?" I ask Alex.

"Of course."

"Can we talk about the specifications?" Henry asks. "How much detail do you want to go into?"

"We don't want to bore them with too much," I reply, "but I think we should at least talk about how the half a million lines of proprietary code control the twenty-seven onboard microprocessors that manage the actuator systems. And mention how we've developed the custom movement control system to ensure stability throughout all phases of the movement cycle."

"We should focus on the ease of use," Tyson says. "The exoskeleton looks daunting, and most people think it's going to be clumsy and difficult to get used to, but we should point out that it's fully adjustable to an individual's measurements in minutes, and the joystick feels natural."

"I'll write that," Henry says.

"That leaves the sales stuff for me," I reply. "Do you want me to mention the UK deal?"

"It's all signed," Alex says, "I don't see why not. I'd include Titus Oates' involvement. He's well known in the AI field, and it'll be seen as a coup to have him on board."

"Will do. So, lies, damn lies, and statistics. What do we want to include?"

We talk for a while about our sales numbers, and I go over the latest financial report, highlighting the figures the guys feel it's important to mention.

At ten, the local café delivers our morning tea, and Aroha goes off to collect it, then joins us for a muffin and a coffee. She obviously knows all the guys, especially Alex, but I don't think she's spent any significant time with them. She's quiet and shy at first, but gradually she relaxes, and by lunchtime she's laughing at their jokes and happy to join in the conversation.

She soon proves herself invaluable. She answers the phone, and a couple of times she goes to the door for deliveries. She takes Zelda for a walk for Alex. She makes us coffee and sorts out lunch, runs to the supermarket to stock up on water bottles and snacks, and a few times she gives her opinion when we ask her as a layperson whether a particular detail in the presentation is too detailed.

By the end of the day, three hundred and fifty folders sit neatly in piles on the table, and the A4 sheets have all been collated and stapled.

"Excellent job," I say as I accompany her to the exit. "Tomorrow I might send you to the printer to collect the Kia Kaha brochures, as they're all ready, but they can't deliver until next week, and I'd prefer to have them here earlier."

"Where are they?"

"Over in Addington. You can take my car."

Her eyebrows rise. "What do you mean?"

"I don't expect you to use your own car. We don't have a company car as such here, so you can take mine."

"You don't mean the Porsche?" I nod, and she stares at me as I unlock the door and open it. "James, I'm not going to drive your Porsche."

I laugh. "Why not?"

"You'd seriously let me drive it?"

"Of course. Have you ever had an accident?"

"No…"

"Well, then, you should take her for a spin. She's a nice drive."

"I'm sure she is."

"So you'll take her?"

"No! Oh my God. I'd be terrified."

"You'll take her," I insist. "You won't want to get out. She's *smooth as*."

She meets my eyes, her lips curving up. "You were very impressive today."

"Oh? In what way?"

"All the facts and figures you quote. You know your stuff."

"Not really. I make it up as I go along."

She nudges me playfully. "No you don't. You've surprised me."

"Why?"

Her lips twist, but she doesn't answer.

"Come on," I say, "what do you mean?"

"I don't think I should say it to my boss."

"Say what?"

"It's a bit sexist," she says. "You couldn't say it the other way around."

"Are you going to comment on my nice arse?"

That makes her laugh. "No. Look, you're a good-looking guy. But you've obviously got a brain on you, too. That's all."

"You mean you thought I was all icing and no cake?"

"A bit. But you even seem to have jam in the middle."

"Are you calling me a Victoria sponge?"

"More like a fruitcake."

We both laugh.

"Thank you," I say as graciously as I can. "I choose to take that as a compliment."

"You should." She smiles, then walks past me through the door. "See you tomorrow."

"Have a good evening."

She heads off to her car. It's a battered old Honda, looking a tad incongruous next to Alex's Audi, my Porsche, Henry's Range Rover, and Tyson's BMW.

I close the door and lock it, and walk back to the boardroom thoughtfully.

"All good?" Henry says when I go in.

"Yeah. She just had a fit because I suggested she take the Porsche tomorrow to Featherstone's."

They all laugh. "She's done well," Tyson says, making himself another coffee, "she was pretty quick getting all those folders together."

"What did she do again?" Henry asks.

"She worked at a beauty salon, although she said she's only been there six months."

Tyson brings his coffee back. "What did she do before that?"

"I don't know," I say in surprise, realizing I haven't asked her.

"She worked in childcare," Alex replies.

"Oh, I didn't realize that."

"The center closed after COVID," he says. "Lots of people continued to work from home, and that must have had a knock-on effect on childcare services."

I realize that's why she knew a bit about breastfeeding. I'd assumed she had relatives with babies. "Hmm." I sit back in my seat.

"I've got the first draft of my speech," Tyson says. "Can I run it past you?"

"Sure. Fire away."

We work for another hour, and then decided to call it a day. We lock up, and I get in the Porsche. Ever since I broke up with Cassie, I've been going back to West Melton at night. The apartment no longer holds an attraction.

I arrive home around six thirty, let myself in through the security gates, and cruise slowly up the long drive to the garage. I park the Porsche inside and lock it up, then cross to the house, passing the swimming pool on the way. The water is crystal clear and looks inviting, and I debate whether to have a dip before getting myself some dinner, but as I go into the house, my phone buzzes in my pocket. I take it out and see Maddie's name on the screen, and answer the call.

"Hey."

"Hey." She sounds tired. "Sorry to bother you. Is this a good time?"

"It's the perfect time. I just got in." I cross the living room, go into the kitchen, open the fridge, and fetch myself a cold beer. "How are you doing?"

"I'm okay."

I crack open the beer and have a long drink. Ah, nothing beats it on a hot day. I wipe my mouth on the back of my hand. "What have you been up to?"

"Not much. Trying to get some rest."

"Any improvement on the boob front?"

Normally she'd have made a sarcastic rejoinder, but she just says, "Not really."

I take the beer out onto the deck and sit in one of the chairs that overlooks the garden. "Is Leia okay?"

"She's fine. She's slept a lot of the day. I've tried to sleep when she does, but I just lie there, staring at the ceiling. My heart won't stop racing, and I feel so anxious. I was… I was wondering if you're free tonight."

My heart sinks. I lean back in the chair and watch a fantail flitting around in the nearby lemon tree. I don't say anything for a moment.

"You're busy," she says immediately. "Of course you are."

"No, I'm not…"

"But you're tired, and you want a rest. I'm so sorry to ask."

"Mads, come on. You can always talk to me. If you really need me, of course I'll come over."

"No, I'm okay. I'm lonely, that's all, but I can't expect you to jump in the car every time I feel miserable or you'd have to camp on my doorstep."

I give a short laugh. "Ah, honey…"

"It's all right, don't mind me."

"Mads, please. Think about moving in with me. We'd be company for one another, and I could help out with Leia all the time."

"No, that wouldn't be fair on you."

I don't point out that it's not really fair on me to have to drive forty-five minutes to see her several times a week. I need to get a chauffeur. Or a TARDIS. "Come on, I'm not even seeing anyone."

"But you will, and we all know what that means."

"Not all girls are like Cassie," I say, my voice hard. Cassie made it very clear to Maddie how much she resented her.

"I'm sure most women wouldn't be best pleased to have your twin sister living with you."

I think about Aroha, and her words when I told her I'd been there at Leia's birth: *That was good of you, James. Not every man would have done that.*

"There are some who'd understand what you've been through," I tell her.

"Maybe. I just wish it wasn't an issue. I wish I was a better mother."

"You're a great mother. You love Leia to bits. You're just tired, and you need help. I want to get you another nanny and a new housekeeper. It'll make you feel better if there's someone to do all the washing and cleaning."

"Lots of women have to cope without help."

"And I'm sure they'd give their left arm to have it. What's the point in both of us having all this money and not using it? I'm going to call the agency as soon as it opens next Monday."

"Okay." Her voice is dull. "It's just… I wish…"

I wait for her to finish the sentence. When she doesn't, I say, "You wish what?"

"Nothing."

"Mads…"

"I'm sorry about Cassie. I mean, I didn't like her much, but I'm sorry you're single again."

"I guess I have more cereal grains to sow."

"I wish you'd change your mind about having kids."

I don't point out that her experience hasn't helped the situation. "At least Leia will carry on the family line."

"You need a son to do that."

"I'm not the king of England. And I don't care what Dad says. I don't need an heir. I'm going to give all my money to the dogs' home when I die."

"Forget Dad. You need a wife, Jamie."

"Nah."

"I'm serious. It's no fun being alone."

I study the beer bottle in my hand, and hear her sigh.

"You know I love you, right?" she says. It's unusually soppy for her, and my lips curve up.

"I love you, too," I tell her.

"Bye," she says.

"Bye."

I end the call.

Sliding down in the chair, I look up at the sky. She sounded very down. I probably should drive over to see her. But I'm tired, and hungry, and in the end, like all of us, she's made her bed and has to lie in it. I don't know why she fell pregnant—if a condom broke, or if they chose not to use one. She didn't say. I know that when she found out, it was too late for her to use the morning-after pill. But she chose not to have an abortion. She wanted the baby, and of course I'm glad she did, because Leia is precious, but they were all forks in the road, and she chose her path.

Postnatal depression isn't her choice, obviously. Nor is mastitis. But I can't live her life for her. I've asked her to come and live with me. I've offered to get her more help at home. I spent all Christmas talking to her and trying to convince her to go back to the doctor for help. What else am I supposed to do?

I should go and get myself some dinner. But I continue to sit, as the sun slowly sinks toward the horizon, coating the garden with gold.

*

The next morning, Aroha turns up at eight on the dot. I spend a while showing her how the printer works, and explain how we want the spreadsheets on one side and the color graphs on the other. There's lots to do, and once she's happy, I leave her to it and get back to work in the boardroom.

We stop for lunch, and it's early afternoon before she brings all the copies into the boardroom. We're just sorting through them when the buzzer sounds on the door.

"I'll get it," Aroha says, and she goes out.

"What are you going to get her working on next?" Henry asks me.

"I might send her out in the Porsche, if I can talk her into it. She wasn't keen on the idea."

"You're a brave man," Henry says. "Not sure I'd let anyone else drive my Jag." His 1970 Jaguar E-Type Series 2 is his pride and joy, and he only gets it out for special occasions.

"You let Juliette."

"She doesn't count."

I smirk, and he gives me the finger.

"Uh-oh," Alex says.

I look over at him, then follow his gaze. Aroha is walking back toward us, and behind her are two police officers, one male, one female.

We all glance at each other, then get to our feet as they approach the boardroom, and the doors open. Aroha looks straight at me, her face full of concern. "James, they want to talk to you."

My heart skips a beat, and I walk around the table and approach them.

"James Rutherford?" the male officer says.

"Yes."

"I'm Sergeant Jones, and this is Constable Broughton. Would it be possible to talk in private?"

"Of course." I glance at the others, then gesture for the officers to follow me down to my office. The walls are all glass, so the others will be able to see us, but they won't be able to hear what's being said.

We go into my office, I gesture for them to sit on the sofa, and I take one of the armchairs. I have no idea what this is about. Briefly, I wonder if it's something to do with my father, as he had a Sudden Cardiac Arrest in Australia back in March of last year.

"Mr. Rutherford," the sergeant says, "I'm afraid I have some very bad news."

My heart is banging on my ribs. "Okay."

"I'm very sorry to tell you that your sister has died. Her body was found at the bottom of a cliff in Lyttelton just before eleven this morning."

I stare at him. "What?"

"I'm so sorry," the constable says.

My brain won't work. "Are you talking about Maddie? Madeleine Rutherford?"

"Yes, sir."

"What... how... how do you know it's her?"

The sergeant leans forward, his hands clasped. "Apparently she was walking along the coastal path with her baby, and—"

"Leia?" I inhale sharply. "Is she—"

"She's fine," the constable says quickly. "She was found in her carry seat, still attached to the stroller, by an elderly couple who were out walking. She was asleep, and we don't think she'd been there for long, because it's quite a busy path. Madeleine's purse and phone were tucked beside the baby. Her purse had her driver's license in it, as well as your business card."

"That doesn't mean anything. Maybe—"

"Sir," the sergeant says, "the couple called emergency services. The fire service came out and found your sister's body at the base of the cliff. We will need you to come and identify her, but from the photo on her license, we're sure it's her."

"I'm so sorry," the constable says again.

I feel nauseous. "Oh God. What happened? Did she fall?"

"We don't know yet, sir."

"Jesus, was... was she pushed off? Was anyone else seen around there?"

"We don't think her death was suspicious. May I ask, when was the last time you spoke to Madeleine?"

"Yesterday. About seven p.m."

"I'm very sorry to have to ask this, sir, but how was she?"

I frown. "She's not been well. She had mastitis, and a fever. She's been suffering from postnatal depression, too." The two of them exchange a look, and suddenly I realize why they asked. "Wait—you think she took her own life?"

"We don't know yet, sir."

My jaw drops. "You think she leaped off a cliff and left her four-month-old baby in her stroller?"

"I don't know, sir. But we have to consider it's a possibility."

I can't believe it. I knew she was feeling low, but would she really have taken her own life? And not even dropped Leia off somewhere, or left her with me, but just stuck her in her stroller where anyone could have found her? I don't believe it. I won't believe it.

And yet she had postnatal depression, and last night she rang me because she was feeling low. She said, *It's no fun being alone.* And, even worse, she told me, *You know I love you, right?* She rarely made soppy declarations like that. It was almost as if she knew it was the last time she was going to speak to me.

I should have gone over there. I should have made her come back with me. Oh God. Maddie's dead, and it's all my fault. What have I done?

Chapter Ten

Aroha

I shuffle some papers around on the table, but I'm not concentrating. It's impossible not to keep glancing at James's office. He's clearly visible through the glass walls, and even though I don't want to intrude, it's obvious that the police are delivering some bad news.

The guys aren't even pretending to work—they're all standing, murmuring in low voices.

"Do you think it's his dad?" Tyson asks. "I don't think he's been well since his heart attack in March."

"I think if that was the case, he'd…" Henry's voice trails off. I look up and follow his gaze. James is sitting forward with his elbows on his knees, his head dipped, and his hands sunk into his hair. Slowly, I get to my feet, my heart racing.

"It's not his dad," Alex says. "Someone would have phoned him from Australia. The police wouldn't call personally."

"Oh no," Henry says. "Not Maddie."

I swallow hard, fear rising inside me. He must have other relatives, other friends it could be.

James is motionless for a moment, and I watch him cover his face. When he eventually lifts his head, his expression is full of raw emotion.

He glances at us, then looks back at the police and says something. They exchange a few words, and then he gets to his feet and walks out of his office toward us, and comes into the boardroom, the police following.

He stops in front of the table. He's breathing hard, and he's gone completely white. "It's Maddie," he says. "She was walking along the coastal cliff path. They found her body at the bottom of the cliff."

I cover my mouth with a hand.

"Leia?" Alex queries, looking horrified.

"She's all right. She was in her stroller. An elderly couple found her and rang the police."

"Oh thank God," I whisper. James glances at me, then looks back at the others.

"I've got to go and identify the body," he says. His chest is heaving, and he's struggling to control his breathing. He leans forward, hands on his knees. "Ah, jeez, I think I'm going to be sick."

Alex grabs the wastepaper bin, which is empty, luckily, and about two seconds later James vomits into it.

"Fuck," he says, dropping into a chair, "sorry."

"It's perfectly natural," the constable says. "It's the shock."

Henry takes a serviette from the table and passes it to him. I grab a bottle of cold water from the fridge, run around the table, open the lid, and pass it to him. He takes it from me, his hand shaking, has a mouthful, and spits it into the bin before taking a couple of swallows.

My hands are cool, and I rest one on the back of his neck. "All right, sweetie?"

He nods. "Sorry."

"Jesus, James, don't apologize." I kiss the top of his head and gesture at the bin. "Give me that."

"Ah, Aroha…"

"It's all right." I take it from him and head out to the bathroom.

I go into the Ladies', empty the bin into the toilet and flush it, go out and rinse the bin under the sink, then stand there and look at my reflection. I press my fingers to my mouth again as tears sting my eyes. I mustn't cry—he doesn't need that. But it's impossible to stop the wave of emotion that crashes over me. I can't believe it. What happened? Did she fall? Surely she didn't jump? Oh, poor James.

I think of Leia then, and my hand trembles as I wipe away the tear that tips over my lashes. That little baby… Where is she now? What will James do with her? Will he bring her back with him? Who else does she have? A grandfather in Australia who's not well, by the sounds of it, and an absent father. James is her only family. What other choice does he have?

I take a few deep breaths, make sure my tears have dried up, then collect the bin and return to the boardroom. James is standing again now. As I go in, he looks over at me, a shadow of a smile on his lips. "Sorry about that," he says. He's still white as a sheet.

I put the bin down. "Don't worry about it."

He looks at the others. He came back into the boardroom, so he obviously values their friendship. They're asking questions—what time did the couple call the police, did they see anyone else around, when was Maddie's body found, how was it identified? Good, kind men, giving him what he needs—solid, practical support.

I feel a bit like I'm intruding—we're not close, and I'm not sure he wants me here. I go up and stand next to him, rest a hand on his back, and rub it gently. "Do you want me to go?" I murmur.

He doesn't look at me, but he shakes his head.

"Okay." I keep my hand there. He takes a deep breath and blows it out slowly.

The police are answering all their questions as best as they are able. It's clear they don't know much. They seem convinced it's Maddie, but they obviously don't know whether she fell or if she took her own life.

I think about the fact that she was unwell, unhappy, and probably lonely. It's tough for new mums anyway, when they're full of hormones, physically sore from the birth, and trying to cope with this crying bundle they're repeatedly told they should have bonded with immediately. But if she had postnatal depression, it would have amplified her stress and anxiety to an astronomical level. I feel a surge of anger at the thought that her health provider, nanny, and other mums refused to listen to her request to bottle feed. At least James tried to help.

"So you spoke to her last night?" the sergeant asks. "How did she sound?"

James slides his hands into his pockets. "Low. She's been suffering from postnatal depression, and she's been unwell. I think that made it difficult for her to bond with Leia."

"Did she ever talk about harming herself or the baby?" the constable asks gently.

He shakes his head. "But last night... she asked me to go over. She said she was lonely. I was tired, and I'd been with her all over Christmas, and I was going to drive over Friday night, so I hesitated, and she apologized and said not to worry about it. I talked about her coming to live with me again, but she said no, she didn't want to cramp my style." His brows draw together. "She talked about the fact that I don't want kids." His back stiffens beneath my hand, and I lower it slowly. "She said I needed someone, and that it was no fun being alone.

And then she said she loved me." He swallows hard. "She wasn't the soppy sort. She rarely said that. It was almost as if…" He stops talking, his chest heaving, then he turns and walks across the boardroom and out of the sliding doors onto the terrace. He runs down the steps, then stops at the bottom and sinks onto the bottom step, his face in his hands.

"Leave him for a minute," Henry says to nobody in particular.

Alex looks at the sergeant, who purses his lips. "That doesn't sound good," Alex says.

"No," the sergeant replies.

"Do you think she went up to the cliffs to do it?" Tyson asks.

"Possibly not," the sergeant says. "I'm sure she would have left the baby with someone if that was the case. Asked a friend to look after her or something."

"James said she didn't really have any," I say. "She moved after she found out she was pregnant."

"Postnatal depression is harsh," the constable says. "It's not uncommon for a new mum who's suffering to have thoughts of harming herself or the baby."

We all fall quiet as we think about that. God, at least Leia is okay.

"Where's the baby now?" I ask.

"Social services have taken her to a temporary foster home until everything's sorted," the constable says.

"What's the situation with the father?" the sergeant asks.

"I don't think he's on the scene," Henry says.

I shake my head. "James said he was a lowlife, and Maddie hadn't seen him since she got pregnant."

"They weren't married or living together?"

"I don't think so," I say, and Henry agrees.

"What about other family?" the sergeant asks.

"Leia's grandfather lives in Australia," Henry says. "He has a large family over there. James and Maddie's mother died six years ago. She had a couple of brothers—one lives in Auckland, the other in Napier, I believe. James isn't close to them, but I guess they'll come to the funeral."

I look out at James. He's on the phone now. Maybe he's calling his father. What a horrible conversation to have.

"What are the legal ramifications?" Alex asks. "James would automatically get custody, right?"

"It's complicated," the sergeant says. "He needs to get advice from a lawyer."

We all exchange a look. He told us only minutes ago that he doesn't want children. Maybe he won't want the responsibility of bringing up his niece. So what would that mean, if the father didn't want her either? Adoption, I guess. There's nothing wrong with being adopted, and at least she'd eventually get parents who loved her, but awww... the poor baby.

We look toward the terrace. James is still sitting on the bottom step, near the river, his head in his hands.

"Henry," Alex says, "have you got any brandy in your office?"

Henry nods. "I'll go and get it." He goes out.

"Regardless of whether James ends up wanting custody of Leia," Alex says, "will he be able to take her home tonight?"

The sergeant nods. "At times like this, we always assume that immediate care of a child will pass to the family until guardianship is sorted. The foster mum will bring her into the station, and he can pick her up there."

Henry comes back in with the bottle of brandy. He pours some into a glass, then goes out and descends the steps to James. He lowers down next to him, and we watch him pass the glass to James.

"I guess this isn't your favorite part of the job," Alex says to the two police officers.

They give small smiles. "No, it's not the easiest bit," the sergeant says.

"Can I get either of you a tea or coffee?" I ask, feeling helpless.

But they both shake their heads. "We'll get going in a minute," the constable says.

I look out at the two men on the terrace. James is getting to his feet. The glass is empty. He walks slowly back to the boardroom, listening as Henry talks. They stop outside the window and finish their conversation, and James nods.

When he comes in, he looks more composed. "I called my father," he says. "The police had just rung him." He clears his throat. "So you want me to identify her first?" he asks, and the sergeant nods. "Where do I go?"

"The Forensics Department at the hospital."

"And afterward I can bring Leia back with me?"

"Of course."

"Where do I collect her from?"

"The foster mum is bringing her to Lyttelton Police Station at five, if you could meet us there."

"You'll need a car seat," I tell him and Henry. "And bottles and formula. Clean clothing, and nappies."

James runs a hand through his hair. "Shit. Of course."

"We can call in at Maddie's house," Henry says, "and pick up what we can from there temporarily."

James stands there for a moment, looking at the floor, his hands on his hips. His expression is hard, wracked with grief and, I suspect, an inner fury at what's happened, but despite his initial shock, he's still in control. At that moment, I have no trouble believing he's a billionaire and a successful businessman.

He looks at me, then, taking me by surprise. "I wonder if you'd do me a favor," he says.

"Of course, anything."

"Alex told me you're a qualified childcare assistant?"

My eyebrows rise. "Yes, that's right."

"I need someone to look after Leia temporarily, until everything is sorted, but all the agencies are closed at the moment, and I'm not going to be able to get anyone at this short notice. Could I hire you as her nanny for a few days?"

My jaw drops, but I close it hurriedly. "Um, sure."

"I'll pay you," he says.

I flush. "You don't have to do that."

"It's not up for debate," he says abruptly. "Would you be able to come with me to the station to pick her up?"

For some reason, I feel embarrassed and humiliated that he won't accept my help—that he feels he has to pay me. But that's silly—he knows I'm short of money, and he's probably just keeping it professional and making sure I'm not out of pocket.

"Of course," I say. "I can help you decide what to pick up from the house, too."

"That would be great," he says with relief.

"I'll take you in the Range Rover," Henry says. "You won't get a baby seat in the back of the Porsche."

"Are you sure?" James asks.

"Bro, come on. You don't have to do this alone." Henry claps him on the shoulder. "Do you need to take anything with you?"

"I'll get my jacket. It's got my keys and wallet." James goes out to his office.

As I collect my purse, Alex comes over. "Anything you need, you just call me," he murmurs.

"Okay."

"Cool." He smiles. "Thanks for stepping up."

"It's the least I can do. I feel so helpless."

"Yeah, everyone does at times like these."

"Poor James." I watch him come out of his office, carrying his jacket. "Do you think he'll want custody of Leia?"

Alex watches him as well. "He's always been very vocal about not wanting kids. But if it means someone else bringing up Leia? I don't know."

James comes back into the room and looks around at all the paperwork. "Tyson," he says hesitantly, "I'm sorry…"

"Don't worry about it," Tyson says immediately. "I'll get everything sorted."

James nods. "Okay. Let's go."

He has a final bearhug with Alex and Tyson, and then we head out of the building. Outside, he shakes hands with the sergeant and constable, and they go back to their car, while we go over to the Range Rover. James gestures to the front, but I shake my head and get in the back, and he slides in beside Henry. Before long, we're heading toward the hospital.

James looks out of the window, his elbow on the sill, his fingers resting on his lips, lost in thought. I pull out my phone and send my mum a text, letting her know what's happened. I wonder whether James will want me to stay at his place? If so, I will have to call home and pick up some things.

"I still can't believe it," James says.

"I know." Henry shakes his head. "It's like a bad dream."

"I keep telling myself she wouldn't have taken her own life. But our conversation last night was strange, as if she knew she wouldn't talk to me again." He huffs an angry breath. "I should have gone over there."

"It's not your fault," Henry says.

"But she asked me to go…"

"If it was an accident, it's not your fault," Henry repeats.

"I don't think it was an accident."

"If that's true, it still wasn't your fault. And it wasn't Leia's fault, and it wasn't Maddie's fault. If you have to blame anyone, blame the depression, the black dog, if you will. It's a selfish, horrific condition where the person afflicted is in so much pain that they can only think about themselves and making the pain stop. There's nothing you could have done, James. You couldn't spend every minute of every day with her."

"I should have gotten her more help. I should have been there to save her…"

"The level of support you offered her was based on your understanding of her situation at that time. If you'd known this was going to happen, of course you'd have gone over there, but you didn't. It was her life, and hers to take, if indeed she did. If she was suicidal, she wouldn't have been thinking clearly or rationally. And you still don't know. The police officers didn't mention a note, right?"

James's eyebrows rise. "No."

"I'm no expert, but to me that either means it wasn't suicide, or it wasn't pre-meditated. She didn't go up there planning to do it. So how could you have known, if she didn't know herself?"

James looks out of the window again. "You're so fucking logical."

Henry gives him an affectionate glance. "If you want to blame yourself, there's nothing I or anyone else can do about it, but that's not going to help Maddie or Leia."

James just sighs.

"What are you going to do about Blue?" Henry asks.

"The police will have to find him. I'm not going looking for him."

"Does he know about Leia?"

"No. When Maddie went to his place to tell him she was pregnant, he'd left, and she never saw him again."

"So he's not on the birth certificate?" Henry asks.

"Again, I don't think so."

"Do you think he's going to want her when he finds out?"

"I don't know."

Henry glances at me in the mirror, then returns his gaze to the road. We don't speak again for the rest of the journey.

Chapter Eleven

Aroha

Henry parks out the front of the hospital. We find our way through the maze of corridors to the Forensic Pathology department, and James goes up to the woman on the front desk and explains why he's there. He has to fill out a form, then she asks him to take a seat, and we sit with him in the visitor area. He's gone pale again, and he's breathing fast.

I touch his arm. "You okay?"

"Not really," he says.

"Do you want me to do it?" Henry asks.

"I think it has to be a family member," James says.

"It can be someone else who knew her, if you don't want to do it," Henry tells him.

James inhales deeply, then blows the breath out. I can see him steeling himself. "No, I'll do it."

"Would you like me to come with you?" I ask.

He looks at me. His turquoise eyes are dazzling. I can see him fighting with himself—the half of him that tells him he's a man and he should be able to cope on his own, and the other half that craves support.

"Are you sure?" he asks.

I slide my hand into his. "I want to help."

He swallows, then nods. "Okay."

A man in a lab coat approaches us. "Mr. Rutherford?"

"James, please." They shake hands.

"I'm Dr. Hemara. You're here to identify the body of Madeleine Ann Rutherford?"

James nods.

"If you'd like to come with me, I'll take you to the viewing room."

He's still holding my hand. "Is it okay if my friend comes?"

"Of course. This way."

The two of us follow Dr. Hemara along a corridor, and then he pauses outside a door, his hand on the handle. "Okay, are you ready? I have to warn you that she has a few cuts and grazes from the fall."

James's jaw knots. "Let's just get it over with."

"Okay, this way."

James's hand tightens on mine, although I don't think he's aware of it. I follow him through the door, my heart banging against my ribs.

The room smells strongly of antiseptic. I don't register anything else about it. All my focus is on the young woman lying in front of us. She's covered to her shoulders, so only her face and neck are visible.

James walks forward a few feet and stops.

We both study her quietly. When a member of a Māori family dies, the *tangi*, or funeral, often takes three days, with the body taken to the *marae* or meeting house where they lie in state, usually in an open casket. This happened with my grandfather, so it's not the first time I've seen a dead person. I wonder distractedly whether James saw his mother after she died.

The young woman has a big graze on her forehead, and another cut on her cheek. Her eyes are closed, so I can't see how like James's they are. She looks peaceful, though, and for that, at least, I'm pleased for James.

He stares at her for a long, long moment. Then he says, "It's her."

Dr. Hemara comes to stand beside him. "You confirm that this is the body of your sister, Madeleine Ann Rutherford?"

"Yes. I didn't think it would be. But it's her."

"I'm very sorry for your loss," Dr. Hemara says. "Would you like a moment alone with her?"

James shakes his head. He releases my hand, then he turns and walks out.

I follow him back through to the waiting room where Henry's waiting. Henry takes one look at him and obviously realizes that it's Maddie.

"Ah, I'm so sorry," he murmurs.

James sinks into one of the chairs. "I didn't think it would be her," he repeats. "I thought they'd made a mistake. Ah, fuck." He covers his face with his hands.

"Oh, honey, I'm so sorry." I sink to the ground in front of him and put my arms around him before I can think better of it. I half expect him to pull away, but he doesn't. Instead, he rests his forehead on my shoulder.

"I can't believe it," he whispers.

I rub his back. "I'm sorry." It's all I can think of to say.

He takes a deep, shivery breath. "She was so young."

"I know. Just a girl."

"It's so unfair."

"It is. It's horrible."

"Do you think she did it?"

"I don't know."

"I can't bear it," he says. "I can't bear to think she felt so bad and I wasn't there for her. Why didn't she call me?"

"Henry was right—she wouldn't have been thinking clearly or rationally."

"How could she do that to me?"

"She wouldn't have been thinking of you, James. She would only have been thinking about herself. If she did it, it would be because she was unhappy and in pain, and she wanted it to stop."

"I should have made her come and live with me."

"Against her will?"

He just sighs.

"You did everything you could," I tell him. "She had a disease that got the better of her, and it wasn't your fault."

He lifts his head and rests his lips on his clasped hands as he looks at me. There are tears on his lashes. His beautiful eyes shine.

"She had depression before she got pregnant," he says. "She came off the pills because she was worried they might affect the baby."

"Did you tell the police that?" Henry asks.

James nods and gets to his feet. "What happens now?" he asks as Dr. Hemara comes up to us.

"The coroner will decide whether a post-mortem is necessary. After that, they'll release her, and you'll be able to go ahead with the funeral."

"Any idea how long?"

"Not yet, but of course we'll let you know as soon as we hear."

He nods, and we head back down the corridor.

Outside, the sun seems too bright for such a sad day, and it makes my eyes water.

Henry drives us to Maddie's house in Lyttelton. I have no idea what to expect. Their father is obviously very wealthy, and Gaby told me James's house is more like a mansion, so I expect Maddie's to be the same, and I'm not disappointed. Henry parks out the front of a two-story place that's high on a hill overlooking the harbor with a gorgeous view. We get out, James unlocks the door and turns off the security alarm, and we go inside.

It's not palatial, exactly, but it is huge. Why did she have such a big place when it was only her? I guess wealth buys you space, even if you don't want to put anything in it.

James walks in, stands in the middle of the living room, and looks around. "She loved it here," he says. "She said she felt she could finally breathe." He sighs and meets my eyes. "Leia's room is through here."

Henry and I follow him through the house and up the stairs. It's clear which room is the nursery. It's painted light yellow, and it has a brand-new bassinet with pretty lace drapes above it, and everything a mother could ever need for their baby—a change table, a wardrobe and a chest of drawers full of clothes, packs of nappies, boxes of toys…

James's brows draw together. "I don't know where to start."

"Okay," I say. "Well, we've only got the Range Rover, so you're not going to be able to fit the bassinet or anything big into it. Why don't we take what we need for tonight, and then maybe you could organize a van tomorrow to pick up the rest of it?"

"Okay," he says. "I don't know what her routine is or anything…"

I smile. "She'll wake when she wakes and feed when she feeds. At least she's on the bottle already, that's a good thing. She should have her carry seat—she can always sleep in that, or she can sleep with me tonight, if that's acceptable to you."

He gives me a strange look as if wondering why I need his permission. It hasn't sunk in yet that, at the moment, he needs to make those decisions for Leia until her fate is decided.

"Come on," I say, realizing that someone has to take charge, and the two men haven't a clue what's needed. "Henry, grab a couple of packs of nappies. James, we want the bottle sterilizer and the bottles there, and the tins of formula. I'll start putting everything else together."

Relieved to have something practical to do, the guys begin taking things to the car. I open a bag left beneath the table. It has a portable change mat clipped to it, and it contains baby wipes, muslin cloths, nappy rash cream, and several other items like nail scissors and a thermometer. She didn't take it with her this morning, but maybe she only meant it to be a short trip. I add the bottle teats, rings, and caps, a bottle brush, soft face cloths, baby wash for the bath, and the monitor and receiver.

Beneath the table is a mini fridge. I open it and discover a few baby bottles of water in there. Hopefully Maddie has boiled the water and sterilized the bottles. I add them to the bag.

I find another bag, and next I open the wardrobe and chest of drawers and take out a pile of vests, some onesies, a few outfits, and a couple of cardigans and hats, although it's warm so she probably won't need them. Soft baby blankets. Some bibs. What else? I add the toys from her bassinet as they're probably her favorites, or Maddie's favorites, anyway.

I'm just putting them in the bag when James comes back in. He picks up the Pooh Bear that was in the bassinet. It's very soft, with the usual red T-shirt that doesn't cover his large tummy.

"I bought this," he says. "Maddie loved it. She said she was going to keep it until Leia was grown up." He turns it over in his hands.

I slide an arm around his waist. It's always my first instinct to use touch to comfort. He stiffens at first. I'm just about to move back when he puts his arms around me. I rest my cheek on his shoulder, and we stand there like that for a few minutes.

Henry comes in, picks up the bag, glances at us and smiles, then goes out again. James sighs, then releases me and walks through to what I presume is Maddie's bedroom. "What do I do with all her stuff?" he asks.

"Don't worry about it now," I advise. "Let's concentrate on Leia."

He looks around the room, then comes back out, hands in his pockets. "This is so fucking horrible," he says bitterly. "My father wanted to know when the funeral will be. I think he's coming over." He huffs a sigh, looking out of the window.

"Was he close to Maddie?" I ask.

"No. She hated him."

My brow furrows. "Really?"

"Our mother suffered with depression too, and Dad was unsympathetic—he just told her to pull herself together, and he'd yell at her when she couldn't motivate herself to get out of bed in the

101

morning and call her lazy, stuff like that. Eventually she plucked up the courage to leave. Their breakup was extremely acrimonious. He didn't want her to leave the country with us, and he tried to get a court order to stop her. He was furious when the court found in her favor. He made her life a misery, and Maddie never forgave him. She hadn't seen him in years."

"Is your relationship with him better than hers was?"

"Fractionally. He's not an easy man to love."

I'm shocked, because somehow I'd imagined that rich people didn't have the same problems as poor ones. They have the resources to pay for therapy and health programs and private hospitals. And yet, obviously, even billionaires have their issues.

He looks around the room. "Anything else?"

"A car seat?"

"She had one of those that clips to a stroller. I'm guessing that's what Leia was found in."

"So it should be with the foster mum."

"I hope so."

"Okay, that's it then."

Henry comes back in. "Are we done? We should get going if we're supposed to pick up Leia at five."

James looks around the room once more. Then, without saying anything, he walks out.

*

Henry parks out the front of the police station.

"I'm just going to visit the Gents," James says.

"I might get a coffee," Henry says, pointing to a nearby café. "Do you want one?"

"Please." James picks up his jacket, gets out of the car, and walks over to the public lavatories.

Henry and I lock up the car and cross to the café.

"Poor James," I say. "He must be so upset."

"Of course, although he's been brought up not to show it."

"You're talking about his father?"

"Yeah. I've met him a few times. If you look up the definition of toxic masculinity in the dictionary, it'll have a photo of him. Imagine a man showing emotion! Appearing weak and vulnerable! There's no worse thing in the world, according to him."

"James isn't really like that, though, is he?"

"Well, he's not a racist, sexist homophobe, if that's what you mean. But the guy's his dad. He brought James up, taught him how to be a man. Sons emulate their fathers, until they know better."

Henry's expression is dark—he has his own issues there. I feel for these guys. Our society celebrates those with power, wealth, and ambition, and at the same time criticizes men for using dominance and control to assert their superiority. Our young men are under tremendous pressure to walk that fine line. It's no wonder the suicide rate for them is so high.

James must be feeling awash with sadness and grief and guilt. I hate that they have to hold it all in. My father has been the same. Although my family is very open, he has been putting on a brave face, even though I know he's desperately worried about how he's going to pay the bills.

At the café, we order three coffees to go, and sit at a nearby table to wait for them to be made.

"Tough day," Henry says.

"I know, it's awful for all of you. Did you know Maddie very well?"

"I've met her a lot socially."

"Did she and James look alike?"

"Same dark hair. Same turquoise eyes, from their mother. Both smart—Maddie worked in finance, too. They got that from their dad. Both ambitious and driven. But she had a kind of... I don't know... wistful quality, I guess, that James doesn't have. She didn't have a lot of luck romantically, whereas James..." He glances at me, and his lips twist.

"Yeah," I say wryly. "I know what you're trying to say."

"She always seemed sad." He sighs.

"He implied they were close."

"Yeah, not in a lovey-dovey way, never heard them say I love you or anything. I guess that's why it shook him up that she said it last night."

"It doesn't mean she killed herself."

"No, true. But yeah, they supported each other because they didn't have anyone else around, I suppose. She didn't like Cassie."

My eyebrows rise. "Really? Why?"

"Cassie made it very clear that she didn't want James seeing Maddie so much. He told her it was none of her business how often he saw his sister. Cassie didn't like coming second. Especially when James asked Maddie to move in with him. Maddie said no. She didn't want to come between them. I think Maddie felt to blame when they split. Wasn't her fault, though. Cassie wanted kids and James didn't. That's why they broke up."

"Oh." That explains a lot.

"Well, Cassie *said* she wanted kids," Henry adds. "I think it was more that Cassie wanted the money, and she thought marriage and children would be a way to make sure that happened."

"Seriously?"

"Oh yeah. She was definitely after his cash. Partly, anyway. And he knew that, I think. It's the main reason he didn't ask her to move in with him."

He goes on to tell me a story about how James brought Maddie as his plus-one to his wedding, and how Maddie got drunk and went off with one of the groomsmen, to James's chagrin, as he hadn't managed to pull any of the bridesmaids. I smile, because I'm meant to, but I recognize Henry's need to reminisce and think about Maddie.

It's the most I've ever heard him say in one go. He's normally a quiet guy, happy to sit back and let others lead the conversation. Māori men can often be reticent and shy, but I think it's more that Henry just listens more than he speaks, which is a rare talent in people nowadays. I know he's Head of HR at their firm, and his easy manner becomes evident the more we talk—he has a way of looking at you that makes you feel as if you're the most interesting person he's ever met.

Gaby told me that he and Juliette headed off together after the trivia night, but she also said that neither of them will talk about it, and they're clearly not together. I think Juliette is still with Cameron, even though he didn't go to Damon's wedding with her.

Henry finishes his tale and sighs again. "Of course," he says, "that was six years ago now."

"How long has it been since you and Shaz broke up?" I ask. "If you don't mind talking about it?"

He leans forward with his elbows on his knees, the coffee cup dangling in his fingers. "Our divorce came through just before Christmas."

AROHA AND THE BILLIONAIRE BOSS

I stare at him. I know you have to be separated for two years to get a divorce in New Zealand. "Oh, I'm so sorry, I didn't know."

"Nobody did. We kept it quiet. She moved into the west wing of the house two Christmases ago, and the court agreed to make that the start of the two-year period. We tried to rekindle things a couple of times, but it didn't work out, and in the end she met someone else and moved in with him."

"Aw. That must have been hard."

"Yeah, but she's happy, and I'm glad about that. It wasn't acrimonious at any point. We sort of had the same problem as James and Cassie, except it wasn't that I didn't want kids—I can't have them."

"Oh, Henry." I bump shoulders with him. "You couldn't have adopted or anything?"

"She really wanted her own children, and she didn't want to use a sperm donor. I don't know, I say it's the reason we broke up, but it's a symptom, not the cause. If we'd been right for each other, we would've been able to work through it, wouldn't we?"

"I guess."

He sighs, looking out to sea. "It doesn't seem that long ago that we were all so young and carefree."

"You're only twenty... what? Six? Seven?" I tease.

"Eight. Yeah, I know it's still young, but it's different from being twenty-one, when even thirty seems like old age. And now Maddie won't make thirty. She'll never see Leia grow up. That fucking sucks." He stops, and I can see he's fighting emotion, too. I put my arm around him and kiss his shoulder, and he sighs.

The coffees arrive, and we rejoin James and pass him his, drink it while we wait until it's nearly five, then head into the police station.

Chapter Twelve

James

We're shown to the office of Detective Inspector Maddox.

"Thank you for going to identify Maddie, and I'm so sorry for your loss," she says as we enter, so the mortuary has clearly called her.

"Thank you." I indicate the two others. "These are my friends, Aroha and Henry."

Everyone says hello and shakes hands.

The DI sits in her chair on the other side of the desk. "Okay, so I believe the sergeant who came to see you at your place of work told you that we discovered Maddie's body this morning just before eleven."

"Yes."

"We have a little more information to share with you now," she says. "We've discovered that Bruce Clarke, Leia's father, wasn't listed on Leia's birth certificate. Because Maddie didn't live with him, it means that he is not Leia's guardian, so if he wants to be involved in her life, he's going to have to apply to the courts. We also discovered that Maddie saw a lawyer and named you, James, as Leia's testamentary guardian."

I stare at her, shocked. Maddie hadn't told me she'd done that. "What does that mean?"

"That she wanted you to be the one to make decisions about her daughter's upbringing if something happened to her."

I'm Leia's guardian. Jesus. I don't know how I feel about that. Pleased for Leia, I guess. And panicky in equal measure.

"Does it mean he has custody of Leia?" Henry asks.

She shakes her head. "Guardianship and custody—what we now call day-to-day care—are two separate things. I recommend you see a lawyer yourself soon, and he or she will be able to explain the difference in more detail."

"Have you spoken to Blue—I mean Bruce Clarke—yet?" I ask.

The DI shakes her head. "We're trying to find him. We should hear tomorrow whether the coroner believes a post-mortem is necessary. My guess is that it will be, as we still don't know the reason for her death. We're also carrying out an investigation at the site. We're questioning people who were there around the time of the incident to try and put together a picture of what might have happened. Of course we'll let you know as soon as we know anything."

Her mobile rings, and she says, "Excuse me a moment," and answers it. She jots down a few notes, then thanks the caller and hangs up. "We've accessed Maddie's mobile phone records," she says. "She made a phone call this morning at 9:52 a.m., about an hour before her body was found."

"What number was it?" I ask.

"It's registered to Bruce Clarke."

Fire rushes through my veins. "What?"

The DI looks thoughtful. "Do you know when Maddie last spoke to Bruce?"

"They only hooked up a few times, and he didn't treat her well—I think he was also seeing another girl at the same time. When Maddie found out she was pregnant, she went to his place, and his mate said he'd left and wasn't coming back."

"And she didn't hear from him again?"

"Not as far as I know. She didn't try to track him down. She said she wanted someone who wanted to be with her, not some arsehole who didn't give a shit." I know my voice is harsh, but the DI doesn't blink. "You think Maddie called him to tell him about Leia, and he said he didn't want anything to do with her. And Maddie was so upset she killed herself."

The DI doesn't reply.

"She wouldn't do that," I say. "Not over a piece of shit like him. She had more self-worth than that." The DI still doesn't say anything, and I go cold. "You don't think he… pushed her?" Next to me, Aroha gasps at the notion.

"I'm not speculating," the DI says. "We're not treating her death suspiciously at the moment. But we definitely need to find him now.

I—" She stops then and looks over my shoulder again. This time she smiles. "Here's someone I think you'll definitely want to see."

I turn and see a woman pushing a stroller through the station toward us. A sergeant opens the door for her, and she comes into the office.

"Hey, Marina," the DI says. "James, this is Marina Serkis, she's a foster mum and looks after children temporarily for the social services at times like this. Marina, this is Leia's uncle, James Rutherford."

"Hello," Marina says, pushing the stroller up to me. "I'm so sorry to hear of your loss."

"Thank you." I can't take my eyes off the baby sitting in the carry seat that's clipped to the stroller. She has a dusting of light-brown hair, bright turquoise eyes, and a freckle on her cheekbone. It's definitely Leia.

Marina lifts her out and passes her into my arms. I hold her stiffly, conscious of everyone looking at me. I should say something to her, but my mind has gone blank. She stirs, and I feel a wave of panic. She's a real, living person, not a doll. I've held her a few times, but mostly I've watched over her in her bassinet or carry seat while Maddie is busy. I feel awkward holding her, and afraid I'll drop her. What do I do if she cries?

Aroha comes over to me and looks down at her. "She has your eyes," she whispers.

"They're Maddie's eyes, too," I reply. My voice sounds strangled. Maddie's eyes are blind now. She won't ever see her daughter again. "Can you take her?" I say abruptly as my own eyes blur with tears.

She glances at me, but just says, "Of course." She lifts Leia from my arms and cradles her. "Kia ora, *Piri Pāua*," she murmurs, smiling at the baby. It's a Māori endearment that refers to how babies attach to their mothers the way the pāua—also known as abalone, a mollusk with a beautiful iridescent shell—clings to a rock. "She's gorgeous, James." She bounces a little from side to side the way many women do instinctively when they hold a baby, looking down at her. She knows what to do. I feel a flood of relief, glad I asked her to come with me. "She's not ginger," she says with a smile.

"Red hair is a recessive trait," Henry says, stroking Leia's hair. "You have to have red alleles or genes from both parents. Leia must have had one red one from her father and one brown one from Maddie."

"I fed her about an hour ago," Marina says. "And I've given her a bath in case you didn't have time today. She's a bonny little thing. So sad about her mum, though."

"Yes," Aroha says. "It is."

"Are you her aunt?" Marina asks.

Aroha clears her throat. "No, I'm James's friend."

"She's a qualified childcare assistant," I add. "She's going to help look after Leia. Is that it?" I ask the DI. "Can we go now?"

She nods. "I'll keep in touch regarding the investigation and the coroner's report."

"Thank you." I nod at Marina. "And thank you so much for looking after Leia."

"You're very welcome. I'm glad I could help." She goes over for one last look at the baby. "Take care, precious." She kisses her little hand, then steps back.

Henry pushes the stroller and Aroha carries Leia, and we leave the station and walk back to the car. Aroha instructs us how to fix the car seat into the back with the seat belt, and then she places Leia in it carefully and clips her in. She gets into the back beside her, Henry and I get in the front, and he starts heading back to Christchurch.

"I wonder if you could drop me off at Kia Kaha," Aroha says. "I'll pick up my car and call home to get a few things, then I'll meet you at your house, James. You want me to stay the night with her, right?"

"If you could."

"Of course."

Leia starts grizzling a little. Aroha entertains her with Pooh Bear for a while, but Leia soon starts crying again.

"What are your views on giving her a dummy, James?" Aroha asks.

"Sorry, what?"

"I didn't find any at the house, but Marina left a new one tucked in the car seat. Do you mind if I give it to her?"

"What do you mean?"

"Some people don't agree with giving babies dummies or pacifiers, that's all. You're her guardian—it's up to you to make those decisions for her now."

And that's when it hits me fully, like a frying pan to the face. I'm completely responsible for Leia. It's up to me to make medical, behavioral, religious, and indeed all other decisions that will affect how she's brought up.

Maddie and I never discussed this. When we were together, we talked mostly about how she was feeling, and rarely about Leia's future. Fucking hell. How did this happen?

"I don't know the first thing about bringing up children," I say, fighting against panic.

"Did Maddie give her a dummy?" Aroha asks.

"I don't know. How do I know what's the right decision?"

"Well, that's the thing about parenting. There are no rules, only guidelines."

"Like being a pirate," Henry says. Then he bites his lip, obviously feeling guilty at making a joke. "Sorry."

It unlocks something inside me, though, and I give a short laugh, then a long, drawn-out sigh.

"Kinda," Aroha says wryly. "The thing is, you can read books that other people have written, and speak to other parents and healthcare professionals. You'll probably get different opinions. And then it's up to you to choose what you think is best for her, which you will, because you're a smart guy and you love your niece."

Henry glances at me and smiles. I turn in the seat and look over my shoulder at her. She's smiling too.

"What do *you* think?" I ask her, wondering if, as she's trained in childcare, she will tend to take the view of what 'should' be done.

She looks down at Leia, who's holding her finger. "Some babies find comfort when they suck, and I believe in doing whatever I can to make a baby comfortable and happy. I think it's better to use a proper dummy made for young babies than for them to try to suck a blanket or something."

I nod. She smiles, opens the packet, and takes out the dummy. Gently, she teases the baby's lips with it, and Leia takes it immediately. She quietens as she starts to suck, and her eyelids droop.

"There," Aroha says, "she feels better now."

"Will Leia miss her?" I ask. "Are babies aware of the person looking after them?"

Aroha covers the baby with a light blanket and tucks it in around her. "I think they can recognize their parents by their smell and their voice. But I'm sure that, right now, all she's aware of is whether she's hungry, needs changing, or wants to go to sleep. The most important thing is that she's with someone who loves her and is going to take care of her." She glances at me.

I look away, out of the window. Leia is my niece. I loved Maddie, and I would tell others that I love Leia, but I'm not sure what that emotion means in her case. She's Maddie's daughter, and I don't want any harm to come to her. I want her to be looked after. But am I the person to do that? She doesn't have anyone else, but I didn't want to have my own children; do I really want to bring up someone else's?

I can't even conceive of what it would entail, only secondhand stories others have told me. The baby crying all day and all night until you can't think straight. Being so tired you can't function at work. Horrid smells. The toddler years: LEGO all over the carpet, your head ringing from tantrums, the carpet stained from spilled juice and muddy footprints, having sticky fingers over your house and your albums and clothes. Bullying and not wanting to go to school. And then all the problems with a teenager—arguments and puberty and periods and contraception and exams. Fuck me—this is one reason I didn't want children. And to have it thrust upon me now? I don't want it.

I suppose I don't have to care for her myself, though. I could hire a nanny full time. Rich people have done it for thousands of years—paid for someone else to bring up their kids. Sent them away to boarding school. But is that best for Leia? To have a succession of paid nannies and a distant uncle like a character from a Brontë novel? Wouldn't she be better off being adopted by a couple who are desperate for their own child, who would love and care for her?

What if Blue wants her once he finds out Maddie's dead? Surely the court would choose him over another stranger? Maybe that would be best though, if he's her father? Maddie called him. Maybe she wanted him to play a part in Leia's life. It would make life much easier for me.

Then I think of what Maddie would say to that, and I feel a wave of shame, so strong it gives me a pain in my chest. She would be so disappointed in me. I can picture the look of shock on her face, the confusion that would appear in her eyes when someone did something that hurt her feelings. "She's my daughter, James. My only girl. I named you her guardian. I thought you'd look after her. Are you really going to offload her to a stranger, or to that arsehole, Blue? Are you that fucking selfish?"

Yeah, Maddie, I really am. Seems you didn't know me as well as you thought you did.

Henry and Aroha talk quietly from time to time, but I don't speak for the rest of the journey. I look out of the window, fighting with fury and shame and grief, glad when Henry finally pulls up outside Kia Kaha.

"She's still asleep," Aroha says softly. "I'll go home and pick up some clothes, and then I'll drive out to you. What's the address?" I tell her, and she programs it into her phone. "Are you going home now?" she asks.

"In a minute," Henry says. "Alex and Tyson are on their way out, so we'll catch up with them, then head off. James, you drive your Porsche. I'll bring Leia."

"See you soon," Aroha says. "Hopefully she'll stay asleep until you get there."

The three of us get out and close the doors as softly as we can. Aroha heads over to her Honda, and soon she's reversing out and heading off with a wave.

Henry looks at me. "You fell on your feet there."

"Tell me about it. There's no way I'd find a nanny at six p.m. on the fourth of January."

We look across as the doors open and Alex and Tyson come out, Tyson carrying my laptop bag. I know that Henry has already texted them to let them know that I identified Maddie. They come over and give me a bearhug, Tyson first, then Alex.

"Bro," Alex says as he moves back, "I'm so sorry."

"Henry told us about the phone call with Blue," Tyson comments.

"They're looking for him now," Henry says.

"They're not treating her death as suspicious though, are they?" Alex asks.

"They said they weren't," I reply, "I think the DI believes Maddie called Blue to tell him about the baby, and he said he didn't want to know, which upset her so much she killed herself."

"Doesn't sound like Maddie," Alex says.

I give him a relieved look. "Thank you. I don't think so either."

"She'd have been more likely to tell him to fuck himself."

I give a short, humorless laugh. "Yeah."

"So he's not on the birth certificate?"

"Nope."

"And she listed you as Leia's guardian?"

"Yep."

"So he'd have to apply to the court to be a guardian?"

"I guess. I need to see a lawyer to sort out the legality of it all."

He gives me a level look. "What will you do if they find him and he wants to play a part in her life?"

"Strangle him? Shoot him?"

"Push him down a flight of stairs," Tyson suggests.

Henry shrugs. "Poison would be less conspicuous."

"I'll rig up a piano to drop on him," Alex says.

We all give small smiles.

"I don't know yet," I say carefully. "I feel like my head's going to explode. I don't want kids."

They all sigh.

"But she's Maddie's girl," I say. "I'd be a fucking arsehole not to look after her, right?"

Alex meets my gaze steadily. "We've all known each other a long time. I think we can be honest with each other, don't you?"

I shrug.

"What's happened to Maddie is sad and unfortunate, but it's not your fault," he says. "You work long hours. You're away a lot. You've never wanted children. I wouldn't think less of you if you were to say that you wanted to remain her guardian and have a say in her future, but that you would prefer it if someone else had day-to-day care of her."

I appreciate his honesty. He's saying what he thinks I want to hear. But I know without having to ask that if he were in my place, he wouldn't be giving Leia away.

I look at Henry, who just frowns. Then at Tyson, who suddenly feels the desire to try to erase a smudge on the car.

All at once, I feel an overwhelming weariness.

"Okay," I say. "Well, I'm heading home. Aroha's picking up some stuff and then she's going to come over and be Leia's nanny until we work things out."

Alex and Tyson exchange amused glances.

"Shut up," I say, only half joking. "I'm not the type of guy to bang the nanny, whatever you might think." I feel myself bristle. I can't take teasing today.

"All right," Alex says softly, "take care of yourself. Call us tomorrow, and let us know if there's anything we can do." He and Tyson head back inside.

"You sure about this?" I ask Henry. "What if she wakes up?"

"I'll manage." Henry gets in his car and waves goodbye. I head over to the Porsche, get in, and follow him out.

My head's buzzing, and I find it hard to think straight as I drive. Everything goes around in my head, emotions tangling like items in a washing machine.

I'm relieved when we finally get to West Melton. We park outside my house and get out, and I walk over to his Range Rover.

"She's still asleep," he says, looking relieved. "What a day."

I glance through the window. Presumably she'll wake up soon. "How often do babies need feeding?"

"No idea. Twice a day?"

"Jesus, even I know it's more than that. Is it every two hours. Or every four?"

"Fuck knows," Henry says. "I know absolutely zero about bringing up kids, and I doubt that's going to change."

I remember then that he can't have children. "Do you think you'll ever adopt?" I ask.

"Depends on the girl, I guess. If she really wants children, and if she's prepared to overlook that I can't have them, then maybe. Lot of ifs there, though."

"Yeah, but if a girl loves you, there'd be no question, would there?"

"I dunno, man. The urge to procreate is a strong one. Women want the whole kit and caboodle—they want their guy to get them pregnant, to take the test, have the bump, to go through the birth, even with all the pain. It's natural. Adoption's better than nothing, of course, but the love's gotta be strong to overcome that basic urge."

Henry paints a harsh picture, but then his experience hasn't been great. Shaz's desire for a child was bigger than her love for him. It's no wonder he's cynical.

We carry in all the bags and equipment, and I'm just lifting out Leia's car seat when she finally stirs, spits out the dummy, and starts crying.

"Fuck." I carry her inside and take her through to the kitchen. "We need to make up some formula."

"How do we do that?"

"What did you do with the bottles?"

"Uh…" We hunt around and eventually track them down. "Here's the formula," Henry says, retrieving one of the tins.

"What does it say?" Leia is now bawling her eyes out. I bend and unclip her harness, then lift her out. She struggles in my arms, her face screwed up as she yells her fury. I feel a surge of helplessness.

Henry reads the instructions. "It says here you're supposed to use boiled water."

"Shit. Put the kettle on, then."

"Boiled, cooled water."

"Fuck. We'll have to boil it, then run it under the cold tap."

"That'll take forever."

"What option do we have?"

He mutters something and fills the kettle.

"I can't do this," I say, my panic rising. I try giving Leia the dummy again, but she spits it out after she discovers it's not delivering any milk. My throat tightens. *Maddie*, I think, *I'm so useless at this. Why did you leave me?*

"Hello, hello." A voice behind us makes me spin around, and I feel a surge of relief as Aroha comes in and closes the door behind her. She looks around the house, eyes wide, but doesn't comment as she walks in, carrying a suitcase. She puts it down. "Someone sounds hungry," she says. "And I don't mean you, Henry."

"I was just boiling a kettle," Henry says.

"Actually, I brought some of the boiled water from Maddie's fridge." She ferrets around in the change bag and brings out a bottle.

I wince as Leia increases her volume. "Why does a baby's shriek cut through you so much?"

"It's supposed to," Aroha says. "She wants to get your attention."

"Can you take her, please?"

"I'll just make the milk."

"No, I'll do that. Just… just take her."

Her eyes meet mine. "All right," she says softly, and she comes up and lifts Leia out of my arms.

Maddie got so anxious when she couldn't quiet Leia—she'd walk up and down, late at night, rocking her and crying at the same time, and saying how she was a terrible mother because she couldn't comfort her own child. I wonder whether Aroha will be the same—will she get stressed and agitated?

But she just kisses Leia's head and says, "It's okay, little bubs." Seemingly unconcerned at the baby's wails, she walks into the kitchen, and says, "Come on, let's make you some milk, shall we?"

Chapter Thirteen

Aroha

"Let's have a look at the tin," I say, taking it from Henry and reading it. "How much water is in the bottle?"

"One hundred and fifty milliliters," Henry says, checking it.

"It's one scoop per fifty, so James, add three scoops of the formula. Yes, like that, but level it off. That's right. Now put the teat through the ring and screw it on. That's it! Put the lid on, and shake it so it all mixes up. Henry, run the hot water. Now, James, just hold the bottle under it for a little while so it heats up a bit. You can pick up the bottle warmer from the house tomorrow."

I cuddle Leia while James turns the bottle beneath the hot water. He looks a little more relaxed now, even though Leia's still yelling.

He glances at me, and I nod and hold my hand out and take the bottle from him. I shake it with my free hand to make sure there are no hot spots in the milk. "Hold out your hand, palm up," I instruct him. When he does, I tip a little of the milk onto his wrist. "How does it feel?"

"Warm. Not hot."

"That's fine. Well done, guys!" I take the bottle and a muslin square and walk into the living room, sit in one of the armchairs facing the TV, and tease Leia's lips with the teat. She starts sucking immediately, and the house falls quiet.

James blows out a breath and exchanges a glance with Henry.

"I feel like we've defused a bomb," Henry says.

I stifle a laugh and look down at Leia. She really is the most gorgeous baby. She could be James's, with those big turquoise eyes. What a shame I never knew her mother; I'd like to have met her.

"Well, I'll leave you to it," Henry says.

"Thanks, Henry," I call, and he waves as he heads to the door. James goes with him, and they talk in low voices for a moment.

I look around the room, taking in the furnishings. Gaby had told me the house was a mansion, but I thought she'd exaggerated. She hadn't. When I pulled up at the front gate, I had to enter a code that James had sent me. The long drive wound through beautiful gardens before widening out in front of a huge house. It looks as if it's in three wings. At the moment we're in the central section, in a glorious living room. It's all open plan, with a dining area to the left, a black leather suite with an L-shaped sofa and two rocking recliners, a glass-topped coffee table, and an absolutely enormous TV. A PlayStation sits on a glass shelf beneath it.

Behind me is a large farmhouse kitchen, with marble worktops, a central square pine table and chairs, and every piece of equipment you could ever need. Does he use it all? Everywhere looks spotless, almost like a show home, and nothing close to being child friendly.

James closes the front door, and he walks into the living room and sits in the chair opposite me. I rock the recliner slowly, watching him.

"You look so relaxed," he says.

"I did a free online course called Mindful with Your Baby. It looked at stress factors and how, when you're anxious, you can transmit that anxiety to the baby. It talked about meditation and other ways to relax, so you and baby can read each other. I found it very useful." His expression hasn't changed. "I'm guessing you think that's all New Age bullshit," I tease.

But he shakes his head. "I can see it's working. Maddie was always so anxious, and I'm sure Leia picked up on that. I wish she'd been calmer."

"It's easier for me. If you don't like the way I care for Leia, you'll tell me and I'll either change what I'm doing, or we'll part ways."

"Jeez, please don't leave."

I chuckle, looking down at the baby. "I'm not going anywhere. I'll be here for as long as you need me."

He doesn't reply. I glance at him, but he's looking out of the window at the gardens. He looks stern and sad, nothing like the joyful playboy who went down on me in the hotel room. His life has been turned upside down in less than a day. Is he wondering how his house would change if Leia were to stay here? Sticky handprints on the glass coffee table, chocolate fingers shoved in his PlayStation, his neat lawn littered with scooters and balls and a swing? LEGO pieces stuck in the plush pile of the spotless carpet? His dining table converted into a tent with blankets? I can't see it, and I doubt he can either.

The sun is low in the sky, and the room is filled with an orange light. It's so quiet here—you can't hear traffic, or any people, or even lawnmowers or motorbikes in the distance.

It strikes me then how different his life is from mine. When my grandfather died, the house was full of people from the moment it happened until weeks afterward. Everyone flocked around, bringing food, giving hugs, eager to help out where they could. His body was in an open casket, and my *whanau* expressed their grief openly, not ashamed to show their sadness at his passing. People played their guitars and sang and cried together. Nobody was alone, and we all found comfort in each other.

James's sister has died, and he's here, in this house, alone apart from me and Leia. All these empty, lifeless rooms, achingly silent. He has so much money, but it can't buy a loving family.

I know he has lots of friends. Alex, Tyson, and Henry will have offered help, and no doubt Juliette, Gaby, Damon and Belle, and lots of others have called or left messages. But a voice on the phone isn't the same as physical touch. A hug is worth a thousand words.

I look back at Leia. Her sucking has slowed down. She's drunk nearly the whole bottle. What a little sweetheart.

I remove the teat and put the bottle down, drape a muslin square over my shoulder, then get to my feet and lift her upright. Singing softly, I rock her from side to side as I rub her back.

"What's that song?" James asks after a while. He hasn't moved, and he's sitting with his long legs stretched out, watching me.

"It's called *Wairua*. *Wairua* is the spirit or the soul, and the song talks about the sun shining and letting the spirit carry you away. I'm telling her about her *māmā*, aren't I, *piripoho*?" It means babe-in-arms, as well as treasured or valued.

James inhales, and I can see the emotion sweep over him as his eyes shine, and he leans on the arm of the chair, resting his fingers on his lips. I look down at Leia and continue singing softly to her, turning away a little to let him deal with his grief.

"Sorry," he says eventually, his voice husky. "I didn't expect you to say that."

I kiss Leia's fuzzy head. "That's okay, *matua kēkē*." I smile at him. "It means uncle. Grief is nothing to apologize for."

"You're very open with your emotions, aren't you?"

"I suppose," I say with surprise. "I hadn't thought about it."

"Emotion isn't welcome in my family," he says with some bitterness.

"What's your father like?" I ask curiously. "Is he like you?"

He doesn't answer for a while. Eventually, he says, "I'm not used to talking about him, or my feelings."

I continue to move with Leia, puzzling over that. "Sorry," I say with some amusement. "We talk about everything in my family."

After a while, he says, "I hope I'm not like him. He wasn't a good father. I don't remember him ever giving me a hug." He looks embarrassed then, as if he thinks it's weak to admit he wanted affection from his dad.

I don't know what to say to that, so I just continue to rub Leia's back. She gives a little burp, and I murmur, "Good girl."

"Māori *tangihanga* last a while, don't they?" he asks, so I guess he's thinking about Maddie's funeral.

I nod. "Often three days, sometimes longer."

"I get the feeling you don't think about death in the same way."

"The dead play an important role in Māori traditions. We acknowledge them at all gatherings, with *whaikōrero*—speeches, and *waiata*—songs. And everyone cries." I smile. "You know the word *whakapapa?*"

"Genealogy?"

"That's right." I show him the tattoo that curves over my forearm. "That's what this shows. The main lines are called *manawa*, which means heart. They represent your life, your life journey, and your time spent on Earth. The *korus* or curls coming off the *manawa* are new life and new beginnings. Each one shows the important people in your life journey: your mother, father, grandparents, siblings, children, and friends. It's a reminder you can carry with you of the people you've loved."

He takes a deep breath in, then lets it go. "I envy you," he says. "Grief, death, and old age is something my family shuts away in boxes. We don't like to think about them." He sighs and takes out his phone. "I should make some phone calls."

"Okay. Would you mind showing me where Leia and I are going to sleep? I'll change her and put her in her carry seat for a while, and then I'll make us something to eat, if you like."

"You don't have to do that," he says.

"I know." I smile.

He clears his throat, then he gets to his feet. "My room's that way." He gestures to the east wing of the house. "I thought maybe you'd prefer a room on the other side." He picks up the change bag and my case and walks off to the west wing.

Is that because he thinks he won't hear Leia as much if I'm that side? I follow him across the living room and then along the corridor.

"There are four bedrooms this side," he says. "Feel free to use whichever you want, but I'd suggest this one. These two have an interconnecting door, so we could convert one of them into a room for Leia temporarily."

Temporarily. So he's not expecting to keep her, then?

I pause in the doorway of one of them. The rooms are both large with king-size beds, both made up with lavender and light-green bedding respectively. It doesn't look as if either of them has ever been used.

I watch him put the bags into the lavender-colored room. "Why do you have such a big house?" I ask, only realizing as the words come out that he might think it a rude question.

"I like space," he says, the corner of his mouth curving up.

"Well, there's definitely plenty of that here."

He glances around as if seeing the house for the first time. "Honestly? I don't know. I wanted somewhere spacious and quiet. Somewhere I could escape if I needed to."

I think of his comment about Maddie's house: *She said she felt she could finally breathe*. It suggests they both felt constrained or constricted in their childhood. Maybe their father was terribly strict. Adulthood brings a certain kind of freedom, I would imagine, if you've had a childhood like that.

"I bet Cassie's missing the house," I tease.

His gaze comes back to mine. "She never came here."

My eyebrows rise. Henry didn't tell me that. "What do you mean? Gaby said you bought it ages ago."

"I did. I always met Cassie in my apartment in town. I've never brought a girl here. Now I have two." He gives me and Leia an amused look.

I don't know what to say to that. He seems to leave me speechless a lot.

He gestures at the door. "I can get a lock put on there tomorrow, if you like."

"Oh James," I scoff, "don't be silly. I know you're not going to come in in the middle of the night and ravage me."

"Probably not," he says.

"Damn it."

We both give a short laugh.

He meets my eyes for a moment, and I remember when he kissed me at the airport, the gentle way his lips moved across mine.

Then he sighs and backs away. "I'll make those calls," he states, as if feeling bad that he smiled.

"Okay." I watch him leave, sigh, then go into the lavender-colored room. Lifting the bag onto the bed, I unpop the change mat and lay it out, then lower Leia onto it. She wakes and mews a little, but I talk to her softly as I change her, and she soon quietens. I clean her and put on a new nappy, then dress her in a pretty lemon-colored onesie with a duck on the front.

Lifting Leia into my arms, I take the nappy into the next room, which I decide will be Leia's room eventually when we get a bassinet, and deposit the nappy in the rubbish bin that has a lid on it. I'll have to remind James to bring back the nappy bin from Maddie's house tomorrow.

Picking up her Pooh Bear and the dummy, I carry her back into the living room. James is out on the deck, walking up and down as he talks into his phone. I bring the carry seat into the kitchen, lower Leia into it, tuck Pooh beside her, and position her so she can see me. Then I start exploring the kitchen.

The cupboards are well stocked—pasta, rice, tins of beans, chickpeas, and tomatoes. The fridge contains cheese, bacon, cooked chicken, bread, butter, condiments, and lots of fresh vegetables, plus there's a box of strawberries and one of blueberries. A bowl of fresh fruit rests on the counter—bananas and apples.

I open the freezer. Handwritten stickers on the plastic boxes proclaim their contents: various pasta dishes, lots of curries, some roast dinners, and a few tubs of expensive ice cream. I've seen his handwriting, and this isn't it. He's also told me he hasn't invited any girl back here. In that case, I reckon someone comes in and cooks for him, then freezes these meals, and he just reheats them as and when.

I could just use a couple of these, but I enjoy cooking and find it calming. He hasn't eaten since lunch and he needs to keep his strength up, plus, I'm hungry too. Tonight we're having a proper dinner.

He's still talking, so I put some music on my phone, not too loudly, then get out the pasta, a tin of tomatoes, an onion, some tomato paste from the cupboard, and the bacon, a red bell pepper, and a green chili from the fridge. I stir fry the onion, add the bacon, pepper, and chili, tip in the tin of tomatoes, and add a sprinkle of herbs from the spice rack.

I've just finished cooking the pasta when James comes back into the house and walks through to the kitchen.

"You're cooking," he says, astonished. "I thought you were going to, like, make a sandwich or something."

"I'm hungry, and you haven't eaten since lunch, plus I enjoy it."

His lips curve up. He puts his phone on the breakfast bar, pulls up a bar stool, and sits, leaning on the counter. "I should have known you could cook," he says.

"What do you mean?"

"You're very homely."

"I don't think it means what you think it means," I say wryly, "or I hope not, anyway. It means plain and ordinary."

"Jesus, I didn't mean that! I mean that you're good in the home—with kids, cooking, that sort of thing."

"I know," I tease, stirring the pasta. "Cassie couldn't cook?"

"I doubt she even knew where the kitchen was."

"Aw."

He sighs. "That was spiteful. I didn't mean to be."

"It's all right. I'm sure she had other talents." I give him a mischievous glance. He doesn't reply.

Deciding to leave it there, I drain the pasta and add it to the sauce, toss it around a bit, spoon it into two dishes, and top it with grated parmesan. "Come on," I tell him, "Let's eat. I'm starving."

I carry the dishes over to the dining table, where I've already laid out two placemats and cutlery. I return to collect Leia and take her seat over so she can see us. I put my phone on the table, leaving the music on, as it's so quiet without it. It's an old album playing, Kiwi artist Bic Runga's *Beautiful Collision*, but he obviously knows it because I hear him hum along to *When I See You Smile* as he opens the kitchen cupboard.

"Do you want a glass of wine?" he asks.

"Not for me. I don't drink when I'm looking after children. But please, have one yourself."

"Actually, I might have a whisky," he says. "Do you mind?"

"Of course not. It's your house, and I think, of all days, you probably need one today."

I sit and sip from a glass of water, watching as he goes into the kitchen and pours himself a large measure from a bottle with a green label. He might be sad, and possibly angry or resentful at what's happened, but he's still gorgeous. He's tall, but he doesn't seem as big as Henry because he's slimmer, lithe and muscular rather than bulky. He's wearing a white shirt today with jeans, but no tie, and he's rolled up the sleeves. The open neck reveals tanned skin a shade darker and warmer-hued than my own light-brown, cool-toned skin. I saw there was a swimming pool outside, so I guess he spends a lot of the summer in there, catching the sun. He has a five o'clock shadow tonight, and his usually combed, neat hair is unruly, reflecting that he's run his hands through it a lot today. He's taken off his shoes and socks, and his feet are brown.

He brings the whisky back to the table and sits opposite me. He picks up his fork and leans on the table, poking the pasta, lost in thought.

Something occurs to me then. "I'm sorry, I should have asked if you mind me eating with you. Would you rather I took mine to my room?"

He lifts his gaze to me with a frown. "Like a servant? Don't be daft."

"Well, technically I am hired help."

"You're my friend." He glares at me. "It's not up for debate."

I poke my tongue out at him. His frown lifts, although he doesn't smile as such. Instead, he leans back in his chair with a big sigh and looks down at Leia.

"You want to talk about it?" I ask.

"Not really."

Okay… Put in my place, I look around the room. "You have a lovely house."

"Thank you. I like it."

"I can't imagine living somewhere so big on my own, though."

"I like being alone," he says flatly. "I come here to escape the world. I don't need family, or children, to make my life complete."

Ooh, that touched a sore spot.

I lower my gaze to my pasta and spear some on my fork. Maybe this was a mistake. I can't quite work out our relationship. I think of us as a similar age, but the three years difference seems bigger at the moment. He's done a lot more than I have—he's traveled, gone to university, he runs a business, and he manages huge amounts of money. I know he's well-respected in the business community, and I met some of the guys he has connections with in Auckland, all of whom are rich, smart, powerful men. He said we're friends, but we're not, really. We have mutual acquaintances, but we have nothing in common. I'm not the sort of girl he'd be interested in dating—I'm not wealthy, sophisticated, or accomplished in any way. I know Cassie works in fashion and is semi-famous in the industry. I'm sure she drives a flash car and owns designer sunglasses, and knows the difference between various wine grapes, rather than buying whatever's on special offer.

We don't have a class system as such in New Zealand, not the way they do in England, but the rich and poor still lead very different lives. His dad's a billionaire; mine has just been made redundant from the meat processing plant. James has hired me to look after the baby—he's paying me to perform certain tasks. I'm an employee—we're not friends, not really.

"I'm sorry," he says.

I lift my gaze to his, surprised.

"That was rude of me," he adds softly. "You've just cooked me dinner, and you've been kind to me all day. Don't mind me. It's nothing to do with you. I'm a grumpy old bastard."

I laugh and eat a mouthful of pasta. "You're not old."

"A grumpy young bastard, then."

"Yeah, that's better."

He chuckles. Then he eats a forkful of the pasta. He chews for a bit and swallows, then says, "Mmm. That's good."

Pleased, I smile, and we eat quietly for a while, while Bic tells us to get some sleep, and the warm evening sun gives Leia a golden crown.

Chapter Fourteen

James

"Is this the first house you've owned?" Aroha asks.

I nod. "I have an apartment in the city as well, although I'm thinking of giving that up. But I saw this place for sale a couple of years ago, and I kept thinking about what it would be like to have somewhere quiet and out of the way, where I could go when I needed some time alone."

"Why didn't you take me to your apartment?" she asks curiously. I have a sip of whisky and just look at her. She reddens. "Oh, of course. I guess Cassie stayed there, and she might have come back. Sorry."

"You don't have anything to apologize for. I'm the arsehole."

"You were on a break," she reminds me.

"Yeah, yeah, I've seen *Friends*."

She gives a small smile. "You're not back with Cassie though?"

"No. We're done," I say firmly.

She leans back, looking puzzled. "You say you bought this house because you needed time alone. That surprises me. You strike me as a sociable kind of guy."

"I am, mostly. But I suffer from migraines, and when I get one I like to come home, pull up the metaphorical drawbridge, and wait for it to pass."

Her eyebrows rise. "I'm sorry to hear that. I've never known a man suffer from them."

"They're not as common as they are with women, but yeah, some men suffer. Maddie has them, too. I mean had them." I correct myself sadly and sigh. "So did our mum."

"It's genetic?"

"Yeah, does seem to be."

"How do they manifest? An intense headache?"

"For me it starts with a blind spot, then an aura, like lots of sparkling triangles. About half an hour later the headache starts. Sometimes I push through it, but usually by the end of the day I'm no good to anyone."

She leans her chin on a hand. "Does it make you sick?"

I scratch at a mark on the table. No girl has ever asked me about them before. If I ever commented to Cassie about having one, she just gave me a speech about how much women had to suffer every month and how lucky I was, so I learned to keep my mouth shut.

"Sometimes I get nauseous," I admit slowly. "The worst thing is that my ears buzz and I have trouble processing sounds—conversations, traffic, it all gets jumbled. I come home here and there's nothing but birdsong. It's like heaven. I just lie on a floating lounger in the pool or on the sofa on the deck and half-meditate, half-doze."

"So that's how you get your tan," she says. "I hope you put on sun lotion first." She glances at my throat, exposed by the open shirt, then lifts her gaze to mine. Her smile is both mischievous and kind.

Ohhh… I'm going to have to be super careful here. Alex knows what he's talking about when he says never to mix business with pleasure. There's something about this girl that fires me up. I don't know if it's because everything about her is gorgeous, from her shiny brown hair to her painted toenails, or if it's because we've been intimate, and my body remembers it and wants to recreate it and take it to the next step. But she's out of bounds now. Any kind of relationship while she's looking after Leia will be inappropriate and messy. Sex with Aroha would be amazing, no doubt, but in the cold light of day we're two very different people, with different backgrounds and different lives. Leia has to come first—for now, anyway, until I get everything sorted.

I look down at my half-eaten dinner. It tasted great, but I have no appetite, my stomach already filled with a heavy stone of grief. My loss keeps hitting me like a gong being struck at regular intervals, reverberating through me. I forget briefly, and then I remember, and it's like my heart has been shocked with a defibrillator. The disbelief is overwhelming. Maddie can't be dead. It's ridiculous. How can it possibly be true?

"Why don't you go and sit outside while I clean up?" Aroha says.

"You don't have to do that. You're not my housekeeper."

"I know." She starts gathering up the plates. "You do have one though, right?"

"Yeah. Ginny. She's in her thirties, and she's nice, you'll like her. She comes Mondays, Wednesday, and Fridays. If you need anything, just ask her and she'll get it for you." I stand and collect the placemats and take them to the kitchen. "Thank you so much for dinner. I'm sorry I didn't do it justice."

"You had a good half. That's something." She begins running the tap.

"I'll wash."

"James…"

I add some washing liquid to the bowl. I have a dishwasher, but it feels good to do something practical.

She doesn't argue with me again. We stand beside one another while I wash and she dries up the plates and cutlery. Her phone is still playing Bic Runga. I can see Leia, playing with Pooh Bear in her carry seat. And there it is again—the fresh reminder that Maddie's gone, hitting me like a tennis racket around the head. I stop scrubbing the frying pan and lean on the sink for a second, catching my breath.

Aroha puts a hand on my back for a moment and rubs between my shoulder blades. Then she continues drying the dishes.

When we first got home, I regretted asking Aroha here. I thought it would feel intrusive, and that I'd be glad when she withdrew to her room. Instead, I find her presence comforting. She's so gentle and capable, with a little touch of sexy mischievousness that I find so appealing. She's relaxed and not stressful at all. Emotion doesn't bother her, which is a very new experience for me. Although she wears makeup, it's light, and I can see she's naturally beautiful. It's like turning off strip lighting and opening the curtains to let the sunshine into a room.

"I'll be back in a sec," she says when we've finished the dishes. She disappears in the direction of her room.

I wipe across the kitchen counter, then drape the tea towel over the handle of the oven. Finally, I walk slowly across the living room to stand in front of Leia. She's dozed off, her long dark lashes lying on her rosy cheeks.

I feel as if we're two survivors of the Titanic, holding onto pieces of broken furniture, drifting in the cold sea and hoping someone will pull us out.

"I guess that makes me Jack," I murmur to her. I think about the time Maddie and I recreated the scene with Rose and Jack at the bow of the ship when one of Dad's friends took us out in his boat. We were nine, and Maddie stood in front of me, arms outstretched, while I stood behind her, the wind blowing in our faces.

It was the same trip when Maddie slipped while trying to climb around the side of the boat and she nearly fell in. Dad yelled at her and told her she'd spend the rest of the trip in the cabin. I went and sat with her, because it didn't seem fair that she was confined when I wasn't. That incident summarizes our relationship with our father—the two of us drawn together by our mutual hatred of him.

And now she's left me to fight that battle alone. Thanks, Mads.

I think back to when I called my father earlier in the day, at the office.

"The police have just contacted me," he stated. "They said they've found Maddie's body."

"Yeah, they're here now."

"Have you identified her yet?"

"No, I've only just found out."

"Do you think it's her?"

"I don't know. They found Leia at the top of the cliff. Maddie's purse was tucked next to her, and it had her driving license in it. They said it looked like her from her picture."

"Jesus."

We were quiet for a moment.

"Do you think she killed herself?" he asked.

I swallowed hard. "I don't know. I spoke to her last night. She was pretty low. She had my business card in her purse, almost as if she left it there so they'd know who to call."

"She didn't usually carry one?"

"I don't think so."

"Ah God," he said. "Maddie..."

I listened to him cry, my chest heaving with resentment. All the years he'd spent criticizing her, not being there for her... His grief felt fake, selfish—he was crying for himself, not for poor, lonely Maddie. And then I felt awful, because all grief is selfish. He's a hard, uncompromising, sometimes cruel man, but even he can't remain untouched by the loss of his daughter. I said goodbye and hung up, leaving him to it. What could I possibly say to make it better?

Aroha comes back into the living room. She's changed out of her pencil skirt and into a pair of yoga pants, and she's carrying the baby monitor and the receiver. She plugs it into the wall and leaves the monitor by Leia, clips the receiver onto the belt of her yoga pants, then says, "Why don't you show me around the house?"

"Okay."

Slowly, we wander through my home. The guys come here often with Gaby and Juliette, but this is the first time I've shown anyone around like this. I take her through the rest of the west wing first. This has four bedrooms in total, with two bathrooms, and a separate lounge.

We walk back through the main living room into the east wing. This has a small gym and a library lined with bookshelves half-filled with my own books, complete with a couple of comfy chairs and sliding doors that lead into a conservatory. A door leads through to my office.

"I'm guessing you spend a lot of time here," she teases.

My lips curve up. It's pretty messy, the tables covered with papers, folders, and books. "How did you guess?"

"It's very masculine." She walks around, looking at the huge wooden desk in the middle of the room, the black leather sofa. "I'm guessing you decorated this when you were in your Ernest Hemingway phase."

"I suppose it is a bit old-fashioned."

"It smells of you," she says, then gives me an embarrassed look. "Sorry, did I say that out loud?"

I give a short laugh and continue walking through. "This is a spare bedroom. And this is my room."

It's the master bedroom, at the end of the house, so two walls are mostly glass, overlooking the gardens.

"Wow," she says, walking into the room. "I've never seen such a big bed!"

"It's an emperor," I say, amused.

"But you don't bring girls here?"

"I sleep like a starfish. I like space."

She looks at the minimal furniture. "I'm beginning to get that." She walks around the room, then stops and looks at the painting on the wall. It's of a Greek goddess, in beautiful white robes, golden hair tumbling down her back.

"Cassie?" she asks.

I know she's teasing me. "It's Phoebe," I tell her. "Titan Goddess of intellect."

"It's wonderful. Did Damon paint it?"

"Yeah."

"He's so talented."

I ignore the flare of jealousy I feel at her compliment. "Yeah, I saw the ones in his office and commissioned him to do one for me."

She follows me out to the last room and stops in the doorway. Her jaw drops. "Oh my God."

I smile and watch her walk in. It's a music room, and the walls are lined with my twenty-six guitars.

"James," she whispers. "Les Paul, PRS, Strat, Telecaster, Flying V, Jag, Gretsch… You've got one of everything!"

I feel a swell of pleasure as she recognizes all the different guitars. "Yeah, I'm quite proud of the collection."

She turns her big hazel eyes on me. "You play?"

"I do. Do you?"

"Well, sort of. Acoustic, mainly. I was going to bring mine, but I'm glad I didn't now. It would have felt really out of place!" She laughs.

I walk over to the Martin, lift it off its hooks, and pass it to her. "Here you go. You can use this while you're here."

Her jaw drops again. "Oh my God. This must have cost you a fortune!"

"About ten grand, yeah. Go on, try it." I want to see her play.

She perches on one of the chairs, resting it on her lap. She forms a C chord, and its beautiful voice rings out, perfectly in tune. Smiling, she starts strumming. To my surprise, she plays The Eagles' *Hotel California*.

As she strums, I lift the Telecaster off the wall and sit opposite her, listening. She plays well, confident with the chords. When she reaches the guitar solo, I start playing. She tries to harmonize with me the way Felder and Walsh did on the original, but can't quite nail it, and eventually we stop with a laugh.

"It's a bit beyond me," she says. "I'm more of a rhythm girl."

"Tough on an acoustic." I replace the Tele on the wall.

She hands the Martin to me, but I say, "Keep it for now."

"Okay."

I pick up a small stand, walk back through to the living room, put it next to one of the armchairs, and she places the guitar on it.

Outside, the sun is very low in the sky. I wander over to the sliding doors, open them, and go out onto the deck. Aroha follows me, and we stand side by side, looking out over the garden. Aroha hums *Listening for the Weather*, one of Maddie's favorite songs.

"Maddie stood right where you're standing only a week ago," I say.

Aroha turns to look at me and tucks a strand of hair behind her ear. "Oh, really?"

"Yeah. I can almost see her. It's so clear to me. But that image I can see is like when you look into a bright light and you see an imprint on your lens. She's gone. And she's not coming back." I shake my head, looking out across the lawn. "I can't believe it."

She doesn't say anything. I fight against a surge of emotion. Jesus. I hate the way it keeps hitting me. I feel as if someone's trying to carve out my heart with a melon baller. I exhale, and it comes out as an involuntary, painful, "Ahhh…"

Aroha turns to me, and she holds out her hand. I look at it for a moment, too miserable to move. I don't want pity, and I don't want her to witness my grief.

But she picks up my hand and then moves closer to me, brings our hands up, and places her left on my shoulder.

"Dance with me," she says simply.

Out of politeness, I guess, I move from side to side with her. My feet feel frozen to the floor for a while, my back rigid. I feel resentful, hating the fact that she's trying to comfort me, and even more that gradually it's starting to work.

After a while she releases my hand and slides her arms around my waist. In response, I lower my arms around her. We're barely moving now, but she's warm against me, and the human touch thaws me completely.

"I'm so sorry," she says, stroking my back.

I just give a shivery sigh.

She retreats a little to look at me. "Tell me a good memory you have of Maddie," she says with a smile.

I study her, surprised, then look out at the garden, thinking. Eventually, my lips curve up. "When we were twenty-one, we had a party at Mum's place for all our friends. Maddie and I did a very bad, drunken performance of *Don't Go Breaking My Heart*."

Aroha laughs. "I wish I'd seen that."

"I'm glad you didn't. It was awful. She couldn't sing for giggling." I smile at her.

She smiles back. Her light-brown hair lifts in the small breeze. I like the way she looks at me, starstruck, as if I'm someone famous.

Unbidden, my gaze drops to her mouth, which looks soft and oh so kissable, and her lips part. It would be so easy to kiss her. I know I could lose myself in her. Let her carry me away on a wave of pleasure, where I wouldn't be able to think about anything except her curves, her smooth skin, the sweet taste of her that I can still remember.

I lift my gaze back to hers, knowing I mustn't, fighting with myself. Her eyes are calm, neither inviting nor refusing, as if she doesn't want to be blamed for it, and she's leaving the decision to me. I know she wouldn't say no, though. If I kiss her now, we'll end up in bed.

Ah… I want that so much…

A knock at the front door brings me to my senses, and we draw apart.

"Who's that?" Aroha asks, startled.

"No idea. Has to be someone who has the code to the gate."

We go back into the house, and she walks over to Leia, while I go to the front door and open it. To my surprise, all the guys are standing there: Alex, Henry, and Tyson.

Alex holds up a bottle of thirty-year-old Macallan that must have cost him close to ten grand. "We thought you might want some company," he says. "If you don't, that's fine, we'll go."

"But we'll take the whisky with us," Henry points out.

I chuckle and move back. "Come in."

Alex gives me a bearhug. "You're sure?"

I nod, pleased to see them, and touched that they've come around. Henry hugs me, then Tyson, and I close the door behind them.

"Hello," Alex is saying to Aroha.

"Hey, guys." She puts her finger to her lips, and they all quieten. She smiles at them all, then at me. "I'll take Leia through to my room."

"You don't have to do that," I protest.

Henry says, "Aw, join us!" and Alex points out, "You've got the monitor."

But she just shakes her head. "I'm tired. No worries at all. Enjoy the whisky." She picks Leia up, gives me a last smile, then disappears down the corridor, closing the door behind her.

The guys look at me, and Henry lifts an eyebrow. "Sorry, did we interrupt something?"

"No," I say wryly. "Not at all. She's just acting as Leia's nanny." Trying not to think about her soft body pressed against mine, I turn away and go into the kitchen. "Whisky glasses all around." I get four out of the cupboard, and Henry extracts some ice from the freezer. Alex opens the whisky, and he pours a generous glug into each glass.

"Who's driving?" I ask.

"We Ubered," Tyson says, taking one of the glasses. "We're here to commiserate." He lifts his glass. "To Maddie."

The others lift their glasses. "To Maddie."

I lift my glass and take a mouthful of the amber liquid. My throat tightens, though, and for a moment I can't swallow. I lower my glass to the counter, holding a fist to my mouth as I wait for the spasm to pass.

Alex puts a hand on my shoulder. "I found a photo," he says, taking out his phone. He scrolls down, then turns it around to show us. It's of all of us at Henry's wedding. Maddie is in the center, half-laughing, half-wincing as a semi-drunk Tyson tries to kiss her cheek.

We all laugh, and I rub my nose as I finally manage to swallow the mouthful of whisky.

"Come on," Henry says. "Bring the whisky, Alex. Let's go and sit on the deck."

I follow them out there, relieved that tonight, at least, I'm not alone.

Chapter Fifteen

Aroha

I change into my summer pajamas—a cotton tee and shorts—and clean my teeth. I haven't bathed Leia, but Marina told me she'd given her one earlier, and anyway it's getting late, and Leia's asleep. Never wake a sleeping baby! I'm happy to live by those rules. Tomorrow I'll try to have more of a routine.

I bring Leia into my bed without waking her. Part of me wants to think about what's happened, and the moment when James looked as if he was going to kiss me, but I'm worn out by all the emotion the day has brought, and I end up dozing off.

It's around eleven thirty when I rouse, conscious that Leia is making noises next to me. I've no doubt her routine is all screwed up, and it's been about six hours since her last bottle, so she's probably hungry and ready for a dream feed.

I pick her up, murmuring to her, and she quietens, looking up at me with her big turquoise eyes. "So like Uncle James," I murmur, lifting the mat onto the bed.

I change her quickly, then lift her into my arms and walk out of my room and down the corridor. As I open the door, though, I stop as I hear laughter and the sound of men's voices. Oh damn, the guys are still here. I should've thought of that. I hesitate, touching my no-doubt-wild hair and realizing I'm not wearing any makeup, but there's nothing I can do. Leia needs feeding, and I'm not here for a beauty pageant.

Muttering under my breath, I go through to the kitchen. The guys are all out on the deck, feet up, talking and drinking. Hopefully I can make her milk quietly.

But as I take the bottle of boiled water out of the fridge, she starts crying. The guys look over, and James puts down his drink, rises, and comes into the house.

"Hey," I say, "I'm so sorry, I didn't realize you'd still be up."

"That's okay." He smiles. His hair is rumpled, and he looks more relaxed than he did earlier. "How's she doing?"

"She's fine, she just needs a feed."

"Want me to make the bottle?"

"Oh. Okay." I rock Leia, watching him scoop the formula in, shake the bottle, then run it under the hot water, an expert now. "How are you?" I ask.

"Yeah, all right." He shakes the bottle and tests it on his wrist. "Good to go." Still holding it, he gestures with his head toward the deck. "Come and sit with us for a bit."

"Oh God, no, I'm not even dressed…"

"Come on." He takes my hand and tugs me.

Reluctantly, I follow him outside. It's a little cooler than it was.

"Hey," the guys all say, smiling.

"Come and sit here," James says, moving up to make room on the outdoor sofa.

"Thank you." I sit between him and Henry and prop my bare feet up on the low table in the middle. Alex and Tyson are in the chairs on the other side. "Um… James, I'm so sorry, would you mind getting one of Leia's blankets from my room? It's a little cool out here."

"Oh, of course." He gets up again and disappears inside.

I start feeding Leia, and she stares up at me with her big eyes as she sucks.

"Would you like a drink?" Henry asks, gesturing at the whisky bottle. A third of it has vanished, so they've made good headway.

"No thanks," I say, "not while I'm looking after Leia."

Alex exchanges a glance with Henry and they both smile—don't know what that's about.

"She looks content," Tyson says.

I straighten her onesie. "Yeah. It's good in one way, and also sad that she doesn't know about her mum."

As one, the guys all sigh.

"How's James?" I ask.

"Okay," Alex replies. "We've been talking about when we first met Maddie."

"Ah, that's good."

"And about Leia," Henry states.

"Oh? Has he decided what he's going to do?"

"Not yet," Alex says. "We were discussing whether duty and guilt should play a part in the decision."

James comes back out and hands me Leia's white blanket, sitting next to me again. I tuck the blanket under and around her, and settle back, curling my toes over the edge of the table. I see him glance at my scarlet toenails, but he doesn't say anything.

"What do you think?" Alex asks me.

"It's not my place to say," I reply awkwardly.

"It's archaic to have a group of men deciding a girl's fate," Alex says. "And Leia doesn't have any other women around to speak up for her."

I glance at James. He's staring into his whisky glass, swirling the liquid over the ice. He doesn't look at me.

These guys are all wealthy, smart, sophisticated, and powerful in their own way. I'm a childcare assistant and beautician—hardly in their league. I've never had staff, board meetings, or international Zoom calls. I didn't know Maddie either.

But Alex is right. Leia doesn't have a woman to speak up for her. I'm sure they'll also ask Gaby and Juliette's opinion. But I'm the only girl here right now, and she's currently in my care.

I look down at Leia—at her big turquoise eyes framed by dark lashes, her button nose, her rosebud lips, her soft cheeks. Her tiny hands, with their miniature nails. She stares back at me, her eyes full of trust.

"I have a large, extended *whanau*," I say, referring to my family, conscious of them all listening to me. "If a parent were to pass away, a child would be cared for by the rest of us. Everyone would flock together to help. We would never give a baby away." I glance at James. His face is expressionless.

"But this is a very different situation," I continue softly. "You're affluent, and if you brought Leia up, she'd want for nothing, which is great. But you're a single guy. You've admitted you don't want kids, and if you were to keep her, the majority of Leia's care would be done by a succession of nannies. We care for our charges, but it's not the same as being brought up by loving parents."

He looks up at me then. I meet his gaze openly.

"I don't think you should keep her out of duty or guilt," I continue. "You could still be Leia's guardian, keep in touch with her, be the kind of uncle who takes her to the cinema on her birthday and tells her about her mum, if you wanted to play a part in her life. But there's no shame in admitting you'd prefer someone else to care for her day-to-day."

He meets my eyes then. His lips curve up, just a little. "Thank you," he murmurs.

Nobody says anything for a moment. Leia sucks contentedly at the teat, her eyes closing.

"Do you remember at my wedding," Henry says, "you dared Maddie to do a dance with you that you used to do as kids?"

James rolls his eyes. "I knew you were going to bring that up."

"What dance?" I ask, amused.

"It was like the one that Ross and Monica do in *Friends*," Alex says. I giggle.

"I was a bit tipsy," James protests.

"Seems to be a theme," I comment. He just gives me a wry look.

Tyson changes the subject, asking about the funeral, and the guys chat for a bit, discussing options. I concentrate on Leia, thinking how beautiful she is. I know she's not James's child, but I like the fact that she has a blood connection to him. It's like holding a little piece of him. I guess this is how it feels when you have your own children with a guy, and the baby is part of you and part of him. It's not in my future, but I can see the attraction.

Leia seems to have had enough milk. I lift her over my shoulder and rub her back. James watches me. His gaze lifts to my hair, and his lips curve up.

"Don't mock me," I say. "I didn't know you lot were going to be out here when I got up."

Henry chuckles. "We'll be off soon."

"Well judging by the whisky bottle, you—" I stop as Leia gives a loud burp. "Ooh! Sweetie, that wasn't very ladylike." I look at James. "I can tell she's related to you."

The others chuckle. James just meets my eyes, amused.

"Would you mind holding her for a minute?" I ask him. "I want to go to the bathroom, and get myself a drink. Then I'll take her back to bed."

He sits up. "Ah… okay." Clearly, he'd rather not, but he doesn't want to say no in front of the others.

I rise and pass Leia to him. He takes her awkwardly and sits back, and I get to my feet. "I won't be long," I say, and I head off to the bathroom.

Afterward, I return to the kitchen, pour myself a glass of water, and have a long drink. I can see through to the deck. Part of me had wondered whether James might have handed Leia over to one of the others. But he's still holding her. He's standing now though, facing the garden, rocking her a little.

I rinse the glass, then cross the living room. As I approach the deck, Alex lifts a finger to his lips. Nodding, I tiptoe out and lower myself quietly onto the sofa.

Henry's talking, and he sees Alex's gesture but continues to talk, covering the fact that we're watching James as he holds his niece.

James is looking at Leia as he moves from side to side, rocking her. I can just see his face in profile, and his expression is tender. My heart gives an unexpected bump. When you hold that tiny, defenseless figure in your arms, it's impossible not to feel fiercely protective. Is he thinking about Maddie, and how she named him Leia's guardian? She wanted him to have her daughter if something happened to her. If he gives her away, he'll be going against her wishes. That must be haunting him.

As he supports her with one arm, he lifts the other hand and strokes a finger across her forehead, feeling her fine, downy hair. Alex stretches out his legs and links his fingers, then winks at me and gives me a subtle thumbs up.

James turns then, looking surprised as he sees I'm back. He walks slowly over to the sofa and bends to put her back in my arms.

"She smells nice," he murmurs. "I didn't expect that. And she seems very content. Maddie always seemed so frenetic." He runs a hand through his hair. "And now I feel mean for saying that."

"Ah, don't worry," I reply. "My body's not recovering from childbirth. I'm not in pain. And I have no social pressures to contend with—I don't have to prove anything to well-meaning friends and family. I think many new mums think they should know instinctively what's wrong with their baby when it cries, and they feel guilty when they can't figure it out. Add to that raging hormones, pain, and people constantly giving advice, and it can lead to a pretty miserable time."

"And she didn't have a partner to help," Henry adds. "Obviously lots of women cope just fine on their own, but it must be nice to have someone else to share the load."

James slides down in his seat, rests his head on the back, and gives a big sigh. "I should have done more."

"You did what you could," Alex says.

"She called me," James states. "She asked me to come over. I should have made the effort. I let her down." He brushes a hand over his face. Dark shadows mar the skin under his eyes.

My heart goes out to him. On the surface, he's a businessman, successful, capable, who's learned to deal with things on his own, But inside he's just like any other young guy. He doesn't have a wife, a girlfriend, or a mother to comfort him or help him through this, and I do believe that women are, in general, more compassionate in these situations.

"Can I make a suggestion?" I ask.

He lowers his hand and looks at me.

"It's late, you've had an awful day, and you're exhausted. You totally needed a drink, but any more and you're going to sink into melancholy and blame yourself for everything, and that's not what Maddie or Leia need right now. Leia needs her uncle to be clear-headed and strong for her. Like Alex said, you have to make big decisions that will define the rest of her life, and you owe it to her to put aside your guilt and self-criticism, at least until you've decided what you're going to do. So go to bed, get a full night's sleep, and we'll start again tomorrow."

He frowns. Alex looks from him to me, then finishes off his drink. "Time we got going," he says.

"You don't have to—" James begins, but Alex waves a hand, already taking out his phone to call for an Uber. The others finish off their drinks too, and they all get to their feet.

I go to rise, but James instructs, "Stay there."

I bristle a little at the way he says it, but I don't reply, and sit back, exchanging a glance with an amused Alex.

"Take care," he says softly before heading for the door. The others say goodbye to me and Leia, then follow him.

James says goodbye to them all, and then they head out to the front gate, and he closes the door behind them.

Tucking Leia's blanket around her, I hear his footsteps as he comes back to me.

I stiffen as he stands in front of me. Is he going to berate me for trying to tell him what to do? Make it clear that I'm just Leia's nanny, and I'm not his girlfriend, and I can't pass comment on his life and his choices?

I wait for him to yell at me. But instead, he lowers down onto the sofa, leans an elbow on the back, and rests his head on his hand.

I watch Leia blow a tiny bubble, and dab the muslin square at the corners of her mouth. Then I look at James.

To my surprise, he's watching me, not her.

"Are you going to yell at me?" I ask.

"Why would I do that?"

"For bossing you around."

"Maybe I like that."

We both smile.

"Thank you," he says.

"What for?"

"For agreeing to look after Leia, especially after I was such an arsehole to you."

I sigh. "You weren't an arsehole."

"I was, and I'm sorry for it. But it's done."

"It's okay. Don't be so hard on yourself."

He stares out at the dark garden moodily.

"What's bothering you?" I ask after a while.

His gaze comes back to me. "What do you mean?"

"You're angry. I can see that. Is it just because Maddie died? Or is it something more?"

He gives a short, humorless laugh, then runs a hand through his hair. "Yeah, I'm angry."

"Why?"

"Because she named me Leia's guardian even though she knew I didn't want children."

"I doubt she ever envisaged this happening."

"Unless she took her own life."

I hadn't thought of that.

"Last night," he continues, "she berated me for not wanting kids. Talk about have the last laugh."

"She wouldn't have taken her own life just to teach you a lesson."

He scowls. "You don't know Maddie."

I know he doesn't mean it, so I don't berate him. Instead I say, "Can I ask you a question?"

He pours himself another shot of whisky. "I guess."

"Why don't you want children?"

He has a mouthful of the amber liquid, just looking at me.

"I'm not having a go," I say, amused.

"Women always say that, and then they try and talk you into it."

"Not me, James. I don't want children either."

His eyebrows rise in surprise. "Seriously?"

"Yes."

"Why not?"

"I asked you first."

He studies me, clearly taken aback. Then he shrugs. "Because I'm afraid I'd be like my father. Arrogant, dismissive, and controlling. On the verge of violent. An all-round arsehole."

Violent. Did he hit James's mother? "You're not like that," I point out.

"You don't really know me. I hit Blue when he wouldn't leave Maddie alone."

"Alex told me. He also said, 'We all become Neanderthals when the women we love are threatened.'"

"That doesn't excuse being violent."

"So you should have stepped back? Let Blue harass her?"

He gives me a wry look.

"We're all animals at heart," I continue. "We may think we're civilized, but at heart we're just cavemen and women. It's your role to protect your partner and children, should you choose to have them."

"Maybe. I guess what I'm saying is that I don't like how it makes me feel. I'm afraid it's a very small step from protecting to being violent toward them." He has another mouthful of whisky. "So why don't you want kids?"

I adjust Leia's blanket. "I told you that my brother has autism with high support needs."

"Yes."

"I love him with every bone in my body. But he needs twenty-four-hour care. He has epilepsy. He can be aggressive, and he doesn't speak. It's been very, very hard on my parents, especially my mum, as she stays at home to look after him, and I've seen how hard it is for her physically and emotionally."

"I'm guessing it's hereditary?"

"Yes. Highly hereditary."

"Is there prenatal testing for it?"

"Blood tests during early pregnancy can show if a woman has a low risk or an increased risk of having a baby with Down syndrome or another condition. If she shows an increased risk, she can then have diagnostic testing. But what do you do if you discover the baby has a likelihood of a condition? Terminate the pregnancy? Mum chose not to be tested, because she says she believes that a fetus with a condition like Down Syndrome or autism has the same right to life as a fetus without."

"Do you?"

I don't answer for a moment, and like James, I look out into the darkness. It's so quiet here. It's odd that we're discussing these deep issues. I've never vocalized my thoughts on this to anyone. Somehow though, because of what he's gone through, it feels easy to discuss it with him.

"I'm not sure how I feel about the ethics of disability prevention," I say slowly. "Does my mum's point of view hinge on the fact that she can't bring herself to admit her life would have been easier without my brother? I don't know. I believe in a woman's right to choose. But the right to terminate a pregnancy just because the baby isn't society's definition of normal or perfect? Would I terminate because it would make my life easier? I suppose I don't want to put myself through having to make that decision."

He sighs. "I understand."

I look at Leia's beautiful rosebud mouth. "If I'm honest, I know what decision I'd make, because I don't want to go through what my mum has been through."

"I think that's a very human reaction."

"Maybe. But I'm ashamed of myself." My throat tightens, and it takes me a moment to gather myself. I think he notices, because he doesn't say anything for a moment.

Eventually, he sighs again. "They didn't mention any of this in sex ed at school, eh?"

"No." I get to my feet. "I'm taking Leia back to bed."

"Okay."

"Are you going to bed soon?"

"Yeah, in a bit."

"You want me to stay?"

He smiles. "No, but thank you. I appreciate everything you've done for me and Leia today."

"You're welcome." I meet his eyes, and he holds my gaze for a moment.

I want him to get up and kiss me. To ask me if he can lose himself in me tonight. But he doesn't, of course. I know him well enough to understand he won't make a move on me while I'm working for him, and I would be stupid to push it.

"Goodnight," I say.

"'Night."

I walk back through the living room to the corridor to my bedroom, and close the door behind me.

Chapter Sixteen

James

I know Aroha's right, and that if I stay up, I'll just sink further into gloom. I lock up and turn out the lights, then head off to my room at the opposite end of the house.

It was cool when I got up this morning so I turned off the aircon, and now it's hot and sticky in the room. I turn it on, then go over to the window and stare moodily at the garden. It's like a scene from an old black and white movie, the silvery moonlight on the trees and bushes making them shine like ghostly figures.

I'm not religious anymore, and I'm a very practical guy, too concerned with getting on with life to worry about what happens when you die. But at that moment the full force of Maddie's death hits me like a wrecking ball. I inhale, something squeezing inside me, taking my breath away. She's gone, and she's not coming back. Extinguished like a candle flame, so easily. I've never believed in ghosts, but for the first time I wonder whether there is more to life than this. Does she exist somewhere in spirit form? Is she watching me at this moment, feeling my pain? Will we meet again one day in the afterlife? Or is that it? I'll never see her again?

I can't bear to think about it. I'm tired, but my body and brain are still buzzing. If I hadn't drunk so much, I'd go into the gym and work out for a while, but I know that would be a dumb thing to do after drinking so much alcohol.

I take off my shirt and toss it in the laundry bin, hang up my suit trousers, and take off my underwear. Then I go into the bathroom and turn the shower on. I clean my teeth as I glare at my reflection. Finally, as the room begins to fill with steam, I go into the cubicle and stand beneath the hot water.

My head feels stuffed full with the enormity of the day's events, as if someone's inserted a balloon in my skull and is slowly pumping it up. I can feel it pressing on the back of my eyeballs and my eardrums. I don't want to think about Maddie. If I imagine her on that clifftop, if I ponder on whether she fell or jumped over the edge, and how she felt when it happened, how scared she must have been, I'm going to lose it. Think about something else, James...

The hot water pours down my body, silky smooth. Ahhh... I really, really wish I could have sex. My body needs it, desires the release of tension.

I can't help it; I think about Aroha, remembering how incredibly soft and smooth her light-brown skin was when I held her in my arms. I sigh, closing my eyes and thinking about how I kissed her breasts, then pressed my lips slowly down over her stomach to between her thighs. She was hairless and smooth there too, swollen and glistening. I can still recall the taste of her—sweet and musky, so enticing.

I want you to fuck me into next week. Ah, man, I was such a fool to miss out on that opportunity. I'm hard now, aroused with the thought of sliding inside her. I take myself in hand and start giving long, slow strokes as I think about how she clutched her hand in my hair, and how she moaned when I sucked her clit. She's a beautiful girl. Nice, high breasts, a soft, shapely body, big hazel eyes, and those full lips with the intriguing, angular Cupid's bow and large bottom lip. I can imagine her mouth closing around the tip of my erection, those lips sliding down the length... ahhh... yeah...

My hand moves faster as I imagine her on her knees, her large eyes looking up at me as she sucks. I want to come in her mouth, and feel her swallow it down... or would it be better to toss her on the bed? On her back or her front? Front, I decide. Push her legs wide and slide inside her. Then plunge down into her as I drive us both to a climax. Ahhh... yeah... that's working... She'd bury her face in a pillow and cry out with pleasure as I fuck her, begging me to go faster, harder... I'd do my best to hang on until she comes, clenching around me, moaning my name, and only then would I let go. My hand curls into a fist on the tiles as my climax hits, and I can't hold in a groan as I come, imagining erupting into her until I've filled her, and I'm completely empty.

Afterward, I stand under the hot water for a few minutes as my heartbeat slows, then turn off the shower and leave the cubicle. I dry myself, then go out into the bedroom.

I should feel sated and calm, but I don't. It hasn't helped at all. I'm exhausted, but I'm furious, and I have no way of venting it. I'm angry with myself for fantasizing about Aroha, and cross that I can't have her for real. I know myself well enough to guess that I'm not going to be able to sleep. There's no point in lying in bed staring up at the ceiling, tossing restlessly.

After pulling on a pair of track pants, I go through to the kitchen, retrieve my glass from the sink, pick up the whisky bottle, and return onto the deck.

I stand on the edge, looking out at the garden, then go down the steps onto the lawn. I feel feverish, burning with resentment and anger, and I welcome the way the grass is cool and crisp on my bare feet.

Glancing around at the manicured bushes, the flower beds, the carefully tended lawns, I swear. I have a small blind spot in the center of my eye. Of course I'm going to have a fucking migraine. If anything was going to bring one on, it would be a day like this.

I should stop drinking, get myself some painkillers, and go to bed, but I don't want to. Instead, I splash a few inches of whisky into the glass and take a big mouthful.

I wonder how long it's going to take the police to find Blue, and what he'll say when they do track him down. Maybe Maddie told him about Leia and demanded he play a part in her life, and he was so angry he pushed her over the cliff. Part of me wants to believe that rather than she took her own life, but it doesn't ring true. He was an arsehole, but I can't see him as a murderer. No, I'm beginning to think she walked off that cliff of her own volition, which hurts a thousand times more than the notion of someone else taking her life.

I've fucked everything up. My relationship with my parents for a start. I couldn't save my mother. My father hates me. And now I've let my sister down big time. I wasn't there when she needed me. If I'd gone over there that night, I would have been there in the morning when she thought about calling Blue, and I could have either gone with her to meet him or talked her out of it. Instead, I was too lazy to respond to her cry for help, and now she's gone.

I welcome the almost-pain of the firewater as it sears inside me. Maddie, why didn't you tell me how bad you felt? How could you do this to me? And now you've left me with your baby—you fucking coward. You couldn't cope with her yourself so you take the easy way out and leave it all to me? *Fuck you.*

I throw my glass with all my strength and feel a twinge of satisfaction as it smashes against the trunk of a nearby tree. The joy dissipates immediately, though, to be replaced by misery so immense I can't bear it. My failures feel so huge they're like a weighted blanket that's so heavy I can't move.

The blind spot has turned into a tiny ring of shining triangles in the center of my vision. I press my fingers into my eyes until it hurts, then have a swig from the bottle. If I'd been a normal guy, I'd have a girl by my side to help see me through this, but I'm not. I screwed up the one long-term relationship I've had. I'm not so drunk that I don't realize Cassie wasn't right for me. I chose badly, and it's no surprise it didn't end well. I should have chosen someone like Aroha, who's gentle and caring and homely, qualities I realize with some surprise that I value very much.

But I fucked that up too. Falling asleep while making out. Jesus, I'm such an idiot. I'm completely alone, and I'm probably always going to be.

My heart's racing, and my skin feels as if it's on fire. I drop to my haunches, tip back onto my butt, then lay back on the grass. The damp seeps into my track pants, but I don't care. The ring of shining triangles is widening, shimmering. I feel nauseous, but I still lift my head and have another mouthful of whisky. I want to blot it all out—Maddie, today, what happened with Cassie and Aroha, in fact erasing my whole life would be good.

A morepork hoots in the trees, a haunting, mournful lament. I haven't cried for years, since my mother died, I think. I don't like crying. It makes me feel weak. I fight the tears, but the grief and unhappiness is too strong, and in the end I just let the tears slide out of my eyes and down my cheeks, as I look up at the silver triangles sparkling around the moon.

*

"James?"

My arm is resting across my eyes, but I recognize Aroha's voice. "What?"

"How long have you been out here?"

"Go away."

"Have you been here all night?"

I lift my arm a little. I'm still lying on the grass. The whisky bottle lies beside me, empty. The sky is lightening—it must be around six a.m.

Maddie. The memory comes back in a rush, along with the grief that crashes over me.

The light makes my head bang, and I cover my eyes again. "Leave me alone."

She touches my arm. "You're freezing."

"I don't care. Go away."

"James…"

"For fuck's sake—" I lift my head, then immediately groan and let it fall back, pressing the heels of my hands into my eyes. "Ahhh… shit…"

"What? Have you got a hangover?"

"Migraine."

"Oh, honey…"

"Just leave me alone."

She waits a moment, then gets up and disappears.

Half relieved, half disappointed, I cover my face with my arm again. I should move onto the deck, at least, out of the sun as it comes up, but I can't bring myself to move. I'm such a fucking idiot. Alcohol often brings on a migraine—I should have known. Jesus, I feel rough. I just want to die. Drift into oblivion. With Maddie.

Fresh tears prick my eyes, and I give a long sigh.

I assume that Aroha has returned to her room with Leia, but after a few minutes I hear footsteps on the deck, and then feel her at my side as she bends down.

"James?"

"What?"

"Come with me."

"Fuck off."

"Yeah, yeah. Come on. I've run the bath. Closed the blinds. You need to warm up, have something to eat, then get some proper sleep."

I don't reply. Actually a bath sounds great, but I can't force myself to move. It's easier just to lie here and stew in self-pity.

But she says, "Come on, up," rises, takes my hand, and pulls. Grumbling, I let her tug me to a sitting position, then slowly get to my feet.

"Oh God…" I bend forward, hands on my knees. My head pounds, and the garden spins around me. I think I'm still drunk.

"Come on," she says again, quietly, a hand on my back. "This way." She guides me up the steps and into the house.

I don't know if I'll be able to cope with a screaming baby. But the house is quiet, dark, and cool. "Where's Leia?"

"She's fine—I've fed her and she's happy in her car seat for now. She's in the bathroom." She pats the receiver on her hip. She takes my hand again and leads me through the house to my bedroom, then through it to the bathroom. It's my favorite room in the house—the large sunken bath faces the garden, and I often have a soak in the evening sunlight after a workout. Today, though, she's lowered the blinds, shutting out the light. Leia sits in her seat to one side, her Pooh Bear tucked beside her, sucking on a dummy. She looks at me, and I give her a weak smile.

The bath is deep and filled with bubbles. "It smells nice," I mumble.

"It's lavender—it's good for headaches. I learned a bit about aromatherapy at the salon. Have you had any painkillers?"

"No."

She opens the bathroom cabinet. "Okay, what do you normally take? Triptans?"

"Mm."

"Paracetamol or Nurofen?"

"Paracetamol."

"How bad is it? Do you want a couple of these codeine as well?"

"Please."

"Do you feel sick? Do you want one of these anti-nausea pills too?"

I blow out a long breath. "No, I should be okay."

She tips the others into my hand, then passes me a glass of orange juice. "Drink it all," she says.

I swallow the pills with the juice. It relieves the sour taste in my mouth, but it makes me realize how cold the rest of me is, and I start shivering.

"In the bath," she says. "Come on."

"I'm not stripping in front of you," I protest.

"All right, I'll look the other way." She turns around.

I glare at her, but she's obviously not going to leave. Ah fuck, I don't care. I take off my clothes, get gingerly into the bath, then slide into the hot water. Ooh shit, that's hot. My feet tingle as they react to the heat. Slowly, I begin to thaw. Ahhh…

"Done?" she asks.

I slip lower, making sure I'm covered with bubbles. "Yeah."

She picks up a towel, rolls it up, and puts it behind me. I rest my head on it, still watching her.

She bends down to look at me. "Better?"

I nod.

"I'm going to make some breakfast. Try to relax and warm yourself up. Come out when you're ready."

I lift my gaze to hers. Her big hazel eyes study me with gentle concern. "Thank you."

She smiles, leans forward, and kisses my brow. Then she rises and picks up Leia in her seat. "Come on, *Piri Pāua*. Let's go and make Uncle James something to eat." Still talking to her, she leaves the room, half-closing the door behind her.

I close my eyes.

The hot water is soothing and comforting. I inhale the pleasant smell of the lavender, and when I sigh, some of the tension leaves me for the first time.

Even though I'm still over the limit, the raging fury I felt last night has dissipated. Now I just feel tired and sad, but maybe not quite as hopeless as I did. I was wrong when I told myself I was completely alone. Of course I'm not. I have my friends—Henry, Tyson, Alex, Damon, Saxon, Kip, Juliette, Gaby, Missie, and lots of others. And I appear to have Aroha, which has surprised me no end considering how I treated her. Nobody's ever looked after me like this, not since I was a kid, anyway. I kind of like it. Best not to think of my fantasy about her in the shower last night. That was just a by-product of the grief and alcohol—first port in a storm kind of thing. At least I didn't act on it.

And, of course, I also have Leia. Once I feel better, I need to give some serious thought to what I'm going to do about her. *There's no shame in admitting you'd prefer someone else to care for her day-to-day.* Aroha's words rang true. It wouldn't be fair to keep Leia out of guilt or duty. It would be better if she went to a family who would give her the love and attention she deserves. So many people can't have children of their own and want to adopt. I could stay in touch, if they'll let me, and make sure Leia's all right financially, pay for her university fees, or whatever she wants to do, that kind of thing.

I open my eyes and imagine Maddie sitting on the side of the bath, looking at me accusingly. "I don't know what else you want me to do," I whisper. "What did you expect? I'll never make father of the year. She deserves a lot better than me."

She doesn't reply, and I sigh.

The pills are starting to work, and I feel the familiar loosening of the band around my head, and a light-headedness not related to the hangover. At the same time, I become aware of the enticing smell of frying bacon filtering from the kitchen, and my stomach rumbles. Aroha's right—I need some food inside me to soak up the alcohol and pills.

I give myself another couple of minutes, dip under the water to wet my hair, then get out of the bath and dry myself. She's hung my damp track pants over the towel rail to dry, so I go into the bedroom and find another pair, along with a plain gray tee. I comb my hair, then walk through to the kitchen.

She's in the process of transferring the crispy bacon to two rolls, along with a fried egg and a slice of cheese. "Well, you look a lot more human," she says, adding a squirt of ketchup before pushing it across to me with a cup of coffee.

"You're a goddess," I mumble, pulling up a stool, then having a big bite of the roll. Oh my God, it's amazing.

She chuckles, lifts Leia up onto the worktop in her seat, then sits across the breakfast bar from me and has a bite of her own roll. "How are you feeling?"

"Better. Head's thumping, but not as bad as it was."

"Does alcohol trigger your migraines?"

"Sometimes. You probably won't believe me, but I don't drink very much."

"You're right. I don't believe you."

I give a short laugh and have a swig of coffee. It's strong and piping hot, just how I like it. "Dad is teetotal," I admit, "and he sees alcohol as a weakness. I always feel guilty when I drink."

She glances at me, but she doesn't say anything.

Leia chews on a teething ring, and Aroha talks to her while we eat our rolls. "All right, baby girl?" she asks. "Look at your gorgeous blue eyes. Your *māmā* is going to be so proud of you when you grow up!"

She talks as if Maddie's still here, sitting beside me, sipping coffee and listening to us. It's not the first time she's spoken matter-of-factly about things that other people seem to struggle with.

"Are you religious?" I ask.

"My parents go to church, and they told me both Christian and Māori stories while I was growing up. I don't go to church now, but I suppose I have faith, of a kind."

"Do you believe in life after death?"

"I don't know whether we end up as angels sitting on clouds, but I don't believe a mother who's just given birth to her baby girl would be anywhere but by her side, do you?" Her eyes are wide and clear.

My throat tightens, and I struggle to swallow my mouthful of coffee. "No, I don't."

"Are you religious?" she asks.

"Not now. Our mother took us to church when we were young, but I stopped going when we came to New Zealand, and I stopped believing completely when she died. Maddie still went, sometimes."

She has another mouthful of her roll. "Eat up," she says, gesturing to mine. "I want to see all that gone."

I roll my eyes at Leia, but I do as she says, because I kind of like being bossed around.

Chapter Seventeen

Aroha

James looks a damn sight better now. For a moment, when I first found him sprawled on the lawn, I had the horrific thought that he'd died out there in the night. His skin was pale and icy cold, and I couldn't see his chest moving. But then he'd stirred, and I realized he'd either passed out from all the alcohol, or from exhaustion and grief, or likely a combination of all of those.

Now his skin has returned to its natural light brown, and the pain lines scored into his face have lessened, although his headache is obviously still bad. I wait for him to finish his roll and coffee, then I lift Leia out of her chair, take James's hand, and lead him back to his room.

"Get in," I tell him, drawing the duvet back. I try not to think about the last time I was in a bedroom with him, when I fell back onto the bed, and he kissed down my body before he sank his tongue inside me. How it felt to be wanted by this gorgeous guy, even if only for one night. Ahhh… no… don't go down that road. Don't torture yourself.

He glances at me, and I wonder whether he's thinking the same thing, but he doesn't say anything. I wait for him to protest that I'm watching, but he surprises me by grabbing a handful of his tee at the nape of his neck and tugging it over his head, exposing his muscular torso, then sliding off his track pants, giving me a glimpse of his toned butt in the black boxer-briefs before he slides beneath the duvet. Falling back onto the pillows, he presses the heels of his hands into his eyes again.

Still holding Leia, I go over to the window and pull the curtains, and he sighs. "Thank you."

I sit on the side of the bed. "Are you okay?"

"Yeah." He lets his arms fall above his head. Wow, a girl could break a tooth on his biceps. He's definitely the best-looking guy I've ever seen in real life. Usually he's well-groomed, but right now his hair is ruffled and messy, he looks weary, and his face is etched with grief.

I'd love to lean forward and kiss his frown lines away. I don't, of course. But I fantasize about it for a few seconds.

He reaches out and picks up Leia's hand, and his lips curve as her fingers curl around one of his. "She looks content," he says.

"Can I get you anything?" I ask.

He shakes his head. "I'm sorry."

"What for?"

He lets his arm fall back. "All this. I'm not normally like this. Or, at least, there's never anyone around to witness it." His lips twist.

"You should be around people right now," I tell him. "Grief should be shared."

"I've always found it to be a very private thing." He studies me, then smiles. "That puzzles you."

"A bit."

"Who did you lose?" he asks softly.

"My grandfather, when I was twelve. My *whanau* flocked around and filled the house. Everyone grieved openly. I wasn't alone for weeks."

"I can't imagine that."

"Henry said you have some family though? Two uncles? And more in Australia?"

"Yeah. I'm not close to any of them, but I guess some of them will come to the funeral."

"Do you think your father will come?" I ask.

He hesitates. "I don't know. He said he'd let me know. He had a Sudden Cardiac Arrest in March last year. He used to travel a lot, but I don't think he's left Australia since."

"Did he remarry after your mum died?"

"Yeah. To Arabella. She already had two sons. She hates me because at the moment I'm due to inherit Dad's fortune. Which of course will be even more now Maddie won't be taking half of it." He speaks matter of factly, obviously used to his stepmother's feelings toward him.

I feel inordinately sorry for him, something I didn't expect considering how rich he is. "You said 'at the moment.' Do you think your dad will change his will to include his stepsons?"

"He's threatened it a couple of times if I don't toe the line." His mouth curves up.

I give him a baffled look. "How are you not toeing the line? You seem as if you're doing fabulously to me."

"He wants me to get married and have children. A son, specifically. An heir."

"Oh…" I say softly.

"Yeah, it's positively medieval. I refuse to comply. I'm going to leave my fortune to the SPCA."

I give a short laugh. He's right, it is archaic, but I'm practical enough that I can understand why his father wants the money he's earned to stay in the family. "Has he been pressuring you more since his heart problem?"

"Yeah. He told me that if I don't get married by the end of this year, he's going to cut me out of the will."

Understanding slowly sinks in. "Is that why you went steady with Cassie?"

He doesn't answer immediately. He looks up at the ceiling, breathes in, then lets out a long sigh. "Kinda."

"You don't need the money though, surely?"

"No, I don't need it. But I could do a lot with it. Invest it in Kia Kaha and Kingpinz—that's Damon's company. I could help a lot of people with it." He's not being sarcastic. I think he genuinely means it. I hadn't realized he was so altruistic. He comes across as a player, but of course he created Kia Kaha with Alex and the others, so he's obviously interested in helping people.

"And you want his approval?" I ask, wondering if that's part of it.

His lack of reply tells me I'm right.

"We're hardwired to desire the approval of our parents," I tell him. "You're not unusual in that."

"Fuck him," he says, which tells me everything I need to know.

"How old were you when your parents split?" I ask. I keep expecting him to tell me to mind my own business, but he doesn't.

"Fourteen."

"What was your mum's name?"

His expression softens. "Emma."

"What was she like?"

"A lot like Maddie. Gentle, and kind, but she had her demons. She suffered from depression too."

Something occurs to me then. "Do you have depression?"

But he shakes his head. "I don't seem to have inherited that gene, thank God. I remember getting home from school when I was a teenager and finding Mum still in bed. She'd cry for hours." He sighs.

I think about that fourteen-year-old young man, still a boy really, telling himself he was the man of the family now, that he had to look after his twin sister and mother, and I feel ashamed. I thought he was just a pretty face, just a playboy, but he's obviously crafted his carefree attitude to cover the layers of unhappiness and problems he's had over the years.

I glance down at Leia. She's looking sleepy, having woken around five today. I'd like to shift that to a little later if I can, and get her in a proper routine, so I want to try to keep her awake a little longer.

"I'd better leave you," I say to James. "Try to get some sleep and hopefully you'll feel better when you wake up."

I walk to the door, then stop and turn as he calls, "Aroha."

"Hmm?"

"Thank you."

He looks sleepy and gorgeous. I have to fight not to go back to the bed, climb on the mattress, and crush my lips to his.

Instead, I smile, go out, and shut the door.

I blow out a breath as I walk back into the kitchen. "Not sure I should have taken this job," I say to Leia. She hiccups and nuzzles my neck, and I chuckle. "But then I wouldn't have had a chance to meet you, would I?"

I look around the kitchen—I need to clean the breakfast things and tidy up. But there'll be time to do that when Leia's asleep.

Instead, I go through to her bedroom, change her, and dress her in a pretty lemon-colored dress with white spots. I add a cute sunhat that looks like the top of a bear, with a smiley face and two ears on top. I rub a little baby sun lotion on her arms, legs, and face, chatting to her while I smooth it in. I place her in the baby carrier and clip it on to myself so she's facing out. She's just big enough for it, and she waves her arms and kicks her legs, suggesting she likes it. Then I grab my own sunhat and sunglasses, return to the living room, open the sliding doors, and go out onto the deck.

It's a beautiful day, warm and sunny. I walk down the steps to where I found James this morning, and then follow the path across the lawn.

I walk slowly around the gardens. A gap in the hedge around the main lawn leads through to a rose garden, with winding paths through the rose bushes, a sundial, a fountain, and a bird bath. I talk to Leia while I walk, pointing out bumble bees, sparrows, and blackbirds. I'm getting her used to the sound of my voice and trying to build a connection with her, and you never know how much babies can understand.

A middle-aged woman in shorts, tee, and sunhat is working on the rose bushes, clipping off the dead flowers and tying them up. "Hello," she says, smiling as I approach.

"Morning," I reply, holding out my hand. "I'm Aroha. I'm the nanny to James's niece, Leia." The baby is currently holding my finger, and I lift it as if she's waving.

"Oh, how lovely to meet you." She shakes my hand, then reaches out to chuck Leia's cheek. "I'm Sue, I'm the gardener. I heard about his sister. I'm so sorry."

"Thank you, Sue. I'll pass it on. He's asleep at the moment. He was up very late."

"Hmm. I... ah... found a broken glass by the jacaranda. I've picked up all the pieces, but just be careful if you walk that way, okay?"

"Okay, thanks. He was very upset last night."

"Of course," she says. "Maddie was a lovely girl. She came here quite a bit. I think he was hoping she'd move in with him, but..." She shrugs. "Was it an accident, do you know? Or did she jump?"

"I don't know." I understand her curiosity, but I wouldn't discuss the details with her even if I knew anything. "Well, have a good morning!"

"You too. Enjoy your walk."

I continue, going through the gate, astonished to find myself in a tennis court. I love tennis and was in the school team. Does James play, or did it just come with the house? The net's up, which suggests it's used. Who does he play with, though? Maybe one of his friends.

I circle the court, heading back toward the house, go through the gate at the far end, and discover the swimming pool. Ooh, what a luxury. It's large, with a section meant for doing lengths and then a shaped area with a deep end that leads up to a shallow end for children that's sheltered by a shade sail. The water sparkles in the sunshine. I'll definitely make use of this, if he doesn't mind. I can't imagine that he will.

A man approaches the gate and looks at me in surprise. He's in his fifties, graying, dressed in shorts, a faded tee, and a sun hat with a wide brim to protect his neck. "Hello," he says.

"Oh, hi. I'm Aroha. I'm the nanny to James's niece." I wave her hand.

"I'm Nick," he says, coming into the enclosure. "I look after the pool a couple of times a week." He's carrying a pipe and a brush on a long pole.

"You do a great job. It looks beautiful."

He smiles. "Discovering the estate?"

"Yes, just out for a morning walk." I go through the gate. "Bye."

"Bye." He bends and starts fitting the pipe to the plate, and I leave him to it.

It must be funny to have staff—a housekeeper, a gardener, a pool assistant. I'm not so proud that I could say I'd be any different if I had money.

It's warm and bright, and Leia's starting to grizzle a little. Not wanting her to get overstimulated, I head back to the deck and go inside and through to our room. Hopefully soon we'll be able to get her bassinet transferred here. For now I take off her hat, place her in her carry seat, and give her the dummy, then take her with me into the kitchen. She sucks quietly and closes her eyes.

I boil the kettle, tidy up a bit, then pour the cooled, boiled water into a few bottles and place them in the fridge ready for later in the day.

Ginny arrives then. James has obviously told her about me and Leia because she doesn't look surprised when she walks in. She comes straight up to me with a smile and says, "You must be Aroha," and shakes hands with me, then looks at Leia and says, "Oh, she looks so content. Isn't she gorgeous?"

She's in her thirties with blonde hair she wears in a ponytail, and as we chat briefly, it doesn't surprise me to learn she has three kids, as she has a brisk but kind, no-nonsense manner about her. "You look tired," she says, "why don't you go and have a snooze while I clean up?"

"Are you sure?" I ask, embarrassed to have another woman tidy up after me.

"Of course. I'm sure you were up early. Go on." She starts to clean the kitchen.

It's still early, but I was up at the crack of dawn, and I am a little tired. I lift Leia out of her seat and take her onto the deck. It's warm without being hot beneath the shade sail, and there's a nice breeze blowing across the lawn. In the distance I can hear Sue using a hedge trimmer, but it's far enough away to just be a pleasant summer sound. The birds are singing in the trees, and the air smells of mown grass and lavender.

Despite the sadness behind my reason for being here, I can't help but feel there are far worse things to be doing than looking after a beautiful baby in such a gorgeous house.

I pile the cushions in the corner of the outdoor sofa, then curl up on it with Leia lying on my chest, stopped from rolling off by more cushions.

I sigh, enjoying the peace of the summer morning. I'd much rather be doing this than working in the salon. Of course I have no idea how much James is intending to pay me, or how long he's going to want me here. Will he offer Leia up for adoption? Even if he does, it's still going to take time before it all goes through. Surely he won't put her into foster care until then?

I feel a surge of affection and tenderness for her that surprises me. I'm going to have to be careful not to get too attached to her because I'm sure my relationship with her won't continue long term. It's impossible to remain distant, though. She's warm and soft against me, and she smells of that beautiful, sweet, milky smell that all small babies have.

I'll just have to make the most of her while I have her. *I hope you approve of how I'm looking after her,* I say to Maddie in my mind.

Then I close my eyes, and after only a few minutes I doze off.

*

When I open my eyes, it's to see James sitting in one of the armchairs, elbow on the arm and his chin propped on his hand, watching me.

I blink, and my eyes widen. "Oh!"

He smiles. "Morning."

"What time is it?"

"Still early." I go to push myself up, but he holds up a hand. "Don't disturb her."

I settle again, resting a hand on her back. "Sorry, I dozed off."

"Sleep when the baby sleeps, right?"

"So they say. I think it's easier when you have a housekeeper."

He chuckles.

"How are you feeling?" I ask.

"A bit better. The headache is still there, but the pills have kicked in."

I rub Leia's back. He watches me, his expression unreadable.

"You have a very calming influence," he says. "It's no wonder she seems so content."

"She's a good baby." I stroke her silky hair. "What do you have planned for today?"

He sighs. "Phone calls: the police, the funeral home, Dad, some relatives. I don't know whether I'll find out about the coroner's report today. They might wait until they find Blue."

"When do you want to get Leia's bassinet?"

"I might ask Henry to go over and get it. He won't mind. If there's anything else you need, just let me know."

"Are you going into the office?" I ask.

He shakes his head. "Not today. My head's not in the right space. The guys might come by later. Gaby and Juliette both want to see me and Leia."

Leia stirs, then mewls. "Hey sweetie," I murmur, sitting up and laying her on my shoulder. "Are you hungry, *pēpe*?"

"Want me to make a bottle?" he asks.

"Are you sure?"

"Yeah. You stay there." He gets up and goes inside.

I've brought her bag out with me, and I lay her on the mat and change her while I think about the look Alex gave me last night, the way he put a finger to his lips when I came out to see James holding his niece, and then winked at me. He wants me to encourage James to have a relationship with Leia. I'm guessing he thinks that James shouldn't give her up for adoption, judging by the way he asked me my opinion as to what James should do.

I wasn't lying when I said that James shouldn't keep her out of duty or guilt. I believe a child is better with people who love her. I have a cousin who has adopted two children, and she doesn't love them any less than she would if she'd given birth to them.

After saying that, I think it would be too easy for him to say that because he's single and young and knows nothing about handling a baby, he should just give her up. Maddie named him Leia's guardian for a reason. She obviously wanted him to have Leia should anything happen to her.

I put the used nappy in one of the lavender-smelling bags and place it in the change bag, then lift her into my arms. She starts crying, and I stand and rock her while I wait for James. A few minutes later, he comes back onto the deck and holds out the bottle. "Actually I need to pop to the bathroom," I say. "Can you hold her for a minute?"

"Sure," he says, although his voice doesn't hold much enthusiasm.

I wait until he's seated, then turn Leia and place her in his arms. She's still wailing, and he winces as her cries obviously cut through his headache, and looks up at me in alarm.

"She's just hungry," I say.

He tips the bottle up and touches the teat to her lips. She takes it and starts sucking, quieting immediately.

"There." I bend and kiss her forehead. "I'll be back in a minute."

Leaving him to it, I go to the bathroom, taking my time. I return to the kitchen and call through, "Want a coffee?"

"Please," he calls back.

I use the machine to make us both a cup, then bring them through to the deck.

He's sitting quietly, looking down at his niece as she takes the bottle.

I put his coffee beside him and sit on the sofa. He doesn't ask me to take her, seemingly content to watch her feed.

"You should play us a song," he says.

My eyebrows rise. "Oh, okay." I go in and collect the acoustic guitar and bring it back out. I check the tuning quickly, then strum a few chords. "Any requests?"

"I don't know any songs for children."

"Well, firstly, I'm sure you do. Twinkle, twinkle, little star? Yeah, I thought so. But the songs don't have to be for children." I start strumming Stevie Wonder's *Isn't She Lovely*.

James laughs. "*Songs in the Key of Life* is one of my favorite albums."

"Mine too."

He sings along as he feeds her, and for some reason my face warms as he tells her that we've made her from our love. She's not ours, of course. He didn't plant his seed in me, and it didn't grow into a baby in my womb. But Leia has connected us in a way I don't think either of us expected.

I change to Taylor Swift's *The Best Day*, and James and I sing to Leia, while the blackbird joins in from the jacaranda tree.

Chapter Eighteen

James

I spend the next couple of hours in my office. The first person I call is my father.

"It's me," I say when he answers the phone, even though I know my name will have appeared on his screen.

"Your watch broken?" is his curt greeting. I glance at my computer—it's nine thirty, which means it's seven a.m. in Adelaide.

I stiffen at his tone. "I'm aware what time it is. I thought you were always up by six."

He's a driven man with a fixed routine, and he's usually at the office by seven. If he were any other person, I'd have assumed he would've had a few days off following Maddie's death, but he worked through his ex-wife's death and his own parents' passing, so I'd expected him to be in as normal.

But he says, "I had trouble sleeping, and I missed the alarm." He sighs.

Bitterness rises inside me like stomach acid. I want to say *Why are you so upset?* Or *It's a bit late to pretend to care!* But I bite down on the words. I'm not going to let him provoke me. I refuse to lower to his level.

"I wondered whether you've decided if you're going to come to the funeral," I say. "I haven't heard from the coroner yet, so I don't know when they'll release her body, but I'm going to start making arrangements."

"I'm coming, and so is Arabella."

My heart sinks. Part of me had hoped he wouldn't be up to it.

I lean an elbow on the desk and rest my head on my hand. Maddie, I think sourly, how could you leave me to cope with him alone? At least when she was here it felt as if I had someone on my side.

I don't want him at the funeral. And I certainly don't want to see Arabella. It's going to be a hard enough day as it is without them being present. But I can't stop Maddie's father from attending. It's just another part of the event I'm going to have to get through.

"I'll let you know when it's all arranged, then. Gotta go. Bye." I hang up, toss my phone on the table, and lean back with a curse.

There's a gentle knock at the door, and I turn the chair to look over, annoyed at being interrupted. It's Aroha, holding a mug of coffee. The intercom receiver is clipped to the belt of her cut-down jeans, so I'm guessing Leia is asleep in her seat.

"Sorry to disturb you," she says. She looks nervous. She obviously overheard the last bit of the conversation. "I thought you might like a drink."

My irritation fades at both the sight of her and the smell of the coffee. "I would. Thank you."

She comes into the room and places it on the desk. I pick it up and sip it, welcoming the slide of the hot liquid down inside me, thawing out the coldness that a conversation with my father always leaves behind.

"Are you okay?" she asks.

"Yeah. I was just talking to my father."

"Ah. What's his name?"

"Vincent. He's bringing my stepmother, Arabella, to the funeral."

"Oh."

"Yeah." I let my head fall back. I'm tired, and my head's hurting again. The light's too bright, and even the most distant sounds—a lawnmower, a plane overhead, the washing machine in the laundry room—hurt my ears.

She rests her butt on the edge of the desk, inches from my hand. I have to fight not to move so I'm touching her.

"I met Sue and Nick," she continues. "It's funny to think of you having staff. It makes me feel as if I'm in Downton Abbey."

"This place is too big for one person to look after on their own."

"Yes, I can see that. Are you going to hold the wake here?"

"I guess. Maddie and I held one when our mother died. I don't know how I feel about having it here, though. Having them in my house."

She obviously realizes who I mean by 'them'. "Has your father been here before?"

"No."

"It's a gorgeous house, James. It makes you look successful and wealthy. It's a chance to show him how well you've done for yourself."

"He'll just think it's all down to him and the opportunities he gave me. He won't see it as my success." My voice drips with bitterness.

Her eyes spark. "Well, fuck him then. If you hold it here, it's on your territory. Show him the cub's ready to challenge the sire."

I meet her eyes. She's been here one day, and I think she already understands me and my relationship with my father better than Cassie did after nearly a year.

I sit up and pull my phone toward me. "I'm going to make some more calls."

"Okay. I'll make us some lunch at one."

"You don't have to. You're Leia's nanny, not my housekeeper."

"I know. I want to help."

I study her for a moment. Her cut-down jeans are tight, showing off the curve of her hips and shapely calves. She's twisted her hair up and secured it with a butterfly clip, revealing her slender neck. I want to kiss the soft skin there, and feel her pulse against my lips.

She's wearing a sleeveless, crew-neck, white tank top with a large flower on the front. Each petal of it is filled with a paisley-style colored pattern. Underneath it says, 'Life is good.'

"Are you looking at my boobs?" she asks. Her smile suggests she's teasing me.

I give her a wry look. "No. I was reading the words."

"I know you've had a terrible loss," she says softly, "and things seem dark at the moment. Just remember that feeling or showing grief doesn't make you weak, whatever your father says."

Her astuteness shocks me. I watch her go up to the door. "See you later," she says. "Let me know if there's anything I can do." She goes out, closing the door behind her.

The scent of her perfume—something light and flowery—remains in the air, stirring my senses. I purse my lips, leaning my chin on my hand, staring moodily at the door for a while. Then I sigh and turn back to my computer.

I Google 'what needs to be done after a family member dies,' and start making a list. Tell close family, friends, and work colleagues. Maddie worked as Director of Finance at a software development company, although she was on maternity leave. I spoke to the company

CEO yesterday and told him what had happened, but I might call him again and keep him up to date. He'll want to come to the funeral.

I'll need to arrange for a death notice in the newspapers. Get a medical certificate or Coroner's Authorization. Register her death. Contact the funeral director to organize the cremation, and sort out the wake.

I'm guessing the coroner will request a post-mortem as the cause of death isn't clear. I wonder whether there'll be a hearing or an inquest? I might not find that out for some time—it depends on what the post-mortem shows and what Blue says when they find him.

I continue with the list, remembering some of it from when our mother died: tell the Inland Revenue, her bank, cancel her passport at the Department of Internal Affairs, cancel her driving license at the Transport Agency. I'll need to go through her house and sort out the contents. That's not going to be easy. Then I'll have to put it up for sale. Sell her car. See my lawyer about her estate and her will, if she had one. I presume everything will go to Leia. He'll also be able to help with sorting out Leia's future.

I'll need to make an announcement about Maddie's death on my social media, and maybe hers before closing all her accounts. I know she was active on Facebook and Instagram. I'm not sure what other sites she frequented.

It's a lot to do, and I'm kept busy for the next few hours. It's not easy work, either. I lose track of the number of times I explain what's happened, and say thank you for the other person's expressions of sorrow and best wishes. Many times it's me comforting them rather than the other way around. At first it hurts every time I say it, but in the end I lock my grief away deep inside me, and it gradually becomes easier.

Around one o'clock, I get up and stretch. My head is thumping. I visit the bathroom and take some more pills, then wander out to the kitchen.

Aroha is in the process of making sandwiches. Leia sits in the carry seat on the counter. Her bright eyes turn to me, and she watches me, sucking contentedly on her dummy, as I sit on a stool and lean on the counter.

"Kia ora, *Piri Pāua*," I say, echoing Aroha's first greeting to her.

Aroha smiles. "How are you feeling?"

"*Rough as*, actually. I've remembered why I don't drink much."

"How's the head?"

"Pounding."

"Have you taken some more pills?"

"Yeah, just now."

"They should start working soon." She places the sandwiches on a plate and pushes it over to me. "What would you like to drink?"

"I'll make myself a coffee."

"I'll do it. You eat." She starts the machine. "Are you drinking plenty of water?"

"Yes, Mum."

She pokes her tongue out at me. "I'm only trying to help."

"I know. I'm teasing you." I have a bite of a sandwich. Chicken and grated cheese with pickle, one of my favorites, don't know how she knew that.

She finishes making our coffee and passes a mug to me, then draws up a stool opposite. "How did you get on with your phone calls?"

"Not bad. I'm making a To Do list. It's pretty long. I'm going to have to sort through everything in the house. That's going to be hard." I stare at the sandwich for a moment as I think about going through Maddie's cupboards and wardrobes, her clothes, her intimate things.

"I could always help, if you like," Aroha says.

"You've got enough on your plate without taking on tasks like that." I take another, bigger mouthful of the sandwich. I'm hungrier than I thought, despite the headache.

"Well, the offer's there." She sips her coffee. "I was thinking about making a cake for this afternoon."

I stare at her, bewildered. "Why?"

"You have the guys coming around, don't you?"

"Yes, but… Aroha, you're Leia's nanny. All you have to do is look after her."

"I know." She frowns and studies her sandwich. She was trying to do something nice for me, and I've hurt her feelings. That's the last thing I want to do.

I lean on the worktop and sigh. "I'm sorry. I'm extremely grouchy, and it's not your fault."

"It's okay, you don't have to apologize. You've been through a lot."

"That's no reason to take it out on you. You were kind enough to jump in without hesitation to help me with Leia. Of course, you're welcome to make a cake, if you wish. You took me aback, that's all. I've never had a girl offer to bake a cake for me before."

Her eyebrows rise. "Really?"

"Yeah." I try not to laugh at the thought of asking Cassie to produce a Victoria sponge.

"Then I'm definitely going to make one." Aroha gives an impish smile. "What's your favorite kind?"

I eat my sandwich, watching as she takes small bites of hers. "Chocolate."

"Chocolate it is, then." She nods, apparently satisfied.

I finish the sandwich, then sip the last of the coffee, closing my eyes for a moment. This migraine is a humdinger. Even after taking the pills, it feels as if I have a full brass band inside my head.

"Still thumping?" she asks, her voice low and gentle.

I open my eyes. "Mmm."

"I have an idea. Come with me." She rises from the stool, walks around the counter, picks up Leia, and then takes my hand. I let her pull me through the living room and out onto the deck.

"Lie down," she instructs, placing Leia's carry seat on the deck beside the sofa.

I frown. "What for?"

She just points at the sofa.

Muttering, I sit down in the middle and go to turn.

"Head this way," she says, pointing to the end nearest her.

I switch the other way and lie down, resting my head on the cushion she's just placed there. She kneels on another cushion at the end, so that when I look up, I see her face upside down.

She places her hands on my forehead, then runs her fingers lightly over my skin. "Does it hurt to touch?"

"No."

"How about here?" She threads her fingers through my hair, sliding them across my scalp.

I stifle a shiver. "No."

"Okay. Close your eyes and try to relax."

She proceeds to move her fingers with a light touch, so she's stroking firmly rather than massaging. At first, I feel too self-conscious, slightly turned on by it and worried I'm going to end up with an obvious erection. But gradually, as she works the muscles of my face and neck and strokes through my hair, my eyes close, and I surrender to her touch.

Ohhh… it feels magnificent. She spends ages working across my face, sliding the pads of her fingers across my forehead, down my cheeks, and across my nose and chin. She massages the tops of my shoulders where they meet my neck, and the muscles around my clavicle and upper arms, then returns to my face and eventually back to my hair. She strokes up from the nape of my neck up to temples, then slowly massages my scalp. She takes her time, splaying her fingers out, then drawing them together.

Everything tingles, and I can feel the tension ebbing from my jaw and teeth, which often ache during a migraine. She applies light pressure with the tips of her fingers around my eye sockets, around my eyebrows, at my temples, and at other points across my skull, a technique which I'm sure is akin to acupuncture.

"Did they teach you this at the salon?" I murmur eventually, impressed.

"Yes. It's called Indian Head Massage or Champissage."

"You're very good at it."

"Thank you."

"I bet my hair looks a mess."

She laughs and runs her fingers through it. "It might need a comb through." She strokes a finger across my forehead, then down my nose and across my mouth. It doesn't feel like part of the massage. Her nail scrapes on my bristles, and I'm sure I hear her sigh.

Then, finally, she sits back. "Let me know if that helps," she says. "It's supposed to be good for relieving migraines."

I sit up slowly. I feel lightheaded and a bit out of it.

"What time are the guys coming around?" she asks.

"After work, five-ish."

"Well, can I make a suggestion? Why don't you lie out here for a while, maybe with some sunglasses, and rest? You're going to need some energy over the next few days, and it would be good to get rid of this headache."

I want to protest, to say that I don't need handling or organizing, but the idea of an afternoon nap appeals, and she's right—the next few days are going to be stressful and busy.

"All right," I say, a little grouchily.

"Where are your sunglasses?"

"On the coffee table." I go to get up, but she's already walking off. She fetches them for me and brings them back. "Lie down."

I lie back, the other way around this time, so I'm leaning on the cushions, and slot the glasses on.

"Good boy," she says. I snort, and her lips curve up. "Try to relax," she adds, switching the fan on. Then she picks up Leia and goes inside, pulling the sliding door almost closed behind her.

I tuck my right arm under my head and look out at the garden. I inhale deeply, then let out the long breath over ten seconds.

This is possibly my favorite place in the world right now. I know the house is too big for me, but I love how peaceful it is. I feel isolated and safe. The deck is north facing and catches the rays from sunrise to sunset, but the shade sail keeps it out of direct sunlight. The fan sweeps across me, brushing cool air from my head to my toes.

I wonder whether Aroha is baking her cake.

Closing my eyes, I think about her fingers gliding through my hair. No girl has ever done anything like that for me. They've expected me to lavish attention on them, and I've always been happy to do so, believing it to be the guy's role. I guess Freud would have something to say about it. But I'm not looking for a mother. It's just been a long time since I've been cared for. Having a housekeeper helps, but it's not the same as personal affection. I loved my mother dearly, but depression is a selfish disease, and her mental issues meant she was always focused on herself. Maddie also had too many problems of her own to help me with mine. I've learned to cope alone. Maybe that's why it feels like such a surprise to have someone doing things for me.

I wish Maddie had met Aroha. I think they would have gotten on.

*

I doze as the sun slides down in the bright-blue sky. I'm half-aware of my surroundings, but I let my brain meander where it wants to, in and out of a dream world full of memories and emotions. At one point I hear Leia crying, but it cuts off fairly quickly, and I guess Aroha has stopped whatever she's doing to feed her. Not long after, I become aware of the magnificent smell of baking filtering out through the crack in the sliding door. I guess the cake is in the oven. My lips curve up, even though I don't open my eyes.

I must fall into a deeper sleep then, because I dream that Maddie and I are at the beach our parents used to take us to as kids. We're adults, though, sitting beside one another on the sand as the water rolls up over our feet. She's wearing her favorite pair of blue shorts, and her legs are brown.

In the water, a young girl is playing, maybe six or seven years old. She looks up and sees me watching her, and splashes through the water toward me. "Daddy!" she says, and she leaps on me and throws her arms around me.

I snap awake. The sun is much lower, and even the fan can't disguise the baking heat of the late-afternoon sun. I blink, startled by the dream. Who was the little girl? Was it Leia? If so, why did she call me Daddy?

It takes a second for me to remember that Maddie is dead. Grief hits me like an arrow to the chest, taking my breath away.

"Hey." It's Aroha, opening the sliding door and coming outside, carrying Leia. "Are you okay?" she asks. "I heard you cry out."

"I was dreaming." I clamp down on the grief. "Something smells nice."

"We've had fun baking the cake, haven't we?" She kisses Leia's forehead. "It's four thirty. I guess the guys will be here soon."

"Yeah. I'll get changed." I sit up. My headache has dulled to a low, bearable throb.

"Are you all right?" She moves forward and places a cool hand on my forehead. I close my eyes, touched by her concern. "Is your head bad?"

"No. It's better." I don't move, though. Neither does she. Instead, after a moment she caresses my temple with her thumb, a soft brush that sends the hairs rising on the back of my neck.

Then she drops her hand, and I get up. I look at Leia, whose big turquoise eyes stare back at me, and I smile at her. To my surprise, her lips curve up in response.

"I'm guessing that's just wind," I say.

"Not at all. She's returning your smile. Aren't you, bubs? Are you saying hello to Uncle James?" She waves Leia's hand and holds it close to my face. I kiss the tiny fingers obediently, and Leia laughs and swats my cheek.

"Typical woman," I say. "I show her some attention and she slaps me around the face."

"I'm sure you deserved it." Aroha chuckles. "We're going to put the butter icing on the cake, aren't we?" Still talking to Leia, she goes back inside.

I watch her go, still thinking about the little girl throwing her arms around my neck. Daddy… Frowning, I follow them inside.

Chapter Nineteen

Aroha

Henry and Alex arrive first, in a van they use at Kia Kaha, and James helps them in with the bassinet. They take it through to the bedroom that adjoins my room and put it up in there, along with the other items they've brought—the change table, the nappy bin, the mini fridge, the bottle warmer, a rocking chair, and a couple of bags full of clothes, toys, and other items.

At this point, Gaby and Tyson arrive with Juliette and Missie. Gaby, already tearful, goes up to James, slides her arms around his waist, and buries her face in his shirt, and they stand there like that for a minute, James with his chin resting on the top of her head. He doesn't say anything, but his eyes meet mine across the kitchen before he closes them and kisses the top of her head.

"What would everyone like to drink?" I ask, dragging my gaze away. "Tea, coffee, something stronger?"

They all reply with coffee, and I get to making them, glad of something to do.

"Something smells nice," Henry says, looking pointedly at the cake.

"I made it." I pass him a knife. "Would you mind cutting it into slices?"

Missie comes up to where I'm making the coffee and smiles. "Hey, Aroha."

"Hey, Missie." I like Alex's girlfriend. She comes from a normal background, like me, and there's something natural and friendly about her that makes me warm to her.

"How's the little one doing?" she asks, tickling Leia where she's sitting in her carry seat on the counter. Leia grizzles a little.

"Can I have a cuddle?" Missie asks.

"Of course," I reply, and she unclips Leia and lifts her out of the seat into her arms. Gaby and Juliette come over and coo while Alex starts distributing the coffees, and Henry puts slices of cake onto plates.

"No Cam today?" Gaby asks Juliette.

She shakes her head. "He's in Australia at the moment, for work."

"You didn't want to go with him?"

She swallows. "We thought it would be best to have some time apart."

Missie reaches out and rubs Juliette's upper arm. "Aw, I'm sorry to hear that."

"When's he coming back?" Gaby asks.

"Saturday. We're going to sit down and have a talk." She wrinkles her nose.

Missie frowns. "Do you want to stay together?"

Juliette hesitates. "It's complicated."

Gaby glances at Henry, then back at Juliette and lifts her eyebrows.

Juliette blushes. "Sort of. But there's something else. I—"

Tyson interrupts though as he comes over to collect the kitchen roll, and Juliette shakes her head and walks away. Gaby, Missie, and I exchange glances, but I have no idea what she was going to say, and clearly neither do they.

We all move outside to the deck. Missie sits with Leia, and Alex watches her, a tender expression on his face. I wonder whether they'll have children together? Her son is something like eleven or twelve, I think, but she's only in her late twenties, so it's plausible that they'll want to have a family.

I glance over at Gaby, my best friend. For a long time after Tyson's accident, she wasn't sure whether they would be able to have children. But he's walking now, albeit a bit stiffly and occasionally with a stick, and she confided in me a few weeks ago that he'd given a sperm sample to the fertility clinic, and they'd said his sperm count was on the low side but that he was perfectly capable of fathering children. She was thrilled, and happy to leave it in the hands of Fate, for the moment at least. She's a believer that if it's meant to be, it will be. I'm not sure if I agree with her, but I'm happy that there's a possibility they might not have to undergo fertility treatment.

"This is fantastic," Tyson says, tucking into his piece of chocolate cake. "I love the frosting." The others murmur their approval, too.

"Thank you, I'm glad you like it," I say, a tad shyly.

"It's a comforting smell," James murmurs, and Gaby reaches over and rubs his arm.

"No news from the police yet?" she asks.

He shakes his head. "They were carrying out an investigation at the site, but I don't know what they found out yet. I'm guessing they haven't found Blue either, or I presume they'd have called."

"Have you spoken to your father again?" Alex asks.

James sighs. "Yeah. He is coming to the funeral, with Arabella." Henry pulls a face, and James gives a short laugh. "Yeah, that was my reaction. Aroha said if I hold the wake here it means at least it'll be on my territory."

"I agree," Alex says. "And we'll all be around to help."

"Is there anything we can do?" Gaby asks. "For the funeral, I mean."

"Not at the moment," James replies. "I can't finalize anything until the post-mortem is done."

"We can organize the catering for you, if you like," she continues. "That would be something you can cross off your list."

"That would be great, thank you."

They go on to talk about Maddie, telling stories and exchanging memories. After a while, someone suggests ordering Uber Eats, and we settle for half a dozen large pizzas and place them in the center of the table so we can all help ourselves.

Leia dozes off in Missie's arms for a while, and when she wakes, it's Gaby's turn to hold her, then Juliette's. Eventually even Tyson and Alex request a cuddle, and it's heartwarming to watch their partners' faces as they see their men interacting with a baby.

I don't say much, and I'm happy to listen to them all talking. I like them all, and of course I know Gaby well, but the more I listen to them, the more I feel the great divide between us that money has carved. They talk about vacations abroad—in Fiji and the other Pacific Islands, in Australia and Japan and even to Europe, places I've never been and will probably never go. They have stories involving skiing and scuba diving and flying lessons, and tales about parties where they drank too much champagne.

The more I hear, the more it reminds me how different the lives are that James and I have led. He's been very kind, and he treats me like an equal, but it's clear to me that I really am just like his gardener and his pool man. I'm a member of staff, and I'm only here with the others because I'm looking after Leia. They know I'm not wealthy. I can only imagine what they think about me staying here. Do they assume we're sleeping together because we're in the same house? That maybe I'm after his money? As much as I like him, the thought embarrasses me.

It's seven-thirty p.m., and the sun is heading toward the horizon, filling the garden with light the color of treacle. I've lit several citronella candles to keep away the insects, but I don't want Leia to get bitten.

I go into the kitchen and make her up a bottle. Then I return to the others. "I think I'll take Leia in for a bath and feed," I announce, going over to Missie, who's having another sneaky cuddle. "I'm trying to get her into a routine."

"Makes sense," Missie says, handing her over.

"Is there anything you need?" James asks.

"No, I'm fine, thanks."

"Want some help?" Gaby asks.

"No, I'm good."

"Come back out when you're done," James adds.

I just smile and head inside.

I take Leia through to the bathroom adjoining my bedroom, put her in her carry seat for a moment, and retrieve the small baby bath that Henry and Alex brought from Maddie's house. I put it in the main bath, run some lukewarm water, and add some No Tears baby bath foam with chamomile. Then I strip Leia and lower her in, talking to her as she splashes about, apparently enjoying the sensation of the water on her skin. I clean her face and ears, all the creases in her skin, and her fingers and toes, and then I wash her hair.

When she's clean, I lift her out and wrap her in one of James's big soft towels. I dry her thoroughly, then look through the bottles that Henry brought from Maddie's house. She has some baby lotion, so I take Leia through to my room, lie her on the bed, and use a little of the lotion to give her a massage.

As I stroke her tiny arms and legs, I wonder whether she misses her mum. My eyes sting, even though I didn't know Maddie.

"Poor little bubs," I murmur, kissing her toes. She's such a beautiful, contented baby. She deserves parents who'll treat her like a princess.

I start singing to her as I turn her onto her tummy, smiling as she lifts up her head, her tiny neck strong enough to support it now. I massage her back and shoulders, then turn her back over, put a nappy on, and dress her in a cute white onesie with a yellow duck on the front.

I put the bottle in the warmer and switch it on, then give her a cuddle and dance with her for a bit while I sing to her. When the bottle's done, I sit in the rocking chair and feed her. While she's feeding, I retrieve the first Harry Potter book that I glimpsed in the bag and open it up. It's well-thumbed and has obviously been read many times. Was Maddie planning to read it to her daughter at some stage?

"No time like the present," I tell Leia, opening the book up. "You're going to love this one about the boy who lived." I begin reading to her while I rock slowly.

Mmm, this is nice. The room is pleasantly warm and smells of the chamomile lotion I bathed her with. Leia sucks contentedly, looking up at me with her big turquoise eyes, her eyelids beginning to droop. I feel a little sleepy myself. Well, it's been a busy few days, and I know how exhausting emotion can be.

When she's finished her bottle, I put down the book and rock her for a little longer, looking at her fingers with their tiny nails and her long dark lashes. I should put her in her bassinet and get her off to good habits from the start, but suddenly I don't want to part with her. Maddie won't ever be able to hold her again, and I feel a sweep of sadness at the thought.

"Come on, *ātaahua*," I say, which means beautiful, rising from the chair. I take her over to my bed and, still fully dressed, curl up with her there. I stroke her back for a while until she settles, and then my eyelids drift closed.

*

I jerk awake, not sure what woke me, and glance up to see someone standing in the open doorway. It's James, and he's watching us, his hands in his pockets, leaning on the door jamb, although he pushes off as he sees me look over.

"I'm sorry," he murmurs, "I didn't mean to intrude. I wondered where you were."

I sit up. How long has he been standing there? For some reason, I think it was more than a few seconds. "It's okay. I was tired and I dozed off, sorry."

"It's not a problem. Everyone's gone. They all said to say goodbye." He tips his head to the side. "Why didn't you come back out?"

"They're your friends, James, I didn't want to intrude for too long."

He frowns. "Gaby's your best friend."

"I know. But she's part of your world."

"What do you mean, my world?"

"She's used to mixing in different circles. She's not intimidated."

His eyebrows lift. "You feel intimidated?"

"A little."

"By whom?"

"Nobody in particular."

He studies me, puzzled. "Is this about… money?"

"Of course it's about money. I know it's hard for you to understand, but I haven't traveled, I don't eat in posh restaurants, I don't know the difference between different wines and whiskies, I don't run my own business. Your experiences are very different from mine. It just reminds me that I'm… well… staff."

He gives me an exasperated look. "You're not staff."

"You're paying me to do a job, so yes, I am, and that's fine! I'm happy with that. I'm not complaining. I'm just trying to explain why I feel a bit uncomfortable."

He glares at me. "I don't see it like that. You came to the trivia night with us, and to Damon's wedding. You're Gaby's friend, and you're my friend now who happens to be helping me out with my niece. I might be compensating you for your time, but you're not staff."

We study each other for a moment. He folds his arms and lifts an eyebrow.

"Is this you putting your foot down?" I ask.

He runs his tongue across his teeth, fighting not to smile. "Maybe. Look, the contents of our bank accounts are irrelevant. We're friends, aren't we?"

"Yes, but that's a very naïve comment to make."

"Are you going to give me a speech about being entitled and privileged now?"

"Of course not, I wouldn't be so rude. But money does give a person a different outlook on life. It gives you confidence and a sense that you can do anything."

"Are you saying you think I'm powerful and masterful?"

I give him a wry look. "Definitely not."

He smirks. "I think that's what you're saying."

Embarrassed, I decide to say what's on my mind. "James… come on, don't be dense. I'm staying in your house. I don't want the others to think I'm sleeping with you because I'm after your money. I know what they all think of women like that."

He stares at me. Then he says, "I don't give a fuck what anyone else thinks. And anyway, for all my faults, they know I'm not the kind of guy to bang the nanny."

My face warms. That very declaration puts me in my place. Whatever he says, he sees me as staff, and because of his strict, self-imposed rules, he's never going to be interested in me.

I think of how I gave him a massage today, and the feel of his skin and hair beneath my fingertips. I so badly wanted to lean over him and kiss him at the time. I like this guy so much. But I'm not in his league, and we both know it.

"Come and have a cup of coffee," he says.

I look down at Leia. "No, thank you. I think I'll go to bed."

"It's only nine p.m."

"I'm tired. It's been a busy few days."

He watches as I pick up Leia. "I've upset you."

"I'm just tired, James. I'll see you tomorrow." I stop in the doorway to Leia's room. "Goodnight."

He hesitates, and for a moment I think he's going to argue with me. But he just says, "'Night," and then he goes out and closes the door behind him.

*

The next day, there's a subtle shift in James's attitude toward me. He's pleasant and polite, but I can feel his detachment, his slight coolness, as though he's made a personal vow to keep a distance between us, the same way he would if I were someone he'd never met who he'd hired to look after Leia.

I suppose I should be relieved that he understood what I was saying, but it makes me sad. I don't say anything though, and I don't argue when, as I make myself some breakfast, he doesn't join me, but instead retires to his office to work.

I prepare a bottle and take it out onto the deck with Leia, and sit on the sofa in the shade, watching the fantails hopping along the branches while Leia quietly sucks. I kiss her forehead, feeling a surge of tenderness for the tiny baby. James still hasn't said what he plans to do, but I have a feeling he's going to offer her up for adoption. The thought makes me sad, but I guess it'll be better for her in the long run. A couple somewhere who have been childless up until now will get the chance to have this beautiful baby girl, and that has to be a good thing.

Chapter Twenty

James

It's around twelve thirty when I finally leave my office and walk out into the kitchen, my hands in the pockets of my jeans.

I find Aroha on the deck, Leia lying on her tummy, asleep. Aroha is reading *Harry Potter and the Philosopher's Stone*. For some reason, it makes me smile.

"I'm going to make myself a coffee," I say to her. "Would you like one?"

She looks up, surprised. "Oh. Yes, please."

"Stay there, don't get up. I won't be long." I go back into the kitchen, make the two coffees, then take them out onto the deck. I place hers on the table and take the seat opposite her.

Our conversation yesterday revealed that she doesn't think of herself as a friend who's helping me out, but rather as a member of my staff. I can understand that, and in essence she's right. I'm paying her for a service, so in that sense she's no different from Ginny or Sue. It disappointed me, though, and made me angry at myself that I've somehow made her uncomfortable by flirting with her. Determined to make up for it, I've distanced myself this morning, keeping to my office, but now something's happened, and I need to talk about it, and to my surprise my feet brought me to her.

"I heard from the police," I say, warming my hands on the mug. Even though the good weather is continuing and it's a beautiful day, I feel cold all the way through. I sip the coffee—its earthy flavor grounds me and takes away some of the lightheadedness I feel.

Aroha's eyebrows have risen. Man, she looks amazing today. She's wearing a plain light-blue tee and a denim mini skirt. Her feet are bare, and her toenails are still cherry red. I know her light-brown skin is soft all the way up her thighs, and that she's hairless and smooth in all the places that matter.

My brain wants to linger on her because it stops me thinking about Maddie. But I have to tell her what happened.

"What did they say?" she asks.

"They've found Blue and interviewed him this morning. Blue said Maddie called him and told him about Leia. He said he was shocked, but they agreed to meet in the afternoon at a local coffee shop. But she never turned up."

Aroha sips her coffee, stroking Leia's back with her other hand. "Did they believe him?"

"Yes."

"How do you feel about that?" she asks. "It puts a different perspective on things, doesn't it?"

I lean forward, elbows on my knees, cradling the mug. "Yeah. And that's not all. The results of the post-mortem have revealed that she died from injuries she sustained after the fall. The police have also investigated the top of the cliff. They found that part of it had crumbled away, and they discovered loose stones around her body. They've sent the results to the coroner, but the DI said it's likely the report will conclude her death was accidental."

She's silent for a moment. Eventually, she says, "So, for some reason, she called Blue to tell him about Leia, agreed to meet him, then went for a walk to think about things. And she just went too close to the edge, and fell?"

"That's what they're thinking."

She dips her head to catch my eye. "Are you okay with that?"

I drop my gaze to my coffee. "I don't understand why she'd contact Blue. But of course it's possible that after I spoke to her that night, she spent a while thinking about him, and decided she should tell him that he had a daughter. It's plausible that she'd go for a walk to think about things—she did that a lot. And she happened to pick an unstable part of the cliff. Apparently they've sectioned it off, and they're going to investigate why there weren't any signs indicating it was unsafe. But it's too late now. It's done."

"How did Blue react to the news that Maddie had died?"

"The DI said he was shocked. She also said that he wants to talk to me about Leia."

"Are you okay with that?"

My jaw knots. "He's Leia's father."

"That doesn't answer the question."

I blow out a breath. "The DI said that if I want, she'll facilitate a meeting on neutral ground. If I'm going to put Leia up for adoption, surely it would be better for her biological father to adopt her than two strangers. Right?"

Aroha looks down at Leia and strokes her downy head. "So you've decided to give her up?"

I grit my teeth. "I'm not a natural father."

She gives me a look that says *Don't start*. "James—"

"I'd already decided I didn't want kids. I'm not married or in a long-term relationship. Being wealthy isn't enough. I know Maddie named me Leia's guardian, but that's only because she didn't have anyone else."

"She named you to stop Blue having Leia, didn't she?"

"I don't know that. I don't know anything. I don't know why she named me, and I don't know why she called Blue that morning. He doesn't have any rights by law, but that doesn't seem fair to me. Men never have a say in pregnancy or fatherhood. I understand why, and I fully believe in a woman's right to choose, but… I don't know. He had no say in the fact that she chose to have the baby. I… feel for him, I guess." I frown. I'm uncomfortable with having any sympathy for the guy when I would happily have punched his teeth down his throat before now. But I can't help how I feel.

"I suppose you can meet with him and see how you feel afterward," Aroha suggests.

I nod slowly. "Would you come with me?"

"Yes," she says without hesitation. Then she gives a shy smile. "I feel protective of Leia. I'd want to make sure she's all right."

I look at where she's stroking Leia's head. Aroha has elegant hands with long, slender, fingers. She's gentle in both the way she moves and her manner. She's very calming, and I think that's why she's so good with children. I like that about her.

I'm touched that she feels protective of Leia, and that she wants to make sure she's okay. But I can't let that distract me from the bigger picture. Blue is Leia's father. He deserves to meet his daughter, if nothing else. My personal dislike of the guy is irrelevant. Maddie arranged to meet him. She must have changed her mind and wanted him to play a part in Leia's upbringing, or else why did she phone him?

"All I can do is meet with him and trust my instincts. The fact is that, by law, right now I'm Leia's guardian, and he'll have to apply to the courts to get any kind of access to her. All we can do is play along and see how it goes."

She nods. "When will you organize the meeting for?"

"Soon as."

"Okay." She sighs, stroking Leia's back. "It looks as if we might have even less time together than I thought, little bubs." She looks sad. Is it because she'll miss the baby, or because she was hoping the gig would last longer? She is in need of money, after all.

"You need to give me your bank details," I tell her. "So I can pay you."

She continues stroking Leia's back, not looking at me. "Sure. I'll text them to you."

"Thanks." I hesitate. She glances at me and catches my eye, the way we seem to do, and we hold each other's gaze for a moment. But even as my pulse picks up, she looks back at Leia. And she's right to do so. I have to stop sending mixed messages.

I clear my throat and stand. "I'm going to get back to work."

"Do you want some lunch?"

"No, thank you, I'm good."

"How's your head?" she asks as I begin to walk away.

"Better, thank you. I think your massage helped."

"Good." She flashes me a smile.

I return it, then head back to my office.

I phone the DI and ask her to contact Blue to arrange a meetup. She calls back in fifteen minutes with the details of a café not far from Kia Kaha in the center of the city, and a time—Sunday at ten a.m.

After that, I find it difficult to put my mind to anything. I spend an hour trying to work, but I can't concentrate. In the end, I put it aside and go out to the kitchen. There's no sign of Aroha and Leia. Maybe they're having a lie down.

I find a muesli bar and a bottle of water, don my sunglasses and a baseball cap, and go into the garden, barefoot. I can hear Sue around the back of the house, trimming hedges. I can also hear singing. Surprised, I cross the lawn and go through the garden gate to the swimming pool. Aroha's in the shallow end, holding Leia as she bobs about in the water. She's singing to the baby, who's wearing a brightly colored swimsuit with ducks on it and a sunhat.

I lean on the barrier fence and watch them for a moment, finishing off my muesli bar. Aroha hasn't seen me. She's wearing a bikini that's a luminous orange color and showcases her magnificent figure. Wow. I blink in slow motion.

She's singing 'Wheels on the Bus'. As she tells Leia that the wipers go "swish, swish, swish," Leia smacks the water with her hand, sending a spray over Aroha's face. She just laughs and says, "Good girl! Do it again!" She moves Leia's hand to splash her, and Leia laughs and kicks her little legs, making me smile.

Aroha turns at that point and sees me, and her eyebrows rise. "Oh, hello."

"Hey." I'm suddenly embarrassed she's caught me watching. "Sorry, I wasn't spying on you. I heard singing, and…"

"Come in," she says. "The water's lovely."

I have a swig from the bottle. She's obviously spotted that I'm wearing swim shorts. "I was going to have a dip later."

"Aw, come on. You have to see Leia—she's really enjoying it."

I give in. It's too hot, and the water—and Aroha—look too inviting.

I go through the gate, leave the bottle, sunglasses, and hat by one of the loungers, and strip off my tee. I don't miss the fact that Aroha watches, and I feel a surge of pleasure as her gaze skims down me. Trying not to show that I've noticed, I go down to the deep end and dive in, swimming all the way underwater to the shallow end, where I see Aroha's tiny bikini bottoms outlining her tight butt, and her brown skin glimmering in the water. Fighting the urge to slide my hands across it, I surface right in front of the two of them.

Leia bursts out laughing and splashes me, and Aroha giggles. "Good girl!"

I chuckle and shake my head so droplets of water from my hair scatter them both, and Leia laughs again.

"She's having a great time," Aroha says. "She loves the water. It's so warm."

"It's solar heated. The panels are on the roof." I point to the house.

"That makes sense. How wonderful." She gives me a hopeful gaze. "Would you mind holding her for a minute so I can swim a few lengths?"

"Oh. Er, sure." I take her from Aroha, feeling all fingers and thumbs.

"You're holding her like a rugby ball," she says with a giggle.

"I'm worried about dropping her and drowning her."

"You won't," she scoffs. "She holds up her head now, so you can turn her facing out. Look, slide your hand around her, under her arms, and put one hand under her legs. That's it!" She pushes off the side. "Back in a minute." She dives under the water and heads toward the deep end of the pool.

I look down at the baby in my arms. She smacks her hand on the water, splashing me in the face. "Nice one," I tell her. She's clearly enjoying the feel of the silky water on her legs, and kicks them enthusiastically. I move about from one side of the shallow end to the other, so the water passes over her skin. The suit she's wearing is tight around the tops of her legs, so I think it doubles as a nappy.

"Look," I say to her, "you've got ducks on your tummy."

She turns her head at the sound of my voice and looks up at me. I catch my breath at the blueness of her eyes. It's like looking in a mirror. This little girl shares the same blood as me. She's a little piece of Maddie, and of my mother, who also had turquoise eyes.

She lifts a hand to my mouth. Her fingers are so tiny, the nails minute. She brushes them against my lips, and I open my mouth and pretend to nibble them, which makes her lips curve up.

"Nom, nom, nom," I say. "I'm having your fingers for lunch."

She smacks the water and looks away, then rubs her eyes. Maybe the chlorine makes her eyes sting, because she screws up her nose and her chin wobbles.

In alarm, I look for Aroha, but she's swimming lengths at the moment, moving fast through the water. I'm not even sure she'll hear me if I call.

I look back at Leia and carefully, awkwardly, turn her in my arms so she's facing me. Then I lift her against my shoulder. Pulling her arms to her chest, she nestles against the crook of my neck and sighs.

Aroha sang to her, so maybe she likes music. I start singing, continuing to move, letting warm water stroke our skin.

Not long after, Aroha swims up to us under the water, then appears and smooths back her hair. Droplets glisten on her lashes.

"Are you really singing an AC/DC song to her?" she asks.

"It was the first thing that came to mind."

"Not sure of the appropriateness of *Highway to Hell*, but whatever." She laughs and moves closer to peer at the baby. "She looks half asleep. How did you manage that?"

"Skill. Do you think she'd prefer John Mayer?" I start singing *Slow Dancing in a Burning Room*.

Aroha joins in, and we sing together, turning circles in the water.

I'm a very driven guy, and I don't have many pastimes. If I have a spare minute, I tend to spend it working. I don't enjoy vacations. I get bored and restless unless I'm doing something. So I'm surprised how content I feel right now, in the warm water, holding a baby, and doing nothing except moving around, singing to her.

Then I think of Maddie, and it's like a cloud passing across the sun. She won't get to do this with Leia. She won't be able to watch her daughter taking her first steps, or hear her saying her first word. She won't see her put on her first uniform and go to school, or watch her excel in art or music or sport. She won't hear Leia tell her about her first kiss, or be able to hold her when she breaks up with her boyfriend.

She won't see her graduate from university, or get engaged and married, or hold her first grandchild. So many firsts, and Maddie's going to miss them all.

"Are you thinking about Maddie?" Aroha asks.

I look up, surprised she's picked up on it. "Yeah."

Her hazel eyes survey me thoughtfully. "Tell Leia a story about when you were young."

Leia is almost asleep. "She can't understand me."

"It doesn't matter." She smiles.

I look back at Leia. "I guess not." I turn from side to side, thinking. "When your mum and I were five," I say, "your grandparents took us to the beach. We had a dog at the time—a Labrador called Malfoy."

"From Harry Potter?" Aroha asks in delight.

"Yeah. Maddie and I both loved the books. Anyway, Dad bought us both an ice cream, one of the soft whipped ones in a cone. Maddie only had a few licks of hers when she dropped it. She started crying and asked Dad for another, but he said no, it was her fault she dropped it, so she had to do without. So I said she could share mine, and we sat there eating it—one lick for her, one for me, and one for Malfoy." The memory makes me chuckle. "Mum was horrified, but we still did it. One lick each." I smooth down a strand of Leia's hair that's sticking up. "I don't know what made me think of that."

"I'm reading her Harry Potter now," Aroha says.

"You're a fan too?"

"I've seen all the movies a dozen times. So, uh, yeah." She smiles.

"Maddie would like that," I murmur. My eyes meet hers. "She would have liked you."

"I hope so. I wish I'd met her."

"She would have liked that you're down-to-earth. She hated pretentiousness of any kind. She would have been pleased that you were reading to Leia. And that you were singing to her."

"I'm sure Leia's missing her mum, even though she can't say so."

I sigh and kiss the baby's forehead. "I don't know. Maybe it's better that she won't remember her, or anything of this time." She won't remember me, unless I choose to play a part in her life. The realization makes me frown.

Aroha watches us for a moment. Then she says, "She's falling asleep. I think I'll take her in."

"Okay." I hand the baby over. Aroha sits on the steps, retrieves the towel she left on the side, and wraps Leia in it. Leia grizzles, but Aroha has her dummy ready, and Leia sucks on it contentedly.

"I'll dry her off indoors," Aroha says, "and then put her down for a nap. I'll catch you later."

"Yeah, see you."

I watch them walk away. The wet bikini clings to Aroha's skin.

Sighing, I push off the wall and dive into the warm water.

Chapter Twenty-One

Aroha

I don't see James for the rest of the day. At six, I'm in the kitchen looking through the cupboards when he finally appears.

"I'm going into Kia Kaha to catch up with the guys," he says.

"Six p.m.? On a Saturday?"

"Yeah, it'll be nice and quiet. We're going to get some food brought in." He pauses. "Would you like to join us?"

I know he's just being polite. "No, thank you." I chuckle. "I'm sure the last thing you all want is a screaming baby in the middle of a meeting."

"She doesn't seem to scream very much."

"No, she's a good baby, I have to say."

"Or maybe it's her excellent care."

I warm through at his compliment. It means a lot that he believes I'm taking good care of her.

"You're sure you don't want to come?" he asks. "Honestly, nobody would mind, and it must get pretty lonely here on your own all day."

"I'm not on my own—I have Leia. Anyway I'm trying to get her into a routine, so it'll be bath and bed at seven."

"Are you okay being here alone?"

"Of course!" Privately, I think I'll enjoy having the house to myself without feeling nervous that I'm going to bump into him around the corner. Every time I do that, it makes my stomach flip.

"All right." He picks up his keys. He's already dressed in jeans and a white shirt, unbuttoned at the neck. "I don't know what time I'll be back."

"I'll probably be in bed. I hope you have a nice evening."

"Help yourself to anything in the cupboards or freezer. And if you want to order in Uber Eats, you can use my credit card."

"No," I say hastily, "it's fine, I'll make myself some dinner."

"Okay. I'll see you tomorrow, then." He gives me a nod and leaves.

I hear the front door close and then, not long after, his car starts and heads off down the drive. I release a long breath. "It's just me and you, girl," I tell Leia, who's sitting in her carry seat on the counter. "Time to let our hair down!"

It turns out that party time consists of a portion of spaghetti Bolognese reheated in the microwave and a few scoops of chocolate fudge brownie ice cream for dessert. I eat it while I rock Leia's seat with my foot, watching an episode of *Friends*, while I tell her all about Ross and Rachel, and the wonder that is Chandler Bing. Afterward, I wash up the dishes, then put Leia on her playmat and lie beside her, smiling as she knocks the mirrors and toys that dangle from the frame above her.

At seven I take her in for a bath, dress her in a pretty pink onesie, and feed her, sitting in the rocking chair, while I read her Harry Potter. I burp her, then lie her down, turn on her monitor, and leave the room.

She cries for a while, but I know she can't get used to sleeping with me, and she has to learn to fall asleep on her own, so I sit in my bedroom for a while, reading and fighting the urge to go in and pick her up. Sure enough, eventually she quietens and dozes off.

After clipping the receiver to my waistband, I go into the kitchen and make myself a cup of coffee. I'm tempted to be nosy, wander around the house, and poke around in all the drawers and cupboards to see if I find anything interesting, but that feels sleazy, and besides, what am I expecting to find? He's a single guy, living on his own. He's told me he's never brought a girl here. We're not like the older generations—we don't tend to keep photos in frames around the house, so I doubt there'll be much to see anyway, and I don't feel comfortable invading his privacy.

Instead, I call my mum, and we chat for half an hour. She knows where I am, and that a friend has asked me to stay while I look after his niece. We chat about Leia for a bit, and then she talks about Dad and the fact that he hasn't been able to find another job. She doesn't ask me about James, and I don't volunteer any information. What would I say? That I have a huge crush on my employer? She has enough on her plate at the moment—she doesn't need to worry about me.

After I finish the call, I help myself to a small bar of chocolate from the cupboard and eat it while I watch a movie. By the end, I'm dozing off too, so I turn off the TV and lights, leaving on the one by the front door, and go to bed.

When Leia wakes around midnight, I change her, then go into the kitchen to make her a bottle. I've just finished warming it through when a voice says, "Hey."

I jump—I hadn't seen James sitting in the living room, in the semi-darkness.

"Oh, hello." My heart racing, I walk toward him, carrying Leia and the bottle. "You're back." I frown. "Why are you sitting in the dark?"

"Just thinking."

Leia grizzles, so I lower into one of the armchairs and start to feed her. "About Maddie?"

He inhales, then lets it out slowly and looks away, out at the garden, not replying. His feet are bare, crossed at the ankles and resting on the coffee table. I think he takes his socks and shoes off every time as soon as he enters the house. He has smooth, tanned feet. I've never been attracted to a guy's feet before.

He's holding a whisky glass in his right hand. He looks back at me and lifts it. "I'm only having the one."

"I wasn't judging you, James."

"Some people would." His father, no doubt.

"Not me," I say softly. "It's none of my business." I tip my head to the side. "Are you feeling sad?"

"You're not afraid of emotion, are you?"

"No."

"I envy you." Frown lines seem etched into his face. He's grieving, but he's scared of giving into it, because his father has told him that he always needs to be in control.

I feed Leia for a while. James sips from his glass, watching us, but not speaking. The only sounds are the occasional slurp when Leia sucks on the teat, and the rattle of ice in his glass when he lifts it. I would have thought I'd feel uncomfortable with such a prolonged period of silence, but I don't, and I don't think he does either. He doesn't take his eyes off me, though. Or maybe he's watching Leia; I can't tell.

When the bottle's empty, I lift her onto my shoulder and pat her back gently. "What's your favorite memory of Maddie?" I ask.

He narrows his eyes. "I know what you're doing."

"I'm not doing anything."

"Yes, you are. You're trying to get me to open up."

I don't reply. I concentrate on Leia, straightening her onesie.

"Most of my memories of Maddie are difficult ones," he says eventually, surprising me. "She wasn't an easy person to be with." He lets out a long sigh and brushes his hand over his face. "And now I feel like a heel."

"Death doesn't make someone into a saint. We all have our faults, and it's okay to remember them. But tell me a nice memory. Something she said that made you laugh."

He looks up at the ceiling. He's quiet for a while. I think he's suffering. Maybe it's only just sinking in that she's gone.

Eventually, he says, "One evening, when we were sixteen, we went to a friend's birthday party. When we got home, Maddie told Mum that she'd seen me snogging a girl. Mum said, 'What's her name?' I couldn't remember—I said she and her sister were named after birds, and Maddie said, 'Tits,' and I said, 'Probably a B cup,' and Mum told me off."

I giggle, and his lips curve up. He meets my gaze. "I can't believe she's not here anymore," he whispers, his smile fading. His beautiful turquoise eyes turn glassy. His jaw knots as he clenches his teeth hard, refusing to let his emotions show while I'm there.

I get to my feet and, carrying Leia, go over and kiss the top of his head. Then I take her back to bed, leaving him to his grief.

*

The next day, I check my bank account while I'm having breakfast and discover it's over ten thousand dollars in credit.

I nearly fall off my chair. "Holy shit."

He looks up from where he's eating cereal across the breakfast bar from me. "What?"

"You've paid me ten thousand dollars?"

"I told you I would," he says.

"I didn't think you were serious."

"Of course I was serious." He points at himself. "Look at my face."

Speechless, I watch him spoon cornflakes into his mouth. "Nannies earn around twenty-five dollars an hour on average."

"And you're working twenty-four hours a day."

"Well, kinda. But that's still only six hundred dollars. And I've only been here a few days."

"Aroha, you honestly have no idea how relieved I was that you dropped everything to come here and look after Leia."

"I didn't have to drop anything. I was out of a job."

"Yes, but even so, you didn't bat an eyelid before saying yes."

"That's because you're my friend," I say awkwardly.

He pokes his cereal. "I wanted to compensate you, and I know you need money. Do we have to argue about it?"

I look at my phone and think about my parents. Am I really going to tell him I'm not going to accept the money? I have to put them first, and their rent needs paying. "All right. Um… what should I do about tax?"

He waves a hand. "I'll sort it."

I give him an exasperated look. "James, you can't just say 'I'll sort it.' We should do it all by the book."

He gives me a look. "I have a degree in economics and finance. When I say I'll sort it, I mean it. I'll organize the employer deductions when you give me your IRD number, and I'll print you a proper contract."

"Oh. Okay. I forgot you have two degrees."

He has his last spoonful of cornflakes and stands up. "One more and I'll be singing *When Will I See You Again*."

The Three Degrees—that makes me laugh. He gives me a wry look and brings his dish over to put in the dishwasher. Then he checks his phone. "Ready to go by nine thirty, okay?"

"Yes, sir."

His eyes meet mine, and my pulse leaps at the sudden heat in those turquoise orbs. Ooh. He watches me a lot, but I assumed he was assessing my care of his niece, rather than because he was still interested in me sexually. That heat tells me something different. He still wants me.

I won't act on it. But it warms me through to know.

*

Ten o'clock finds the three of us—me, James, and Leia—standing outside Café Muse in the bustling Riverside Market.

"He's not here yet." James is wearing a business suit, even though, as far as I know, he's not intending to go into the office. I wonder whether he's worn it to intimidate Blue. I've never seen a man wear a suit as well as James. Clearly, it's bespoke, because the jacket fits his shoulders and is snug without being tight all the way down. The white shirt looks as if he took it out of the packet this morning, crisp and clean. His tie bears a silver pin. His hair is neatly combed. His emotion from the previous night has vanished, and he looks cold and stern.

I've also dressed smartly, and I'm wearing a pair of black trousers and a pink blouse. I've braided my hair and taken time over my makeup, even though I'm not expecting anyone to pay any attention to me. I washed Leia this morning, and I changed her and fed her before we left, so she's dozing in her carry seat. She's wearing a gorgeous floral dress with little white socks that have a lacy frill around the tops, and I've tied a matching scarf around her head, so she looks super cute. If Blue is going to play a part in her life—and maybe he'll even get custody of her—I want him to love her immediately.

"Let's go in and order a coffee," James says.

We enter the shop and find a table near the window. I'm super nervous to the point of queasiness and don't want a drink, but it'll give me something to do, so I ask for a cappuccino, and he goes up to order.

He comes back and sits next to me, leaving the two seats opposite us for Blue and his partner, who is apparently accompanying him. James leans on the table, his arm a fraction away from mine. I can feel the warmth of his body even through his suit, and smell his cologne.

"You look nervous," he says.

"I am nervous. Aren't you?"

"Yes, but then I have skin in the game. Why are you anxious?" He seems genuinely puzzled.

"I have skin in the game too," I say quietly, looking down at Leia. "I know I shouldn't, but I've grown very fond of her already. She's such a sweetie. I'm going to miss her if—when—she goes."

His lips curve up. "You have a big heart. I guess you were called Aroha for a reason."

I love the way he says my name, softening the 'r', the word tender in his mouth, like a kiss.

The waiter comes over with our coffees. Once he retreats, James has a sip of his, then studies the cup. "I keep thinking that apparently

AROHA AND THE BILLIONAIRE BOSS

depression is approximately fifty percent hereditary, so there's a likelihood that Leia will have it too."

"It also means there's a 1 in 2 chance she won't. I would imagine there's a nature versus nurture element to it, too. Maddie would have watched your mum and copied her behavior to some extent. Leia won't be able to do that. She'll grow up emulating the behaviors of the women around her."

A frown flickers on his brow. He opens his mouth to speak, then stops as something catches his eye. I watch as his expression changes. The friendly guy I've been talking to fades away, his spine stiffens, and he morphs into James the stern businessman again.

Two people are approaching the table. One is obviously Bruce Clarke, known as Blue because of his extremely bright ginger hair. He's average height, stocky, and I guess that when he was younger he could have challenged James with his looks. Now, though, he has the fleshy look of someone who's overindulged too often. He has thin lips and a hint of meanness about his features. And, worse than that, I can smell marijuana on his clothes. His eyes are red, and something about his manner tells me he's high. I stiffen, my hand tightening on Leia's carry seat.

He's with a woman who's also overweight, mainly because she's very short, with long bleached-blonde hair. She also smells of weed. She looks at James with interest, and the interest in her eyes suggests she finds him attractive.

"Blue," James says tersely, holding out his hand.

Blue shakes it, then glances at me.

"This is Aroha Wihongi," James states. "She's looking after Leia at the moment."

Blue nods and shakes my hand. "This is my wife, Jasmine," he says.

"Wife?" James says. "You got married?"

"Yeah, a few months ago."

Jasmine stretches out her hand to shake ours. Next to me, James stiffens, but I'm not sure why.

"Can I get you a coffee?" he asks politely.

"No thanks," Blue replies. "We won't be staying long."

James waits a moment, as if he's expecting Blue to display at least some sign of grief or to say he's sorry that Maddie died, but he doesn't.

"Okay," James says eventually, his tone clipped and curt. "I can see you don't want to be here any more than I do, so shall we get straight to business? DI Maddox told me that Maddie called you on the morning of the day she died. Can you tell me about the phone call?"

"She rang to tell me about the baby. She said she'd been giving it a lot of thought, and whether or not I wanted to be involved, she thought I deserved to know."

"And you arranged to meet?"

"In town, in the afternoon, but she never showed up."

"What did you do?"

He shrugs. "Went home. I assumed she'd changed her mind."

"Did you call her again?"

"No."

"You didn't want to see your daughter?"

Blue shrugs again.

James's knee is bouncing next to mine. He's agitated. "What did you think when she told you that you were a father?"

Blue's expression flickers with irritation. "I didn't believe her. I used a condom. I told her I wanted a paternity test. That's why we agreed to meet—she said she'd bring a kit to take a saliva sample."

"Do you still want a test done?" James asks. "As far as I know, Maddie wasn't seeing anyone else."

Blue leans forward. "I'm prepared to forgo the test, if the price is right."

"The price?"

"What do we get?" Jasmine asks. "If we take the baby?"

James and I both stare at them. It occurs to me then that neither of them has looked at Leia once.

"You get custody of your daughter," James says carefully.

Blue taps on the table. "Let's stop beating around the bush. You're a rich playboy, and the last thing you need hanging around your neck is a kid that isn't yours. You want me to take her off your hands. Fine, I'll do it. If the price is right. So what are you offering?"

A surge of fury makes me inhale. "You piece of shit," I say before I can think better of it. I'm absolutely aghast. "She's not a secondhand car. She's your *daughter*."

"Fuck off," Jasmine spits. "What's this got to do with you?"

"I want half a million up front," Blue says, lifting his chin, "and a hundred thousand every year after that."

James just stares at him.

Blue narrows his eyes. "I know you have the money. You and Maddie were fucking loaded. If I'm going to take on her kid, I expect to be compensated."

Her kid, not *my* kid. He's not even sure Leia's his. But Jasmine's eyes gleam with excitement. They don't care about Leia. The two of them just think she'll be their ticket to a fortune. It wouldn't surprise me if they offload her as soon as they get her.

James gets to his feet. The rest of us rise quickly.

He looks at me and says quietly, "Pass me Leia."

I stare at him in horror. He's going to give her to them. "Oh my God, James, no. Don't do it. I beg you."

He meets my eyes and gives a small smile. "Pass her to me, please."

I swallow hard, then lift Leia's seat and hand her to him. He takes the handle in his left hand. Then he moves closer to Blue.

When he speaks, his voice is soft and menacing. "I wouldn't give her to you if you were the last man alive." He trembles, and I realize it's with anger. Oh, thank God.

Blue's jaw drops. Then his eyes blaze. "I'm her father. She's mine by right."

"Oh, so now you're claiming you're her father?" James moves closer and towers over him. "Maddie might have slept with you in a moment of madness, but that does not make you Leia's father morally or legally. A father cares for his partner when she's pregnant, he holds her hand when she gives birth, and he's there to support her when the baby's young. She didn't put your name on Leia's birth certificate. And she named me Leia's guardian. I don't know why she called you that morning—if it was to involve you in Leia's care, I'm sure she would have changed her mind if she'd heard what you just said to me."

"So what?" Blue scoffs. "You're going to give up your parties and your whores to stay at home and play Daddy?"

"He can give her up for adoption," Jasmine says warily.

Blue snorts. "Any lawyer worth his salt would convince the Family Courts to give the kid to me over strangers. And he'd also be able to persuade the judge to give us part of Maddie's fortune to bring the baby up."

"I promise you, you won't get a single cent of Maddie's money." James's voice is like ice.

"We'll see," Blue says.

James turns on his heel and, carrying Leia, marches out of the door.

Chapter Twenty-Two

James

I stride back to the car so fast that Aroha has to run to keep up with me. I own a Jeep as well as the Porsche, and when we arrive at it, I clip Leia's seat securely in the back, then get in the driver's seat, and Aroha slides into the passenger seat.

I sit there for a moment, holding the steering wheel, my knuckles white. Then I start the car, and I head for home.

We don't say a word on the way. I'm too angry to talk, and she seems to understand that. Instead, she takes out her phone and examines it while I negotiate the traffic.

When we finally arrive back home, I park the car by the garage, get out, unbuckle Leia's seat, and I carry her through to the house. She wakes at this point, and, without asking, I start preparing her a bottle, while Aroha unclips her harness, lifts her out, and gives her a cuddle.

When the bottle's warmed, she takes it from me and carries the baby out onto the deck to feed her.

I make us both a coffee, then I take the mugs out onto the deck, place one in front of Aroha, take a seat in the chair opposite, and flop back.

I stare out at the garden. The sky has clouded over, and it's raining lightly. Sue will be pleased—the lawn and flowers need it.

I take a deep breath and huff it out.

"You all right?" Aroha asks.

"Yeah."

"I know you're upset but try to calm down." She arches her eyebrow. "Don't glare at me. You don't want another migraine, that's all."

I grit my teeth, knowing she's right, but I'm furious. I want to smash my fist into the wall or yell until I'm hoarse. But I learned long ago that giving into anger makes a man weak. Instead, I lean forward, elbows on my knees, and press my thumbs into my eyes.

"Talk to me," she says.

My chest heaves. "I feel as if I've let Maddie down."

"Why?"

"She contacted him, and she was going to meet him. She must have decided to involve him in Leia's life." I clench my hands into fists. "I don't understand. The guy's a fucking arsehole. Why would she want anything to do with that wanker?"

"Maybe it was guilt. He is Leia's father, after all. Perhaps she thought Leia deserved to know him as she grew up."

I lower my hands and look at her. "Is that what you think?"

She studies Leia, who's staring up at her adoringly as she sucks from the bottle. "I understand why she might have thought that. And I can see why she was attracted to him. He's a charmer. One of those guys who thinks he can talk his way into any woman's underwear."

Jealousy flares inside me. "You were attracted to him?"

She wrinkles her nose. "I'd never go out with a ginger." She hardens the 'g' and rhymes it with 'singer'. That makes me give a short laugh.

But despair isn't far away, and as it sweeps over me, I bend my head and sink my hands into my hair.

"What's bothering you?" she asks gently.

"I feel as if I've fucked it all up," I mumble. "I should do what she would have wanted. But I can't be sure what that was. I can't trust what Blue said about their conversation. What if she just contacted him to demand he contribute financially? I mean she didn't need the money, but maybe she thought he should still do it for Leia? What if she didn't want him involved in any other way? How do I know?"

Aroha's silent for a moment. Then eventually she says, "Do you want my opinion?"

I lift my head and rest my lips on my clasped hands. I can't trust myself to speak, so I just look at her.

She adjusts Leia's dress. "Maddie's gone." She looks at me, her eyes gentle as she sees my emotion. "You can't second guess what she did or didn't want. She made you Leia's guardian. That means she trusted you to make the right decisions for her daughter. You're Leia's whole world now. She's relying on you to make the choices that will affect the rest of her life. It's a huge responsibility, and I'm not surprised you feel overwhelmed. All parents feel like that, and that's what you are, for all intents and purposes. For the moment, anyway. You have to decide what's best for Leia, and what's best for you. Forget everyone else. Don't think about what anyone else wants or is advising you to do."

I swallow hard. "I don't know if I can bring up someone else's child." I'm embarrassed and ashamed to say it. I wouldn't have said it to anyone else, but oddly, I feel as if I can be honest with her. I'm not trying to impress her, and I don't have a reputation to uphold. And somehow, I know she'll give me her honest opinion back.

She seems unfazed by my emotion. "Okay, let's break it down. Let's talk about you first. As I see it, you have two main options. Basically, you keep Leia, or you don't."

I nod. That much is obvious.

"So," she continues, "let's talk about you not keeping her. A child is for life, after all, not just for Christmas."

My lips curve up. "That's true." Glad she isn't telling me I'm a terrible person for wanting to think about it, I blow out a breath and have a big mouthful of coffee.

"Again," she says, "you have two options. First, you let Blue have her. And here I think you have to forget about trying to decipher what Maddie did or didn't want. Maybe she felt guilty that she hadn't told him. She could have been thinking about Leia growing up, or perhaps she just felt he deserved to know. We'll never know. I think all you can do is trust your instincts and decide whether you think he'll be a good father."

I don't miss that she says '*we'll* never know,' not '*you'll*.' She told me she has skin in the game, too. I remember what she said to Blue in the café. *You piece of shit… She's not a secondhand car. She's your daughter.* At the time, I felt a surge of relief that she agreed with me. And so I'm not surprised that she looks relieved when I say, "Honestly? I don't want him anywhere near her."

"Thank God." She blows out a breath. "I could smell marijuana on them both really strongly. I mean, I know lots of people smoke weed, but when there are kids around…"

I smile. Henry told me he offered her a whisky the first night they were all here, and she refused, saying she didn't drink alcohol when she was looking after children. I admire her for that. "It wasn't just marijuana," I tell her. "I'm sure I saw needle marks on Jasmine's arm."

Her jaw drops. "No... oh James. We can't let them have her. Neither he nor Jasmine looked at Leia once all the time we were in the café. That annoyed me more than anything else." She strokes the baby's downy head with such tenderness it makes my chest tighten.

"I think we can agree that we don't want them to have her," I say firmly. "I don't believe Blue is the slightest bit interested in the fact that he has a daughter. He just wants the money."

"Absolutely." She's pleased I've come to that conclusion.

"If Maddie did change her mind about him playing a role in Leia's life, she did so because she was feeling low and vulnerable. But the fact is that he slept with her and then ditched her and refused to return her phone calls. He treated her like shit, and he's obviously not interested in Leia. He doesn't deserve anything." I speak bitterly.

She nods her agreement. "So the other option is that you give Leia up for adoption."

I nod slowly. "Would I get to meet the couples who were interested?"

"Yes. Birth parents make the decision on who they want to care for their child, so I presume as guardian that decision would transfer to you."

"That's something." I look at the tiny baby in her arms, and suddenly I feel as if I've been punched in the stomach. It's Maddie's little girl. How can I hand her over to strangers?

"Or you could keep her," Aroha says.

I study Leia's little hand where it lies on the bottle. "I'm seeing my lawyer tomorrow about Maddie's will. I guess he'll explain what options exist about caring for Leia."

"You could just continue to be her guardian. She'd be like a medieval ward."

"Like Theon Greyjoy," I say, naming the character from *Game of Thrones* who lives with the Stark family.

She laughs. "Yes, but hopefully with a happier outcome. You'd make the decisions on how she's brought up—anything involving her health or education, for example. But you could stay her uncle, if that made you feel better."

"Or?"

"Or you could adopt her. Take her on as your own. You'd be her daddy." She smiles.

Daddy? I shift in the seat. I'm not sure if I'm comfortable with Leia calling me that.

Leia has finished the bottle, and Aroha puts it down. She lifts Leia and gets to her feet. Then she comes over to me. She drapes a square of muslin cloth over my shoulder. Then she hands the baby to me.

"Hold her upright," she says, moving Leia so she's against my shoulder. "That's it. And just rub her back gently to get rid of any wind. Don't worry if she brings up a little milk, that's normal. I'm just going to the bathroom." She strokes Leia's hair, then disappears inside.

I sit stiffly for a moment. Then I stand and move to the edge of the deck, looking out at the rain.

Leia is warm in my arms. I rub her back, worried about patting in case I use too much force. She feels so tiny, like a doll.

But she's not a doll. She's a living, breathing human being. The responsibility of deciding what to do presses down on me. I live on my own because I don't have to worry about anyone but me. Even when I was dating Cassie, I liked that we lived apart because it meant I wasn't responsible for her. She had her life, her friends, her job, and I had mine. I'd help her if she was in trouble, of course, but I had no real input into the decisions she made about her own life.

If I took on Leia, every decision that would affect her would be up to me, until she grew of age, anyway. Jesus. How do people do this? I suppose if the child is your own, you feel you have the right to bring them up your way and to make decisions for them. But how do I stop wondering what Maddie would have wanted?

Aroha said, *She'll grow up emulating the behaviors of the women around her.* Leia could do worse than emulate Aroha. But of course, Aroha won't be around forever. She's just looking after Leia while she's a baby, and eventually she'll want to move on. Then it'll just be me and Leia.

I don't think you should keep her out of duty or guilt. There's no shame in admitting you'd prefer someone else to care for her day-to-day.

Leia squirms in my arms, and panic rises within me. I don't know what to do if she starts crying.

My thoughts are cloudy, like the summer sky, and I can't see clearly. What am I going to do?

Chapter Twenty-Three

James

Ten o'clock the next morning finds me at Fuller & Blade's law firm. The rather heroically named Ethan Blade is actually fifty-two, on the short side, tubby, and gray-haired, but he's smart and direct, and I've known him a long time. He's my personal lawyer, and he also acts for the firm.

"I'm so sorry to hear about Maddie," he says as I enter his office and we shake hands. He leads me over to the sofa and chairs on one side and gestures at the sofa. I sink onto the end seat, and he takes the chair opposite me.

"Thank you. Yeah, it was a bit of a shock, as you can imagine." I smile at Julia, his secretary, as she comes in.

"Would you like a coffee, Mr. Rutherford?"

"Please."

"Ethan?"

"Yes, please."

She leaves, closing the door behind her.

"Did the police contact you when she died?" I ask.

"Yes, they rang all the lawyers in the area to see whether we had Maddie on our books. I was able to tell them she'd named you her guardian in her will."

"When did she make the will?"

"Two weeks after Leia was born."

"Did she come into this office?"

"Yes. She brought Leia with her. She sat where you are now." He gives a sad smile.

I feel oddly lightheaded at the thought that my sister sat here only a few months ago. Then she was alive—now she's dead. How much your life can change in such a short space of time.

The door opens, and Julia brings in our coffees, along with a plate of biscuits. I take one, feeling the need to ground myself.

"Where's Leia today?" Ethan asks, sipping his coffee.

"With Aroha, a friend of mine. She's a childcare assistant, and she was kind enough to agree to look after Leia until I sort out what I'm going to do."

He nods and opens the manila file on his lap. "So, shall I go through her will?"

"Please."

He reads through the will that Maddie organized with him. It's short and to the point. It names me as Leia's guardian should anything happen to Maddie. It doesn't mention Blue once, nor does it say anything about how she'd like Leia brought up.

She talks about her funeral and requests a cremation, and it makes me wonder whether she somehow knew this was going to happen. But her death was an accident, so she must have just wanted to provide for her daughter, that's all. Still, the thought that she had to envisage what she wanted done with her body chokes me up for a moment.

Ethan keeps his gaze on the file and continues talking until I recover.

Like me, she had a considerable fortune. She's given generous sums to several charities but left the majority to Leia. She explains that I'm to manage the funds until Leia comes of age, and invest it as I see fit.

She names some jewelry items she wants me to give to the few friends she had.

She doesn't mention our father at all.

"That's it?" I ask when Ethan stops talking.

"That's it."

A whole life contained in several short paragraphs. It takes my breath away.

"So we need to talk about Leia," I say when I can finally gather my scrambled thoughts. "I don't know if the police told you, but Maddie called Bruce Clarke—Leia's father—the morning that she died."

His eyebrows rise. "I didn't know, no."

"She didn't name him on Leia's birth certificate, and as far as I know they didn't have any contact from the moment he left, before Maddie found out she was pregnant. She was very scathing about him to me. He broke her heart, she said, and she didn't want him anywhere near Leia. But, of course, he is her father. He says that Maddie called him and told him she'd had his baby, and they arranged to meet that afternoon, but she never turned up."

"The police are saying her death was accidental, right?"

"Yes, there's no talk of foul play, and they seem to think it wasn't suicide."

"Why do you think she contacted Mr. Clarke?"

"I don't know. She could have felt guilty for not telling him he had a daughter. She could have done it because she thought Leia should know her real father. Or she could have been angry and thought that he should contribute financially to Leia's upbringing."

"Did Mr. Clarke give any indication which it was?"

"He said he'd used a condom and he wanted a paternity test, and that was why they were meeting. It implies to me that their conversation wasn't friendly."

"Hmm." Ethan jots down some notes. "Is Mr. Clarke saying he wants to take over care of Leia?"

"He said something along the lines of, 'You want me to take her off your hands, I'll do it if the price is right.' He asked for half a million dollars up front and a hundred thousand every year after that."

Ethan's eyebrows rise, and he gives a short, humorless laugh. "Jesus."

"Yeah. Fucking arsehole. Look, I need to know where I stand legally. Do I have custody of Leia?"

"No. Guardianship and custody are different things. A child's birth mother is automatically a guardian. The father will only be a guardian if he's named on the birth certificate, or if he was married to or lived with the mother, otherwise he has to apply to the court. Maddie named you Leia's testamentary guardian. A testamentary guardian acts as an overseer and is only involved in big decisions. Their role is to provide input into all the important decisions about a child's upbringing. These would include where they go to school, any religious preferences, major decisions involving health, and where they live. These responsibilities end when the child is eighteen."

"Right."

"Custody—what we now call day-to-day care—cannot be provided for in a will. A guardian needs to apply to the court for a Parenting Order to get day-to-day care of the child. The court will assume that Leia's family will take care of her until her fate has been decided. But whoever wants to look after her permanently will need that Parenting Order."

"It sounds as if Blue is going to apply for one. What are his chances of getting it?"

"If I were his lawyer, I'd ask him to take a paternity test to prove he is Leia's birth father. Then I'd ask for the court to appoint him as a guardian. The court has to do that unless it would be against the welfare and best interests of the child, which is obviously what we'd argue. But as his lawyer I'd explain to the court that he had no knowledge that Maddie was pregnant, and it wasn't his fault he played no role in the pregnancy or birth. Does he have a partner?"

"He got married the day after Leia was born."

"Then I think he stands a good chance of getting the Parenting Order."

"Even against my wishes?"

"If the court thought it was best for Leia." He leans forward. "Look, having a child is a huge responsibility. Giving her over to her birth father would be easier all ways round. I wouldn't blame you for doing it."

"Ethan… The two of them stunk of marijuana, and I'm pretty sure I saw needle marks in his wife's arm."

He leans back and gives a humorless laugh. "Christ."

"Yeah. I don't want him to have her. But I'm guessing there's a slim chance that even if I accuse him of taking drugs, the court might still choose him over giving her to strangers."

"There's always a chance. A clever lawyer can always find ways around anything, like say you were mistaken, or put him into rehab, say he's given it up for Leia, he's a reformed character…"

So if I don't fight for Leia, there's a good chance she'll go to Blue. Will he still want her even if I refuse to give him the money? God, can I risk that?

I get up and walk over to the window. Take a deep breath and wait for my emotions to stop spinning.

Okay, let's think this through.

Leia is Maddie's girl, and Maddie entrusted her to me. I let my sister down by not being there when she needed me, and I don't want to let her down again.

But that's not all it is. Leia has Maddie's blood, my mother's and father's blood. My blood. She's a part of me. What kind of person would it make me if I just gave her away like an unwanted pet? I'm a bigger person than that. I'm scared about bringing up a child, but I don't back away from the things that frighten me. I face them head on.

So… that means…

I inhale deeply.

I'm going to keep her.

I let out a shaky breath.

So how will it work? Do I stay as her guardian? Would that mean that my life would carry on the way it is? With me as some kind of distant uncle? I envision a future scene where her nanny brings her in for half an hour in the evening so I can inspect her school report. Fucking hell.

You have to decide what's best for Leia, and what's best for you.

I'm not a person who does things half-heartedly. This isn't the path I would have chosen for my life, but it's happened, and it's all or nothing. If I'm keeping her, I'm going to adopt her. I'm going to be her father. I'm going to give her everything, a hundred percent. It's what would be best for her. Like all women, she deserves to be loved, to be adored.

I inhale a shaky breath, overwhelmed. I'm suddenly incredibly scared. I've lost my mother, and I've lost my sister. I know how precarious childhood can be. Kids get sick and sometimes die. What happens if I bring Leia into my life and lose her, too?

Loving someone is a risk I've done my best not to take since my mother died. I realize that now. I kept Cassie at arm's length because I wanted to stay in control of my feelings. Whether or not we were suited is irrelevant—it wasn't fair to her, and I let her down. I can't do the same to Leia. If I'm not prepared to give her my all, she'd be better off being adopted by someone else.

Can I do this?

For Maddie, for Leia, I have to try.

I turn from the window. Ethan sits patiently, eyeing me as I return to my seat.

I take a deep breath. "Okay. That's it. I'm going to adopt her."

A smile spreads across his face. "Well done," he says, and even though he's not my father, it gives me a little glow inside.

"What's the likelihood that the court would grant me the Parenting Order?"

Ethan doodles on his notepad. "You have some things going for you. You're Leia's guardian—that's the most important thing. Maddie didn't name Mr. Clarke on Leia's birth certificate—another bonus for you. You're wealthy and would obviously be able to provide Leia with a good standard of living." He eyes me with a wary look.

"Go on," I say wryly. "Spit it out."

"All right. I'd brush Blue up, put him in a suit, make him act suitably contrite, and get him to explain how he and his wife would be able to provide a stable environment for his daughter."

"Whereas I…"

"Am a confirmed bachelor with a…" He gives me an apologetic look. "Somewhat notorious reputation as a ladies' man, shall we say."

I haven't blushed since I was about twelve and forgot the words during a stage performance at school, but my face heats under his steady gaze. "I see."

"I'm not saying I believe that," he adds, "but that's how someone else could spin it—that you're a playboy with a revolving door, and it would be an unsuitable atmosphere to bring up a baby girl."

I try not to wince, remembering Aroha mentioning a revolving door. "You make me sound as if I live in a brothel."

"I'm just saying how they could phrase it. Let's face, it James, you're a young, extremely good looking guy."

"Stop it, you're making me blush."

He gives a short laugh. "I'm saying it wouldn't be difficult to convince the judge that you don't have trouble securing female attention. I have to add that usually sole male applicants cannot adopt female children unless there are 'special circumstances.'"

Cold filters through me. "I didn't know that."

"But I would argue that these are special circumstances," he continues. "You're Leia's uncle and her guardian. You're well respected in the business community."

"Despite being a manwhore," I say sarcastically.

His lips twitch.

I blow out a breath. Compared to many guys I know who use Tinder on a weekly basis, I don't actually sleep around that much. "I went out with my last girlfriend for nearly nine months," I protest.

"And before that?"

I glare at him and don't reply. I might not sleep with a different girl every week, but it's true that I haven't had many relationships that have lasted longer than a few months.

"Look, the courts will always put the child first," he says. "Obviously, Maddie's wishes would be taken into account, which means her naming you Leia's guardian is a huge benefit for us. But I have to make it clear that a clever lawyer could make a good case on Mr. Clarke's behalf."

I lean forward, elbows on my knees, hands linked. "Are there any ways I could stop him getting her?"

"You want my honest opinion?"

"Always."

"The best way to ensure you get Leia would be to get married."

I stare at him. "Married?"

He shrugs. "It would make you look respectable and trustworthy. Then we'd apply to the Family Court for a Parenting Order. I'm relatively confident the court would grant it, and you would take over day-to-day care. Parenting orders specify the care arrangements for a child, but they don't change parenthood. To do that, you would then apply to adopt her. Adoption is where a child legally becomes the child of someone other than a birth parent. The child's birth certificate would be altered to reflect this. That would be the surest way of keeping her."

"Marriage and adoption… Jesus, that's pretty drastic. I'm not even seeing anyone at the moment."

He clears his throat. "Could you rekindle the romance with the girl you were dating?"

"Cassie? Christ, no. She'd take me for every last cent."

He chuckles. "We'd get her to sign a pre-nup. Give her enough to make it worth her while."

I stare at him. His gaze is even. He can't say in so many words, but I think he's implying that I don't need a soulmate—I need a wife. A girl to marry me, in order to get Leia.

I feel queasy. I don't want to marry Cassie, even in name only. And I don't know anyone else who could fulfil the role…

And then it comes to me.

Slowly, I sit up. I rest my lips on my knuckles, meeting Ethan's gaze.

"What?" he asks, amused.

"I've got an idea."

I know the perfect person to help me out.
The only question is… will she?

*

Aroha

James is gone for several hours.

I put Leia on her playmat with the frame over her, and lie beside her as I watch her play with a toy lion that dangles above her. I know I have no say in what happens to her, and I'm just her nanny temporarily. But the fact that her mother died has left me feeling responsible for her. Alex's words struck a bell that won't stop ringing in my head. *It's archaic to have a group of men deciding a woman's fate.* And Leia doesn't have any other woman around to speak up for her. Of course she has Juliette and Gaby and Missie, but I'm the one looking after her.

Leia has lost interest in the lion, and she's reaching out for a mirror to her right. She grasps it in her right hand and brings her left hand over to join it—and then, all of a sudden, she rolls over! I inhale with delight and move closer to say, "Oh, you clever girl!"

She looks at me with astonishment to find herself on her tummy. She's holding her head up well now, and I know it won't be long before she's rolling over on a regular basis.

The front door opens, and I sit up as James comes in. He's wearing his suit again, and he tosses his keys on the kitchen counter, takes off his jacket, shoes, and socks, then walks through to the living room.

Mmm, barefoot James in a suit. Is there anything sexier?

"You just missed it—she rolled over all on her own," I say, conscious of my pulse picking up speed.

His eyebrows rise, and he lowers down onto the sofa and smiles at the baby as she looks up at him. "Did you really? You clever girl."

"She'll start doing it more now," I tell him. "And it'll probably only be a few months before she'll begin crawling."

"Wow." He studies her for a moment. Then his gaze slides to me.

I get up and sit in the armchair opposite him. "You were gone a long time."

"I went for a walk after the appointment. I had a lot to think about."

"So… how did it go?"

He leans back, resting an ankle on the opposite knee, and strokes the bristles on his face. "Okay."

"Come on, tell me what he said."

He takes off his tie and undoes his top button as he runs through his meeting. He explains the contents of the will, and then he summarizes what the lawyer said about Leia.

"So…" He swallows hard. "I've decided. I'm going to keep her."

My lips slowly curve up, and I give a delighted smile. "Really?"

He nods. "You think that's the right decision?"

"I do, I really do."

He blows out a breath. "The thing is, it's not going to be easy." He tells me what the lawyer said about him being a ladies' man. He looks most put out.

"You're shocked by that?" I scoff. "Come on. You look like a model, and I know you've had plenty of girlfriends. Another lawyer would easily be able to twist that into something more scandalous." He scowls, and I chuckle. "So what can you do to make yourself more respectable?"

"He joked that I could get married."

I laugh, although I feel a slither of cold slide through my veins as I say, "So are you going to pop the question to Cassie?" Oh God. The thought of him marrying her feels like he's stabbed my heart with an icicle.

He doesn't react, but he does say, somewhat flatly, "No."

Relief floods me. "Oh, good." Then I blush. "I mean…"

He's looking away, though, across the garden, lost in thought, and he misses my comment. He doesn't smile when he eventually looks back at me and says, "The important thing you need to understand is that Leia has got to come first now."

I nod. "Of course."

"I need to get the Family Court to grant me a Parenting Order, and then I can apply to adopt her."

"Right."

He hesitates. Then he says, "I have a business proposition for you."

My eyebrows rise. "Oh?"

He pauses for so long I wonder whether he's forgotten what he's going to say. Then, finally, he says, "I'd like you to marry me and pretend to be my wife."

I stare at him. "What?"

211

"It would be in name only," he says, "although for the court's sake we would tell everyone we fell in love and didn't want to wait. You'd have to live here with me. But of course we'd have separate rooms."

My brain is refusing to work. "What?" I say again.

"I'd make it worth your while," he says, leaning forward. "You'd get your own car, a new wardrobe, anything you wanted. And I'd pay you." His eyes gleam. "One million dollars."

I blink. My face burns so hot, I know I've turned scarlet. "You want to pay me to marry you?"

He shrugs. "Yeah."

"One million dollars?"

"Yeah. Is that enough?" He's teasing me.

I'm so insulted, I'm speechless.

He leans back and waits. He looks almost amused at my bewilderment, and that finally brings the words rushing to the surface.

"Absolutely not!" I say indignantly.

He stares at me. I can see he's stunned. "You're turning me down?"

"Of course I'm turning you down. It's a stupid, offensive idea."

He looks puzzled. "Why is it offensive? You need the money, right? I wouldn't ask you to do it for nothing."

And I realize then. Of course, he thinks of me as an employee, and he knows my father's out of work, and I'm broke. To him, it's the perfect solution. I can continue to look after Leia, and I'm sure a million dollars is a drop in the ocean to him. It hasn't occurred to him that I might like him, and I might see his offer as degrading or hurtful, because he has no interest in marrying me for real.

What am I saying? Of course he has no interest in marrying me for real. I know he finds me attractive, but that's irrelevant in this situation. He's thinking about his niece. He wants to keep her out of Blue's hands, and this is the only way he can think of to do it.

A million dollars. The terrible thing is that I'm tempted. It would make a huge difference to my family. I could pay my parents' rent for years. I could even buy them a house. I'd be able to pay for a carer for Rua to give my mum some time off.

"You could keep the car and clothes and whatever else you buy afterward," he says helpfully.

My face burns even more. He obviously has no idea how cheap that makes me feel.

But I'm being ridiculous. This is a hell of an opportunity. I'd get to live here, in this gorgeous house, use the pool and the gym, buy whatever I wanted, drive a fantastic car, and make sure my family are settled and happy. Am I really thinking of saying no?

But of course, we're not addressing the bigger issue. "I'm not sure what to say," I begin carefully. "Marriage isn't something two people should enter into lightly. The vows say it's a solemn and binding relationship, a union of two people to the exclusion of all others, for life."

His lips twitch. "Well, yeah, that's what they say…"

"James, you're asking me to stand up in front of witnesses and swear to love you for the rest of my life."

"They're just words," he says.

"Not to me."

"Not even for a million dollars?"

I give a short laugh and look away. My eyes sting with tears. He has no idea that for me, marriage is sacred. He means this as a business proposition. Can I treat it the same way?

I swallow down my emotion and look back at him. "So what would the arrangement involve?"

"Well, that's the only issue. Unfortunately, in New Zealand couples have to be separated for two years before they can divorce. We would have to wait for the Parenting Order and adoption to come through. I'm expecting that to take anything up to six months. After Leia is legally mine, you could then move out, and we would start the process of applying for a divorce. I appreciate it's a long time to wait, especially if you meet someone else. That's what the million dollars is for. The inconvenience."

I clench my teeth to stop my bottom lip trembling. *Especially if you meet someone else.* This guy has no fucking idea how women's hearts work.

"And for that six months, would you be bringing other women here?" I ask.

For the first time, he looks embarrassed. "Of course not."

"Well, it wouldn't matter, would it, if it's just a business proposition? If the vows don't mean anything. If they're just words."

"I wouldn't bring anyone here," he reiterates.

"Oh of course, you have your apartment in town for your Tinder hookups."

He looks bemused. He has no idea why I'm upset. "I thought you'd jump at the chance to make some serious money. I thought you enjoyed looking after Leia."

"I do." I bite my bottom lip. My spine is so stiff it's close to snapping. I really liked this guy, but he's just brought all my hopes and dreams crashing down around my ears.

It's my own fault, though. Apart from our fling on the trivia night, he hasn't led me on or implied he's interested in me. He hasn't flirted, not really. It's all been in my head.

He's a businessman, and he's doing this for Leia. He's putting her first. Wasn't that what I told him to do?

I think of the money. God help me, but I don't think I can pass up the chance of a million dollars. Not for my family.

I get up and smooth down the fabric of my capri pants. "All right."

His eyes light up. "You'll do it?"

"I'll do it."

He grins. "Excellent." He rises, too, and comes to stand before me. "Thank you," he says sincerely. "I really appreciate you helping me out like this."

"It's not every day a girl gets the offer of a million dollars." I meant it to sound sarcastic, but it just comes out kind of sad. He frowns, so I say quickly, "I presume you'll tell the others it's just for show?"

He purses his lips. "Only Alex, I think." He runs a hand through his hair, looking relieved. "I'm thrilled that Blue won't get his own way. That fucking wanker thought he could play me. It's about time he realized who he's up against." His smile fades, and his eyes are cold enough to make me shiver. Ooh, he can be ruthless when he wants to be. It reminds me that this is strictly a business proposition. It's all about Leia. It's not about me at all.

"Excuse me for a minute," I whisper.

He opens his mouth to reply, but I'm already walking away.

I go through to my bathroom, lock the door, then sit on the toilet and burst into tears. I hate myself for it, but I can't stop. I told myself he'd never be interested in me, but a small piece of me hoped that if I stayed for a while, he'd find the attraction I knew was between us was too strong to fight. But he'll be even more determined to keep me at arm's length now.

I'm going to have to promise to love him forever, tell my friends and family I'm married, then go through a divorce, and all for money. I feel like a cheap whore who's sold herself to the highest bidder.

But it's done. I've painted myself into a corner, and there's nothing I can do about it now. My desire for money is greater than my need to preserve my self-respect.

And I hate myself for it.

Chapter Twenty-Four

James

When Aroha comes back into the room, I tell her that the funeral is organized for Friday, the twelfth, and it makes sense to organize the wedding for the following week.

"I'll just get the celebrant to come here," I say to Aroha. "We'll tell everyone we couldn't wait and didn't want a big do and just wanted to get it done. I'll ask Alex and Missie to be witnesses. We can tell everyone else afterward."

She nods, eyes downcast, picks up Leia, and walks away, talking quietly to the baby.

I'm puzzled by her manner. I know her parents were having trouble paying their rent. Now she's going to be a millionaire! I thought she'd be singing and dancing and, I have to say, showing a little gratitude. It's an easy way to make a million dollars. Say a few words, sign a bit of paper, wear a ring for six months or so, and then you're free! What's not to like?

Instead, she's quiet and withdrawn, and I have a feeling I've upset her. I don't have the time or patience to work out why, though. I have the funeral to organize, and I need to get back to work.

I don't see Aroha much for the rest of the day. She keeps to her rooms, or sits on the deck with Leia, and I spend the afternoon and most of the evening in my office, organizing the funeral and the wake, and telephoning friends and distant family. When I eventually take a break, I come out to find she's cooked a stir fry, dished it up, and left a portion on a plate under foil for me. I go over to the door to the west wing, open it, and listen. I can hear her singing, and a quiet splash of water. She's bathing Leia. I close the door again, reheat the stir fry, and eat it alone. I don't see her again for the rest of the day.

The next day, I rise early and discover the kitchen and living room empty and quiet. When I go out onto the deck, I hear her singing to Leia and realize she must be sitting out on the patio in front of her room. She's choosing not to see me.

Frowning, I go into the kitchen and find that she's moved the bottle warmer and formula, presumably into Leia's room, so she can prepare her bottles in there. Puzzled, I eat breakfast alone. While I crunch my cornflakes, I muse over what I could have done. When I first put the idea to her, she said no, and she called it a stupid, offensive idea. I still don't understand why. It was a business proposition. I make ten of them a day.

James, you're asking me to stand up in front of witnesses and swear to love you for the rest of my life.

They're just words.

Not to me.

I frown and poke my cornflakes. I suppose the problem is, at that moment, she was thinking of marriage as a sacred religious bond, whereas I was thinking about it purely as a means to an end. But I'm not asking her to marry me in church. It's nothing to do with religion or God. It's not sacred, for crying out loud. I know the stats—half of all first marriages end in divorce. Half! And that statistic goes up for second and third marriages. Couples promise to love one another until death parts them, then conveniently forget that commitment when they're tired of one another. Vows not taken in a religious context are meaningless words. When not carried out in church, marriage is just a legal contract that can be severed by another piece of paper, and the emotional connection between the two people is irrelevant. It's no more binding than when you buy a car.

But I understand that for some people it is, and she told me her parents go to church. I suppose my proposal must have appeared somewhat shocking if she thinks of marriage as a holy order. Maybe she thought I was degrading the religious institution. Well, hopefully she realizes now that I just meant it as a business arrangement, and I didn't mean to upset her.

It is a long commitment, and I guess that might also have worried her when she first thought about it. She's young, and single, and the notion that she might have had to wait two years before she started dating someone new could have upset her.

Is that what I'm saying?

I frown. I hadn't considered that bit of the arrangement. I wouldn't want her to bring men home because it's important that we maintain a semblance of a happy marriage until Leia is legally mine. But I guess she could still go out on dates, if she was subtle about it.

I glare at my cornflakes. A million dollars is a lot of money. I don't think it's too much to ask that she waits until Leia's mine. Six months isn't long. After that, she can move out and do whatever she likes.

I push the bowl away, feeling irritable. I need to clamp down on my emotions right now, or this whole venture is going to drive me mad. Yeah, I would have made more sense to pick a partner I had no attraction to. But unless I advertised and interviewed strangers for the role, there is literally nobody who fits the bill. The women I'm closest to—Juliette, Gaby, and Missie—are married or have partners. I don't want Cassie or any other previous girlfriend who might cause me no end of emotional trouble. I want someone calm and practical, who understands the situation, and I thought Aroha fitted the bill perfectly.

She'll be fine once she gets her mind around the idea that this is just business, I'm sure of it. She told me her family comes first, and I'm sure the notion that she'll be able to help her parents out of a financial hole will smooth things over between us eventually.

Talking of which, I need to tell her a few things. As she's keeping to herself, I'll have to write them down. I fetch my laptop, and compose a letter to her while I finish my coffee.

Dear Aroha,

I'm off to work in a minute. I hope the two of you have a good day at home in this lovely weather.

I just want to jot a few thoughts down. First, I wanted to say thank you for agreeing to do this for me. I appreciate that it's a long commitment, and also that I might have upset you by treating marriage so lightly. I do apologize for that. I realize I have quite different views about it, and I honestly didn't mean to trivialize what you obviously see as a serious institution. I was focused on Leia, and after deciding to raise her myself, my thoughts were only on what was the best way to achieve that, and to stop Blue getting her. I picked you because you're so down to earth and calm and good with Leia, and I like you, and I thought we could work well together to ensure that Leia remains here with me.

I stop for a moment. Does that sound a bit manipulative? I purse my lips. Oh well. It's the truth.

I continue writing.

I am sorry if I hurt your feelings or insulted you though. That was never my intention, and I hope you can forgive me.

Now, about the money. It's best if I pay you the million dollars once we're married, as I can open a joint account and transfer the money into it, and you won't have to pay tax on it that way. I'll open the account and get you a debit card for it once you're Mrs. Rutherford.

I stop again and stare at the screen. I wasn't sure I'd ever type those words. For the first time, it strikes me that Aroha is going to be my wife.

I give a short laugh. Wow. My missus. The old ball and chain. I never thought I'd have one of those. I chuckle as I continue typing.

In the meantime, I've left one of my credit cards under this note, and the pin number. Feel free to use it to buy anything you or Leia need. You can also use it to get cash out, if you need some to give to your parents.

Mid-morning, a guy from the local garage is going to be delivering a new Range Rover. It's in my name for tax purposes, but it's going to be your car. If you'd rather have a driver, I can arrange that, but you're named as the main driver on the insurance. Just sign for it, and feel free to take it out for a spin.

Later, maybe we can talk about Leia's room and making things more permanent. Have a think about how you'd like to decorate it as a nursery, and we can organize some decorators to repaint it.

I try to think of what else to say. What would she like? What might cheer her up?

Would you prefer to get her another bassinet, or new equipment? What about clothes and toys? And for yourself, too. What do you need? Why not treat yourself to some clothes or jewelry today. You can do a fashion show for me later!

I wonder whether I'm being sensible. I don't think she's likely to dash off to the nearest jeweler's and splash it all out on a six-carat diamond ring, but maybe the thought of having so much money will go to her head. Ah, it doesn't matter. My credit card has a limit of a hundred thousand dollars. Even if she reaches the limit, she can't go past it.

I realize I'm rambling and end the note.

I'm off to work, see you later. Call me if you need anything at all.

I sign it 'James', print it out, and leave it on the counter with the credit card.

Pleased I've at least attempted to apologize and put things straight between us, I put the bowl and mug in the dishwasher, clean my teeth, grab my jacket and briefcase, and head to work.

When I arrive at Kia Kaha, it takes me a while to walk through the corridors as I'm stopped regularly by people wanting to offer their condolences. Maddie visited me here many times, and so I'm not surprised that many of the staff seem genuinely upset. By the time I get to the row of offices at the end, I feel as if I've done a day's work.

I stop outside Alex's office and knock on the glass. He looks up, smiles, and beckons, so I go in.

"Morning," I say.

"Hey." He leans back. "I didn't expect you'd be back until next week."

I sit in the chair in front of his desk and stretch out my legs. "I wanted to get the presentation sorted with Tyson, and I have a few things to catch up on."

"How are you doing?"

"Yeah, okay. I saw my lawyer yesterday." I summarize the first bit of what Ethan told me.

"So he's hopeful about you getting the Parenting Order?" Alex says at the end.

"Yeah. He says I have a lot of things going for me. And some things against. Like my… ah… reputation, compared to the fact that Blue is recently married."

Alex frowns.

I hesitate. Then I give a mischievous smile. "So… I have an announcement."

"Okay…"

"You need to keep it under your hat for now."

"Sure."

"I've asked Aroha to marry me."

He stares at me. He's a smart guy, and I can see him working out the whys and wherefores behind that decision. He'll realize the legal implications behind it, and he'll know it'll be easier for me to adopt if I'm married. I wait for him to smile and say he understands.

Instead, after a long pause, he says, "You fucking idiot."

Alex never swears, and my eyebrows rise. "What?"

He looks out of the window, shaking his head. Then, eventually, he looks back at me. "And she said yes?"

"Yeah. I did offer an incentive."

"Which was…"

I hesitate, for some reason beginning to feel as if I've asked her to prostitute herself. "Um… a million dollars."

He laughs. "Right."

Anger floods me, and I get to my feet. "Jesus, don't you start. You didn't see Blue. He's married. He and his wife are using hard drugs. He told me he'd take Leia off my hands for half a million dollars up front and a hundred thousand each year."

He blows out a breath. "Jesus."

"Yeah. I think he's going to push for custody. He's married, and he's her biological father. Ethan said a smart lawyer can easily make it look as if I'm a womanizing rake."

To his credit, Alex obviously realizes how upset I am, and he doesn't laugh. "Sit down," he says instead.

I lower back into the seat. "If I put Leia up for adoption, there's a likelihood the court will think her father is the better bet than handing her to a couple of strangers."

"I get it."

"I can't let him get his hands on her, Alex. She's Maddie's girl. I can't let her down again." I stop, too emotional to carry on.

"I understand," he says, rising and retrieving a bottle of water from the mini fridge behind him. He slides it across the table toward me. "So what's the plan?"

I unscrew the lid and have a couple of mouthfuls. "Thanks. We're going to wait until after the funeral on Friday. It only takes three days to get the license, but I need to organize the celebrant and the location. Apparently you can't get married in a registry office anymore."

"I didn't know that." He plays with a pen, turning it in his fingers. "So… you'll just have a basic registry ceremony, not a fancy personalized one?"

"Yes. But I want to be prepared in case Blue's lawyer tries to prove we only got married to keep Leia. The story is that Aroha is a friend and we've been attracted to each other for a long time. The guy on the front desk of the Clarence saw Aroha on the trivia night, so he'd be able to vouch that we started seeing each other then."

"That was when you fell asleep, right?"

I give him a sarcastic look. "Yeah. The story will be that we've been dating since then, and Maddie's death showed us that life is short, and so we decided to tie the knot."

"Very romantic."

"It has to appear to be. So to everyone else, it's the truth."

"Even Henry and Tyson?"

"Yeah, for now, although I expect they'll find out eventually."

He nods slowly. "Fair enough. And so Aroha knows all this?"

"Yeah."

"And she's okay with it?"

I hesitate. "I think she's a bit shocked, to be honest. You know what girls are like about marriage."

"Some would say rightly so."

I roll my eyes. "Don't tell me you think of it as a sacred oath."

He looks at the pen in his fingers. "I didn't. Then I was best man at Damon's wedding. I'd always dismissed it as just words—a legal document. But… I'm not so sure after that. There was something… magical about it." He looks up then and his lips twist. "But anyway, I understand where you're coming from. I'm just saying… I get why Aroha might have been taken aback."

Moodily, I pick at a piece of lint on my suit trousers. "Well, anyway, I want to at least attempt to make it appear genuine. You're the only one who knows the whole story. So I wanted to ask if you and Missie would be witnesses."

He meets my eyes, and we study each other for a while.

He's going to say no. He disagrees with what I've done. I'm surprised, and a little bit angry.

"It's for Leia," I emphasize.

He drops his gaze. "Missie won't like it."

"So don't tell her the truth."

That makes him give me an exasperated look. "We don't have secrets from each other."

"Oh bullshit."

His gaze sharpens. "Just because your marriage is going to be based on a lie doesn't mean mine will be."

Ouch. That stings.

"You're going to marry her?" I ask after a moment.

"Yes."

"Have you asked her yet?"

"No. I was thinking of doing it on Valentine's Day."

It's my turn to drop my gaze. I feel surprisingly envious of his obvious happiness, and his disapproval makes me feel an inch high.

But he didn't see Blue and his wife, and those suspicious marks on her arms. And he's a better man than I am. He didn't let Maddie down. He isn't responsible for her four-month-old baby. I'll do anything to keep Leia now. Whatever it takes.

I get to my feet again. "Tell Missie if you want. If she refuses to be a witness, let me know. I'm sure I can pull a couple of strangers off the streets." My voice is bitter. I turn to leave.

"James."

I stop and turn back.

"We'll do it," he says softly. "Missie will be all right; she'll understand."

I hesitate, tempted to tell him to shove his offer. But that would be childish, and oddly, for some reason I can't fathom, I do want him there. "Okay. Thank you."

"Have you organized a celebrant yet?"

"No, I was going to do it this afternoon."

"Leave it with me. I'll do it."

Surprised, I say, "Okay, thanks."

"Just… be careful. It's a big thing Aroha's doing for you. Don't forget that."

"You don't think a million dollars is enough of a thank you?"

He tips his head from side to side. "I'm not sure you can put a price on a broken heart."

I laugh. "I'm not going to break her heart."

He gives me an amused look as he picks up his phone. "I wasn't talking about her."

I stare at him, but he puts the phone to his ear and says, "Close the door on your way out."

I leave and head to my office, already dismissing his words. Nobody's heart is going to get broken. We both know it's a business decision, and that Leia is the only thing that matters.

Chapter Twenty-Five

Aroha

I wait until I hear James's car roar up the driveway, then, carrying Leia, I go through to the living room.

In the distance, I can hear Sue already at work, mowing one of the far lawns. Otherwise, the house is quiet.

I inhale, then let the breath out slowly. Leia looks up at me, and I say, "It's just us, baby girl."

Leia looks disappointed, but I'm relieved. When James is here, I'm acutely conscious of him, whether he's in the same room or at the other end of the house in his office. I can smell his cologne everywhere, and it makes me nervous that I can walk around any corner and discover him there, watching me with those unnerving turquoise eyes.

Tired of being on edge, I've transferred Leia's bottle warmer to her room, which means I can feed her in there without worrying I'm going to bump into him.

I'm sure eventually we'll be able to coexist in this house without feeling we have to avoid one another. But right now, I'm so angry and hurt, I can't bear to be in his presence.

The worst thing is that I know I'm being ridiculous. Whilst his proposal was bizarre, and an incredibly long commitment, a million dollars is a huge amount of money. It's very generous. So is it odd that I wish he'd not offered it? That he'd just asked me to do it as a friend? I would still have hesitated, but I wouldn't have felt so insulted. So cheap.

But I need the money, so I'll have to get over my indignation. Just not today. I need time to calm down.

"Let's get some breakfast," I say to Leia, and I put her in her seat, clip her in, and give her a toy to play with, then start making myself some toast.

It's only when I turn to put a plate on the counter that I discover a letter, typed and printed, sitting on the counter, with a credit card on the top. I pick it up and read it.

When I'm done, I sink onto a barstool, my hand covering my mouth.

He thinks I'm upset because he's trivialized marriage, boiled it down to a legal contract. And that is partly why I was upset. So his apology means a lot to me. *I am sorry if I hurt your feelings or insulted you though. That was never my intention, and I hope you can forgive me.* My throat tightens. I'm glad he realized I was upset, even if he doesn't understand the whole reason why.

I'll open the account and get you a debit card for it once you're Mrs. Rutherford. Oh God. I'll be Mrs. Rutherford. I get a funny feeling in the pit of my stomach. It doesn't matter that it's in name only—we're really getting married. Will we both wear a ring? I imagine he'd want that, if he's intending to project the image that it's a love match.

I've done my best not to think about it since our conversation, but now I let myself imagine the moment where he slides a ring onto my finger, and he promises to love me and be faithful to me for the rest of our days. My face heats. How can I pretend it doesn't mean anything to me? That the words are empty?

But I must. He's right—they're just words. If there's no love behind them, of course they're meaningless.

I read the rest of the note. He's having a car delivered. A new Range Rover. *If you'd rather have a driver, I can arrange that.* Dear God. What would the poor man do all day while he waited for me to go out? I couldn't possibly deal with that.

I can go into town and buy anything I want with his card. Some clothes or jewelry. I laugh out loud. Clearly, he doesn't know me at all. I'd never spend any of his money on myself. The million dollars is one thing—I'll take that to make a better life for my family. But I won't be spending it on myself.

Jeez, I'm so dumb. What's the point in having principles? Why not take everything he offers and run? Cars and clothes and flashy diamonds? I'll never get a chance to live like this again.

It's a job, that's all—a very well-paid job. It's not demeaning. I'm not selling myself. I'm helping him keep Leia out of that awful couple's hands. I look down at her, sitting in her seat, laughing at the toy in her hands, and feel a swell of affection for her. I'm doing it for my parents, and for her. To make sure she has a wonderful start to life. I've seen James hold her, and I know he'll make a good father. It'll take time, but she'll win him over, and eventually he'll treat her like his own. She'll have a much better life here with him than she would with Blue and Jasmine. That's why I'm doing this.

I feel better after that. He's apologized for trivializing marriage, and that means a lot to me. I can't change how he feels about it, only my own reaction. I still don't like the idea of lying to people about why we're getting married, but I can do it, for Leia.

I pick up the credit card. He's stuck a Post-it Note to it with his pin number. I study it for a moment, then, frowning, I take out my phone and Google Ernest Rutherford. I laugh as I read his Wikipedia page. James's pin number is the year Ernest was born—1871.

Feel free to use it to buy anything you or Leia need… Would you prefer to get her another bassinet, or new equipment? What about clothes and toys? Why not treat yourself to some clothes or jewelry today.

I feel a surge of rebelliousness. Maybe I will. There are a few things I'd like for Leia. Perhaps after the car is delivered, I'll go into town and do some shopping.

Excited at the thought, I butter my toast, make a coffee, then take it and Leia out onto the deck. I've just put her on her playmat and started eating when my phone rings. It's Gaby.

Immediately, I feel nervous. I can keep this secret from everyone else—my other friends and my family—but Gaby knows me better than anyone.

I answer the phone, trying to sound bright and cheerful. "Hello?"

"Hey, you," she says. "Thought I'd catch you before my lessons started. What's up?"

"Not a lot. I thought I might take Leia shopping. There are a few things she needs, and… um… James said I can buy whatever I want for her, so…" I trail off.

"So… How are things in the Rutherford household? Are you carving out a role for yourself there?" She sounds amused.

On the surface, it's an innocent question. I've been texting her, letting her know what's been happening with the situation, so she knows about our meeting with Blue and Jasmine. I told her that James has decided to keep Leia. So it makes sense that she's asking whether I'll continue to be Leia's nanny.

But I know her better than that. "Don't start," I say wryly.

"Aw, come on. Tyson's texted to say they're in their morning meeting, and he asked James how you were getting on, and James said… hold on, I'll read it out… 'She's spectacular. Best thing that ever happened to me.'"

My face turns into a furnace. "Oh, um, that's nice." Of course he's just laying the groundwork for next week, but even so…

"Spectacular?"

"I made him a pretty good chicken casserole the other day. He liked my dumplings."

"I bet he did."

I giggle, and she laughs.

"Come on," she wheedles, "what's going on? The two of you have been together in that house for days. I know you like him. Are you seriously telling me nothing has happened between you?"

"Not like that," I say honestly. Then I give in, desperate to talk about it to someone. "But we are getting married next week."

"Well I thought he'd be—wait, what?"

I give another nervous giggle. "That stopped you in your tracks."

"What are you talking about?"

"It's not what you think." I sigh. "He went to see his lawyer about getting custody of Leia, and the lawyer told him he'd stand a much better chance if he were married. So he asked me to marry him, as a business proposition, and he offered me a million dollars to do it."

Gaby's silent for so long, I start to wonder if I've lost the signal. "Hello?"

"Jesus," she says.

"Yeah, I know."

"And you said yes?"

"After a long deliberation, yeah. I need the money. And, I want him to get Leia. You didn't see that couple, Gabs. They were horrible. They didn't look at Leia once in that café—all they could think about was squeezing as much money out of James as they could. I can't bear the thought of them getting custody of her."

"Aw," she says softly, "you sound as if you've really fallen for… that baby."

I don't miss the pause. My lips curve up. "I didn't do it for him. Well, maybe a little. But my main motivation was Leia."

She hesitates. "It sounds like a good idea... But have you thought it through? You know it takes a two-year separation before you can get a divorce?"

"Yeah. He said that's what the money's for."

"It's a huge commitment."

"I know."

"So what's the plan? You stay in the house for two years? Are you... you know... going to... live together?"

"It wasn't a romantic proposal. He didn't go down on one knee or anything. But he's worried that Blue's lawyer might try to put a case together saying that we did it to get Leia, because it won't make him look good."

"So you're going to pretend it's a love match?"

"Er... yeah. Kinda."

"Oh, this is going to end well. He knows you're religious, right?"

"I'm not religious."

"But you believe in the sanctity of marriage. 'Therefore shall a man leave his father and his mother, and shall cleave unto his wife: and they shall be one flesh.'"

I shiver at the thought of cleaving with James. "Yes, but—"

"'Wherefore they are no more twain, but one flesh. What, therefore, God hath joined together, let not man put apart.'"

"Why are you quoting scripture at me? You're not religious either."

"I don't go to church. But I do believe in the sanctity of marriage. I don't think you should just say 'I do' for cash. God, I'd give you a million dollars right now and you wouldn't have to marry me. You know I would."

"Yes, I know." I draw up my knees and rest my cheek on them, looking out at the garden.

"All the years I've known you, you've never let me give you money." She sounds hurt. "You don't know how hard it is, having a rich parent, seeing your friends struggle, and not being able to help."

"Gabs, come on, you've helped me a lot." At school she often bought me lunch or treated me to clothes or other things I couldn't afford.

"But for you to accept a million dollars... have things gotten worse with your parents?"

I watch a fantail hopping along the edge of the deck. Leia has rolled onto her side and she's watching it too. "My father lost his job."

"Oh, God, when?"

"I found out on the trivia night, just after you invited me."

"Oh, Aroha. Why didn't you tell me?"

"I was trying to sort it myself. I was doing okay until I lost *my* job."

She inhales, clearly shocked. "I can't believe you didn't tell me any of this!" She sounds hurt again. We're best friends, and we're supposed to tell each other everything.

"I was embarrassed," I admit, a little stiffly. "And James happened to be there right when I finished the phone call. I told him what had happened, and he said he needed some help at the office, sorting out a presentation for a couple of weeks."

"I knew you were helping there, but I thought it was just while the salon was closed for the holidays."

"And then of course a couple of days in, Maddie died, and he asked me to look after Leia instead."

"You should have told me."

"I know. I've hurt your feelings, and I'm really sorry about that."

She clears her throat. "It's okay. I understand. But let me give you some money now, if you need it. If your parents need it. Don't sign up for a two-year contract just to sort things out."

"It's not just about the money, though, or I might say yes. It's also about Leia."

She sighs. "There must be another way."

"He could take the risk that his lawyer would win the case even if James stays single, but apparently sole male applicants can't normally adopt female children unless there are special circumstances. James is Leia's uncle, and the lawyer thinks this situation qualifies as a special circumstance, but it's possible the judge wouldn't agree, whereas if James was married…"

"Yeah, I get it." Gaby sighs.

"There's also something else," I add. "James's father has threatened to write him out of his will if he doesn't get married and produce an heir."

"Jesus. It's like Dallas and Dynasty all over again."

"I know. It's archaic. I think it's one reason why James went out with Cassie for so long."

"Oh… that would make sense. They never seemed suited."

"I think he was just desperate to find someone, anyone. And at least this way he can keep it all about business."

"What about producing an heir?" she teases. "Is that going to be in your contract?"

"I might have to draw the line there." She knows I don't want children of my own.

"I don't know. It'd be fun trying."

"Ain't that the truth."

She laughs. "You still like him then?"

I think about how to answer. I don't find him any less attractive than I did on the trivia night. But my feelings for him have… deepened. "I like him a lot. I'm very fond of him, and I want to help him."

"Okay. So… you're going to be Mrs. Rutherford?"

"Looks like it. The thing is, he's apologized for trivializing marriage, and I think he's aware of the fact that there is something insulting about the way he handled it. He did say sorry. But when it comes down to it, it is a business deal that will benefit us both."

"I guess. When's it happening?"

"Next week sometime, I'm not sure."

"Just… be sure. Marriage changes you."

"I'm sure it does if you're really in love."

"No, I mean… saying the words, exchanging the rings… it changes you. It establishes this connection between you both. It's like an invisible thread wound around you. You can feel the other person even when you're apart. And I don't think it's going to be any different, even if you mean it to be fake."

I know all this. But it hasn't escaped me that James hasn't given a moment's thought to it.

And a tiny part of me is very interested to see what's going to happen.

"I'm prepared for that," I tell her. "It's the price I'm going to have to pay for the money, but it'll be worth it, especially if it helps him get Leia."

"And him? Is he prepared?"

"Nope." My lips curve up.

"Oh…" She laughs. "He doesn't have any idea, does he?"

"Not a clue."

"You're a smarter girl than I give you credit for. I'll get the popcorn. This is going to be a lot of fun."

"You mustn't let on that you know," I warn her.

"I'm zipping my mouth shut as we speak."

*

The Range Rover arrives at nine thirty a.m. Leia's down for a nap, and I clip the receiver to my belt, then go out to meet the guy from the garage, who introduces himself as Dan. The car is beautiful—a dark 'Eiger' gray, apparently. Dan runs through the car's specifications, and I do my best to look as if I drive this sort of vehicle every day. I learn that it's not just any Range Rover—it's a top-of-the-range SV. When I see the paperwork, I realize it cost James three hundred and seventy-five thousand dollars.

Holy fuck.

I sign at the bottom, and Dan leaves, saying he'll Uber back to his office.

I've never driven anything that cost more than about five thousand dollars. I glance across at my battered Honda sitting in front of the garage, and hysterical laughter bubbles up inside me.

I open the driver's door and slide into the seat. The Range Rover is sleek and elegant, all natural wood, blue leather, polished chrome, and white ceramic controls. It has a touch screen, and I'll be able to Bluetooth my phone to it so I can use Google Maps and Spotify, amongst other apps.

Carefully, so I don't mark anything, I get out of the car, close the door, and lock it. Then I go indoors.

Leia's starting to grumble, so I go into her room, change her, make up a bottle, and feed her. I haven't really gone out with her much since I started looking after her, but I've looked after babies before, and I know it's a challenge. Still, I'm not in any rush. I empty her change bag, then add everything I think I'll need. I make up a couple of bottles and put them in, then add nappies, muslin cloths, wipes, and a few other bits and pieces I like to have with me. I dress Leia in a pretty dress and clip on her dummy, make sure I have James's credit card in my purse, and head out, locking the door behind me with the keys he also left me.

I stare at the car for a moment. It would be easier to call an Uber. I'm a little afraid of dinging the car. But I'm also excited to take it for a spin.

I put her stroller in the boot, fasten Leia into the back passenger seat, climb in the front, and start the car. It leaps into life with a throaty purr. My lips curve up. It reminds me of James. Sleek, beautiful, and with a mesmerizing voice.

With a little sigh, I Bluetooth my phone to it, then smile as I start playing some Doja Cat. "Sing along," I tell Leia, as I put it into Drive and head into town.

It's a dream to drive. I navigate the busy streets with ease and park in the city center. I retrieve Leia's stroller and clip her carry seat onto it, then head toward the shops.

What follows is, quite possibly, the most fun day of my life.

I spend most of it in Baby Bump, which caters for everything a new mum could ever want. The store is on three floors, and absolutely huge. I steer clear of the maternity section on the ground floor and take the elevator up to the area that sells clothing and equipment for newborns to six months.

Maddie, of course, had everything a baby could ever need, but even so, a few items that are missing that would make my life easier. I spend ages choosing them. A lighter, easier-to-handle, foldable stroller is the most expensive item I could do with. In the past, I've always gone for the cheapest option. This time, I look at them all. The nicest one is four hundred dollars. Will James mind? I'm sure he won't, if he's bought me a car that's three hundred and seventy-five thousand dollars. I take it to the desk and leave it there.

I choose more formula and muslins. A nappy disposal bin. Some infant pain relief and a thermometer. Sun lotion and more baby bath.

I'm not that keen on the baby carrier that Maddie had, so I choose another one that I've seen recommended online. Eek—it's also nearly four hundred dollars! But it's strong and easy to put on, so I decide to take the plunge.

I choose an activity center I can slot Leia into, and a larger high chair, which she's close to being able to use. I choose a larger playmat, another bouncy chair, and a few toys in bright colors, with extremities that rustle or rattle.

I buy her an Eeyore because it's super cute.

A few toys for the bath go in the basket. And I laugh when I find brightly colored rattles with thick Velcro straps you can put around the baby's wrist or ankles—what a great idea!

I take it all to the desk and use James's card to pay. Because it's a store for mums and they know how hard it is to juggle everything with a baby, they have assistants on hand who'll help you take your purchases back to your car, so at least I don't have to worry about carrying it all myself.

After everything's in, I lock the car again and head back to the shops. Leia's fallen asleep, and I probably have over an hour to myself.

Why not treat yourself to some clothes or jewelry today. You can do a fashion show for me later!

I stop in front of a popular store and chew my bottom lip. I could do with a few new items of clothing. Screw it. He offered—he obviously expects me to use the card.

I treat myself to two new pairs of leggings, and I'm really pleased to find a deal for some cool T-shirts that are buy-one-get-one-free. I get four for the price of two. Score!

By the time I'm done, Leia is starting to grumble, so I head back to Baby Bump, and this time go through to the back of the store where they have a baby-friendly café. I change Leia in the mother-and-baby room, treat myself to a coffee, a cheese roll, and a piece of chocolate cake on James's card, heat up Leia's bottle in the bottle warmer they provide for mums, then eat my lunch while I feed Leia in one of the comfortable armchairs.

Afterward, I make my way to the helpdesk and pick up some leaflets with ideas for decorating the nursery. Then, happy with my purchases, I return to the car.

I drive to Hagley Park, leave the Range Rover in the car park there, strap Leia into the new baby carrier, which is much easier to do up than Maddie's one, and take a walk through the park to Victoria Lake, where I sit and show Leia the ducks.

After that, when we're both starting to yawn, I drive home.

On the way, I finally let myself think about my parents, and what I'm going to tell them.

James has said that he doesn't want anyone to know the truth—that it's not going to be a real marriage, and I'm inclined to agree. I'm not sure I want to admit to my parents that I'm marrying an almost-stranger for a million dollars.

There might be some people who would tell me to take the money and run, but my parents aren't two of them. They're both proud, and they would both be horrified to think I was treating the sacred covenant of marriage with such disrespect.

I squirm a bit as I think of their reaction if I told them the truth.

No, I'm going to have to pretend it's for real, as hard as that's going to be. They're still going to be puzzled and hurt when I announce that James and I snuck off to tie the knot without them, but I think they'll believe it if I say he sprung it on me as a surprise, almost as if we eloped, if you can elope in your own town.

I kind of don't want to see them until we've done the deed, because I'm sure I'm going to blurt it all out. No, I'll call her and say I'm super busy, and maybe I can lay some groundwork during the call and say how well we're getting on, and how much I like him.

I try not to look at myself in the rearview mirror, because I know I'm blushing.

Then I'll take James to meet them next week. After we're married.

When we arrive home, Leia's dozed off, so I leave her in the car and transfer all the items into the living room before bringing her in. I'm tired, so I lift her out of her seat and bring her into bed with me, and the two of us doze off for another hour, while the cool air from the open sliding doors blows over us, bringing with it the smell of mown grass.

*

James arrives home at six thirty.

He comes in, tosses his keys and wallet on the table by the door, then walks into the kitchen and stops in surprise.

"Something smells nice," he says. He crouches and kisses the top of Leia's head where she's sitting in her new bouncy seat.

"I'm making a beef casserole." I stir the dish, replace the lid, and slide it back into the oven.

He straightens, takes off his jacket, shoes, and socks, then leans a hip on the counter, folding his arms. "I thought you weren't talking to me."

I remove the oven gloves I'm wearing and stand facing him. I tuck a strand of loose hair behind my ear and give a little shrug. "I wanted to say thank you for writing that note, and to apologize for my reaction yesterday. It was a shock, that's all."

He nods. His eyes are warm. "I saw the car out the front."

"It's beautiful, James. Absolutely gorgeous. And it drives like a dream."

"I'm glad."

"I went shopping."

"Hmm." He runs his tongue over his top teeth in a move that reminds me of a tiger looking at a wounded deer. "I checked my bank accounts."

I stiffen. He told me I could use his credit card. Is he going to berate me now for how much I've spent? In alarm, I think about the new stroller and carrier. And oh God, all those T-shirts. I did go a bit mad.

He surveys me coolly. "You spent just under fourteen hundred dollars."

My face burns so hot, I know I've turned scarlet. "Oh. Um. I'm so sorry. It's mostly bits for Leia. I thought you'd prefer well-made items that will last rather than cheap ones."

He blinks.

"I kept the receipts," I say, fumbling in my pocket, flustered. "And everything's in the living room so you can check it."

"Aroha…"

"I did treat myself to a couple of bits of clothing." God, my face is burning. "I'm sorry, but you did say I could."

"What on earth did you buy?"

"Um… two pairs of leggings and four T-shirts."

"I told you that you could buy anything you wanted," he says softly, "and you bought two pairs of leggings and four T-shirts."

"They were in a buy-one-get-one-free offer…"

"Aroha… are you under the impression that I'm mad at you?"

It's my turn to blink. "Well, aren't you?"

"It crossed my mind that you might have trouble if you spent more than the credit limit."

"What's the limit?"

"A hundred thousand."

I stare at him. "Sorry?"

"Honey, I half-expected you to reach the limit. Most women I've met would have had a field day if given free rein on a rich guy's credit card."

He's not angry. He's stunned that I didn't spend more.

"I did buy lunch," I add.

"I noticed. Twenty-three dollars at Baby Bump Café."

"It was a very nice cheese roll…"

His lips curve up. "You're a strange girl."

I scratch my nose. "So you didn't mind?"

"No, I didn't mind. But I did take the opportunity to get a couple of things, and I'm glad I did now." He bends and takes two items out of his jacket pocket. The first he slides across to me. It's a white box containing a brand-new iPhone.

When I don't move, he picks up the box, opens it, and takes the phone out. It's the newest model, with the biggest screen I've ever seen. He holds it out to me.

I stare at it, eyes widening. "What's this?"

"It's an iPhone."

I give him a wry look. "I can see that. What's it for?"

"I've seen your phone—the screen is cracked and it's a billion years old."

He's right, but I'm still shocked. The phone is like the Range Rover, a thing of beauty, with a gleaming screen.

"And I got these," he says softly. "For next week." He holds a blue velvet jewelry box out. He cracks the lid, revealing two matching gold wedding bands, one slightly smaller than the other. They're engraved and set with a row of tiny diamonds in the center. They're beautiful.

My jaw drops.

He laughs. "They're just rings."

They might be to him, but to me they symbolize eternal love, commitment, and fidelity. I feel a sweep of shame that I'm going to be wearing one of these for money.

Clearly, James has no such problem as he walks past me to open the fridge. "How long is dinner going to be? I'm starving."

Chapter Twenty-Six

James

Over the next few days, I gradually get ready for the funeral on Friday.

As Aroha didn't know Maddie, and I don't want Leia there, I decide it's probably best if Aroha stays behind with her. She agrees and says she can also help out getting the food ready.

"You don't need to do that," I tell her. "The caterers will organize everything, and anyway we need to start suggesting to everyone that our relationship might go deeper than boss and employee."

"Well, anytime you want to stick your tongue down my throat, just give me some warning," she says sarcastically.

"I might, I might not," I reply just as tartly. She sticks her tongue out at me, and I smirk.

We've been like this since I showed her the rings the other night—borderline flirting, pushing each other's buttons. She definitely warmed toward me after I wrote her the letter, but it's obvious that she doesn't know how to act around me. She'd cast herself in the role of nanny and seemed happy there. Now, she's nervous about our wedding next week, and what kind of image to project to everyone.

I should be kinder and more forgiving toward her, but I can't help myself. When I tease her, her cheeks flush, her eyes flash, and electricity jumps between us, setting me alight. It's the last thing I need right now, but it's impossible to stop it. And anyway, I figure that a little spark in front of people will only add to the idea that we're growing closer, ready for our surprise announcement next week.

I'm gradually getting used to the idea of keeping Leia. Aroha still looks after her, but she hands her over to me more and more, encouraging me to play with her and feed her, and also showing me how to change her, saying I should get 'the crunchy with the smooth,' a very Aroha sort of thing to say.

One evening, I even help her bathe Leia, which ends up with all three of us covered in water when Leia decides it's such fun that she kicks her legs in the water, the surprised expression on her face enough to send both Aroha and me into fits of laughter.

Friday finally arrives. I don't go into work as I want to make sure everything's organized for the wake afterward, plus old friends and family are arriving from all over the country and further afield, and there are always last-minute problems that need to be sorted.

The day dawns overcast and gloomy, and around one p.m. it starts raining, bringing down the temperature and the mood. The funeral is at two. Most of those attending are meeting at the funeral home, but the catering team is in the house, and some distant family, as well as Alex and the rest of my close friends from Kia Kaha who want to lend their support. It's nice of them, but I've spent hours talking to people, putting them at ease, and now I take a welcome few minutes to stand on the deck on my own and look out at the rain.

I've tried not to think too much about Maddie over the past few days, filling my time instead with work and organization, but finally I let her slide into my memory. Her dry wit, her infectious laugh, her flashing turquoise eyes, even her wistfulness and dark fury. I miss it all.

I'd hoped to keep my emotion well battened down today, but my heart is racing, my throat is tightening, and I'm fighting to keep my eyes from pricking with tears. At times like this, I wish I smoked to give myself something to do, and it might have calmed me. I don't want to get upset in front of everyone. It's embarrassing, and it makes me look weak.

And now I sound like my father. He's due at the house at any minute, and I'm not looking forward to seeing him. Maybe I should bawl my eyes out and see what he thinks of that.

The door slides open behind me, and I swallow hard, not wanting to talk to anyone right now. But it's only Aroha, and she's carrying Leia, who's just woken up from a snooze.

"Hey, Daddy," Aroha says.

"Don't call me that," I tell her. "I haven't decided what I want her to call me yet."

"Oh, sorry."

It's only partly the reason. She doesn't realize how she sends a shiver down my back every time she says it.

"Hey, baby girl." I say it to Leia, but I don't miss Aroha's glance, as if I'm speaking to her. Does it give her the same shiver?

I take Leia from her and hold her upright against my shoulder. She looks at me with her big eyes and gives me a lovely smile. "Don't you look beautiful today." Aroha has dressed her in a gorgeous red frock with hearts all over it, and a matching scarf around the baby's head. She's a splash of color amongst all the dark outfits in the room.

"Just like you," Aroha says, and smiles.

I look down at myself. I'm wearing a black three-piece suit, white shirt, and black tie. "I look like a waiter."

"More like James Bond. Smart and handsome," she says. "You brush up well."

I give a short laugh. "You could easily be a Bond girl." She's wearing a white blouse and a black pencil skirt, and she's twisted her brown hair up in an elegant chignon. Her makeup is immaculate.

She turns her leg to show me her black stilettos. "I could definitely kill a guy with these heels."

Wow. They're super sexy. I love high heels on a girl.

"I think your father has just arrived," she observes.

I glance through the living room and see him coming through the front door. My heart sinks. "Okay. I'd better go and greet them."

"Just a minute." She tips her head to the side. "Are you okay?"

I nod stiffly, distracted by my grief and the thought of seeing my father.

She studies me for a moment, then drops her gaze and straightens my tie, her fingers brushing my throat. It's a gesture that suggests familiarity and affection, and it takes me by surprise.

"Getting into the role?" I joke.

She smooths my tie down, the light touch of her fingers enough to give me goose bumps.

"I wasn't," she whispers. "But everyone is watching. No, don't look around."

It's an easy instruction to keep my gaze on hers. Her eyes are hazel with golden flecks.

As we continue to study each other, her lips curve up. My gaze drops to them. They look soft and kissable.

I shouldn't. I mustn't.

Then I think about Maddie, who'll never get to kiss anyone ever again. Fuck it. You only live once.

I move an inch closer, turning so Leia isn't between us. We're side-on to anyone watching in the living room.

Aroha's eyes widen.

"Warning," I murmur. "Incoming."

She inhales, but to her credit she just says mischievously, "Tongues?"

I shrug, as if I'm undecided. She stifles a laugh.

Then I lower my head and touch my lips to hers.

It's an innocent kiss, no tongues involved, meant to tease and show off to anyone watching. For the ruse. For Leia.

But the moment our lips touch, I forget everything else but Aroha.

I'd forgotten how soft her mouth is.

I'm transported right back to the night when I took her to my hotel. I think about how I stripped off her clothing. How I laid her on the bed, kissed over her breasts and down her body, and then sank my tongue into her.

How sweet she tasted.

How, when she came, she cried out my name as she curled her hands into my hair.

I don't know how long I stand like that, pressing my lips to hers. Ten seconds? Fifteen? I don't move. I don't even breathe, and I don't think she does either.

Leia sighs, and Aroha's mouth curves up beneath mine.

Finally, I lift my head and look at her.

"Mm," she says. "Naughty boy. You were very restrained, though."

I tuck a strand of her hair behind her ear. "I thought you might run for the hills if I did anything adventurous. In fact, I'm surprised you stayed put."

"You looked as if you needed a distraction." She gives an impish smile. "That should get tongues wagging anyway."

I glance to the side. My friends are all watching. Several heads whip around, as if they're embarrassed to be caught. Tyson gives me a thumbs up, though. Next to him, Gaby's eyes nearly fall out of her head.

Aroha stifles a giggle as she takes Leia from me. Then her expression turns kind. "Good luck. I hope all goes well."

"I wish you were coming." I say honestly. "I should have gotten someone else to look after Leia."

"I'll be here when you get back."

I hesitate. Her gentle support is comforting and makes me feel as if I'm not alone. "Would you come and meet my father?"

I realize as the words leave my mouth that it's a strange request. I went out with Cassie for nine months, and she never met my dad. It's only now that I understand how aloof I was with her, and how I felt the need to keep her at arm's length.

But Aroha says, "Of course."

I hide my surprise and, before she can change her mind, open the sliding doors and walk in.

Alex meets my eyes as I pass, and although he doesn't say anything, he looks amused. I give him a small smile, then continue through the living room, toward where I can see my father in the foyer with Arabella, talking to Henry, who's taken it upon himself to be a kind of MC for the day.

"Hey," I say as we walk up to them.

Dad turns, and I inhale, shocked by his appearance. He's always been a good-looking guy. He's tall, like me, and the discipline and control he exhibits in all areas of his life has extended to his health. He has a personal trainer and dietician, he's teetotal, and he goes to the gym every day. I think that's why his SCA was so shocking. Doctors said it was probably hereditary, but they still don't really know why it happened. My guess is that stress was a significant factor. Dad would say it wasn't, because he does Yoga or some shit, but I'm sure it played a role.

At the time, Dad was angry, I think, that he'd worked so hard to stay fit and healthy, unlike many of his contemporaries, and yet although they smoke and drink, he ended up being rushed to hospital. As a result, he's been on a weight loss kick. Last time I saw him was in December, and he'd already lost twenty pounds; he must have lost at least another ten since then. He looks gaunt and pale, and much older than he did last time I saw him.

"James," he says as I stop in front of him. And, before I can react, he puts his arms around me and hugs me.

I sometimes exchange a bearhug with my friends when we haven't seen each other for a while, or if it's a celebration like someone's birthday. But this is different. Dad's arms clamp around me as if he's clinging to a life raft. I stand stiffly, my arms by my side, resentment pouring through me, making me immovable as a concrete post.

How dare he look to me for comfort? He's never hugged me, and I don't know what to do with this sudden display of affection.

Behind him, Aroha moves into my line of vision and meets my eyes. She gives me a small, tender smile, kisses Leia's hand, and blows the kiss to me.

It's enough to release the chokehold I'm in. My arms rise, and I put them around my father.

"I can't believe she's gone," he whispers.

"I know," I murmur.

"I'm sorry," he says.

Sorry? For what? For making things so hard for my mother that she left the country to get away from him? For never being there for either her or Maddie when they needed him? For not being the kind of father I wanted: someone to play rugby with in the garden, to take me fishing, to show me how to shave, and to tease me about my first girlfriend?

I meet Aroha's eyes again. She's rocking Leia, and her eyes are kind.

I pat his back awkwardly. Then I clear my throat, and he drops his arms and wipes his face.

"Hello, Arabella," I say to my stepmother.

"Hello, James." She's younger than my dad, in her late forties, with blonde-streaked hair cut in a bob, and lots of makeup. She looks drawn, though, and there's no animosity in her face as she comes up to kiss my cheek. "I'm so sorry about Maddie."

"Thank you." I beckon Aroha forward, and she comes to stand beside me. "This is Aroha—she's a good friend of mine who's been helping me out since Maddie died. And this Leia."

"Pleased to meet you," my father says, but he's looking at Leia. Ah, jeez, are those tears in his eyes? "Hello, sweetheart," he says to the baby. He holds out a hand, and she grasps his fingers. "She looks just like her," he whispers.

"Is she a good baby?" Arabella asks Aroha.

"The best," Aroha replies. "Very good-natured, and she only wakes once in the night."

"James is very lucky to have you to help," Arabella says. "I can just imagine how terrible he'd be if he had to look after her himself."

"Not at all," Aroha replies, stiffening on my behalf. She turns and hands Leia out to me, and I take her and lift her onto my shoulder again. "He's going to be an amazing father."

"Father?" Arabella says, and she exchanges a glance with Dad.

"I'm going to adopt her," I tell them. "After the Parenting Order comes through granting me custody."

Dad stares at me. "Seriously?"

I nod. Leia reaches up a hand to touch my lip, and I nibble her fingers, making her giggle. I kiss her forehead. "I'm going to raise her as my daughter."

Arabella is lost for words. To my surprise, though, Dad's eyes continue to shine. "That's a very good thing you've decided to do," he whispers.

We're interrupted by Henry, who comes over and says, "The cars are here."

"Yes, we should get going." I hand Leia back to Aroha and hesitate, on the verge of asking her to come with me.

"Good luck," she murmurs.

I close my mouth and nod. "Thanks." Then I turn and pick up my jacket. "All right. Let's start getting everyone to the cars."

*

We arrive at the funeral home, and I stand near the door, welcoming people as they turn up. I'm touched how many of my friends are here, including all the guys from Wellington and Auckland and their partners, apart from Damon and Belle, who are on their honeymoon. They all give me a hug as they make their way inside. It makes me feel less alone, and I'm just starting to think I'm going to be able to get through this when an Uber draws up and Blue gets out.

I'm shocked to see him. I hadn't contacted him—I don't have his phone number, and I wouldn't have rung even if I had—but he must have seen the date online somewhere.

I once told him I wasn't going to let him within a mile of Maddie, and I'm tempted to tell him that still stands, whether she's dead or alive. But he's dressed in black, and at least Jasmine isn't with him.

He approaches me warily. "I'm not here to make trouble," he says. "I just want to pay my respects."

SERENITY WOODS

I fight the urge to tell him to fuck off. I don't want him here, and I don't think he deserves to be here. But it seems petty, and I like to think I'm a bigger man than that. So I give a short nod, and he walks past me into the chapel and takes a seat on his own at the back.

I take the seat next to my father in the front row, and the service begins.

I find it difficult to shake the thought of Maddie being there somewhere, watching everyone with bemusement as the event proceeds. She didn't have many close friends, but she knew a lot of people through her job, and they've all come to pay their respects. The crowd is a black sea, made darker by the ominous clouds in the sky. Maybe she'd have preferred it if we all wore bright colors, but she made no stipulation in her will, so nearly everyone is in black.

I know that nowadays you're supposed to concentrate on celebrating the person's life, but all I can think is that she's gone, and I've lost her. That doesn't seem like something to celebrate to me. The world has gone from color to black and white, and everything is monochrome. It makes me think of how beautiful Leia looked in her red dress. Is that why Aroha put her in it? A symbol of life among the sadness of the day—a phoenix rising from the flames?

It surprises me how much I miss them both, and I spend most of the ceremony trying not to look at my father sobbing quietly next to me, staring instead out of the window, thinking of the softness of Aroha's lips beneath my own.

After the service, we go out to look at the flowers. People stand in small groups, talking quietly, or bending to read the cards on the bouquets and wreaths. Some of the women are crying.

Blue comes up to where I'm standing talking to Saxon and his wife, Catie. They've left their twins with a friend, and I've just been telling them about Leia.

"Blue," I say to him stiffly.

"Not going to invite me back to the house?" he asks.

I don't bother to answer. We both know that's not going to happen. "Thank you for coming."

He shrugs. "I did my duty." His lips curve up a little, and then he walks off, over to an Uber, and gets in.

I stare at the car as it drives away, his words sinking into my brain. *I did my duty*. He came here because his lawyer told him to. It was part of the play he's putting on for the courts. He's putting his case together, playing the role of mourning lover and doting father.

Fucking bastard.

"James," Saxon says cautiously. "Are you okay?"

"I'm fine." I walk away, a bitter taste in my mouth.

I know I'm supposed to talk to all the guests and play the host, but I stand to one side looking out across the cemetery, feeling hollow inside. My grief is a rock in my stomach, heavy and hard. I'm conscious of some of my friends standing talking to my father, who's still emotional—Juliette is touching his arm, a gesture of understanding for the dad who's lost his daughter. I know he's not putting it on, but it galls me, nonetheless.

"Hey." It's Tyson, with Gaby. He's wearing a black suit, and she's wearing a pretty black dress and sandals. She's carrying a bright pink umbrella that looks incongruous against all the dark outfits. "You're getting wet," Tyson says, moving the umbrella to cover me.

It has started raining heavily, and I hadn't even noticed. I shiver, and Gaby slides her arm around my waist and gives me a hug. "You need a drink," she teases. "Double whisky when you get home."

"Maybe." I blow out a breath.

"He's had a migraine," Tyson tells her. "Alcohol might not be the best thing right now."

"A neck massage, then," Gaby suggests. "We'll see if we can find someone who might be interested in the job."

I open my mouth to reply, but some of Maddie's colleagues come up to talk to me, and I don't get the chance.

When we're done, Henry suggests it might be time to start heading back to the house. I agree, and I travel with my father and Arabella in the car, which soon joins the traffic.

"That was a lovely service," Dad says. "She'd have liked it."

I don't reply. He has no idea what she would have liked. He didn't know Maddie at all.

We don't talk for the rest of the journey.

When we arrive back at the house, I get out of the car and, instead of going in the front entrance like everyone else, I stride out, heading around the house, and go through the unlocked sliding doors into my bedroom.

I rip off my jacket and toss it aside, take off my tie, then flop onto my back on the bed. I want to take off my shoes and socks, but my house is full of people, and I need to stay presentable. I hate that. My stomach feels as if it's bubbling with acid, and my chest hurts. I cover my face, burning with resentment and anger.

I don't want to go out there and talk to a bunch of strangers, or even to my friends, and make polite conversation. I don't want one more person to tell me they're sorry that Maddie's dead, and isn't it a terrible shame, and she was far too young, and oh well at least God has another angel now.

Fuck God. Fuck Blue. And fuck my father. Tears prick my eyes, and I nearly dislocate my jaw as I grind my teeth, refusing to let the tears fall.

There's a soft knock at the door. I freeze, not wanting to see anyone.

Then it opens a fraction. "James?" It's Aroha's voice.

I don't say anything, my hands still over my face.

I hear her come inside, and she closes the door behind her. The carpet muffles the sound of her gorgeous black high heels, but I know she's approached the bed. I can feel her there.

"James?" she asks. "Are you okay?"

I wait a second, then move my hands up and sink them into my hair and open my eyes. "Not really."

She studies me, then lowers onto the bed above me and places a hand on my forehead. I close my eyes again. Her fingers are cool, and something about her touch calms me, as if she's poured aloe vera over all my raw nerve endings.

I inhale deeply, and let out a long, slow breath.

"I should go out there," I murmur.

"In a minute." She strokes my forehead. "How was it?"

"Shit. Blue turned up."

"Ah. I wondered if he might. Did he cause trouble?"

"No. He told me he'd done his duty. I think he came because his lawyer told him to."

She sighs. "What about your father?"

"He cried."

She moves her fingers from one temple, across my forehead, to the other. "Did that make you angry?"

"Yes." I realize she's the only one I can be honest with. "I kept thinking about Maddie standing there watching him, and how she would have hated him pretending to be upset, after the way he's ignored her all these years."

She continues to stroke my forehead. "I doubt he was pretending to be upset. He probably realizes he's lost his chance to make it up to her now."

"Fuck him." I blow out a breath. "I don't know why, but I keep thinking about how she's supposed to be in purgatory now. A place of misery, where you pay for your sins before you're allowed to move onto heaven. How is that fair, when he's the one who turned his back on her?"

She strokes down my nose. "I like to think that purgatory is more like a counselor's room, a place where you get to release all the resentment you've felt in life, and deal with your negative emotions. They'd help Maddie understand that your father is suffering, in his own way. And one day, he'll have to deal with all the things he's done wrong, and understand how he hurt others with his actions."

"He doesn't deserve to go to heaven," I mumble.

"Everyone deserves redemption." She bends and kisses my nose. "Come on. I asked Henry to hold Leia, and he looked as startled as if I'd asked him to split the atom."

That makes me laugh. I sit up and turn to face her. "Do you really believe everyone deserves redemption?"

"I do. Everyone acts the way they do because of holes in their past. If you can try to understand why someone behaves the way they do, it's the first step toward forgiveness."

"I'm not ready to forgive my father."

"Not yet, no. But you will be one day." She gets to her feet and holds out her hand. "Come on. Let's go and rescue your baby girl."

Chapter Twenty-Seven

Aroha

As I lead James out into the living room his skin holds a ghastly gray pallor, and he looks as if he might throw up at any moment. I'm not sure if it's his father's presence that's bothering him most, if it's Blue's appearance at the funeral, or whether it's just the fact that Maddie's death is finally sinking in. Probably all three. I can see he's suffering, and I want to help, but what can I do?

Alex pushes a whisky into his hand, and, after a glance at his father, James has a large mouthful and sighs.

"Eat this," I tell him, giving him a sausage roll. He does as he's told, and gradually some of the color comes back to his face.

"All right," he says, finishing off the whisky. "Let's get on with it."

He rolls up his sleeves, then walks into the center of the living room and calls for everyone's attention.

He gives a speech, thanking everyone for coming, and saying how he knows Maddie would be touched to see so many familiar faces there. He tells a funny story from their childhood, making everyone laugh, and then says that Maddie wouldn't want everyone being upset all day. He gives a toast, then turns the music on, and instructs everyone to drink and eat and dance if they feel like it. A couple of teens—distant cousins of his and Maddie's—start dancing to ABBA's *Waterloo*, and everyone else helps themselves to food and drink.

I know he's the public face of Kia Kaha, and he travels a lot to give talks about their technology and spread the word, but it's the first time I've seen him speak to a crowd. He's confident and composed, and oh so gorgeous, his hair ruffled, the beginnings of a five o'clock shadow on his jaw. He's lost a little weight since Maddie died. He looks good, but I make a mental note to make more casseroles and heartier food to feed him up a bit.

I stay by his side for the rest of the day where I can, rescuing him from conversations when I see he's had enough, making sure he drinks water in between his whiskies, and giving him bites to eat. He talks to everyone there, taking time to move between the groups, and I go with him, bringing Leia with me, so everyone gets a chance to see or hold Maddie's daughter. Leia is marvelous, putting up with being passed from pillar to post like a princess.

Vincent and Arabella catch up with relatives they obviously haven't seen for a while, but I know eventually they're going to want to spend time with James.

"Don't let him talk to his father alone," I murmur to Henry.

"Will do," he says. So when he sees them try to catch James as he passes to get someone a drink, Henry finds them a seat out on the deck where most of James's friends are sitting, and introduces them to everyone. The guys—who are all adept at dealing with awkward conversations—tell stories about Maddie, including them in the conversation, enabling James to move between his other guests if he wants to.

Even though it's going well, I'm relieved when, around seven, Vincent announces he and Arabella should be heading off.

They say goodbye to everyone, and James rises to see them to the door. He glances at me, an unspoken plea, and I collect Leia from Missie, who's been having a cuddle, and follow him through to the foyer.

"How long are you in town for?" James asks his father.

"We're flying back tomorrow," Vincent replies. He looks very tired and wan.

James nods. "Well, take care, and I'm glad you could make it."

He hugs his father, who tightens his arms around him, looking for a moment as if he doesn't want to let him go.

Arabella looks at Leia and smiles. "Such a pretty little thing. I'm glad they both have you to look after them."

Vincent draws back, then turns and kisses Leia's head. "My little girl's little girl," he whispers, stroking her hair. He swallows hard.

Then he turns to me. "Goodbye, Aroha," he says. "Take care of them both. I can see you're very special to him."

I blush. "It was nice to meet you."

They leave the house and head to their car.

James looks at me, relief written all over his face.

"You made it," I say.

He gives a short laugh. "Yeah." He looks tired, but the house is still full of guests, and he can't just leave them.

"Leia needs a feed," I tell him. "Will you take her, and I'll warm the bottle?"

"Of course." He lifts the baby out of my arms. "Hey you," he murmurs to her. "Let's go and watch the birds, shall we?"

I quickly warm up the bottle in her room, then return to the deck. He's sitting in one of the armchairs, Leia in his arms, turning her so she can see the antics of some of his friends—Huxley, the twins, Henry, and Alex—who are on the lawn, throwing a rugby ball around. The rain has eased, and the sun has dried up most of the rain.

Saxon tackles Kip, and the two of them tussle, making everyone laugh. Disco music plays in the background, and Mack turns Sidnie around at the end of the deck, the two of them chuckling at a private joke. It's all very normal and relaxed, just what James needs.

I pass him the bottle, and he sits there quietly, feeding her while the girls talk around him.

There's nothing as healing as holding a baby, and gradually the tension disappears from his shoulders, as he gives a big sigh and stretches out his long legs. The other girls sitting with me glance at him, smiling at the sight of him apparently content.

"Never thought I'd see the day," Gaby teases.

He gives a wry smile.

"It suits you," Juliette states. "So you're going to bring her up as your own?"

He nods.

"Is she going to call you Daddy?"

Everyone looks at him. He exchanges a glance with me and says, "Uh… I'm not sure yet." He lets Leia wrap her hand around his finger. "Do you think it would be weird? She has a real father."

"She has a birth father," I correct.

"Most children call their adoptive fathers Daddy," Juliette states. "I don't think there's anything wrong with Leia calling you Daddy at all."

"You don't think it's odd because Maddie was my sister? It sounds sort of incestuous."

"If Maddie was still here, maybe it would be weird," Elizabeth says, "but with her gone, I think it makes perfect sense for you to call yourself her father."

"Now we just need to find her a mummy," Gaby states mischievously.

James's gaze slides to mine. I glance around the group and discover everyone's looking at me.

I blush scarlet.

Gaby giggles, and the others all burst out laughing.

"Shut up," I say, fanning myself and having a big mouthful of Gaby's wine.

"Oh, are you two…" Elizabeth glances from James to me. "Together?"

"Yes," he says.

"No," I say at the same time.

"Kinda," we both say together, and everyone laughs.

"How lovely," Alice, Kip's wife, states. "You seem so well suited."

I meet James's eyes, and his lips curve up.

"So is she going to call you Mummy?" Juliette asks mischievously.

"It's a bit early for that yet," I reply carefully. I don't know what James is planning, if indeed I'm still Leia's nanny by the time she starts talking, but I imagine she'll just call me Aroha. He'll want to save the title of mummy for the woman he ends up with, right? He's hardly used to being a monk, so I can't imagine it will be long before he wants to start dating again.

The thought makes me sad.

Leia finishes her bottle, and James gets to his feet and brings her over. "A few people look like they're leaving," he says, "will you take her?"

"Sure." I lift her onto my shoulder and pat her back, watching him walk through to the foyer.

"You kept that quiet," Elizabeth says, amused. "After you told us what happened back in December, I didn't think you were going to get together."

"Oh," I reply, "it's… um… very new."

"He looks at you the way that Huxley looks at his forty-year-old bottle of Talisker," Elizabeth jokes. "He's obviously crazy about you."

I blush again, and they all go, "Awwww!"

I meet Missie's eyes. I know James has told Alex the truth, and he said that Alex was going to tell Missie, but that she might not approve of what we're doing. She smiles, but there's a touch of concern in her eyes.

"Shall we make a move?" Saxon asks as he comes over to Catie. "I want to see the twins before they go to bed."

She nods and rises, and gradually everyone else starts getting up, too.

I touch Missie's arm and lead her off to one side. "Um, I know that Alex has told you what James and I are planning to do," I murmur, feeling the need to explain. I like Missie, and I don't want to offend her. "I just wanted to say I understand if you disapprove. I do believe in the sanctity of marriage. But Leia's birth father is a real piece of work, and I'll do anything I can to make sure James can keep her."

"I don't disapprove," Missie says, surprised. "At least, not for that reason. I understand why you're doing it. I'm just worried about you both, that's all."

"Oh. Why?"

She smiles and shakes her head. "No reason. I'm sure it'll all work out fine."

Alex comes up and slides his arm around her. "Are you ready?"

She nods, and we rejoin the others, heading into the living room.

Everyone exchanges kisses and hugs, and gradually people begin heading for the door. Some linger, wanting to talk to James, and I know it's going to take a while for everyone to go.

"I'm going to put Leia down," I tell him.

"All right, thanks." He turns back to his guests.

Waving goodbye to those I know, I head off to the west wing of the house. It's much quieter here, thankfully, and I give a long sigh. Our normal routine has vanished tonight, as Leia has already had her last bottle, so I give her a quick wash and change, dress her in a cute onesie, then sit in the rocking chair and read to her while she sucks contentedly on her dummy and watches the birds pecking crumbs from the feeder on the deck.

When her eyelids start drooping, I kiss her forehead, lift her into her bassinet, and draw the covers over her. I wind up her mobile so the characters move around while the lullaby plays, but she's nearly asleep.

I lean on the side of the bassinet and look down at her. I think she's the most beautiful baby in the world. I know mothers are usually biased, but I'm not her mother, and so I'm surprised by the strength of my feelings for her. I suppose it's because her real mother has died, and she came so close to being snatched up by that horrible man and his wife. I so hope James gets the Parenting Order and custody of her. The judge wouldn't rule in Blue's favor, surely? Not when James—handsome, wealthy, and married—so obviously wants to do this for his sister?

The door opens behind me, and James comes in and walks over to join me at the bassinet.

"Hey," he says softly, leaning beside me.

"Hey."

We both look down at Leia for a while, our arms just touching. I can feel the heat of his skin through the cotton of his shirt.

Eventually, I glance at him. "So are you going to let her call you Daddy?"

He sighs. "I suppose. Better me than Blue, right?"

"I think so."

He sighs again.

"You look shattered," I tell him. "Why not go to bed?"

"I will once the caterers have finished cleaning up." His eyes meet mine. "I wanted to thank you."

I smile. "What for?"

"For being there for me today. I couldn't have done it without you."

"You'd have been fine," I scoff. "I didn't do anything."

"You did more than you realize."

I've released my hair from its chignon, and to my surprise, he reaches out, picks up a strand, and runs it through his fingers. "I'd forgotten how silky it is," he murmurs.

I hold my breath. Even though he's not touching my skin, it still makes me shiver.

He lets the strand curl around his forefinger. "I wanted to say thank you again, for agreeing to marry me."

"I'd do anything for her," I say simply, looking down at the baby.

"I know."

I look back at him. He's still watching me.

His gaze drops to my mouth. He's thinking about kissing me.

I remember how he kissed me out on the deck. It took me by surprise, but I was convinced it was just for show. It was hardly a smooch—despite my teasing, he didn't use his tongue; he just pressed his lips to mine and held them there.

But for some reason it was the sexiest, most erotic kiss I think I've ever had. Maybe it was because I've felt so close to him lately and yet so far away too; he's been tantalizingly out of reach. But it made my nipples tighten in my bra, and other parts of me clench in ways they haven't done in a long, long time.

He continues to look at my mouth. Then he finally lifts his gaze to mine.

We look into each other's eyes for about ten seconds. His are the color of a tropical sea, his thoughts and desires swimming behind them like exotic fish. He wants me—I can feel it. Words desert me. I can't even breathe.

He tears his gaze away. He looks out of the window, at the garden, for a moment. Then he straightens.

"See you tomorrow," he says, and he goes out and closes the door behind him.

*

On Saturday, Alex, Tyson, and Henry come over to the house to work with James on the presentation for Sydney the following weekend. Henry volunteers to go with Tyson, suggesting the two of them do the keynote speech together, and to my surprise, James agrees.

Missie, Gaby, Juliette, and I settle them around the dining table with coffee and plenty of snacks, and then, with Leia, we head into the city to do some shopping.

"This is a gorgeous car," Missie announces as we buckle ourselves into the Range Rover, her in the front, the other two in the back with Leia. "I can't believe James bought it for you." She doesn't come from the rich background that the guys and Gaby do, so she's still impressed by expensive gifts.

"I know. I was hesitant to accept it, but I figured it'll keep Leia a lot safer than my battered old car." I go down the drive, through the gates, then head toward the city. "So, where are we going first today?"

"Coffee shop," Gaby says, and the others nod.

I laugh. "Right." I decide to park near the Riverside Market and take them to Café Kiwi, one of my favorite coffee spots.

"So…" Juliette says once we're on the state highway. "Come on, spill the beans. What happened between you and James? I remember you saying at Gaby's hen night that you really liked him, but I thought he'd blown it after the trivia night."

AROHA AND THE BILLIONAIRE BOSS

I glance at Missie, then in my rearview mirror at Gaby. I could just continue with the ruse and pretend that James and I are so deeply in love that we're getting married, and I'm sure the other two would go along with it. And I know he'd rather everyone wasn't aware of our plan. But I like Juliette. She's honest to a fault sometimes, but she's kind and generous, and she's been nothing but nice to me. I don't want to lie to her.

"Actually," I say slowly, "I have something to tell you."

"Oh?" She glances at the others and realizes she's out of the loop.

"James has asked me to marry him." Before her eyes fall out of her head, I quickly tell her the details behind the arrangement.

"What happens after he gets the Parenting Order?" Juliette asks.

I shrug. "I'll move out, and we'll start divorce proceedings."

"What about Leia?"

My throat tightens. "I suppose he'll find her another nanny."

Silence falls in the car.

Eventually, Missie says, "Is that what you want?"

"No," I say honestly. "I love her, and I'd like to continue to look after her. But I'm not sure I can share a house with James once he starts dating other women."

"What a muddle," Juliette says softly. "Why is love so complicated?"

She's Māori-Indian, with skin a shade browner than mine, and beautiful almond-shaped eyes she outlines with black kohl. She's very proud of both branches of her heritage, and she sports a Māori tattoo on her right arm like me, and a bindi on her forehead. She often wears a sari, but today she's in modern Kiwi summer clothing—a tee and shorts, her hair hanging in one long braid over her shoulder.

"You want to talk about Cam and Henry?" Gaby asks her.

She looks away, out of the window, and just sighs.

"Are you and Cam still together?" Missie asks.

Juliette just tips her head from side to side. Does that mean she doesn't know? Or it's up in the air? "We had a big argument the morning of the trivia night. It had been coming for a while. He wants to move to Australia. He's fed up with his job, and he says there are more opportunities there, and he's right of course. But I don't want to go—I love my job, and all my friends and family are here. We've been arguing about it a lot. He thinks I should understand why he wants to go and support him, and I think he should realize why I want to stay and stop pushing me. So we argued about it, and he was very mean to me."

Gaby's eyes widen. "He wasn't... physical?"

She shakes her head. "No, but he was incredibly cruel. He really hurt my feelings. It's not the first time he's done it. When he walked out that night, I was determined it was over. And I danced with Henry, you know what he's like, he was just so gentle and kind, and he looked at me as if I was something precious..." She sighs. "But they're all like that in the beginning, aren't they? Until they get what they want."

"No," Missie and Gaby say together. "Not always," Missie adds.

"Was it good?" Gaby asks.

Juliette's lips curve up. "You have no idea." It's the first time she's admitted that they slept together. "But when I got home the next day, Cam was there, and he told me he was sorry and wanted to make it up to me, and I was so confused... We've been together a long time and built a life together."

"Does Henry want to see you again?" I ask.

She nods. "But I told him I didn't want to give up on my relationship, and that I wanted to make it work."

"What did Henry say?"

She bites her lip. "He said if I expected him to sit back and let me go, I was going to be disappointed. He said he wants me, and he's going to have me if it's the last thing he does."

We all stare at her.

"Ooh, that's pretty hot," Gaby says, and we all giggle.

"What a naughty boy," Missie adds. "Who'd have thought it? He seems so quiet and reserved."

"He was *not* reserved in bed," Juliette states. She's silent for a long time, looking out of the window. The rest of us exchange glances, but we don't say anything.

Eventually she says, "Anyway, enough about me. We've got something more important to concentrate on today."

"What's that?" I ask.

"Wedding dresses," she says with a grin.

My eyebrows rise. "I'm not wearing a wedding dress."

"Wedding outfit, then."

"I told you, it's all for show. It's just so James can get custody of Leia."

"Yeah, yeah," Gaby says. "James is crazy about you."

"He's not," I scoff, but my face heats at the thought. Is he?

"Definitely," Missie says. "Alex had already told me, but I wasn't sure until I saw how James looks at you. His gaze could melt gold."

My heart swells. They're wrong, surely?

"Tell me right now that you're not interested in him and we'll shut up," Gaby says.

I hesitate, for long enough to make them all laugh. My lips curve up. "You're such a mean bunch."

"No, we're your saviors," Gaby states. "We're the ones who are going to help you turn this fake marriage into a real one. Now. Let's talk outfits."

Chapter Twenty-Eight

James

We work all morning, then stop around one, make ourselves some sandwiches, and take them out onto the deck with a can of Coke Zero each.

I feel as if I'm just starting to relax after the horror of the funeral. The gray skies have cleared, and the heat of the summer sun makes me glad of the shade sail. Nothing helps me more than working hard and using every part of my brain to solve problems. Well, apart from really good sex, and that's not on the table anytime soon. Or on the floor, or in bed for that matter.

And now I'm thinking about Aroha again.

She's strictly out of bounds, I remind myself. I mustn't think about her in that way. I'm not going to make a fool of myself by making a move on her.

Then I think of the way she sat on the bed behind me yesterday and stroked my brow. How she stayed by my side all day, making sure I was all right. How, when I looked into her eyes last night, they were filled with longing.

I blink away the memory. Even if they were, it doesn't matter. If I sleep with her, I might mess everything up again, and my first priority has to be Leia. Once Leia is mine, well maybe then I can start thinking about moving forward with my life. But until then, I have to stay focused.

"I wonder how the girls are doing," Tyson says. "I bet Gaby's bought up half of Christchurch by now."

"Aroha might have spent twenty dollars if I'm lucky," I say wryly, bringing my attention back to the conversation.

"I think you're the only guy I've heard who's disappointed because their girl doesn't spend enough," Tyson replies.

"She's not my girl." I have a bite of my sandwich.

"Of course not." His eyes sparkle.

I glare at him, then at Alex. "What did you say?"

"I haven't said anything," Alex replies, amused.

"Gaby told me," Tyson says.

"Told you what?" Henry asks.

Tyson looks at me. "Ah. I didn't realize he didn't know."

Henry looks insulted. "Am I out of the loop?"

Alex stifles a laugh, and I huff a sigh. "Oh, all right. But please don't tell anyone else." I explain how Aroha and I are getting married next week in the hopes that it'll play well in the courts.

"Shit," Henry says. "And she said yes?"

"For a million dollars, yes."

His eyes widen. "She asked for a million dollars?"

"No, of course not. I said I'd give it to her if she agreed."

Carefully, he leans forward and places his can on the table, then links his fingers and looks at me. "Let me get this straight. You asked Aroha to marry you, strictly as a business deal, and offered her a million dollars."

"Uh, yeah."

"Jesus Christ."

"What?"

"This is the same girl, right? The one you were making out with when you fell asleep?"

I run my tongue over my teeth.

Henry glares at me. "You do realize what an insult that was?"

I frown. "The money, you mean?"

"Yeah."

"Why? I couldn't just ask her to marry me for nothing, could I? It's a two-year commitment, minimum."

"You fucking idiot."

I'm baffled. Alex's face is impassive. Tyson's forehead is creased.

"I don't understand," I say.

"Don't worry about it," Alex replies. "It'll all come out in the wash." He glances at Henry, and something unspoken passes between them.

Henry's lips curve up. "Right."

"I have no idea what's going on," I tell them, "but please, amuse yourselves with my dire predicament."

"When's the wedding?" Tyson asks. "Can we come?"

"No," I say hastily. "I've asked Alex and Missie to act as witnesses, but that's all."

"I've organized the celebrant," Alex announces. "She's free next Friday at four p.m."

"Okay. Is she coming to the house?"

"No," he says. "We're going to Kea Lodge in Arthur's Pass."

Arthur's Pass is a town on the road through the Southern Alps that runs between the west and east coasts. It takes a good two hours to drive there.

"I'll fly us in the helicopter," Alex adds.

"I don't want any fuss," I protest.

"Right. Got it."

"Alex…"

"Look, you said you're worried that Blue's lawyer might be able to make it work against you, right? Paint you as a wealthy playboy who thinks he can buy his way into anything?"

"Are you trying to make me blush?"

"I'm just saying, if it was real, you'd whisk her away for the weekend and spring it on her, right? Plus, that way she'll be able to tell her folks she didn't get the chance to invite them." He lifts his eyebrows. "You had thought about the fact that she's going to have to tell her parents she got married without them?"

I haven't thought about her family at all.

"Yeah," I say.

He gives me a wry look. "They'll be very disappointed. Mums like to be mother-of-the-bride and dads like to give their daughters away. You're not going to be popular."

It strikes me then that Aroha might make me go with her when we tell them. Ah, shit.

"Hopefully the money will smooth things over," I say. I mean it as a joke, but it sounds spiteful when it comes out, and Alex raises an eyebrow.

"I'm not happy about this," Henry says. "I like Aroha. She's a nice girl. I hope you're not intending to take advantage of her." His manner is deadpan. I can't tell if he's joking.

"It's not the fourteenth century," I reply. "She's more than able to handle herself, believe me."

"I'm just saying. This doesn't give you the *Droit du seigneur*."

I know that's the right of the lord to have sex with any female subject, especially on their wedding night.

"'The wife's body does not belong to her alone but also to her husband,'" Tyson says helpfully. "I think that's from Corinthians."

"If you're going to claim *prima nocta*," Alex adds—meaning first night, the other name for the medieval lord's right—"maybe get her to sign a waiver."

"For fuck's sake." I know they're teasing me, and sure enough they all chuckle. "Anyway," I say to Henry, wanting to divert the attention away from my upcoming wedding, "enough about me. What's going on with Juliette?"

He grunts and eats the rest of his sandwich.

"You wanna talk about it?" Tyson asks.

"No," he says.

There's not much we can say to that. Alex clears his throat and starts talking about whether we want Damon's input on the part of the conference speech about how the machinery is paired with gaming software, and the conversation moves on.

The girls arrive back around four p.m., tired but happy, carrying all manner of boxes and bags. Gaby claims that smoke is emitting from her credit card. Juliette's wearing a new sunhat she bought. Missie shyly shows Alex a set of artist's paints she's treated herself to, earning an indulgent smile.

"What about you?" I ask Aroha. She's carrying several bags in one hand and Leia in her carry seat in the other. "Did you treat yourself?"

"I did, as it happens."

"Can I see?"

"It's for the wedding," Gaby announces. "You can't see it before the big day."

"Fake wedding," Aroha and I say at the same time, and both laugh.

"Sorry," Aroha apologizes, "I'm under strict instructions not to show you. But don't worry," she adds hastily, "it's not a wedding dress."

"We tried to make her buy one," Juliette says, "with a veil and a train and everything, but she wouldn't have it."

"I got the confetti though," Missie says.

"She's joking," Aroha replies. "Don't panic."

"You're all having far too much fun with this," I tell them, bending to unbuckle Leia and lift her out of her seat. "Hello, beautiful! Have you had a good day shopping? What did you buy?" I kiss her nose before holding her against my shoulder.

"They all spoiled her," Aroha announces, gesturing to the other bags.

"You can't blame us. Look how cute this is." Missie pulls out a tiny dress with lace around the edge. "Isn't it gorgeous?"

"She already has, like, a hundred dresses," I point out, pretending indignation.

Missie sticks her tongue out at me. "Well, she's got a hundred and one now."

"Aroha refuses to spend your money," Juliette points out, "so we intend to train Leia to drain you dry."

"By the time she's fifteen we'll have to turn the whole west wing into a wardrobe, won't we?" I ask Aroha.

She smiles, but she turns away, and it occurs to me that I shouldn't say things like that. I have no idea how things are going to go over the next six months, let alone fifteen years, but we both know that Leia won't always need a nanny.

In business, I draw up six-month, two-year, and five-year plans. I'm not an impulsive person, and I like to know where I'm going and what the road ahead looks like. So I feel uneasy about the near future. I don't know whether this scheme to get Leia will work. And even if it does, I don't know what would happen with Aroha afterward. Deep down, I'm starting to think I've been a fool for rushing into this and throwing both our lives into disarray. But what else was I supposed to do?

We decide to order in some pizzas and we eat them out on the deck as the sun sinks toward the horizon. Aroha disappears to put Leia to bed around seven, then rejoins us for a while before the others finally say they're heading off. I think they were all aware that the day after the funeral was going to be a difficult one, and I appreciate them spending some time with me.

After they've gone, I make Aroha and myself a cup of coffee. "Fancy watching a movie?" I ask her.

She looks surprised. "Don't you have work to do?" Usually I disappear to my office in the evening.

I shrug. "I've worked most of the day, and it is Saturday. I fancy something with a lot of action and blowing up." Plus, I also want to spend some time with her.

She laughs. "Yeah, all right. If we can have chocolate while we watch."

"Deal."

We discover that Ginny has left a box of truffles in the cupboard, and we stretch out in the armchairs and watch *Extraction* while we drink our coffees and suck on the chocolates.

When the movie finishes, it's only ten o'clock, but Aroha says she's tired and is going to head to bed.

"Thank you," I say to her as we take our mugs into the kitchen.

"For what?"

I shrug. "Everything."

She chuckles. "You're welcome."

She goes to walk away, and I say, "By the way, Alex has arranged the celebrant for next weekend."

"Cool," she says. "Is she coming here?"

I frown. "No. He mentioned that your parents might be upset that they weren't asked to the wedding, and it would be better if we went away, and you could then say I sprung it on you."

She nods. "That makes sense."

"I just wanted to say, I'm sorry that I didn't think about them. Of course they'd want to be there if you got married. It didn't even enter my head."

"That's okay," she says softly. "I understand."

"I wondered if you wanted me to come with you when you tell them."

"Oh, James, you silly boy," she says. "Of course you'll come with me. I'm not dealing with my father on my own."

I give her a wry look. "You're going to punish me, is what you're saying."

"That's exactly what I'm saying. If I'm going to get it in the ear for getting hitched without him, I'll expect you to be there to shoulder the burden."

"I'll be there," I tell her. "At my fiancée's side, as I should be."

Her eyebrows lift. I can see she hasn't thought about the fact that, on paper, she's technically my fiancée now.

"I'll be your wife then," she points out.

"True."

"Does that mean I get to nag you to pick up your socks?"

"Only if I get to claim *prima nocta*."

"*Prima* what?"

"It means first night." I lift my eyebrows. I shouldn't do this, but I can't help it.

She stares at me. Then she narrows her eyes. "You're teasing me."

"I'm allowed by law."

"Only if you get in a time machine and go back to 1348. Just make sure to avoid the Black Death."

My lips curve up. "'The wife's body does not belong to her alone but also to her husband.'"

"'Therefore shall a man leave his father and his mother, and shall cleave unto his wife: and they shall be one flesh'? Yeah, I've already had Genesis quoted at me."

We both laugh.

"All right," she says softly. "I'm off. See you tomorrow."

"Yeah. Good night."

I watch her walk away. She's taken off her sandals, and she's barefoot. Her hips swing a little with each step. I sigh and turn the light off. I'm being tortured, and it's all my own fault.

*

The week passes quickly. On Monday, I call Ethan and announce that I'm getting married at the weekend.

"Who's the lucky lady?" he asked.

"Aroha Wihongi."

"The one who's looking after Leia?"

"Yes."

"Okay. Well, that should work in your favor. So, let's talk about the prenup."

It's an extremely uncomfortable conversation. I know I have to be sensible, and I know the marriage is fake, but I feel like a heel to be implying that she's going to try to fleece me for at least half of everything I own.

I realize that if I'd been marrying Cassie, I'd have been quite happy to sign a prenup. But I can't even get Aroha to spend more than thirty dollars on lunch for herself. Accusing her of wanting half my fortune seems like an insult. Sure, I'm giving her a million dollars, but I still feel about an inch high.

But Ethan insists, and on Tuesday I bring Aroha to the office to sign the contract. She declines independent legal advice, and she sits quietly, holding Leia, while Ethan explains that the contract states she has no claim on my property or the majority of my fortune, apart from the million dollars I'll be giving to her.

"I understand," she murmurs, and signs it without further ado.

I sign it too, and then we head out to the Range Rover.

"I'm so sorry about that," I apologize as she heads back to West Melton.

"Don't worry," she says brightly. "I expected it."

"It wasn't my idea," I tell her, wondering why I feel the need to point that out.

She just laughs. "I'm not going to pout because I'm only getting a million dollars, James." And she changes the subject, as if she's trying to make it clear that she's not offended.

It doesn't make me feel any better, but there's nothing I can do about it now.

We're busy at work, finalizing everything for the conference. We call in a couple of members of staff to help with the handouts, read over the speeches multiple times, and by Friday, Tyson and Henry declare they can't do any more, and they're both ready.

"Good luck," I tell them when we part at our cars that evening.

"Likewise," Tyson says with a grin.

I realize he's referring to the fact that I'm getting married tomorrow. "Yeah yeah."

"Next time I see you, I expect you'll be bald with a pot belly," Henry states as we shake hands.

I give a short laugh and wave goodbye, walking to my Porsche with Alex.

"So, two-thirty p.m. tomorrow at the airport?" he says.

"Yeah, okay."

He grins. "Come on, it'll be fun. We'll have a nice meal and celebrate the fact that we've made sure Leia will be yours."

"I hope it works," I say.

"If it doesn't, you haven't lost much," he says. "Well, I mean apart from a million dollars and two years of freedom."

I blow out a breath. "I don't care about that. I just don't want to lose Leia."

Because if I lose Leia, I'll lose Aroha too, and I'm not ready to let her go.

I don't say it. But I think it.

"You won't lose," he says. "Nobody can prove the marriage is fake, right?"

"They could subpoena you all and make you testify."

"We'd just tell the court you're madly in love."

"You'd lie under oath?"

His lips curve up. "Yes, James, it would be a terrible lie."

I don't quite get why he's amused, but I'm touched. My friends are decent, upstanding guys who would always do the right thing, and the thought that they'd lie for me brings a lump to my throat.

"All right," I say. "See you tomorrow."

"What suit are you wearing for the ceremony?" he asks.

"Ah…" I haven't even thought about it.

"Don't tell me you were going to wear jeans," he says. "You've got to act the part. So bring a suit."

"All right. See you."

I get in the car and start it. As I reverse out of the parking space, I wonder what kind of outfit she's bought, and if it includes underwear.

*

The next day dawns bright and sunny.

All morning, Aroha is flustered and keeps walking in and out of the living room putting things into bags and taking them out again. I think it's because we're staying the night, and so she has to make sure Leia has everything.

"I can manage," she says when I try to help. "Go on, I'm sure you've got work to do."

"Anyway we shouldn't really see each other on the morning of the wedding," I joke.

She blushes. "Fake wedding," she corrects.

"Yes, of course."

We study each other for a moment. She's been a little cool since she signed the prenup. I'm not sure why. I know she wasn't expecting to get half of everything. Maybe it's the notion of divorce she doesn't like. She told me, *Marriage isn't something two people should enter into lightly. It's a solemn and binding relationship.* Perhaps the talk of ending it before it's even begun upset her.

I didn't think about that. Prenups are common, especially when one or both parties are wealthy, but now I come to think of it, it doesn't say much for modern society's attitude toward marriage, does it? Let's get married, but when it all goes wrong, let's make sure that what's yours is yours and what's mine is mine.

I have to fight not to wince.

She clears her throat. "Bibs," she mumbles, and disappears off to the west wing.

Frowning, I leave her to it, and go to my room to pack.

By 2:15 p.m. we're ready. I carry the bags out to the Range Rover.

"We're only going for one night," I say as I squeeze the last one in.

"Babies need a lot of stuff," she protests. "Can you drive?"

"Are you sure? It's your car."

"I'm too nervous," she says mysteriously, and goes inside to get Leia.

Musing on that, I leave her to buckle Leia in, lock the front door, and get in the driver's side. Once she's in, I start the engine and set off for the airport.

It takes us fifteen minutes to get there. Aroha is quiet, and she fidgets with her hands as she stares out of the window.

Something occurs to me, and I glance over at her. "Are you having second thoughts?"

She looks at me then. Her big hazel eyes are wary. "No. Not really."

"Are you sure? You're not going to jilt me at the altar?"

That makes her laugh. "No." She tucks a strand of hair behind her ear. "But it is sobering to think about the commitment."

"Two years is a long time," I conceded.

"Hmm." She doesn't elaborate.

I take the turnoff for the airport. "By the way, I've given instructions to the bank to open a new joint account—we just need to send them the marriage certificate and it'll be done. The million dollars will be in there before the end of the day."

"That quickly?"

"Yeah. Soon you'll discover all the benefits to being a billionaire's wife."

I say it as a joke, but at that moment the realization that we're going to be married slams into me as if she's hit me with a frying pan. She's going to be my wife. Holy fuck.

She glances at me, and our eyes meet.

"You'll be my husband," she says. "Oh God."

"Don't bring him into it," I mumble, "We're in enough trouble as it is."

Chapter Twenty-Nine

Aroha

When we get to the airport, James piles our luggage onto a trolley, and we make our way through to the gate where Alex and Missie are waiting with the helicopter.

Alex reveals that Zelda is staying with Missie's son Finn and his friend, so it's just us and Leia for the night. I'm nervous for many reasons, and climb into the back seat next to where James has buckled her into the middle, feeling his hand warm on mine as he helps me in.

I'm worried the noise of the helicopter might frighten Leia. Alex gives me a special pair of headphones for her, but I'm sure she's going to wail her head off when I put them on. She's as good as ever though, and merely looks astonished as I fit them over her head. Missie, who's sitting the other side of her, exchanges a smile with me, and we don our own headphones as the guys get in the front, and Alex begins to run through his safety procedures.

I've never flown in a helicopter before. I feel as if I'm dreaming as he starts the blades, and the helicopter rises slowly into the air.

James looks over his shoulder at Leia, who's promptly fallen asleep, and then at me. He's wearing sunglasses, but I can see his smile. "You two okay?" he asks into his microphone.

I nod and give him a thumbs up, then turn my attention to the view outside the window.

It's a spectacular trip. Alex flies us up the Waimakariri River valley, with the vast, flat, open fields of the Canterbury region on either side, and then before long we're heading into the Southern Alps. The slopes are thickly forested, and Alex points out landmarks as we go, like the gleaming waters of Lake Coleridge in the distance, and the wonderfully named Devil's Punchbowl Waterfall.

I'm stunned by the scenery. But that's not the main reason why my pulse shows no signs of slowing down. I can't believe I'm getting married today.

It's not how I'd imagined my wedding would turn out. Mum and I discussed it sometimes when I was young, the way I imagine all girls do, talking about my dress and who'd be my bridesmaids, which church I'd get married in, and what kind of reception I'd have.

And, despite the fact that my husband-to-be is a billionaire, I'm not having any of those things. No church, no bridesmaids, no magnificent dress or reception.

I told James that I wasn't particularly religious, but I feel some sadness now at the thought that I'm not getting married in church. I don't know why. I suppose marriage is more sacred to me than I realized. I don't think the undercurrent of shame at what I'm doing is going away anytime soon.

When we went shopping, the girls joked that they were going to help me turn this fake marriage into a real one. I felt a sweep of excitement at the time, but now I just feel embarrassed. James and I have lurched from disaster to disaster, and even though I think he finds me attractive, I'm sure he doesn't view this marriage as anything other than a means to an end. I shouldn't have let the girls talk me into believing I stood a chance.

I think about the outfit in my bag they made me buy and cringe a little inside. Maybe I won't wear it. Perhaps I'll just wear the cream pants I brought with my white tee for going home tomorrow.

But the outfit is beautiful, and I feel a swell of stubbornness at the thought that I won't get to wear it. Screw it. If nothing else, we have to make it look as if this is a real ceremony, right? So I'm going to wear it, and if he thinks it's a little over the top, well, he shouldn't have let me loose with his credit card.

Alex sets the helicopter down south of the Waimakariri River in one of the few fields in the area. A minivan is waiting for us, and the driver puts the bags in the back, we climb in, and then he sets off for the lodge.

When he pulls up out the front, the four of us climb out with jaws dropping. The large wooden lodge is nestled in the forest, with a magnificent view of the snow-topped mountains, and a small stream behind it.

We retrieve Leia, then make our way up the steps to the front desk.

"Mr. Winters," the receptionist says with a smile as Alex approaches. "Welcome to Kea Lodge."

"This is Mr. Rutherford and Ms. Wihongi," Alex tells her. "They're the couple who are getting married this afternoon."

"Oh, congratulations," she says enthusiastically. "You must be so excited."

"Over the moon," James says, amused, and I blush.

She smiles. "Everything's ready for you, and Sharon will be arriving shortly, ready for the service at four. If you'd like to check these forms and sign at the bottom, we'll get you to your lodges and you can rest before the big event."

I exchange a glance with Missie as the two guys check the forms. It's just occurred to me what's going to happen.

We're staying the night here. Oh shit. In the same room?

"Here you go," the receptionist says, and she hands the two guys a key card each. "Mr. Winters, you and Ms. Macbeth are in the Mountain Daisy Lodge. Mr. Rutherford and Ms. Wihongi, you'll be in the Buttercup Lodge."

James takes the key card automatically, then stares at Alex.

Alex stares back.

James puts his hands on his hips.

Alex lifts his eyebrows. "Gotta make it look good, you said."

James runs his tongue across his top teeth and glances at me. I'm too in shock at the thought of sharing a room with him to react.

Conscious of the receptionists trying not to listen, he clears his throat, then says, "Okay, come on."

The four of us follow the porter out. He takes us across to the individual private lodges on the other side, unlocks Alex and Missie's, and takes their cases in.

"Thank you," Alex says. "See you guys in the foyer at 3:45?"

"Sure," James says, throwing him a look. He picks up Leia's carry seat and follows the porter to the farthest lodge from the main building, and we go inside.

All thoughts flee my head at the sight of the beautiful lodge. It's open plan, with the bedroom, living room, and kitchenette forming one big space, with huge windows that look out onto the forest and the mountains beyond. A fancy bathroom contains a deep bath and a shower.

The bed is the room's crowning glory, though, facing the windows, with a large white duvet and numerous white pillows that makes it look as if it's made from clouds. It's a super king. And there's no other bed in the lodge.

The porter retreats and closes the door behind him, and finally, we're alone.

Leia's woken up and she's beginning to grizzle, so I unbuckle her and lift her out, then take her over to the window.

James joins me, and we look out at the view.

Eventually, he turns to me. "I'm so sorry," he says. "I didn't think it through. For some reason I envisaged us having separate rooms. I didn't realize Alex was only going to book two lodges."

I take a deep breath and let it out slowly. Am I really going to act affronted when I get to stay in such a beautiful place?

"Oh, it doesn't matter," I reply. "Come on, we're friends, right? It's only one night, and he was right—we couldn't get married and then spend our wedding night in separate rooms! That wouldn't look very good. And anyway, I've never stayed anywhere like this." I turn and look at the room. "It's absolutely amazing."

He smiles. "Trust you to see the positive side of things."

"Of course. Life must be very tough for people who are glass half empty. I'd much rather be glass half full."

He follows my gaze to the bed, then looks at the suite to one side. "I'll take the sofa tonight."

"Okay." I smile. "Something tells me Alex is having a little too much fun with this situation."

He chuckles. "Yes, me too."

"At least there's a bassinet."

"He asked for one to be brought in."

"Well, that's something. I might change and feed Leia now, so she's all done before the ceremony."

"Okay. Would you like a coffee?"

"I'd love one."

As if we've been married for ten years, we move around each other, me retrieving Leia's bottle, boiled water, and formula and making it up, while James works out the coffee machine and makes us both a cup.

I change her and then sit in one of the armchairs to feed her, and James brings the cups over and sits in the chair next to me.

"It's a wonderful place to stay," I say as Leia sucks contentedly at the teat. "Have you been here before?"

"No, but I've heard about it. There's a five-star restaurant here. I think Alex has booked us in for dinner."

"Oh," I say, feeling a flutter of panic. "Um… I've never eaten at a posh restaurant. I wouldn't know where to start with ordering or what the cutlery is for."

"Start from the outside and work in," he says. "And anyway, this is New Zealand. Nobody cares what fork you use. Half the clientele will be in shorts. And don't worry about the food. We often have platters to share, or we'll order several different dishes, and you can try a bit of everything."

"That would be nice."

He tips his head to the side and studies me for a bit.

Eventually I say, somewhat self-consciously, "What?"

"I'm just thinking how different you are," he says.

"From your other wives?"

His lips curve up. "From the other women I've dated."

"We're not dating," I point out.

"Well, yeah, but you know what I mean. You say you're not used to eating in posh restaurants, and you refuse to spend money when you go shopping, and you act like I've bought you a private jet when you get in the Range Rover, but you take it all in your stride. You're very calm and capable, without having an air of privilege that so many have."

I think of Cassie, and how she expected the whole room to be looking at her when she walked in. She always wore designer clothes, and all her jewelry looked as if it belonged to the English royal family.

"Have you told Cassie you're getting married?" I ask.

He gives me a wry look as he sips his coffee. "No."

"Are you going to?"

"She'll find out soon enough."

"Do you think she'll be shocked?"

He shrugs. "She knew I liked you. That was why she was always so snippy with you."

My jaw drops. He has another mouthful of coffee, his eyes meeting mine over the rim. His lips curve up a little. I can't think what to say.

He notices and laughs. "You're not surprised, surely?"

"Of course I'm surprised. I didn't know… I wasn't sure…"

"I took you back to my hotel and went down on you. I would have thought that was a clue as to how I felt about you."

I blush completely scarlet. "Oh my God."

He laughs. "Sorry was that a bit blunt?"

"You've got to warn me if you're going to say something like that."

"Oh yeah, I forgot. Incoming." Still chuckling, he puts down his cup. "I think I might take a shower. Then you can have the bathroom for as long as you want."

I don't say anything and just watch as he gets up, retrieves his washbag from his case, and heads into the bathroom.

I lift Leia onto my shoulder as the door closes. "I'm not going to make it out of this alive."

She emits a loud burp, and I sigh. Yeah, that about sums it up.

*

James

I shower and shave, wrestle my hair into submission with some product, then pull on my jeans and head out into the bedroom. Aroha is just putting Leia down on the playmat she's brought with her, and she pops the folding frame up and places it over her.

She turns as I walk over to her, and her eyes nearly fall out of her head.

I look down and realize I haven't zipped up my jeans. "Don't look so terrified," I say wryly. "I'm wearing boxers. It's not going to escape."

"Like Godzilla," she suggests, gathering her wits. "And rampage across the room?"

I laugh and start taking out my suit.

"You smell nice," she says.

"Thank you." I send her a smile, then hang up the suit carrier on the outside of the wardrobe.

"You're wearing a suit?" she asks.

"I've had my instructions from Alex," I reply. "He said I needed to dress up."

She scratches her nose. "The girls made me do it. I hope you don't mind."

"Of course not."

"It's not, like, a meringue dress with a veil or anything. It's just an ordinary dress."

"I'm sure it'll look amazing."

She clears her throat. "Are you okay to keep an eye on Leia? I might have a bath."

"Of course. Enjoy yourself."

She retrieves her bag. "Okay. See you in a bit."

She goes into the bathroom and closes the door. Soon I hear music emanating, and the sound of running water.

I check my watch—it's just gone three, so we have about forty-five minutes. I lie on the floor and play with Leia for a while, and then when I hear the bath empty and Aroha drying her hair, I start getting ready. Leia rolls onto her tummy and watches me, and I chat to her while I put on my suit.

I'm just doing up my tie when she comes out of the bathroom. My hands stop moving, and I stare at her.

She's wearing a champagne-colored, satin sheath dress. Tiny pearls line the spaghetti straps. The hem reaches just past her knees, but a split runs all the way up the outside of her thigh. She's matched it with a pair of sexy, high-heeled sandals.

She's swept her hair up into a chignon and pinned it with a clip the same color as the dress. She has pearls in her ears and a single strand around her neck.

It's simple and elegant, and she looks amazing.

As I continue to stare, she glances down at herself. "It was on sale," she says. "And I can wear it afterward, so it'll get more than one use."

"Are they real pearls?" I ask, surprised my voice sounds normal. I'm sure she'd have told me if she'd bought herself some on my credit card. I feel a sudden, sharp, surprising surge of jealousy at the thought that an ex-lover got them for her.

But she laughs and touches them. "No. They're pretty though, don't you think?"

I'm relieved. "You look amazing." I wish I'd bought her some proper pearls, or diamonds to compliment the dress.

"So do you." She admires my navy suit. "It looks different from your normal suits. Why's that?"

"It's Italian. I normally wear British-cut suits to work. Neapolitan styles are closer fitting, without the shoulder padding, and the front panels are curved." I'm waffling, and I clear my throat. "So, it's nearly time."

"Yes, I just want to change Leia." She picks Leia up and kisses her neck, then takes her over to the bed with Leia's bag.

I finish tying my tie, half-watching her in the mirror. The dress may have been in the sale, but it fits her beautifully, accentuating her figure. Hmm. I'm pretty sure from the way her breasts move beneath the silky fabric that she's not wearing a bra…

She glances over her shoulder. I hastily look back at my reflection, tightening my Windsor knot.

When I'm done, I pocket my wallet, phone, and room key card. By this time, Aroha's finished dressing Leia, and she holds the baby up to show her new blue dress with small white flowers and matching headband.

"Well, look at you," I tell her, taking her out of Aroha's hands. "Pretty as a picture." I kiss her rosy cheek, and she swats me.

"She's going to be a boxer," Aroha says, collecting a shoulder bag that's the same shade as her dress. "Are you ready?"

"Yes."

"Do you want me to bring her carry seat?"

"Yes, just in case."

"I've got her dummy, and I've made up a bottle."

We move around the way I've seen other parents do, collecting toys and blankets and bottles, and then eventually we're ready, and head over to the door.

I stop there, still carrying Leia, holding the door handle, and turn to Aroha.

"You look amazing," I say softly.

"Thank you."

My stomach flutters, and I say, "Are you nervous?"

Her eyebrows lift. Then she says, "Actually, no. I was. For days I've been wondering if I'm doing the right thing. But while I was having a bath, I was thinking about Leia, and it just came to me—nothing else matters. Not me or you or my parents or friends or anyone else. We're adults, and we can deal with anything that comes out of it. But Leia's a baby. She needs the absolute best start we can give her. And if this helps, then of course we have to do it."

Her hazel eyes are large and clear—she means every word. I lift a hand, cup her cheek, and stroke her soft skin with my thumb. Then I bend and kiss her forehead.

"Thank you," I say, thinking about Maddie and how much she would have liked Aroha.

Her cheeks flush, and she presses her lips together. Did she think I was going to kiss them? "Come on, or we'll be late."

I release her and open the door, and she closes it behind us.

As we pass Alex and Missie's lodge, they come out and smile as they see us. Alex is wearing a dark-gray suit, and Missie is wearing a pretty floral dress with large hoops in her ears.

"Oh, you look gorgeous," she says.

"Thank you," I reply as we start walking to the main building.

"I was talking to Aroha," she says wryly.

Aroha giggles. "Sorry," she says, "I should have had a glass of wine. I feel a bit wobbly."

"You said you weren't nervous," I tease.

"I should have said I don't have any doubts. I am a bit nervous."

"Would you like a drink?" I ask as we go through the main doors.

"Goodness, no. I haven't eaten, and I might fall off my high heels."

"Oh I'm sorry, we skipped lunch, didn't we?"

"I had a muesli bar, but I don't think it was enough to soak up any alcohol."

Alex grins. "I booked dinner early, for five p.m. because of Leia, so you don't have long to wait. Now stay here. I'll make sure everything's sorted." He heads off to reception.

Missie smiles at me. "You want me to take Leia?"

"Okay." I hand her over, and Missie holds her up, admiring her dress.

"What a little princess," she says, kissing the baby's fingers as she reaches out to touch her mouth. "Give the carry seat to Alex, Aroha."

He rejoins us and takes the seat from her. "Come on. This way."

We follow him through the lodge, past the restaurant and bar, to a smaller room obviously reserved for private events. Two large sliding doors open up onto a wooden deck that looks out at the mountains. Despite it being summer, the weather can be inclement here, but today it's sunny and there's only a little breeze, and the doors are open.

We stop as we walk into the room, taken aback by the decor. White ribbons and silver balloons are pinned around the wooden posts that support the roof over the deck, and ribbons wind through the posts of the balustrade. A white table bearing a bowl of fresh red roses serves as the altar. A woman stands behind it, dressed in a light-gray suit, and she smiles as she sees us.

I hold my hand out to Aroha. Shyly, she slides hers into mine, and I lead her forward.

"Good afternoon," the woman says. "I'm Sharon Hart, the celebrant, and I'll be performing the wedding today."

"I'm Alex Winters," Alex says, "I'm the one who spoke to you on the phone. This is my partner, Missie Macbeth, and we're the witnesses. This is James Rutherford, and this is Aroha Wihongi."

We all shake hands. I glance at the door, seeing a few members of staff there, peering in, wanting to see the ceremony. Suddenly, I'm nervous. My palms are sweating, and I feel flustered. Oh God, I'm getting married, committing myself for two years to someone I don't even know that well. Am I mad?

"Come and stand here," Sharon directs, gesturing for Aroha to stand in front of her on her right, and me on her left. Alex and Missie sit with Leia in the two seats to one side. Sharon asks us to turn off our phones, which we all do. My fingers fumble on the buttons. My heart is beginning to race.

"Alex explained that you only wanted a simple ceremony," Sharon says, "and that you didn't want to write your own vows or have personal readings or music, so I'm going to use the official marriage vows, okay?"

We both nod.

"They're short and sweet," she says, "but no less meaningful for that."

I wonder whether she's going to give us a speech on the sacredness of marriage, but to my relief she doesn't. Instead, she asks, "Is everyone ready?"

Another nod. I look at Aroha. She studies my tie.

Outside, a kea—an alpine parrot that the lodge is named after—sails past the window, and I can hear the sound of the wind in the trees. I can't hear cars or any conversation—even the people watching have fallen quiet. It's very peaceful here. I know this isn't a religious ceremony by any means, but to my surprise it feels it. I feel as if God is watching us. Man, I haven't thought that since I was about twelve.

"*Tēnā koutou katoa*," Sharon begins. "Good afternoon. It is my pleasure to welcome you all to this celebration of marriage between James and Aroha. Thank you for sharing this important day with them. My name is Sharon Hart, and I am authorized by the Government of Aotearoa New Zealand to conduct this ceremony as a registered marriage celebrant."

Aroha swallows. She looks as nervous as I feel.

Sharon continues, "James and Aroha, in marrying you are making a sincere commitment to go forward in your lives formally united as partners, promising support and encouragement to each other throughout your lives together. However, no ceremony can create a marriage; only the two of you can do that—by supporting, trusting, and respecting each other, in all that you share together. Now, please take one another's hands."

Aroha lifts hers into mine. Her light-brown skin is warm. She's painted her nails a pearly color, and they shimmer in the sunshine.

"James and Aroha, we come now to your marriage vows, which are the legally binding words that confirm your choice to marry and declare your commitment to each other. New Zealand law requires that each of you declares before me, and at least two other witnesses, that you are freely entering into this marriage and that you take the other person to be your legally wedded wife or husband. I will ask each of you now to repeat this statement after me."

My pulse is pounding. Aroha's hands tremble in mine. Oh God. Are we doing the right thing?

At that moment, though, Leia laughs and babbles something not unlike, "Mum, mum, mum." We all laugh, but my neck prickles at the thought that maybe she's seen Maddie here, watching the ceremony.

This is why we're doing it. For Maddie. For Leia.

As if she's thought the same thing, for the first time Aroha lifts her gaze to meet mine. In the late afternoon sunshine, her eyes are brown, green, and gold. She smiles, and suddenly all my nerves fade away.

"First, James," Sharon instructs. "I, James Ernest Rutherford, am freely entering into this marriage, and take you, Aroha Jane Wihongi, to be my legal wife."

I repeat the words slowly and carefully. Aroha's eyes stay on mine the whole time.

"Now Aroha," Sharon states. "I, Aroha Jane Wihongi, am freely entering into this marriage, and take you, James Ernest Rutherford, to be my legal husband."

Aroha says the words. Her voice is quiet and shy, but she's smiling.

My stomach flips as she speaks. We're really doing this. We're joining ourselves together legally and… spiritually? No, it's just a contract. It doesn't mean anything.

But it does. I can feel it. Almost as if someone is wrapping a silver cord around us, and it's gradually tightening.

"Now we'll exchange the rings," Sharon says.

Alex stands, takes out the two rings in the black velvet box, and hands the larger to Aroha, the smaller to me.

Sharon continues, "Today you have chosen to exchange rings. A wedding ring is a symbol of the marriage vows you have just made. May these rings always remind you of your commitment to each other. I now invite you to exchange rings."

Aroha holds out her left hand, and I slide her ring onto her finger. I then hold out my hand, and she does the same. The gold bands shine in the sunlight.

"James and Aroha," Sharon says, "it is my great pleasure to pronounce you legally married. Congratulations. *Tēnā rawa atu kōrua*."

And just like that, it's done. We're husband and wife.

Chapter Thirty

Aroha

Behind us, there's a great cheer, and I turn in surprise to see about a dozen people standing there watching. We laugh, and Alex and Missie stand and join in as everyone claps.

"You may kiss the bride," Sharon says, smiling.

I look up at James, my heart racing. He gives me a mischievous smile, then bends his head and touches his lips to mine.

Oh shit, that's it. We're married!

In a daze, I sign the paperwork. My hand shakes, making it almost impossible to write my signature. It doesn't help when James places a warm hand in the middle of my back. I know it's just for show, but heat runs up my spine and pools at the base of my neck. I hadn't lied when I told him I wasn't having second thoughts—I don't regret it for a moment. But I'm more shaken than I thought I'd be. Saying those words… and listening to him say that he takes me to be his legal wife…

I look at the ring on my left hand. It's wide and heavy, a constant reminder of what we've just done. A symbol of our… um…

"Thank you," James says to Sharon, shaking her hand. "Even though it was short and sweet, I was oddly nervous."

"Yes, it's surprising how many people say that," she replies. "Something about the solemnity of the vows, I think." She turns to me and smiles. "Congratulations, Aroha."

"Thank you." I shake her hand, but my gaze slides to James. He's now talking to Alex, and I'm glad. I don't want him to see how flustered I am.

I smile at Missie as she hands me the baby. "I hope this means you're safe," I whisper to Leia, walking away a little with Missie.

"You've just done a marvelous thing," Missie murmurs, putting a hand on Leia's back as she leans forward and kisses my cheek.

"Whatever else happens, you've been incredibly unselfish, Aroha. I admire that."

"I got a million dollars out of it," I remind her. "It wasn't that unselfish."

"Come on, this is me you're talking to. I know you're going to spend most of the money on your family. You did this for other people, and that's no small thing."

As I kiss Leia's head, my gaze slides across the room to James. Mm. I completely did this for other people. It wasn't for myself at all…

The guys join us, and Alex leads us out and across the foyer to the bar. "Let's have a celebratory drink," he says, "and then we'll head into the restaurant." He goes up to the bar. "Can I have a bottle of champagne please?" he asks the bartender.

My eyes widen. "Um… I shouldn't," I begin. I never drink when I'm taking care of children.

He waves a hand. "I'm not saying we should get plastered, but you have to have a drink on your wedding day."

James's lips curve up as he looks at me. "Let him have his fun," he says. "We'll just have the one glass."

"Okay." Happy with that, I follow Missie over to a table. She brings Leia's carry seat, but for now I sit with Leia in my arms and give her a toy to play with.

The guys join us with the champagne, and Alex holds up his glass. "To James and Aroha."

"Oh shut up," James says good-naturedly, and we all laugh and sip the champagne. Mmm, it's lovely. I could get used to this lifestyle.

"By the way," Alex says, "when we finish dinner…"

Missie sends him a mischievous glance. "Alex…"

His lips twitch. "We wanted to say that if you'd like us to look after Leia tonight, we're very happy to have her in our room."

I frown, puzzled. "Why would you want to…" My words trail off as I realize what he's inferring.

"Alex," James warns. "Stop meddling."

"This is purely business," I scold. "You know that."

"I know," Alex protests. "But you want everyone to think it's for real, right? You've gone to all this effort." He gestures at my dress. "I see he even gave you a pearl necklace."

I blush scarlet in seconds at the thought of how James might give me the other kind of pearl necklace. James takes one look at my red face and bursts out laughing.

"Guys!" Missie glares at them both, then throws me an apologetic look. "Sorry, Alex has such a dirty mind. He had a whisky from the minibar. I can't do a thing with him."

"What?" He looks startled, and then his lips curve up. "Now who's got the dirty mind? I was being literal and complimenting the jewelry."

It's Missie's turn to blush scarlet, and then we all start laughing.

"I should buy you a real pearl necklace," James says. "No wife of mine should have a fake one." His eyes meet mine, and he smiles.

"Don't call me your wife," I scold.

"Why?"

"It gives me goosebumps."

He chuckles.

"I've got some ideas for what you can call each other," Alex announces. "I read an article on eighteenth-century names for your significant other."

"Go on then," James prompts.

"You can call Aroha your 'lawful blanket.' Or your 'comfortable importance.'"

"Doesn't exactly slip off the tongue," James says.

"How about 'hussy?'"

"Alex," Missie says, "don't be rude."

"It's short for housewife," he protests. "Or you can call her your 'crooked rib,' because obviously Eve was made out of Adam's rib."

Missie rolls her eyes. "Good lord."

"If you scold him when he's in bed," Alex says to me, "you read him a 'curtain lecture.'"

"I like that," I say. "You can be henpecked now," I tell James.

"I don't mind," he replies. "I'll call you my 'trouble and strife.' Cockney rhyming slang," he tells Missie, who looks puzzled. "Either that or 'me bird.'"

I giggle, and he winks at me.

Leia throws her toy on the floor, and he retrieves it for her. "Sorry," he says, giving it back to her, "are we not paying you enough attention?"

"Quite a demanding little madam, aren't you?" I tease, pressing her nose like a button. She sticks her tongue out, and we all laugh.

"I wonder if Maddie was watching today?" Missie asks, sipping her champagne.

"I thought that too." I brush Leia's fluffy hair where it's sticking up. "I hope she would be pleased that we're doing our best for her daughter."

"She'd be thrilled," James says, his voice a little husky. "I wish you could have met her. She'd have liked you, and she'd be very touched with what you did for Leia today."

A sudden surge of emotion sweeps over me at the thought that Leia will never see her mum again. I clear my throat, not wanting the day to turn sad. "I hope so. I'm tying myself for two years to a man who tried to poison me at dinner yesterday."

Alex and Missie start laughing. "You didn't," Missie says.

"It turns out that mayonnaise looks like whipped cream when it's in a bowl," James says.

"Doesn't taste as nice on apple pie though," I point out.

"I only did it once," he states indignantly, then concedes, "Cooking isn't one of my many talents."

"No shit, Sherlock."

He meets my eyes, his lips curving up. I poke my tongue out at him.

Alex chuckles. "Come on. It's nearly five. Let's go and have dinner."

Leia's dozing, so I put her in her seat, and James carries her through to the dining room. The waiter shows us to the best table in a bow window looking out at the snow-topped mountains, and hands us all a menu.

I'm nervous about what to choose—there are lots of words I don't recognize, some in French, I think. I like cooking, but I mostly cook plain food, and I have no idea what a *Bouillabaisse* is, or a *Velouté*.

But James is there to rescue me, as he says, "I was thinking we could go for the platter, what do you think?"

"Sounds good," Alex says, and Missie and I nod enthusiastically.

What they eventually bring out astounds me. Food fills every inch of a large square board they place in the center of the table. There are thinly sliced cured meats, savory crackers, breadsticks, crusty bread and thick butter, nuts, olives, hummus topped with olive oil and seeds, several different chutneys, figs, grapes, and dried fruits, baked brie with olive oil drizzled over, cheddar and Stilton, rice-stuffed vine leaves, baby peppers filled with soft cheese, and lots more.

We all tuck in, talking and laughing while we eat. Alex and Missie are good company, and they ease the slight awkwardness I feel every time I think about the fact that James and I are married.

Every now and again, I remember that we're sharing a room, and my stomach flutters with nerves. Not that I'm expecting anything to happen. James told Alex to stop meddling earlier, and I know he's determined to keep this strictly business. Still, even the thought of sleeping in the same room as him gives me goosebumps. Is that silly?

Leia wakes and I lift her onto my lap and give her another toy to play with. Even though I eat my fill from the platter, the guys insist on ordering a dessert platter too, and when that comes it's impossible not to pick at the tiny macaroons, freshly made truffles, and the miniature donuts, and I can't resist dipping strawberries, grapes, and orange segments into the white chocolate and dark chocolate sauces.

"You did not just dip a chocolate truffle into a chocolate dip," I say to James.

He licks his lips and gives me an amused smile. "What's wrong with that? I like chocolate."

"I'd noticed. Ginny always makes sure there are bars of Cadbury's available," I tell the others. "And they're always in the fridge."

"You monster," Missie declares.

"I like cold chocolate," he protests.

"Well, if I crack a tooth I'm sending you the dentist's bill," I say sarcastically.

"Anything for my wife." He dips another truffle into the white chocolate sauce and eats it with a grin.

I've had enough to eat, and I bounce Leia on my knees as she grizzles a little.

"Aw," Missie says. "Is she getting bored? How about we go for a walk? There's a path from the lodge down to the stream."

"Good idea," James says. He eats his final truffle, and we rise from the table and head out to the lobby. Leaving the carry seat and bag behind the front desk, he takes Leia from me, and we walk slowly along the path and down to the stream.

It's a beautiful evening, and the late sun has turned the water to beaten copper. We're thrilled as a kea swoops in front of us to sit on a fence and watch us for a while, and a New Zealand falcon floats high in the sky, possibly looking for its supper on the outskirts of the forest.

The breeze blows across me, making me shiver. "Here," James says to Alex, "take Leia for a moment, will you?" Then he slips off his jacket and puts it around my shoulders.

"You needn't do that," I scold, but I welcome the way it's warmed from his body heat, and pull it closer. It smells of him, too, his cologne rising from the material to ensnare my senses.

Is he doing it because he thinks someone's watching from the lodge, and he's keen on portraying the image of the marriage as real? I don't think so, somehow. He's just being kind and affectionate, and that warms me through more than the jacket.

We continue to walk, Alex singing Taylor Swift songs to Leia as he carries her, which makes Missie laugh. When we return to the foyer, James collects the carry seat and bag, and the four of us walk along to the lodges.

"Come in for coffee," I suggest, and so they join us, and James and Alex make the coffees while Missie makes up the bottle and warms it, and I give Leia a quick wash and change her into a onesie. Missie then feeds her, obviously enjoying the chance to get her hands on a baby again, while we sip our coffees and watch the sun set over the mountains.

"It's been a lovely day," I say with a sigh. I've removed my sandals and now I rest my bare feet on the coffee table, crossed at the ankles. "Thanks for suggesting it, Alex."

"You're welcome. Hopefully it'll foil Blue's plans," he replies. He picks up the cups and takes them over to the sink. "Come on," he says to Missie, "let's go back to our place."

Leia is nearly asleep, so Missie takes her over to the bassinet and lays her down gently. We cover her with the thin duvet, and she bends to kiss her goodnight.

"She's a good girl," she says as Leia's eyelids flutter shut.

"She wailed the first few nights," I admit, "but she didn't take long to get used to being left."

She smiles and gives me a hug. "Well, good night."

"'Night."

"Now, you're sure you don't want us to look after her?" Alex asks.

James just gives him a wry look. "Goodnight, Alex."

Alex chuckles and they shake hands. He kisses my cheek, then he takes Missie's hand and leads her to the door. "See you tomorrow," he says.

She waves, and they go out, closing the door behind them.

James goes over and locks it. "I might change into my track pants, if you don't mind?"

"Of course not."

He collects them from his bag and disappears into the bathroom. When he comes out a few minutes later, he's wearing the track pants and a gray tee.

I collect my own yoga pants and tee and walk toward the bathroom.

"You looked lovely today," he says, putting Leia's dress in her bag.

I turn. "You too." I smile, then go into the bathroom and close the door.

I blow out a breath, then slip off the beautiful dress, take off the pearls, and pull on the comfortable pants and tee. When I'm done, I come back out, hang the dress up, then walk over to where he's sitting in the chair, looking at his phone.

He puts it down as I join him, smiles, and gestures at the chair. "It was quite a nice service actually," he says as I sit. "Even though it was brief. It shows you don't have to have a huge, fancy affair to tie the knot."

"I liked the setting," I agree. "On the deck, overlooking the mountains. It was very romantic."

"What kind of wedding would you like to have if and when you do it for real?" he asks. "Would you like a fancy affair?"

"I'm not sure. I've always imagined the big white dress and the host of bridesmaids. I guess it's the thought of seeing all your family, and having the big party, you know."

He nods. "Would you get married in church?"

"I couldn't now," I say softly. "I was raised a Catholic."

He stares at me. "You're a Catholic?" His jaw drops. "Shit, Aroha. Why didn't you tell me?"

I put my finger to my lips and gesture at Leia in her bassinet. "Ssh, you'll wake her. I'm not a Catholic *now*. I don't go to church anymore. I'm just saying that I couldn't remarry in a church. Catholics don't believe in divorce—I'd have to get an annulment. And I've seen the kind of questions you have to answer on the form for that—details about your sex life, problems in your marriage, that kind of thing. So I'm not going down that road. No, if I got married again, it would be a registry wedding, like we've just had."

"But your parents still go to church."

"Yes, most of my family does."

"So they're going to be upset if you get a divorce. You should have told me."

"You'd have changed your mind if I did. I wanted to help. They'll come around. I'll tell them you had numerous scandalous affairs."

I'm teasing, but to my surprise he stiffens and looks affronted. "I'd rather not be accused of cheating."

I meet his eyes, curious. "Why would that bother you?"

"Cassie accused me all the time, and she wasn't the first girl to do so. I'd never cheat, and I find it insulting to be accused of it."

I soften inside like chocolate left out in the sun. "Okay. I'm sorry."

He scratches at a mark on his track pants and mumbles something.

"I didn't mean to insult your manhood," I add, teasing him in the hope of lightening the situation, realizing I've obviously upset him.

That earns me a wry look. "It's a sensitive topic, that's all, and I'd hate your parents to think badly of me."

"Why?" I ask, amused. "You don't even know them."

"Not yet, but I'm going to meet them, right? They're special to you, and I…" He trails off, looking embarrassed.

"What?"

"I want them to like me," he says. "I'm only human."

I'm touched, but I say mischievously, "Dad will think you're a pretty boy."

That makes him laugh. "I've heard worse." He looks at me curiously. "You've never spoken about your exes. I presume there have been some?"

"I'm not a virgin, if that's what you're asking."

He chuckles. "How long have you been single?"

"Nearly five years."

He looks startled. "Jesus. How old are you?"

"Twenty-five."

"And you haven't dated since you were twenty?"

"Um, briefly, last year, but it didn't work out."

He studies me, curious now. "Why did you go so long without seeing anyone?"

I wasn't going to tell him. But it's late, and it's dark in the room because we haven't switched the lights on, and the sun has almost set. And lastly, I realize with some surprise that I trust him.

I take a deep breath. "Because the guy I was dating back then assaulted me."

Chapter Thirty-One

James

I stare at Aroha for a long time.

She sits there quietly, bearing my gaze with patience, while horror, pity, and fury blend together inside me.

"I wasn't going to tell you," she admits eventually. "I'm guessing you want to challenge him to a duel." Her lips curve up. She's trying to lighten the moment because she can see the emotions on my face.

"I want to kill him," I say eventually, when I can trust myself to speak.

Her expression softens. I think she likes that answer, although she doesn't respond.

I can't think what to say. Eventually I opt for, "Did you go to the police?"

"No."

So the bastard got away with it. "Why?" I ask, aghast.

"Because he was my boyfriend. And I didn't say no. It's hard to explain. I don't really want to talk about it."

She doesn't have to. I think I can guess. He wanted sex and she didn't, so he took it by force, and she let him because she was young, and for whatever reason she didn't feel she could resist. And because of that, she assumed the police wouldn't count it as assault.

"Who else knows?" I whisper.

"I've never told anyone."

"Not even Gaby?"

"No."

"Not your parents?"

"Definitely not. Mum has enough on her plate. Dad would have murdered him and gone to prison for it."

And yet she's told me. I'm touched, and also confused. We don't know each other well. I'm hardly a counselor. I have no experience in a situation like this, and no idea what to say. How can I possibly understand what it was like? Nobody's ever forced me to do anything since I was a kid.

"I'm so sorry," I say eventually.

She just gives me a small smile.

I think about what she told me before. "You said you dated briefly last year, but it didn't work out?"

She sighs. "Yeah, I met a guy through a friend of a friend, and we dated for a few weeks. I liked him. But when we went to bed…" She looks embarrassed.

I read between the lines. "You found it difficult because of what had happened before?"

She nods and sighs. "Have you heard of vaginismus?"

"No."

"It's an involuntary tightening of the vagina. I have no control over it. It made sex impossible." She fiddles with the hem of her tee. "I hadn't told him about what my ex did, and he got impatient, and that just made it worse. In the end we gave up, and I didn't see him again." Her lips twist, and she gives a slight shrug.

My heart goes out to her. "And you haven't dated since?"

"No. I've had other things on my mind."

I think back to the trivia night, when I took her back to my hotel room and made her come with my tongue. I slid my thumb inside her, and I remember her being tight, but not impenetrable. "But when we… you know… you were okay then." She didn't seem frightened or panicky.

"I'd had a lot to drink," she reminds me wryly. "And…" She meets my eyes for a moment, and her expression turns impish. "You warmed me up first."

I can't summon a smile. "And the guy you dated last year didn't?"

"No." She doesn't elaborate.

My head's spinning. No man with any sense of humility would label himself good in bed, but I like to think I'm considerate. I know that women take longer to achieve an orgasm than men, and they therefore need more foreplay. I've never resented that—it's hardly their fault, and anyway, I like foreplay. I like kissing and touching—it makes it more pleasurable for me, as well as for them. Why get it all over with in two minutes when you can make it last an hour? And while it's more fun if the girl doesn't just lie there expecting me to do all the work, I do feel it's the guy's responsibility to... warm the girl up, as Aroha put it.

It's not onerous work. It's not difficult. And it's hardly a big secret. So I get annoyed when I hear that other guys expect girls to be ready at the drop of a hat.

And as for her ex who assaulted her... I want to demand she tells me where he lives so I can go down there, drag him out of his house, and beat him to a pulp with my bare fists.

But she doesn't want to talk about it, and I'm going to have to honor that.

"Have you had counseling?" I ask, wondering if she's talked to anyone.

"Yes. It helped, a bit." She gets up from the chair. She looks a little emotional. "I'm just going to the bathroom," she says quietly.

I rise too. "I need a drink," I announce. "Would you like a whisky?" I hold up a hand as she goes to protest. "It's fine if you don't, and I won't push you, but Leia's asleep now, and we're both right here for when she wakes. Say you'll have one with me?"

"All right," she says. She goes into the bathroom and closes the door.

I choose a couple of miniatures from the minibar, pour them over ice in two tumblers, and add a splash of water. Then I stand there, my hands on the counter, and glance around the room.

We're practically strangers, and she's been assaulted in the past. I'm expecting her to stay in a room with me, and now I'm plying her with alcohol. Jesus. Could I be any more insensitive?

She comes out of the bathroom, looks around the room to find me, then walks over to the kitchen. She glances at my face and asks, "Are you okay?"

"Am *I* okay?" I give a short, humorless laugh. "I was just thinking how insensitive it was to offer you alcohol when you're alone in a room with a stranger."

"You're not a stranger," she says, amused. "You might be a strange man, but you're not a stranger."

I can't smile, too upset at everything she's told me tonight, and I'm angry with myself. "You know I didn't offer you a drink because I expect... I mean because I thought it might..." I trail off, furious at my apparent callowness.

"James," she says softly, "I know."

"It's just... I can't bear to think... of you being..." My hands clench into fists on the counter.

I half-expect her to get cross and tell me to stop making it about me. To ask if she can have another room. Or to demand I stop talking about it.

To my surprise, she does none of those things; instead, she walks around the counter and comes up to me. As I straighten and face her, she slides her arms around me and rests her cheek on my shoulder.

"You're such a nice man," she murmurs.

I give a choked laugh and bring my arms up around her. Gently, half afraid to hold her. "I'm really not."

"You are. You're gentle and kind and sensitive. I trust you."

It's possibly the nicest thing she could have said to me. "Thank you," I whisper, my voice almost a squeak.

"I shouldn't have told you," she says, a little puzzled. "I don't know why I did."

"I'm glad you did."

"I don't want you to look at me differently."

"I do, but not in the way I think you mean. You're brave and courageous. I have nothing but admiration for you for picking yourself up and getting on with your life and making such a success of it."

She snorts. "I didn't even have a job until you gave me one."

"That was unfortunate, and it wasn't your fault. You qualified in childcare, and when COVID took that away, you changed tracks and found work in the beauty salon. When that closed, you came to work for me, and now you've married me to help me out, even though you know it's going to upset your parents if and when it comes to an end. You were ready to do anything for your family, and for Leia. I have nothing but admiration for you."

She sighs. "You always make me feel worthy. I don't know how you do that."

"Because you are. You're very special, Aroha."

We stand there like that, our arms around each other, for a while. Without her high heels, she feels small and fragile. I rest my lips on the top of her head and inhale—her hair smells of mint.

Eventually, she releases me, and I lower my arms. I push the whisky glass over to her. "Come on, let's sit down."

As we return to our seats, I say, "Do you want me to put a lamp on?"

"No," she says. "The moon is just gorgeous."

The sun has now set, and the moon is close to being full and hangs in the sky like a Christmas bauble someone's forgotten to take down on Twelfth Night. It fills the room with a silvery glow.

"It's strange," I say, sitting back down, "but I realize how little I know about you. We haven't really talked like this, have we?"

"I suppose not."

"Or at least when we have, we've talked about me and my problems. I'm sorry about that."

"It's okay. There's not much to say about me!"

"Aw, I don't believe that. Come on, tell me about yourself."

"Like what?"

"Everything," I say, and to my surprise, I mean it.

In the end, we talk for hours.

Despite the fact that I'm rarely lost for words, I don't normally have conversations like this. When I'm with my friends, we either chat about work, or rugby, or movies, or we tell stories and jokes and anecdotes.

For ages, I listen to Aroha talk about herself. She's hesitant at first, shy and reluctant to open up, but I ply her with questions, and she gradually tells me about her life and her family. She talks about her sister, and what it's been like for them growing up with a brother who has autism with high support needs. She tells me about her parents—her strong, silent, Māori father who's so ashamed of losing his job and not being able to support his family. And about her stoic, patient, English mother, who's also a touch stubborn, and never wants to ask for help, even when she's struggling.

She tells me about her extended family in England—her grandparents, aunts, uncles, and cousins. She's never been there, and they've never come over—it doesn't sound as if any of her family have enough money to travel. But she talks to them weekly on Zoom, and she says she'd love to visit them.

She talks about her relatives in New Zealand, and reminisces about her school, meeting Gaby, and about a few boyfriends. She hasn't had many—only two before He Who Shall Not Be Named. I get the feeling she hasn't had any one-night stands, although I don't ask her directly.

She's not been to uni, and hasn't experienced that lifestyle. She's worked all her adult life, and has always given a large portion of her money to her mother.

I don't sit there mutely—she asks me questions, and we trade experiences and stories as the moon rises higher, turning the tops of the mountains silver.

It's close to midnight when Leia first stirs and grizzles.

"She's tired of listening to us," Aroha jokes, getting up and going over to the bassinet. "There, there, *pēpe*." She lifts her up and gives her a cuddle.

"I'll make the bottle," I tell her, and while she changes Leia, I go into the kitchen, tip the formula out, and warm it up, just like she showed me.

"I'm a bit tired," Aroha says. "I might feed her lying down, if that's all right."

"Of course."

She places Leia in the middle of the bed, slides beneath the duvet on Leia's left, turns on her side, and props her head on a hand. I bring the bottle over, and she takes it and starts feeding her.

I sit on the other side of the bed and watch Leia suck dreamily, her eyelids already drooping. I yawn. "I can see why they call it the dream feed."

Aroha smiles. "Me too. It always makes me sleepy."

"I'm going to brush my teeth."

"Okay."

I go into the bathroom. When I come out, she says, "Will you finish feeding her so I can do mine?"

"Sure." I stretch out on the bed, on top of the covers, and hold the bottle while Aroha disappears into the bathroom.

I rest my head on a hand and watch Leia's tiny rosebud mouth suck at the teat. She looks up at me, her turquoise eyes silver in the moonlight. *I trust you.* I hope Leia does, too. I want to make sure no man ever hurts her the way Aroha has been hurt. I hate to think of women feeling vulnerable. I did a little jiu jitsu when I was younger, and I decide I might teach Aroha some self-defense moves, and Leia too, when she's old enough.

She'll start walking and talking, and I'll be able to help teach her colors and shapes, and read her stories, and show her how to ride a bike. I can take her to ballet lessons, or rugby lessons, whatever she wants to do. And as she grows older, I can teach her about computers, and sport, and how to play the guitar. It's going to be fun to play Daddy.

The only fly in the ointment is that there'll be no Mummy to help me out.

I realize I don't like the idea of having another nanny bring up Leia. Aroha loves her, and she's so good with her. Leia will miss her, and it seems cruel to take her away after she's already lost her mother.

But what's the solution?

Aroha comes out, and I do a double take as I see she's carrying her yoga pants, and she's just wearing her knickers and a tee. She tosses the pants over a chair, then slides beneath the duvet again. She takes the bottle from me. "Thanks."

She's removed her makeup, and she's released her hair from the chignon, brushed it through, and braided it over her shoulder. She looks younger without her makeup. I'm touched that she doesn't mind me seeing her *en deshabille*.

Leia's finished the bottle, and I pick her up, chuck the muslin square over my shoulder, and walk with her over to the window. "Look at the mountains," I murmur. "There's Aoraki Mount Cook. It's three thousand seven hundred and twenty-four meters tall. That's over twelve thousand feet."

Behind me, Aroha laughs. "You're going to be a great dad," she says.

I pat Leia's back. "She's not so sure." She's snuffly tonight, and a bit grizzly, which is unlike her. I wait for the obligatory burp, and when it comes, I go to lie her down in the bassinet, but she starts crying. "Aw," I say, picking her up again. "There, there." I glance at Aroha. "What should I do?"

"Normally I'd let her cry for a bit," she says, "and she'd probably settle eventually. But maybe she realizes she's not at home. She's had a lot of change lately. Perhaps she's a bit lonely."

"Shall I bring her over?"

"Yeah, okay."

I take her to the bed and place her back beside Aroha. She gives her a dummy, then strokes the baby's head.

I get up and say, "I'll leave you to it." I spotted a spare blanket in the wardrobe. The sofa is ultra firm and isn't going to be comfortable, but it's the only option.

AROHA AND THE BILLIONAIRE BOSS

"James," she says as I turn away. I look back at her. "Don't sleep on the sofa," she says. "The bed's huge. Come on."

I hesitate. Should I refuse? Insist on taking the sofa? But the bed looks soft and inviting, and I'm tired. "You're sure?"

"Of course. No point in being uncomfortable. And we are married." She gives a mischievous grin.

My lips curve up. "Um… do you mind if I lose the track pants? It's quite warm in here."

"As long as you keep your boxers on, we're all good."

I chuckle, take off the track pants, then slide beneath the duvet. Turning onto my side, facing them, I prop my head back on my hand, mirroring Aroha.

Leia sucks her dummy, and Aroha rubs her tummy, while I hold the baby's hand.

"Sing to her," Aroha whispers.

I start singing *Miracle* by Foo Fighters, and Aroha hums along, still rubbing Leia's tummy. When I finish the song, Leia's eyes are still open, but she's looking drowsy.

Aroha pulls a pillow down and rests her head on it. She looks like a Greek statue, turned to marble in the moonlight.

"You look sad," she says.

"I was thinking about the future."

"And it makes you sad?"

"The thought of you leaving does."

"I don't have to leave."

My heart lifts at the thought.

"I could stay on as Leia's nanny," she adds sleepily.

I look at Leia's tiny fingers. That's not what I meant.

What did I mean?

I'd like us to be more than boss and nanny.

Friends?

I look at her mouth, and think about kissing her. No, I want us to be more than friends.

But I've screwed up any chance of that by making her marry me for money. I've done it all backwards, when we haven't even gone on a date. I can't count the trivia night. I don't want to count the trivia night. That was a complete disaster. I don't even really know how she feels about me. She says she trusts me. But does she mean like a friend, or a brother? Now she's said that, I can hardly make a move on her.

God, I've really fucked up this situation.

I look back up at her. Her eyes are closed.

I sigh and rest my head on the pillow. Her hand is resting below Leia on the duvet. I move mine next to it. Then I move it an inch closer, so our fingers are touching.

Looking up at her, I see her lips curve up, just a little.

I close my eyes, and within a few minutes, I fall asleep.

Chapter Thirty-Two

Aroha

The next day, Sunday, we finally go to see my parents.

I called Mum this morning and explained that James and I have fallen in love, and that yesterday we went away for the night. I said that he told me while we were there that he'd booked a celebrant and wanted to marry me. As I expected, she was shocked, but she also seemed to find it romantic, and when I said he wanted to come and meet them that afternoon, she replied that she was excited to meet this guy who'd captivated her daughter.

I hate that I've lied to her, but I don't want to tell her the truth. She'd be horrified that I've married for money, even if I explained how it will help James get Leia. It's going to be hard enough to get her to accept any of the million dollars that appeared in my new account this morning. She and my father are very proud, and so although I originally told them I was working for a wealthy guy, I haven't told them *how* wealthy he is. I think their heads would explode.

"There's no bell," James says when we walk up to their front door. "Shall I knock?"

I shake my head. "The noise upsets Rua. They'll hear us, don't worry."

He nods. I've explained that Rua is very sensitive and finds loud noises overwhelming, and that he doesn't speak much. I'm a bit nervous for James to meet my brother. I love Rua with all my heart, but strangers struggle with how to talk to him, and he can sometimes get anxious and aggressive with those he doesn't know.

James is holding Leia's carry seat in one hand. She's had a nap and I've fed and changed her, so she's bright and perky. He has her change bag in the other. He passes it to me, though, as the door opens.

Dad looks at us, pinning a smile on his face, although his eyes are cool when he looks at James. "Hello," he says, "come in."

I kiss him on the cheek as I pass him, then say, "Dad, this is James. James, this is my father, Mik."

"*Tēnā koe*," James says, a formal greeting, as he holds out his hand. Then in Māori, he proceeds to say that I've told him a lot about him, and he's been looking forward to meeting him. He speaks fluently, without faltering. I look at him in astonishment—I didn't know he could speak Māori beyond a word or two.

My father lifts his chin, accepts the handshake, and then, to my surprise, comes forward to give James a *hongi*. It's a common practice amongst Māori—the pressing of noses—especially in the *marae* or meeting house, but I'm sure James isn't expecting it, and I wait for him to look surprised or unsure. He doesn't—he dips his head, and the two men solemnly exchange the Māori greeting. Of course—I forget James is a businessman, used to traveling and speaking to all kinds of people. Still, I'm so touched that my throat tightens.

"Come in," Dad says gruffly, closing the door behind him.

I glance at James, who winks at me, and I lead the way into the living room. The place is spotless, and there are fresh flowers from the garden on the dining table. My sister is there, sitting with Rua, and Mum stands as we come in.

"Mum, this is James," I say, keeping my voice low so I don't agitate Rua. "James, this is my mum, Samantha."

"Pleased to meet you," he says, shaking her hand.

"Hello, James," she says, eyes sparkling. "So you're the man who's captivated my daughter."

He gives me an amused glance, and I blush and clear my throat. "This is Marie."

He shakes hands with my sister, smiling as she giggles.

"And this is Rua," I say, gesturing at my brother.

"Nice to meet you, Rua," James says in a low voice. He doesn't try to shake Rua's hand. Rua keeps his gaze fixed on the robot toy he adores that never leaves his side.

"Please, come and sit down." Mum gestures at the sofa.

James and I sit side by side, and he places Leia at our feet in her carry seat.

"Would you like a cup of tea or coffee?" Marie asks. She has obviously had her instructions.

"Coffee please," we both say.

She nods and goes into the kitchen.

Dad sits in his chair. There's an awkward silence, and Rua fidgets, obviously picking up on the atmosphere.

"I have something for you, Rua," James says quietly. "It's a toy I've been working on for a while." He glances at my parents. "You're welcome to look at it first to see if you think it's suitable for him, or save it for later if you want."

Surprised, I watch him rummage in Leia's bag. He brings out a round object, maybe eight inches in diameter, that sits comfortably in the palm of his hand. A white sphere rests inside a clear one, and as he turns the clear one in his hands, the white sphere inside stays the right way up. The front has a cutaway section with two large cartoon eyes and a simple smiling mouth. "It's for children with autism," he says, "to help them learn and communicate with others."

Mum and Dad stare at him.

"Caregivers can control how much noise and light it emits so it doesn't overstimulate," he continues. "Its responses are predictable and stable, so the child feels safe. I also used a cartoon face as I've read that they prefer that to a more realistic face."

They continue to stare at him. Mum presses her fingers to her mouth.

His gaze slides to me, worried. "Have I made a mistake?"

"You made this?" I can barely get the words out.

He nods. "When you told me your brother was autistic and liked robots, I came up with the idea, and Henry helped me with the design. I… ah… thought Rua might like it…" He looks embarrassed now, as if he thinks he's committed some faux pas.

"James," I say, my voice husky with emotion, "we're all incredibly touched. Nobody's ever done anything like that for Rua before."

He blinks. "Oh."

"Show us how it works," I suggest.

"To turn it on, you can just say Hello *Kare* or Kia Ora *Kare*." He pronounces it the Māori way—kah-reh, rolling the 'r' so it's almost a soft 'd'. It means friend, but it's also used to attract attention, and it's a lovely name for the toy. As he says the phrase, a line of soft blue lights appears around the toy. "Or you can press this button on the top," he says, obviously realizing that many autistic children struggle with speech. He turns it off, then on with the button.

The blue lights reappear. He places it on the floor, then pushes it, and the ball rolls along the carpet, while the face inside stays upright. Rua watches it, wide-eyed.

James then claps his hands gently twice, and the ball rolls toward him. Rua stares, his jaw dropping.

James does it again—he rolls the ball away, then claps twice, and the ball rolls back to him. He rolls it away a third time, then says, "Do you want to try, Rua?"

Rua looks uncertain. James repeats the action—he claps, takes the ball, rolls it, and does this two or three times, nice and slow.

Eventually, as he rolls Kare away, Rua claps his hands twice, and the ball rolls toward him. He grasps it, thrilled.

"Well done, Rua," James says with a smile. "Kare is your friend."

Rua picks up the ball and hugs it to him.

"Can you give him a kiss?" James asks. "On the top of his head?"

Rua frowns and puts the ball down. James picks it up and gently presses his lips to the top, and Kare gives a playful chirp, its lights changing to pink hearts briefly before returning to blue, while on the front its 'face' beams a smile. James rolls it away, and Rua claps his hands so it rolls toward him, picks it up, and kisses it. When Kare chirps and glows pink, and Rua laughs, my mum nearly bursts into tears. I understand why—Rua struggles to show affection, and he doesn't enjoy playing with other children, and therefore has few friends.

"James," my dad says, "I can't believe you designed this."

"It does lots of other games," he replies. "I'll go through them with you, and you can decide which ones you think Rua might like."

"How much will it cost?" Mum asks, wiping beneath her eyes. "It must be very expensive."

"Toys that improve cognitive development often cost thousands of dollars," James says, "but we're hoping to offer it for much less than that, maybe a couple hundred dollars."

Mum nods. "We'll do our best to save up. I think it will be an amazing toy for him."

"No, I'm sorry, you misunderstand me," James says. "This one is a prototype specifically for Rua. It's yours. You'll be doing me a big favor if you can help me work out any kinks and improve the design."

They're both speechless, and just nod their thanks. He glances at me, and I smile and reach out a hand. He grasps it for a moment, then lifts it to his lips and kisses my fingers.

It's an innocent gesture, but my face heats at the touch of his lips on my skin. Mum says, "Aw..." and I remember then that he's doing it for show, but my face stays warm for a while.

Marie brings out our drinks, then sits with Rua, asking him to show her the ball.

"So, this is Leia," Mum says as Leia waves the toy she's holding. "She's your niece, James, right? Aroha told me about your sister. I'm so sorry to hear of her passing."

"Yes, it was very sad," he says. "I'm hoping to adopt Leia and bring her up as my own."

"Where's her birth father?" Dad asks.

"He's not in the picture," James says. He doesn't elaborate.

"So you'll be her daddy?" Mum asks. When he nods, she continues, "And Aroha, you'll be her mummy? I'm finally a grandma! How wonderful."

I look at James, taken aback by her comment. I should have guessed she'd say something like that. He quirks an eyebrow and smiles at her, but he doesn't look at me.

"Can I hold her?" Mum asks.

"Of course." My fingers fumble at the harness, and then I lift Leia out and pass her to Mum. Leia stares at her, wide eyed. Mum says, "Hello sweetheart," and kisses Leia's hand as she holds it up to Mum's mouth. Leia giggles, and Mum laughs. "Oh, you're just adorable," she says.

I warm through. I was worried that Mum might be hostile toward her, but I should have known better. She loves babies, and she was so disappointed when I said I didn't want my own.

"So, Aroha tells us that you own your own business," Dad says to James. "Kia Kaha?"

James nods. "With four of my friends, plus one woman who's our chief physio. Amongst other things, we design exoskeletons that help people to walk again."

"You should see their building, Dad," I say. "One of them, Henry, is a member of Ngāi Tahu, and he worked with the local *kaitiaki* to plan and design the building so it connects with nature and the local culture. There's a wonderful painting of Rangi and Papatūānuku as you walk in."

"I'd like to see that," Dad says.

"Actually," James replies, "I have something to ask you. Our Building and Grounds Supervisor handed in his notice before Christmas. Aroha mentioned that you have experience with handling staff and maintaining equipment, and that you're in between jobs at the moment. I wondered whether you would be interested in the position? I'd like you to come in and meet the other guys. It's so hard to get trustworthy staff, and you'd be doing me a favor."

Oh my God, this guy. How did he manage to make it sound as if my dad's skilled and honest and perfect for the role in the same sentence?

Mum looks at me, and I can see immediately that she's crazy about James. And who can blame her?

Dad looks embarrassed, though. "I don't know what Aroha told you, but I'm just a process worker."

"You were in charge of your shift though, right?" James asks.

"Well, yes..."

"And you've received an award for your contribution to the company for eight years running?"

Dad nods, but I stare at James. How did he find that out?

"You're just the type of guy we're looking for," he says. "Would you be available to come in tomorrow?"

"I'll check my calendar," Dad says, then laughs, the frown lines that have been there for so long disappearing from his face.

James grins. "Shall we say ten o'clock?"

Dad nods. "I'll be there."

"Excellent." James sips his drink. "This is an excellent cup of coffee, by the way."

Marie blushes, and I stifle a laugh. He's such a smoothie. But I love him for it.

"So..." Mum sits back, obviously enjoying her cuddle with Leia. "Tell me all about what happened yesterday. You're such a naughty boy, James. I can't believe you sprung a wedding on her, and we hadn't even met you!"

"I know," he says guiltily, "I'm so sorry about that. I wanted to grab her before she got away."

"Aw, that's so romantic." Mum sighs. "What did you wear?" she asks me.

"Um… I'd brought a champagne-colored dress for dinner, so I wore that." I bring a photo up on my phone that Alex took for me. James has his arm around me, and we're standing by the altar with the mountains behind us. They all look at it and murmur their approval.

"She looked amazing," James says. "So beautiful."

I bump his shoulder with mine. He bumps it back.

"It's a shame you didn't get married in church," Dad says.

"Come on, Dad," I scold, "you know that was never going to happen."

"You're not religious?" Dad asks James.

He shakes his head. "We went to church when I was young, but I haven't been for years."

"Oh well," Dad says. "I suppose I can't have everything. You'll look after her, though? She's my girl, and she means everything to me. You'll understand now you have your own daughter."

James looks at Leia, and I can see understanding filter through his expression. He's just starting to get to grips with what it means to be a father. It's for life—it never goes away.

"Yes, sir," he says, and that's it, my father's convinced.

*

On the way home, I sit quietly, glancing over at James from time to time. He's driving the Range Rover today, lost in thought.

"Are you okay?" I ask. "That wasn't too bad, was it?"

He glances at me, smiles, and shakes his head, but his eyes remain preoccupied.

"Thank you for what you've done for Rua," I say. He went through how to work Kare with my parents, explaining how to charge it, and what kind of games it does. "They were very touched."

"It was my pleasure," he says. "We're hoping to get it out to schools and centers by the end of the year."

We fall quiet again. I clear my throat. "And thanks for offering Dad a job. You didn't need to do that."

"He's a solid worker. We'd be honored to have him."

"Wow, James, I don't know how you do that. How do you make everyone feel special?"

"Everyone has something to offer. You just have to look for it."

He's so offhand about it—he has no idea how he made my dad feel special.

"How did you know about his awards?" I ask.

"I… ah… made enquiries." He flicks me a smile.

He sinks into thought again, though, and it's a few minutes later before I say, "Are you annoyed about something? Did they say something to upset you?"

His eyebrows rise. "No, of course not. They're lovely people. They gave me a lot to think about, that's all." He doesn't elaborate.

He doesn't say much more when we get home, and after dinner he excuses himself and disappears into his study, claiming he has work to do. Knowing he'll be there for the rest of the evening, I bathe and feed Leia and put her to bed, play the guitar for a while, then watch a movie, hoping he might come out and want to join me. He doesn't though, and around ten I finally go to bed.

I'd hoped the fact that we're married now might have changed things between us. That it might make him look at me differently. But now I realize everything is going to stay the same, and it makes me sad.

*

The next day, Leia sleeps in until seven, which is unusual for her, and by the time I'm up and dressed, James has gone to work. I have a quiet morning—I chat to Ginny while she cleans the kitchen, then when she goes off to vacuum the house, I take Leia for a walk around the gardens. At ten I picture Dad arriving at Kia Kaha and wonder how he's getting on, and I'm pleased when James texts me around eleven to say the guys loved him, and they've given him the job, starting tomorrow. Henry has taken him off to show him around the place and introduce him to some of the staff, and he says that Dad loves the building and thinks Henry's great.

What are you doing for lunch? he says at the end. *We're ordering a working lunch, but Missie and Gaby are coming in, and you can join us if you like?*

Delighted, I reply, *I'd love to!* That cheers me up no end. I make sure that Leia has a nap and feed, then head out in the Range Rover, arriving at Kia Kaha just before one.

AROHA AND THE BILLIONAIRE BOSS

I get out of the car, unbuckle Leia's seat, and carry her across the car park to the front entrance. I've just reached the top of the steps when I realize a man is standing there, watching me.

I stop walking and stare at him. It's Blue. My heart immediately doubles its speed. Not just because of who it is, but because of the look on his face. He looks absolutely furious.

"You married him," he snarls. "You fucking bitch, you went and married him!"

My jaw drops, and I look around hurriedly for support, but although I can see people walking through the foyer, there's nobody close by to help.

Holding Leia's carry seat, I try to walk around him, but he moves to block my way.

"My lawyer will show the judge that it's all fake," he snaps. "You're just a fucking money grabber—you married him for his money, and my lawyer will prove it."

"Leave me alone." Shaking, I try to walk around him to the right, but again he steps in my way. Although he's not as tall as James, he's bigger than me, and he's wearing a vest that reveals alarmingly big biceps.

I'm angry and determined not to be intimidated. I take my phone out of my back pocket and, with one hand, start dialing. "I'm calling the police."

Before I can react, though, he knocks the phone out of my hand, and it skitters across the floor. That upsets me—the phone is new and now it's going to be all scratched, or worse, broken. "Get out of my way!" I say sharply.

Leia, unaccustomed to hearing me raise my voice, starts wailing.

Then, to my alarm, Blue reaches down and wraps a meaty fist around the handle of Leia's carry seat. He tugs it, trying to wrench it out of my hand.

"Give her to me!" he yells.

"Blue, stop!" I'm frightened now. He yanks at the seat, but I hold it with both hands. As Leia is tossed about, she screams, striking fear into my heart. I can't let her go. I can't let this sorry excuse for a man have her.

"Fuck off, you fucking cunt!" He yanks the seat hard.

I stumble, then trip up the last concrete step and tumble onto my knees. Ooh, that hurt, but I still refuse to let go of the seat.

"Let go!" I yell.

He moves back, pulling me forward, and I fall onto my elbow, but continue to hold onto the seat as he drags me a few feet across the ground.

Infuriated, Blue kicks out at me, his shoe meeting my ribs with such force that it forces air out of my lungs. I scream until my throat hurts, terrified of losing Leia.

Oh God, I don't know how much longer I can hold on…

Chapter Thirty-Three

Aroha

Blue kicks me again, harder, and it hurts so much... I curl around the carry seat, trying to protect Leia and myself. There's blood on the concrete and on my clothes... Leia's still wailing, and Blue's cursing...

And then suddenly, there are voices and feet all around me. Someone wrenches Blue up and away, propelling him back to the wall, and James's voice cuts through my pain. He says something I miss, but I hear the second bit: "You fucking piece of shit!"

There's a smack like the sound of a fist striking a piece of meat, then another, and then someone—Henry I think—says, "James, enough." Feet scuffle, but I'm distracted by a female voice, and then Missie appears in my vision, bending down.

"Aroha. Aw, sweetheart, come on, sit up."

Gaby also appears, and she helps me to a sitting position. "Leia," I say immediately, gasping for breath.

Missie unclips her harness and lifts her out. Leia's still wailing, but Missie ignores it, checks her over, then gives me a relieved look. "She's fine."

I take her and hold her to me tightly, then burst into tears.

"You're okay." Gaby lowers onto the step beside me and rubs my back. "God, what a terrible shock."

Alex bends down beside us, his face full of concern. "Where's all the blood from?"

"Her elbow and knee," Gaby says. "She's grazed them quite badly."

"Have you called 111?" Missie asks him.

"Rachel did before she called us," Alex replies, naming their receptionist, who must have seen the whole scene from her desk. "I can hear the sirens already. She asked for the police and an ambulance."

"Here's a first-aid kit." Tyson passes one to Alex, who opens it and takes out a pad of gauze. He hands it to Gaby, who presses it to my knee.

I only half-process what they're saying. All I can think is that I came so close to losing Leia. I'm holding her too tightly, but she's quietened, and she snuffles as she curls up against me. I rest my cheek on the top of her head, my tears soaking her hair.

"Aroha." It's James. He drops to his haunches before me, and I look up into his eyes. They're blazing with fury, but they soften now as he looks at me. "Are you all right?"

"She's okay," Gaby says. "A few cuts and grazes. Nothing too bad, I think."

"Jesus." He cups my face, brushing my cheeks with his thumbs. "I'm so, so sorry."

"Where is he?"

"Henry has him," Alex says, and I glance over my shoulder to see that Blue is on the ground, and Henry's kneeling on his chest, one hand on his throat. Blue isn't going anywhere anytime soon.

James's face is white. "I can't believe what he did."

"He wanted to take Leia," I say with a sniff. "He tried to pull her seat out of my hands."

"You could have been badly hurt," he snaps. "What were you thinking?"

I stare up at him. What was I supposed to do? Let Leia go?

The sirens are growing louder, and he straightens as two police cars and an ambulance pull up at the base of the steps. "Alex," he says.

"I'm on it." Alex runs down the steps to talk to them.

Gaby is in the process of trying to stop the bleeding on my knee and elbow. Two police officers walk up the steps, along with two paramedics. They all stop in front of us, and James goes to speak to the police officers.

The paramedics put down their bags and one of them bends and smiles at me. "Aroha," she says, "my name's Janie. Can we have a look at the baby?"

"Her name's Leia," I mumble.

"What a wonderful name, a real princess," she says. "Can I take her?"

I hesitate, fear turning me to rock.

Her expression softens. "It's all right. I'm just going to check her over. She was in her seat the whole time?"

"Yes."

"I'm sure she's fine. I won't take her away, I'll do it here, okay?" She sits beside me.

Reluctantly, I hand Leia over to her. I watch her while the other paramedic cleans my knee and elbow and patches them up. Janie chats to Leia as she examines her limbs, torso, and back, looks into her eyes, and runs a gentle hand over her scalp.

"She looks just fine," she says. "What a lovely baby you have. And you're a lucky girl having such a brave mummy, aren't you?"

"I'm not her mum," I say, my bottom lip trembling. "I'm just her nanny."

Janie frowns, clearly puzzled, but James interrupts whatever she's about to say as he walks up and asks, "Is she all right?"

"A bit shaken up," the other paramedic says. "Are you hurt anywhere else?"

"No." All I can think is that I'm so relieved Leia is okay.

"Rest and TLC," Janie says cheerfully. "You'll be right as rain tomorrow."

"What about Blue?" I ask as I see a police officer walking him down the steps toward the car.

"I'll call my lawyer later," James states. "That man will never come anywhere near you or Leia again." He speaks firmly, with authority, and both police officers just nod.

"We'll need you both to come in and make a written statement," one of them says. "Tomorrow will be fine."

"Thank you." James walks away with them, and they chat for a few minutes before the officers finally head away.

The terrace is still full of people, mainly staff from Kia Kaha, talking amongst themselves and looking horrified by the turn of events.

"Is there anything we can do?" Missie asks.

"I think we'll be okay," James says. "I'll take them both home now."

I let him help me to my feet. Ooh, I feel as if I've been run over by a bus.

"Give me Leia," he says. He takes her from me and clips her into her seat. She doesn't want to go and starts squealing.

"She's upset," I say tearfully.

"She'll be all right," he says. "Come on." He slides a hand beneath my elbow.

"Call us if you need anything," Alex states.

"Will do," James says.

Gaby gives me a hug. "Call me later, okay?"

I nod. James takes me over to the car, opens the passenger door, and helps me in. Then he buckles Leia into the back seat before getting in the driver's side.

He waves to everyone watching as he pulls away and heads for home.

Leia is still wailing, and I wish I'd thought to give her a dummy. I ferret in my purse and find one, then twist in the seat to give it to her.

"Ow," I say as a sharp pain stabs my side.

"What is it?" he asks.

"Just my elbow." I give Leia her dummy, and she quietens.

"I want you to tell me what happened," he says. "Step by step. You don't have to do it right now if you don't want to, but I need to know. I'm going to call Ethan and take out a restraining order. With any luck Blue will do some time for assault, too."

"I don't mind telling you now." I go through it with him, explaining how Blue was standing there waiting for me. "He was angry that we'd gotten married," I say. "I think he decided on the spur of the moment to take Leia. I don't know why—I don't know if he was thinking about asking for a ransom, or if he just thought that because she was his, he deserved to have her, but—"

"She's not his," James says curtly. "She's mine. And I'm not going to let him within an inch of her again."

I look at him. His face is white—he's furious, and also, I think, terrified at the thought of what happened.

She's mine. Not she's ours. Of course he wouldn't say that. I'm not blood related to Leia. She's not my daughter, and she's not my niece.

When we arrive back at the house, he comes around and retrieves Leia, puts her seat on the ground, then helps me out. He carries Leia in, and I follow him, feeling tired and sore.

Leia is close to dozing off. James takes her out of her carry seat and says, "I'll put her down for a bit."

I nod, watching him take her through to the bedroom. Sighing, I go into the kitchen, open a bottle of water from the fridge, and drink a quarter of it. Ooh, I'm sore. I investigate my elbow and knee. My knee is okay, but my elbow is already bleeding through the pad. Ouch.

It's my side that feels really tender, though. Why's that? Oh of course, Blue kicked me in the ribs. I guess I'll have a nice bruise there. I'm wearing cropped jeans and a tee, and I lift the tee.

"Jesus Christ!" James strides across the foyer, carrying the baby receiver. He puts it on the counter and comes up to me. I've dropped the tee, but he pushes aside my hand and lifts the hem. He obviously glimpses where my ribs are marred by a fresh graze that's already starting to turn a nasty reddish-purple before I move away.

"What happened?" he asks in horror.

"He kicked me," I say reluctantly, not wanting him to fuss.

His jaw drops. "He kicked you?"

"Twice."

He takes my hand and leads me to an armchair. "Sit down."

"But—"

He glares at me, and I lower down.

"Stay there," he barks. He slides a hand into his trouser pocket, then frowns and looks around. "Have you seen my phone?"

"No."

He curses. "Can I borrow yours?"

"It's in my purse." I gesture at the kitchen counter. "Blue threw it away. The police officer put it in there. I hope it's not broken."

He goes over and retrieves it. "It's fine, don't worry." He gets me to unlock it, then dials a number.

Relief that the phone isn't damaged makes me feel oddly tearful.

I watch him as he paces. "Hello?" he says after a while. "It's James Rutherford. Yeah, I'm using someone else's phone. I'm fine, thanks, but I need a favor. Not for me, for my... wife."

He hesitated, and my throat tightens. He didn't want to use the label.

"Yeah," he continues as the person on the other end of the phone obviously queries it. "Long story. You heard about Maddie? Yeah, that's right, hoping to adopt her. Aroha was looking after her for me, and we fell in love and ended up eloping, kinda. Anyway, Leia's birth father has just attacked Aroha outside Kia Kaha. She saw a paramedic, but she didn't mention that he kicked her in the ribs. I think he might have broken a couple. Yeah. Do I need to take her to the Emergency Department?"

He listens for a moment. Then he walks over to me. "Are you short of breath?"

I shake my head.

"Do you have pain in your tummy?"

I shake again.

"You're not coughing up blood?"

"No."

"Did you hear a crack when he kicked you? Or can you feel a bump there?"

"No."

He presses a hand to my forehead and says into the phone, "No, I don't think so."

"I'm all right," I say. "I don't think my ribs are broken."

He ignores me. "You sure? I can bring her in if I have to. No, right. Okay. Five's fine. What can I do in the meantime? Yes, I have plenty of those. Right. The bruise is coming out. Yeah. Will do. All right, see you after five. Thanks, Josh. Bye." He hangs up. Then he walks over to me.

"A doctor will be calling in later to check up on you. He's a friend of mine. He said you might have just bruised your ribs rather than broken them, but you need to tell me if the pain gets worse or you have trouble breathing, and I'll take you straight to the hospital."

"I'm okay—"

"I mean it, Aroha," he barks. "I want you to tell me if you start to feel worse."

"Okay," I say meekly.

"For now, I think a lukewarm bath is in order to make sure the wound is clean, and then we have to put ice packs on it. I'll go run the bath and get you some painkillers. You're not allergic to anything?"

I shake my head.

"Stay there," he says. "You need to rest." He stalks off in the direction of the bathroom.

I sit back, puzzled as to why he seems angry with me. I feel a bit shaky and tearful. I curl up in the armchair, wincing at the stab in my ribs, and hug a cushion to my chest. Suddenly, I miss Leia, and I feel a surge of panic at the memory of Blue tugging the handle of her carry seat, and my fear that he'd win the tug of war and run off with her.

I get up and go through to the bedroom, only feeling better once I see her in her bassinet, sound asleep. Leaning on the side, I swallow hard. I don't know why I'm so upset. I'm not her mummy. One day in the not-so-distant future I'm going to have to tell my own mother that I'm getting a divorce and she won't be having grandchildren after all. She'll be so upset—she's already knitting Leia a blanket for the winter, and talking about how wonderful it will be when she's old enough to be taken to the playground. And what about my father? Will James continue to employ him after we've split up? Tears well in my eyes.

"What are you doing?" James has appeared at the door, and he looks cross. He comes over and takes my arm, turns me, and propels me back into the corridor.

"I missed her," I say, knowing I sound pathetic.

"She's asleep. She'll be fine." He marches me through the living room and then into the east wing, toward the big bathroom. Walking so fast hurts my ribs, but I'm not about to tell him because I think he'll bundle me in the car and spirit me off to the hospital.

When we get to the bathroom, he makes me sit on the toilet seat, then proceeds to get a big fluffy towel and a robe. He tests the water. "Best to have no bubbles," he says, "it might sting." He adds some cold, waits until it's a third full, then tests it again. "Right." He goes to the cabinet, retrieves a bottle of Nurofen, takes out two, and gives them to me with a cup of water. "Take these now. When you get out, we'll put an ice pack on. Now, in you get."

I swallow the pills with a mouthful of water, then get to my feet, my shoulders hunched and my arms wrapped around me. I glare at him, irritated by his bossiness. "I'm not stripping off while you're standing there."

"And I'm not leaving—you might fall over."

I don't move. He crosses his arms and glares back.

Why is he so angry with me? I feel cold and anxious, and I know I'm trembling. I can't just strip off in front of him. He reaches out a hand, I'm not sure why, but instinctively I take a step back. He lowers his hand, looking puzzled. Does he really have no idea why I'm nervous of men right now?

"Just go," I say tiredly. "I'll be careful."

He hesitates, and I think he's about to speak, but then he backs away and leaves the room, although he leaves the door open a crack.

Feeling sorry for myself, I peel off my clothes and look in the mirror. Ooh, it's a good job I waited until he'd gone. My whole side is going to be black and blue.

Gingerly, I lower myself into the bath. It's not too hot, and although my side stings a bit, I welcome the warmth on my skin. I take a sponge and clean it carefully, then take off the dressing on my knee and clean that too. I make sure my elbow stays out of the water, not wanting to get it wet.

When I'm done, I lean forward with my elbows around my knees and rest my cheek on them. My eyes sting. I hope Blue is enjoying his stay in a prison cell, I think spitefully. I hope he's damaged his chances of ever getting Leia. How long will it be before James knows if the court has granted him a Parenting Order?

I lift my head as I hear a knock at the front door. The doctor? I didn't think he was coming until five. The police, then? Why would they come here?

"Beware Greeks bearing gifts," I hear James say.

"I haven't been near the Mediterranean." It's Alex. "I thought you might need some whisky. And your phone. You left it on the boardroom table. How are you doing?"

I hear a dog bark, and a boy's voice telling it to be quiet. Presumably Missie, her son, Finn, and Zelda are there too.

I'm too tired and upset to make polite conversation. Hopefully they won't stay long. I rest my cheek on my knees and close my eyes, shutting out their voices, but tears filter through the lashes and run down my face.

It's only a few minutes later though that I hear a knock on the bathroom door. "Aroha? It's Missie. We just came to see how you're doing. We're worried about you."

"I'm all right," I say, but it comes out as a squeak. "I'm in the bath."

"James said you've hurt your ribs."

"Yes. They're... very sore."

"Sweetheart, can I come in? I just want to make sure you're all right."

I sigh. "Yeah, if you want."

Missie pushes the door open. She comes in and closes it behind her, and walks over to the bath. Immediately, she sees the red marks on my ribs and my tearful face, and she drops to her knees beside the bath.

"Aw, sweetie," she says. "Are you okay?"

I give a humorless laugh, trying to wipe my tears away, but it's impossible. "It's all right, I'm just feeling sorry for myself."

"Of course you are. I think you're perfectly entitled to. Are you in a lot of pain?"

"No, it looks worse than it feels. I don't think they're broken, just bruised."

"I'm so glad. What a terrible thing to have to go through."

"It could have been worse. He nearly got Leia." Emotion rushes through me, and for a moment I can't speak.

"But he didn't because you were so brave," Missie whispers.

"I just didn't want to lose her," I squeak.

"And you didn't, you saved her. James is so proud of you."

"Then why is he so angry with me?" I sob.

She looks startled. "He's not angry with you."

"He is. He said, 'You could have been badly hurt, what were you thinking?' I don't know what he expected me to do. He yelled at me, and now he's cross with me, and I don't know why." I start crying for real.

"Aroha, honey, he isn't cross with you. He's furious with Blue, and terrified at the thought of you being hurt."

"He's not, he's just worried about Leia…"

"Sweetheart, didn't you hear what he said when he strode up to Blue? He yelled, 'That's my wife!' before he hit him."

I blink and sniffle. "Did he? I didn't hear him."

"He was livid—Henry had to drag him off Blue. I swear, he isn't cross with you." Her expression softens, and she smiles. "He's crazy about you."

"He has a funny way of showing it," I grumble, wiping my face.

"Everyone knows how he feels about you," she says. "We're all just waiting for him to realize it."

I shake my head. "You're wrong. He doesn't have feelings for me, not in that way. I'm sure of it."

"We'll see," she says. "I'll have a word with him."

Chapter Thirty-Four

James

After leaving Aroha in the bath, I change into a tee and track pants, and now I'm sitting on the carpet, fussing Zelda as she tries to lick my face.

"Have you called Ethan yet?" Alex asks.

"No, but I will now that I have my phone, thanks. I'm going to take out a restraining order, so even if he doesn't stay behind bars, he won't be able to come within a mile of either Leia or Aroha. I still can't believe he tried to take Leia, or that he kicked Aroha. The fucking cunt." I glance at Finn. "Sorry."

"He doesn't sound like a nice man," Finn agrees. "Aroha was really brave to hold onto Leia's seat."

"She was." I cover my face with my hands, then slide them into my hair. "She was crazy. Can you imagine if he'd pushed her down the steps?" I shudder at the thought of her falling and hitting her head.

"She's okay, though?" Alex asks.

"I think so. She was pretty shaken up."

"You're as white as a sheet too," Alex says. "I'm going to pour you a whisky."

I don't protest. I sit there on the carpet and watch Finn playing with Zelda while Alex moves around the kitchen, throwing ice in a glass and pouring a small amount of the expensive whisky he brought over it. He brings the glass back and gives it to me.

"What if I have to take her to the hospital?" I ask.

"Ring for an ambulance. Or call me."

I study the glass. "All right." I have a mouthful of the pale amber liquid. Ah, man, I needed that. It shoots down through me, warming the iciness that had filtered through me when I saw Aroha on the ground and Blue looming over her.

We talk for a bit about the legal issues surrounding adoption, and whether we think Blue stands any kind of a chance of adopting Leia. Neither of us is versed in the law. Alex has a more positive view of it than I have after the hassles my mother went through with my father.

"Blue will have scuppered his chances of adopting her," he says. "No judge in his right mind is going to give a baby to a violent drug user."

"He is her birth father, though, when it comes down to it. I'm sure a clever lawyer could spin it—make it seem he was distraught at losing his daughter, and that's why he lost control."

"If it comes to it, I'll testify that I saw the needle marks on his and his partner's arms."

"Did you?"

"No, but you said you did, and I believe you."

"Alex Winters," I tease weakly, "that's the second time you've said you'd lie for me. And I thought you were an honest man."

"I believe in the truth, and that good things should happen to good people. Bruce Clarke is not a good person, and he doesn't deserve baby Leia. It's not what Maddie would have wanted. I don't care that she called him—she named you Leia's guardian, and that's all that matters."

My throat tightens, and I study my whisky before having another mouthful. It means a lot to me that my friends have my back.

Missie walks across the living room and sinks down onto the sofa.

"How is she?" I ask.

"She's okay. Badly bruised, but she insists the ribs aren't broken." She eyes me. "She thinks you're cross with her."

My eyebrows rise. "What? Why?"

"Apparently you yelled at her, asked her what she was thinking when she didn't let go of Leia's seat."

"Well, yeah, but only because I was terrified of her being hurt…"

"James…" She sits on the edge of her seat, looking like the schoolteacher she is, about to give a pupil a lecture. "I think it's time we talked about this situation you've gotten yourself into."

"What do you mean?"

"Marrying Aroha. We all thought it was funny at the time, because we knew how you both felt about each other, but I think she's really screwed up about it."

I brush a hand over my face, thinking about the fact that her parents are going to be furious when they find out the truth. "I know. I've fucked up big time." I'm too exhausted to apologize to Finn again.

"How?" Alex asks.

"All I could think about was keeping Leia, and I was so thrilled that Aroha agreed to help me. I didn't think about what it might mean, and now I've dishonored her, and—"

"Wow," Missie says, "I blinked and ended up in the eighteenth century."

"Don't mock me," I say, conscious of Alex trying not to laugh. "I'm dying a thousand deaths here. I feel really bad."

"You didn't dishonor her," Missie says. "She's your wife, isn't she?"

"No…" I mean to say it wryly, but it just comes out kind of wistful.

"I beg to differ," Alex says. "I definitely saw you exchange rings."

I glance at where it sits, heavy on my finger. "I married her, but she's not my wife. Not in the Biblical sense."

Alex snorts. "Don't go all Old Testament on us. You spent most of your time at university with girls while Tyson, Henry, and I were sitting in the dark, eating family-sized bags of chips and wrestling with computer code. Are you really telling me you can't work out how to seduce the woman you're married to?"

I glare at him. He raises an eyebrow.

"Why don't you just tell her you love her?" Finn suggests helpfully. "Girls like that, apparently."

I flop onto my back on the carpet and cover my face as Zelda tries to stick her tongue up my nose. "It's not as easy as that."

"I kinda think it is," Missie says. "Gaby told me that on her hen night, they played a game where they had to go through all you guys and say which they wanted to kiss, marry, um… sleep with, and…" She bites her lip. "Murder."

"Don't tell me," I say gloomily, "she wanted to murder me."

"Oh… that was definitely not what she wanted to do to you."

Finn giggles.

I lift my hands, push Zelda away, and look at Missie. "Really?"

She smiles. "She's crazy about you, James. When she told us you two were going to have a fake marriage, we said we were going to help her turn it into a real one, and she bloomed like a rose. For God's sake, she loves Leia as if she's her own. You've already tied the knot. What's stopping you from making it real?"

I blink. Making it real?

Is that what I want?

I've done it all back to front. I should have dated her for months, gotten to know her intimately, let her find out all my faults, before I asked her to commit to me for two whole years. But I didn't, and now I'm somehow stuck in the friend-and-boss zone, too afraid to make a move on her in case I screw it all up.

I think of how, on the night of our wedding, she admitted what her ex had done to her, and how it has affected her.

"She's been through so much," I say. "Her ex..." I glance at Finn.

"Finn, why don't you take Zelda out into the garden?" Alex suggests. Finn nods, goes over to the sliding door, and leads the dog out onto the grass. Alex looks back at me.

"Her ex assaulted her," I say softly. "Five years ago, and she hasn't dated since."

"Jesus," Alex says.

Missie looks upset. "Oh no."

"It's affected her deeply," I continue. "And I'm no counselor. I'm like a bull in a china shop. I told her to strip in front of me and get in the bath." Missie winces, and I cover my face again. "I'm such an idiot. I reached out to her in the bathroom, and she flinched. She's terrified of me."

"No, she's not," she scoffs. "She's had a rough day, that's all. And... look, I'm speaking from experience. Women can move on after being assaulted."

My gaze slides to Alex. He returns it calmly. Is she talking about her late husband? I knew that Alex waited a year after her husband died to date her, but I didn't know anything about her marriage.

"You just need to treat her gently," Missie continues. "Be patient and respectful. Lots of hugs and kisses, and don't push her too fast. And Finn's right—tell her you love her, and all will be well."

"Chocolate helps," Alex says.

Missie nods. "Definitely."

"She said she trusts me," I murmur.

They both smile. "Of course she does," Missie says. "You're one of the good guys, James. I think you forget that sometimes." She laughs. "You look so surprised. Come on. You've dedicated your life to making equipment to help people walk again. You're kind and generous, warm and funny. Are you really so surprised that Aroha's in love with you?"

"In love?"

"Of course." She sighs. "Silly boy."

I think about my father, and the way he brought me up to believe that men should be hard, unyielding, and ambitious. How he made me feel that I was weak to show emotion, or a failure if I admitted I'd done something wrong. Talk about toxic masculinity.

"Talk to her," Alex says. "Be open and honest. It's the only way."

I look up at the ceiling. Will she listen? Or have I waited too long?

"Why are you lying on the floor?" Aroha's face appears above me, upside down.

I sit up quickly and turn around to look at her. She's in the white bathrobe I left for her, and barefoot.

"How are you feeling?" I ask.

"I'm okay. A little sore, but not too bad."

"I'll find you an ice pack." I get to my feet.

"We'll head off," Alex says, going over to the sliding doors and gesturing to Finn. "I just wanted to drop off your phone and make sure you were okay. Call me if you need anything, okay?"

"I will."

Zelda comes bounding in, but Finn has clipped on her lead and restrains her as she approaches Aroha.

"Zelda, sit!" he declares, and the puppy obediently puts her bottom on the ground.

"Good girl." Aroha bends and fusses her. I note that she winces as she moves, though, so she's obviously still sore.

"Come on." Alex leads the way to the door. Missie gives us both a kiss on the cheek, and murmurs something to Aroha before she heads out, and I close the door behind them.

Aroha blushes.

"What did she say?" I ask, amused, as we head back into the kitchen.

"Nothing."

I purse my lips. She meets my eyes, then drops her gaze again and fiddles with the tie of her robe.

"All right," I say softly. "Let's get your ice pack."

I retrieve it from where I keep it in the freezer for sports injuries, and wrap a tea towel around it. "Have a seat out on the deck," I tell her. "I want to talk to you. And I'm going to pour you a small whisky. I think you need it."

Her eyes have widened, but she doesn't say anything as she heads out. I avert my gaze as she tucks the ice pack into the robe and curls up in the corner of the sofa on the deck, and concentrate on pouring her drink. Then I take it out, along with Leia's monitor, so we can hear when she wakes up.

"Can you do me a favor?" Aroha whispers as I put the glass and monitor on the table.

"Of course."

"Can you check that Leia's okay?"

I go to tell her that she's fine, but I can see the fear in her eyes, so I just nod. "Okay." I walk back through the house. I've just entered the west wing when my phone rings in my pocket.

I take it out and look at the screen—it's Ethan. I answer it. "Ethan? I was going to call you."

"I've just spoken to Blue's lawyer," he replies. "Do you know Terry Campbell? He's been at the police station. Terry knows that Blue's fucked up big time. The fact that you've gotten married, followed by his antics today, has blown up in his face. Terry has advised him to drop his claim for custody."

Joy flows through me. "Jesus. That's fantastic."

"He said that Blue isn't interested in Leia. He's even saying he's probably not the father, as he's not on the birth certificate, and if he's not getting any money, he doesn't want anything to do with her."

"Fine by me," I say.

"Yeah. Basically, he knows that all a court case is going to do is cost him a fortune. So Terry has put forward a suggestion—that Blue relinquishes any attempt to name himself Leia's guardian, and that he drops his application for a Parenting Order or adoption. He'll even sign a document stating as much."

"What does he want in return?"

"That you drop all charges and don't take out a restraining order, so he doesn't get a police record. And that you pay him a significant sum of money."

"How significant?"

"A hundred thousand."

I grit my teeth. It goes against the grain to give the man anything. But if it means it makes sure he has no claim on Leia…

323

"I want the document to state that he's not going to come anywhere near Leia or Aroha again," I tell Ethan.

"Fair enough. And regarding the money, we can probably get that sum reduced, and—"

"No, it's fine. I'll do it to get him out of my hair."

"You're sure?"

"Yep. Draw it up. I'll come in tomorrow and sign it."

"All right. I'll get going on it now."

"So… it's over?"

"Looks like it." Ethan's tone suggests he's smiling.

I blow out a long breath. "Thank you."

"You're welcome. I'm just sorry you had to go through this today. How are mum and baby?"

I smile at his use of 'mum'. "Leia's fine. Aroha has bruised ribs where Blue kicked her."

"Jesus. Fucking bastard."

"Yeah," I say vehemently. "But she's okay. And she'll be thrilled to know it means Leia is… ours." I tingle at the word.

"All right. I'll email the document to you when it's done for you to check over."

"Thanks, Ethan. Bye."

I end the call and stand there for a moment. Then I walk through to Leia's bedroom, and go over to her bassinet. She's fine—sleeping soundly, her skin a healthy pink, blowing bubbles as she breathes.

I lean on the side of the bassinet and look down at her. For the first time, I let myself believe that she's really going to be mine.

Mine and Aroha's.

We'll be Leia's mummy and daddy.

I swallow hard. My father was wrong. He might have tried to teach me to keep my heart out of things, but I can't do that. I loved Maddie, I love Leia, and I love Aroha.

I love Aroha. It's true. Or at least, I'm in love with her. I know it's not been long, but I love everything about her. The way she forgave me for falling asleep on her in bed. How she immediately said she'd help with Leia when I found out Maddie had died. How she agreed to marry me, even though she knew it would upset her parents, and it also went against her own beliefs of marriage, because she knew it would help me get custody of Leia.

AROHA AND THE BILLIONAIRE BOSS

I love how she looked after me on the day of the funeral. And how she's been a mother to Leia in everything but name. It's only now that I realize how I thought I wanted someone like Cassie, who's wealthy and accomplished, who enjoys travel and parties and is successful in business, and who's semi-famous on social media, with hundreds of friends.

But I don't. Aroha's beautiful and smart, but she's so gentle and kind. She's a homebird, happy cooking, playing guitar, reading, and doing crafts. I didn't value those things before, but I do now. She and Leia have made my house into a home, something I never thought would happen.

I didn't think I wanted children, and I'm still not sure I want my own, but I have Leia, and I'm excited at the thought of being there when she grows up. Of showing her all the wonderful things the world has to offer. Her innocence has cleansed me of much of my cynicism—not all, I acknowledge, but I think I'll get better. Who could remain cynical and pessimistic when faced with beauty like this?

As I look at her, she stirs and opens her eyes. She blinks as she looks up at me, and then she gives me the most beautiful smile. My eyes sting, and my throat tightens as I say, "Hello baby girl."

I lift her up into my arms, and she snuffles and buries her face in my shirt. I chuckle. "Are you hungry? Why don't we change you and make you a bottle, eh?"

I haven't changed her on my own before, so that's a challenge, but I manage it, and I lift her up again afterward, ridiculously pleased. I take her out into the living room and through to the deck.

"Well done," Aroha teases, and I grin and lower Leia into her arms.

"Are you okay to hold her without it hurting too badly?" I ask.

"It's okay if I rest my arm on the cushion." She nestles back.

"I'll make a bottle," I tell her, "and then I've got a few things to discuss with you."

I head into the kitchen, my heart lifting, and start to spoon the formula into the bottle.

Are you really telling me you can't work out how to seduce the woman you're married to?

My lips curve up. Okay, Alex. Challenge accepted.

Chapter Thirty-Five

Aroha

My heart races as I wait for James to return with the bottle. What's he going to say?

When Missie left, she murmured to me, "Don't worry, I've put him straight," but I didn't have a chance to ask what she meant by that. I'm still reeling from her announcement that James is crazy about me. *Everyone knows how he feels about you. We're all just waiting for him to realize it.* I heard him shout something at Blue, but was it really 'That's my wife!'?

I feel emotional and all over the place. I guess that's not unusual, considering what kind of a day I've had. It's impossible for it not to stir up all the feelings I had after my ex assaulted me. Fear, fury, embarrassment, shame, resentment, and hate. But I don't want to be ruled by such negative emotions.

Leia lifts a hand, and I kiss her tiny fingers, trying to hold in my tears. Right now, she's not aware of anything negative in the world. She doesn't understand darkness or fear or pain. For her there's only light and promise. I hold her tightly, trying to let her beauty wash over me and wipe all the bad memories away.

"Here." James has returned, and he holds out the bottle.

I take it, knowing he'll have tested the temperature, and tease Leia's lips with the teat. She opens her mouth, and soon the air is filled with the sound of her gentle sucking.

I wait for him to sit in the armchair opposite, where he normally sits when we're out here on the deck, but to my surprise he sits beside me on the sofa. I turn and prop my feet on the coffee table, making more space, not disappointed when he moves a little closer. I look at his strong, bare feet, brown from the sun. I find them really attractive. That's odd. I've never considered myself to have a foot fetish before.

I look back up at him to see his bright turquoise eyes focused on me. To my relief, he gives me a mischievous smile. He's not cross with me anymore, then.

"I've just spoken to Ethan," he says.

"Oh?"

"He's in the process of drawing up a document that I'm going to sign tomorrow. I'm going to promise to drop all charges and not take out a restraining order, so Blue won't get a police record. I'm also going to pay him a large sum of money."

I stare at him, shocked. "Seriously?"

"In return," he says softly, "Blue will agree to relinquish any attempt to name himself Leia's guardian, and he'll drop his application for custody and adoption." He smiles. "Leia's ours."

My jaw drops.

We stare at each other for a long, long time.

My heart is soaring. Blue has obviously realized he's blown any chance of adopting Leia. This way he'll get the money, which is what he wanted, and we get Leia.

"I'm so sorry he attacked you today," James says. "I'd do anything if I could rewind time and make it so that hadn't happened. The only comfort I can give you is that because you were so brave, you've made it so that Blue will never have a claim on her."

My bottom lip trembles, and I look down at Leia, who stares back up at me with big, trusting eyes so like her uncle's.

No, her father's. Her eyes are just like her father's.

"Did you hear what I said?" James adds. "Leia's *ours*." He emphasizes the last word.

Ours. Not mine.

"I've been an idiot," he murmurs. "I've done everything back to front, and made a complete hash of things. I should have asked you out and dated you properly. And I should have asked you to marry me for love, not for money. In my defense, I did it for Leia. But it's affected me in ways I never imagined."

I frown. "What do you mean?"

He lifts his left hand up and examines it thoughtfully. "It's just a metal ring. A symbol of a contract. That's what I thought." He looks at my hand then where I'm holding Leia, and he reaches out and touches the gold band on my finger. "Today, when I was crossing the lobby and I saw you on the floor and Blue standing over you, all I could think was that you were my wife. And I felt this incredible surge of protectiveness for you and Leia."

I can barely breathe. Around me, the summer day continues—fantails twittering in the lemon trees, the sound of a lawnmower in the distance, music playing faintly where Nick is cleaning the pool. But here, on the deck, with James, it feels as if time has stopped.

He takes a deep breath. "I've fallen in love with you." He stops, then gives a short laugh and murmurs, "Turns out it *was* that simple."

"Sorry?"

"Nothing." He smiles. "I've fallen in love with you, Aroha Rutherford." His smile broadens at the use of my married name. "I know when I asked you to marry me, I said it would be in name only. And I'll understand if you want it to stay that way. I know I've been an arsehole, and that I have no idea how women's hearts work. But I want to say that I'd like to be married properly."

I finally remember to breathe, and I inhale deeply, then exhale. My head is spinning. "What do you mean?"

He tips his head to the side and reaches out to remove a thread from my robe. "When you feel better… when you're ready…" He lifts his gaze to mine again. "I'd like us to be married for real."

"You mean…"

His gaze drops to my mouth.

My lips part. "Oh…"

He looks back up. "Only when you're ready," he says sternly. "If you want, we can start all over again. Begin dating for real. Go out for dinner, to the theater. Get to know one another first. And then, when it's time… We can consummate the marriage." He chuckles.

I swallow hard. "I don't think I'm a bad nanny, but I know I'm not the sort of woman you'd choose for a wife, James. Are you only saying this because you're stuck with me?"

He looks startled. "What? No!"

"I'm not a businesswoman. I don't wear expensive, fashionable clothes. I don't have thousands of followers on Instagram."

"If you're trying to say that you're not Cassie, I'm very much relieved. I've fallen for you because of who you are. You're kind and gentle. And really, really hot."

That takes me by surprise and makes me laugh, and he grins.

I press my fingers to my lips as tears spill over my lashes. "Do you mean it?"

His expression softens. "Of course I mean it. I'm just sorry it's taken me so long to say it."

I can't brush the tears away because I'm holding Leia, so he picks up a muslin square and wipes my cheeks gently.

"Alex said we need to be open and honest," he says, "and I know he's right. I'm not used to being like that. My father brought me up to believe a man should deal with his emotions himself, and not air his dirty laundry in public. But I don't believe that anymore. And I want to learn how to talk about things with you. If that's what you'd like, too."

I press my lips together and nod hastily. "I'd like that."

He looks relieved. Then he glances at Leia. "So, do you think you'd like to be Leia's mum? To help me bring her up?"

"Very much," I squeak.

His brows draw together. "You're sure?"

I nod, trying to hold my tears in.

He looks emotional too. "Can I kiss you?" he asks, his voice husky.

I nod again.

He moves a little closer to me, putting his arm around my shoulders. Leia continues to suck and look up at us as he slides his other hand into my hair. He holds my head, then lowers his lips to mine.

It's an innocent kiss, gentle and caring, but it lights a spark inside me that flares and warms me all the way through, as if I've swallowed a piece of summer. It feels like the start of something wonderful, and I can't believe my luck.

He lifts his head and studies me. "You have the softest mouth."

I feel as if I've looked at the sun bouncing off metal, and all I can see is bright light. "Kiss me again," I murmur, sliding down a little on the sofa, nestling in his arms.

So he does. While Leia drinks her milk, and the fantails jump across the deck, he kisses me leisurely, his lips moving across mine, until eventually I feel his tongue brush my bottom lip. I open my mouth and allow him access, and his tongue slides against mine, teasing, gentle, firing all my nerve endings, and leaving me full of tingles and sighs.

*

The doctor arrives just after five. A little shy to strip off in the living room, I take him into the bedroom and remove my robe. He takes his time inspecting my elbow and ribs.

"I don't think anything's broken," he tells me. "Just bruised. Continue to use the ice packs for a few days, take regular painkillers, and you should see some improvement by next week. If you have any trouble breathing, though, or the pain gets worse, you need to go to the hospital straight away."

He repeats the instruction to James when we return to the living room. "Will do," James says firmly. He sees him to the door, and they exchange a few words quietly before the doctor finally leaves.

"What did he say?" I ask when James comes back in.

"That you have to do everything I say."

I give him a wry look. He smirks. "I'm going to cook dinner now," he says. "Go and make yourself comfortable."

With a fresh ice pack, I retreat to the living room, and I sit and play with Leia while James cooks pasta with a tomato sauce. It's delicious, and he gives a delightful, bashful smile when I compliment him.

Afterward, he helps me bathe, dry, and dress Leia, and then he gives her the last feed before placing her in her bassinet.

She doesn't even bother grizzling tonight when we leave—she's asleep in seconds.

"What would you like to do?" James asks. "Watch a movie?"

"Actually, I'm nearly dead on my feet. I might go to bed now, too. Would you mind?"

"Of course not." He pulls me into his arms and hugs me. I bury my face in his tee. Part of me had hoped he'd invite me into his bed, but he doesn't. He does kiss me, though. He cups my face and searches my eyes, then lowers his lips to mine in a gentle kiss with a touch of heat in it, like the dash of chili he put in the pasta sauce.

Eventually, though, he wishes me goodnight and disappears into the east wing.

I go back to my half of the house. It's dark and quiet, and a ripple of nervousness runs down my spine. Blue won't come here, I scoff, he wouldn't dare, but even so, I catch myself glancing in the dark corners, and jumping at the slightest sounds.

Quickly, I change into my pajama top and shorts, check on Leia, do my teeth, then get into bed. While we were watching the movie, James gave me one last ice pack, two Panadol, and a couple of codeine because I was sore. The codeine worked, and I feel sleepy now, and I curl up around a pillow.

I can't imagine I'll be able to sleep after the events of the day. The image of Blue standing over me, face filled with anger as he kicks me, blooms in my head, but I push it away and think instead about James. *I've fallen for you because of who you are. You're kind and gentle. And really, really hot.*

It's a lovely thing to say, and I'm filled with joy at the thought that he wants to try to make this marriage work. But it's impossible not to feel anxious about it all.

He's young, and gorgeous, and I'm sure he's used to sleeping with girls who are confident and knowledgeable in bed. I'm not a virgin, but I'm not exactly swinging from the chandeliers either. I haven't had sex for ages because of the vaginismus.

He did comment that he didn't notice when we went back to his hotel, and it's true that because we spent a long time kissing, I half forgot my nerves. So maybe, if we take time, everything will be okay.

How patient is he likely to be? And what if it happens while I'm with him? I cuddle the pillow, wincing at the pain in my side. He might have signed the marriage contract, but he didn't sign up for this. I wish I could just be normal. I like him so much.

Despite my fears, I'm exhausted. My eyelids flutter closed, and in less than a minute, I doze off.

When I jerk awake, it's completely dark. The duvet is twisted around me, and I feel hot and sticky. I was in the middle of a nightmare, and I feel relieved to be back in the land of the living. Something was chasing me down darkened corridors, and I could feel its hot breath on the back of my neck.

I sit up and realize that I'm not just sticky because of sweat—my elbow has bled through the gauze, leaving dark patches on the sheet. Dammit. Now I'm going to have to change the bed. I check my phone—it's nearly midnight. In the other room, Leia grizzles. That's probably what woke me.

Rising, I stretch and sigh, sore and stiff, and walk through to her room. She's really wailing now, hungry and tired. I lean over to pick her up, then cry out. It hurts too much to lift her. I didn't think of that. Shit. What do I do now?

I need to change her and feed her, but I'm not sure if I can get her out of the bassinet. I try again, but a dull ache spreads across my ribs, and I grunt with pain. No, it's not going to work. I'm going to have to go and wake James.

I turn, and walk straight into someone. I hadn't heard them come into the room, and I squeal before I can think better of it.

"Hey, it's me." James holds me by my upper arms. "I'm sorry, I didn't mean to make you jump. I heard you on the baby monitor—it's still switched on." He bends his head to look at me. "Are you okay?"

"My elbow's bleeding." I press trembling fingers to my lips. "I was having a nightmare. And it hurts too much to lift Leia out of her bassinet." I'm usually so calm and collected. Why am I so emotional and useless right now?

He thinks for a moment, then says, "All right. I'll change Leia, then I'll make her a bottle. Go and clean up your elbow."

I go into the bathroom, swallowing hard and trying not to cry. Don't be such a wuss! I take off the soggy dressing, clean my elbow as best I can, then put a fresh dressing on it.

When I come out, James and Leia have gone. I walk through and discover them in the kitchen, where he's putting the bottle in the warmer. The living room is dark, lit by a single lamp. A book rests on the coffee table. He must have been reading.

He's holding Leia, and she's sucking on a dummy, eyes wide as she snuggles up to him.

"I need to change the bed," I say.

"Tomorrow," he states. "You're both coming to bed with me."

Relief floods me, and I don't argue.

He retrieves a tumbler from the cupboard, takes out a bottle of brandy, unscrews the top with one hand, and splashes a small amount into the glass. Then he holds it out to me. "You look like a ghost," he says. "Drink this."

I take it and down the spirit in one. It sears through me, and I cough.

He nods. "That'll do the job."

The bottle warmer beeps, and he retrieves the bottle, shakes it, then gestures with his head for me to follow him. "Come on."

As we walk, he says, "How's the pain?"

"Seven out of ten." It was six earlier.

"You're not short of breath though?"

"No. I think it's just the bruise coming out."

He stops by the bathroom. "Take two Nurofen."

"Yes, Dad."

He lifts an eyebrow. "Go on."

Muttering, I do as he says while he watches. Then I follow him into his bedroom.

He flicks on a lamp, then pulls back the duvet. "Get in." After I slide beneath the cover, he places Leia beside me and hands me the bottle. I take out her dummy, and she starts drinking straight away.

"I'll just lock up," he says. He disappears, and I snuggle down. A whisper of his cologne rises from his sheets.

I hear him moving about the house, checking and locking doors and windows. Eventually he comes back in and closes the door. "Do you need anything else before I get in?" he asks.

I shake my head.

He goes into the en suite bathroom for a few minutes, then comes back out. I watch him grab a handful of his tee at the back of his neck, tug it over his head, and toss it over the chair, then run a hand through his hair. Muscles ripple in his arms and torso. Mmm, he's so gorgeous. He pushes his track pants over his hips and takes them off, too, and then, in just his black boxer-briefs, he slides beneath the duvet.

"I'm sorry you had a nightmare," he says, moving closer to Leia. He props his head on an elbow, then holds the bottle for me. I pull my arms closer to me, wincing at the pain.

"Before I went to sleep, I kept thinking about Blue," I whisper. "I had the horrible thought that he might try to break in and get Leia."

"He won't. He doesn't have any interest in Leia. He only wants the money. Tomorrow he and I are meeting at Ethan's office with his lawyer to sign the document, and I'll transfer the money over then."

"How much are you paying him?"

"A hundred thousand. Ethan said he thought he could get the price down, but I'd rather give him all of it and keep him off our backs."

I swallow hard. "I just hope I'm worth it."

He frowns. "What do you mean?"

"I'm sure you didn't think I'd be this high maintenance when you suggested we get married."

Humor lights his eyes. "You think this is high maintenance? Aroha, you're the least high maintenance woman I've ever met. All this is nothing to do with you. Jesus, you're not even complaining after being kicked in the ribs twice. I'd be in a hospital bed asking for morphine if I was in your position."

I give a short laugh, and he smiles and says, "That's better. By the way, part of the document states that he's not to come within a mile of either you or Leia. I should have told you that."

My eyebrows rise. "Oh."

"There's also the code on the gate, and the walls around the grounds are very high. There are visible security cameras everywhere, so anyone who broke in would know they were being captured on film. But if you're still worried, I'll hire a security firm to patrol the grounds."

That makes me smile. "You needn't do that."

"I would, if it'll make you feel better."

"I know."

"The safety of you and Leia is all that matters to me now." His eyes meet mine, shining in the light of the lamp. "My wife and daughter." He gives an impish smile. Then he says, firmly, "Anyone who wants to get to either of you is going to have to come through me now." He looks determined. Then he says, "You're mine now, and no other man is going to touch you."

I lift my gaze to his as a shiver runs down my spine. I suppose I should bristle at his possessive tone, but I don't. It makes me weak at the knees.

I want to kiss him. I want to make this marriage real. I've wanted him for so long, and now he's mine, and he's like one of those chocolate fountains that you're supposed to dip strawberries in, but I just want to lie my head under it and let it coat me all over.

"Tomorrow," he says, "we're going to convert the bedroom next to this one into the nursery. I'll move the bassinet in there, and I'll bring her change table and all the rest of her stuff through."

"What about me?"

He rolls his eyes. "You're going to sleep in here with me."

My eyes widen. It feels like Christmas Day, my birthday, and Valentine's Day have all come at once.

His lips slowly curve up. "No," he says.

"No what?"

"No, we're not going to have sex."

"What, never?"

"For a while," he clarifies. I blow out a breath, and he chuckles. "I don't want to make love to you and have to worry about hurting your ribs."

"I'll be fine."

"Yes, you will be, because we're not doing it." He looks at Leia. Her eyelids are drooping. I remove the teat from her mouth, and James says, "I'll do it." He sits up and lifts her, and she snuggles up to his shoulder.

I watch him as he rubs her back.

"Don't sulk," he says.

I poke my tongue out at him.

He grins and kisses Leia's head. "Everything I knew about babies were horror stories from movies and other dads about screaming and bad smells and getting no sleep. But nobody mentioned this part. The feeding in the night. The quiet cuddles. How damn beautiful she is." She gives a big burp, and he laughs. "That's my girl."

I smile as he lowers her back between us. He leans across to turn out the light, then settles down.

We look at each other in the moonlight.

"How long is a while?" I ask.

"A few weeks."

"Weeks!" I stare at him, aghast.

He tries not to laugh. "I'm not going against the doctor's advice."

"What does he know?"

He chuckles. He's obviously determined not to give in.

Hmm. I'll have to see what I can do about that.

He lifts a hand, touches two fingers to his lips, then presses them to mine. "Go to sleep."

I know nothing's going to happen tonight. But tomorrow is a whole new day.

Dutifully, I close my eyes, and I sleep soundly for the rest of the night.

SERENITY WOODS

Chapter Thirty-Six

James

The next day, Gaby comes over in the morning and stays with Aroha while I go to Ethan's office. I meet Blue and his lawyer, Terry, there. Blue has a large bruise on his cheekbone where I hit him. He meets my eyes, and I smirk. I don't speak to him, though, and he doesn't say a word either. The two lawyers talk, we sign the document, and then I transfer the money over to Blue's account on my phone. When it's done, Blue walks out without another word.

I feel a wave of relief, and a lightening of my heart. He's gone, and I doubt I'll hear from him again. I shake hands with Ethan, who informs me that we should hear about the Parenting Order soon, and then he'll help me start the adoption process.

I walk out of the office a new man.

In celebration, I decide to take the following week off work—the first time I've done so for ages. Tyson and Henry are back from the conference, which went great, and as the guys are there to cover, and the rest of January will be quiet in the office, I know I won't miss much.

It's not just to look after Aroha and Leia. I feel the need for a break. I need to really deal with Maddie's death before I put it behind me. And I also need to get to know my new wife and child. It's a huge change for me, and a big adjustment in the way I view my life. I'm no longer James the bachelor, the playboy with no ties. I'm a married man with a baby, and I haven't had the preparation that most men have—of watching their wife get pregnant, of seeing their child born. Leia is starting to wind her way around my heart, but I know I need time for love to sink in.

In the afternoon, I take down the bassinet and transfer it into the room next to mine, then spend a while moving the change table and all the other paraphernalia down there. Afterward, I carry Aroha's clothes through and help her put them in the wardrobe I've emptied in my room for her. She doesn't have many. I know she's left some at her parents' place, but even so… I announce that I'm going to buy her a whole new wardrobe, a hundred pairs of shoes, and lots of expensive jewelry.

"I'd love a pearl necklace," she says.

"Jesus." I blow out a breath at the thought.

"I'm serious. Don't you think it would look nice? A row of shiny pearls, right across here…" She draws a semi-circle across her throat, giving me an innocent look.

I sigh. I'm enjoying being with her, but I didn't expect it to be such torture.

Yesterday, when I saw Josh, the doctor, to the door, I asked him how long it would take her to recover.

"Just be careful with any bedroom gymnastics for a week or two," he teased.

I almost blushed, and he laughed as he walked out. But his words made me determined to wait until she's healed before we have sex.

Aroha, however, seems to have other ideas.

I have the vague feeling that I'm being seduced. She's very subtle about it. But it's her eyes. She looks at me as if she's constantly thinking about doing erotic things to me. She's doing it right now. Her words were innocent, but her eyes are suggesting she's thinking about something much saucier.

"Stop it," I scold.

"I'm not doing anything," she replies. But her lips curve up, and I have to stifle a groan.

Every time I walk past her, she looks at me as if she can see right through my clothes, and it's impossible not to stop, slide my arms around her, and nuzzle her neck. I do it gently, so as not to hurt her ribs, but the way she sighs and tips her head to the side sends tingles all the way through me.

And when she lifts her arms around my neck and rises on tiptoes to kiss me, it pushes my willpower to its limits. Her lips are so soft, and the way her tongue teases mine makes my head spin.

That evening, after we've put Leia down in her bassinet, we watch a movie together. Aroha curls up beside me, and I put my arm around her, and we proceed to make out for the length of the movie.

Afterward, I can't recall a single thing about it. All I can remember is kissing her, and the heat in her eyes every time I looked at her.

That night, for the first time, we have the bed to ourselves.

We brush our teeth together, then slide beneath the duvet—she in her pajama top and shorts, me in my boxers.

She lies back, her brown hair spilling over the pillow like chocolate-colored satin.

"Well, well," she says. "What shall we do now to entertain ourselves?"

I'm determined not to give in. She's had ice packs on and off all day, and she's taken regular painkillers, but I know she's still in a lot of pain.

Still, it doesn't mean I can't kiss her, right? So I don't fight her off when she snuggles up to me, and I slide a hand into her hair and hold her gently with my other arm while we indulge in a long, sensual kiss.

Then I sigh, lean back, switch off the light, and say, "Turn over."

Her eyes widen. "Seriously?"

"I told you. We're going to wait until you're better."

Her jaw drops. Then she turns away from me, gingerly, so I know I'm making the right decision. She heaves a big, sulky sigh, though, letting me know her disapproval.

I stifle a chuckle and move closer to her, wrapping my arms around her, and she nestles back against me. Her hair smells of mint again, and her perfume is something spicy and musky... I stifle a groan.

"Are you sure you don't want to?" she murmurs. She wiggles her butt in my lap, obviously feeling my erection.

I stuff the duvet between us. "Stop tempting me."

"James..."

I kiss her ear. "No. Now go to sleep."

*

The next two days follow a similar pattern. As hard as it is to keep our hands off each other, we spend the time together, talking, which was what we should have done in the beginning.

We have a picnic in the garden one afternoon—we sit on a blanket on the lawn, under the shade of an angled umbrella, and eat sandwiches and strawberries while we listen to music and talk. The next day, we drive to the beach and walk along the water line in bare feet, holding hands. Aroha makes sure Leia has a sunhat and is covered in sunscreen. I carry her in the baby carrier on my chest, facing outwards, and she's fascinated by the sound of the sea and the seagulls swooping overhead.

In the evenings, we watch movies while we make out, teasing each other with kisses until we're both sighing. And then we go to bed, and I wrestle with my self-control as I insist she turns over and goes to sleep.

I last for three days.

On day four, we sit at the dining table to eat dinner. Aroha, protesting she feels better, has cooked us a stir fry. Leia, now able to sit upright on her own, sits in her highchair with a couple of toys.

I tuck into my dinner, then stop, my fork halfway to my mouth, as I look at Aroha and see her watching me while she eats.

Her eyes are undressing me again.

I close my mouth around the piece of chicken, then chew while I lift an eyebrow.

"Stop it," I scold, my phrase of the moment.

"I'm only eating my dinner." She has a mouthful of rice, but her gaze, as it slides down me while she eats, is hotter than lava.

"You make me feel naked," I complain, fighting the urge to cover myself up.

She snorts. "I should be so lucky."

I give a short laugh. "I'm not taking my clothes off at the dinner table. The last thing I want is to find a fork in my sausage."

That makes her giggle, and soon we're both laughing. Leia joins in and bangs her rattle on the tray.

"It's so warm in here, though," Aroha states, getting up to take our empty plates to the kitchen.

I pick up Leia's rattle when she throws it on the floor. "Want me to turn up the aircon?"

"No, it's okay," Aroha says. "I'll just take this off."

She's wearing a short dress made of T-shirt material. My eyes almost fall out of my head as she lifts it up her body and over her head, then drops it to the floor.

She's wearing a pretty cream teddy. Oh, checkmate, Aroha. It's incredibly sexy, but it covers the bruising on her side.

"That's sneaky," I tell her.

She brings back two glass dishes of dessert she's made—Tiramisu, no less—places mine before me, then slides back into her seat. She scoops up a spoonful, then eats it, her eyes dancing.

I narrow my eyes. The material of the teddy clings to her breasts, and her nipples protrude through like two buttons. "Are you cold?" I ask, somewhat sulkily.

She glances down at herself, then looks back at me, amused. She doesn't attempt to cover herself up.

I give her a helpless look. "I'm only doing what the doctor said."

"And I'm very touched. I'm not trying to entice you. It's hot, that's all." She points at my dish. "Eat your dessert."

I glare at her. "Tiramisu?"

"I was going to give you oysters and asparagus, but I thought that might have been a bit obvious."

I give a short laugh and delve my spoon into the dessert. "Why is this supposed to be an aphrodisiac? I mean, it tastes fantastic, but…"

"It was invented inside Italian brothels," she says. "It was served to reinvigorate exhausted clients. Especially after orgies." She turns her spoon upside down and sucks it, her eyes fixed on mine.

I purse my lips. Then I have another spoonful. "You're a temptress."

"Is it working?"

"A little bit."

We both laugh, but it's true. I've kept my desire locked away over the past few weeks, but now I feel like a lazy bear waking up after hibernating. Everything's stirring, and it's difficult not to groan as an internal battle wages between my conscience and my lust.

When we've finished the dessert, she says, "Bath time," to Leia. Then she lifts her out of the highchair.

"Careful," I say. I've been lifting Leia for her the last few days.

"I told you, I feel much better," she teases. Then she walks away, still just in her teddy, murmuring to Leia, and leaving me with the view of her beautiful bottom.

I return the dishes to the kitchen and put them in the dishwasher. Tidy up a bit and wipe down the counter.

Then I give in and follow her to the bathroom.

I lean against the door jamb and sigh at the sight of her bending over the bath. "Let me," I scold, kneeling beside her to hold Leia.

She leans on the side of the bath, her arms touching mine. "You should take your T-shirt off," she suggests. "So it doesn't get wet."

I give her an amused look, and she giggles, but it's impossible to resist her, so I strip off my tee and toss it away, then continue supporting Leia as she sits there and splashes in the water, playing with the rubber ducks and other toys. I'm conscious of Aroha's heated gaze on my skin like lasers.

"You have a beautiful body," she says, brushing her fingers down my back.

I shiver.

"Sorry," she murmurs, not stopping. "Is that not nice?"

I lean on the bath and run a wet hand through my hair, her touch firing every nerve ending in my body. Leia splashes me, and I sigh. "You two are determined to make life a misery."

"Does this make you miserable, then?" Aroha strokes down my back.

I lower down, resting my chin on my hand on the side of the bath, supporting Leia with my other. "No," I mumble.

So she continues, stroking up my side, across my shoulder, and then down my back again, her fingers feather light. She circles them around the nape of my neck and draws them up into my hair, making my scalp tingle.

I know I should be the one doing the seducing, but the way she's touching me is so innocent, and yet so erotic, I can't bear for her to stop. I want to kiss her. I want to take her in my arms and feel her soft body against mine. But I'm not taking my eyes off Leia while she's in the water.

"I should get Leia out," I say eventually, my voice husky.

"Mmm." She leans forward and kisses my shoulder. "I'll go prepare her bottle."

I sigh as she leaves the room, then get the towel ready and lift Leia out onto it. I dry and powder her, then wrestle her into a onesie before picking her up and taking her through to the living room.

Aroha's just removing the bottle from the warmer, and we go over to the sofa, where she sits and starts to feed Leia.

I sit beside her, and she nestles up close and looks up at me with those eyes that beg me to do wicked things to her.

So I kiss her. Slowly, languorously, taking my time. I kiss from one corner of her mouth to the other, then up her cheek, across her eyebrows, and back down her nose to her mouth.

She parts her lips, and her tongue slides against mine, slow and sensual, and I sigh, knowing I'm nearly beaten.

"I don't want to hurt you," I murmur, cupping her face.

She looks into my eyes, and hers are gentle. "I know. And if you'd really rather wait, that's okay. But I feel better. My ribs are tender, but not painful now. If you don't mind… um… taking it slow… you know… taking our time…"

That does it. The thought of making love to her slowly, drawing out our pleasure, makes me crumble.

"Well, I've had blue balls for, like, two hours now, so I don't think I'm going to be able to resist you any longer."

Her eyes flare. "Oh…"

"How's Leia doing?"

She looks at the bottle. "Nearly done."

I wait until all the milk has gone, then take Leia from her and hold her against my shoulder, and we go through to Leia's room. We're going to paint it over the next few days, because Aroha wanted to do it herself, so we've already made a few marks on the walls where we're going to put stickers, and the pots of paint sit in the corner, ready for us to start.

After a few minutes and a final cuddle from us both, I put Leia down in her bassinet. Aroha closes the curtains and sets her mobile playing, and then we go out, taking her monitor with us.

We go into the living room, laughing as Leia talks to herself for a bit. "I wonder if she'll say Mama or Dada first," I tease.

Aroha flushes and slides her arms around me. "You really want her to call me Mummy? I don't mind if you'd prefer Aroha."

I shake my head. "We're married. If I'm her Daddy, you're her Mummy."

She smiles and nods. "Okay."

I look away, out of the window at the garden. It's been a gorgeous summer, hot and sunny most days. In the evenings, the late sun turns the lawn to gold and floods the living room with treacle-colored light. The sliding doors are open, and I can smell the lavender and jasmine growing around the base of the deck.

I feel unbelievably happy, full of hope and anticipation. I haven't felt like this for a long, long time, maybe ever.

I look back at the beautiful woman standing before me. Her hair is down today, and it shines like chocolate silk. Her mouth with its full bottom lip looks soft as rose petals. Her big eyes stare up into mine, a little worried, I think, that I'm going to change my mind.

Taking my phone out of my pocket, I bring up Spotify, choose Khalid's *Outta My Head*, turn it up to max, and start it playing. It's slow and sultry, with a mesmerizing beat, and Aroha's eyes light up.

Without saying anything, I slide my hands around her, and she lifts her arms up around my neck.

We begin to move to the beat, and I tighten my arms, keeping her hips close to mine. It takes me back to the night before Damon's wedding, when we danced to Paua of One and Nine Inch Nails. We've come a long way since then—we've gotten to know one another better, and we've grown so much closer. She's helped me through those terrible first few days of grief, and she's been there for me continually, a raft I could cling to when I felt as if everything was going to sweep me away.

As Khalid tells us there's romance in the atmosphere, we move together, and the hazy air seems to sparkle with promise.

She slides her hands into my hair and pulls my head down, and I kiss her obediently. "I can't get you outta my head," I murmur. "I don't know how you've done it, but you're all I've been able to think about for weeks."

"I'm in love with you," she whispers. "I think I have been for a long time. I've tried to ignore it, but you're all I want."

"My wife."

"My husband."

We both chuckle. She's still wearing the silky teddy, and my hands slide over her body to hold her hips as they wind close to mine.

She kisses me, pressing up against me, and I brush my hands lightly over her bruised side and up to her breasts, cupping them for the first time. She murmurs her approval, arching her back to push them into my hands, making my heart race. Her nipples are soft, but as I tease them with the pads of my thumbs, they harden into tight buds, and she sighs against my mouth.

God, this song is sexy, and the girl in my arms is driving me crazy. I know she must be aware of my erection; our hips are pressed so close together.

It's been less than three minutes, and I want this girl so badly I feel as if I'm going to explode.

Pocketing my phone and giving her the baby monitor, I then bend and pick her up in my arms.

"Sofa?" she asks hopefully.

I shake my head. I haven't forgotten that as much as she wants me, any memory of past trauma might make it uncomfortable for her, and I don't want to hurt her.

"Bed," I tell her huskily. "I want you to feel comfortable and safe."

"I always do with you."

Chapter Thirty-Seven

Aroha

James carries me through to the bedroom, pulls back the duvet, and lowers me onto the mattress. I lie back on the pillows and watch him remove his track pants. Then, in just his very tight boxer-briefs that cling deliciously to his erection, he climbs on the bed next to me and stretches out.

We lie on our sides facing each other, and he moves closer so we're pressed close from our chests to our thighs, our legs tangled together. He puts his arms around me, and I slide mine around his back. Then he starts to kiss me.

I'd been semi-teasing him when I said about taking it slow, trying to entice him and turn him on, but he seems to have taken it to heart. While his mouth moves across mine, and he teases my lips with his teeth and tongue, his hands wander across my body, his fingers stroking light as feathers. He brushes them down my back, over my hips, and along the outside of my thighs, then back up the insides, just missing the sensitive area between them, and traveling instead back up over my tummy to my breasts.

He strokes them, drawing a finger across the tops of them in the lacy teddy, then cupping them and squeezing them before teasing my nipples with his fingers oh-so-gently. I don't know how he's so in control—I want to push him onto his back, slide onto him, and ride us both to a climax, but he definitely has other ideas.

I'm sure part of it is my confession that I've struggled with sex since the incident with my ex. He wants to make sure it doesn't hurt, and I love him for that.

Even though I'm turned on and I'm crazy about him, I'm worried I'm going to tense up, and that's stupid because anxiety is one thing that will make it worse. But it's impossible not to feel nervous.

He must be able to feel the tension in my body, but he doesn't comment on it. Instead, he kisses me for what feels like hours, until I'm dizzy with longing, and sighing against his mouth. Only then does he rise and start pressing his lips down my body. He starts with my neck and kisses down to the fabric of the teddy. Then he slips the ribbon straps off my shoulders and peels them down to reveal my breasts, sighing as they come into view. He trails the tip of his tongue around my nipples, then sucks them gently. He plays with them for ages, nibbling the tips with his teeth, sucking and then blowing on the wet skin, and teasing them with the pads of his fingers, and I ascend higher and higher, feeling as if I'm floating amongst the clouds.

Eventually, he kisses down my belly, then moves between my legs. I feel him undo the fastenings underneath me, and then he moves the fabric aside and lowers his mouth to slide his tongue into me.

Ohhh... I'd forgotten how amazing this is. My eyelids flutter closed as he begins to lick and suck, and the pad of his forefinger circles over my clit, followed by his tongue.

"James..." I say with a sigh, "that feels so good..."

"You taste amazing," he murmurs. He slides his thumb down, and I feel him tease my entrance. I tense and curse myself silently, but he doesn't stop. He keeps his thumb there, pressing slightly while he continues to lick and suck. Each time I tense, he stops and waits, concentrating on teasing my clit. He doesn't seem in any hurry. Eventually he turns his hand palm up and slides the tips of two fingers inside me, just a few millimeters, and gradually eases them in as I relax.

"Good girl," he says, and I flush at his praise. I can do this. If he's gentle and slow, we're going to be okay.

He continues to flick my clit with his tongue, and eventually I feel the tiny muscles inside me begin to tighten. "Mmm..." My lips part as I wait for the orgasm to build, but at that moment he withdraws his fingers and lifts his head.

I blink and stare up at the ceiling, and exhale in a rush.

He chuckles, bending his head to blow gently across the sensitive skin. Only when the ripples have died away does he lower his head again, and begin to lick while he teases me once more with his fingers.

He does this a few times, until I'm gasping with need, aching for release. Then he sits up, reaches across to his bedside table, and withdraws a condom and some lube.

"Sorry," he murmurs at my hazy look. "There's a method to my madness." He gets rid of his boxer-briefs, then rolls on the condom. Finally, he squeezes a big dollop of lube onto his fingers.

"I'm surprised you need that," I say wryly, knowing I must be swollen and wet. I don't normally have an issue with lubrication.

"Pain might be a turn on for some people, but not for me, or you, I suspect." He covers his erection with lube, then brushes the reminder down over my sensitive skin to my entrance, making sure I'm slippery.

Pushing up my knees, he leans over me and presses the tip of his erection into me. Then he lowers down, doing his best to support his weight on his elbows to avoid my ribs, and looks into my eyes.

"Hello, wife," he says, and smiles.

I wrinkle my nose. "Husband."

"Do you trust me?" he murmurs as he kisses me.

I sigh. "Yes."

He moves his hips, pressing into me just a little. I can't help it though; I tense, and he stops.

I swallow hard. "I'm sorry."

But he just chuckles and kisses me again. "Don't apologize. This is the most erotic thing I've ever done." My eyes widen at his smug smile. "I don't care if I have to take you a millimeter at a time," he declares.

I try not to laugh at his obvious delight. "You're not supposed to enjoy my affliction."

He pushes forward another fraction and groans, closing his eyes. "You're so tight. Ah God."

"Is it like trying to fuck a tube of toothpaste?"

That makes him laugh, and he opens his eyes. "I'm so crazy about you," he says, and kisses me, plunging his tongue into my mouth.

I groan as heat engulfs me, unable to do anything but lie there as he kisses me senseless. I feel him press into me a little more, and shudder at his answering growl.

"Come on Aroha," he teases, kissing around to my ear, his hot breath making my skin sizzle. "Let me in. You know you want to." He cups my breast with a hand and tugs my nipple, and at the same time he moves his hips from side to side a little. He's pressing on my clit and, as it's already sensitive, desire ripples through me.

"Oh yeah," he says, and slides halfway into me, his eyelids fluttering. "Ah, Jesus. I feel like I'm in a vise."

"Don't make me laugh, that won't go well."

He pulls back, and this time, when he pushes forward, he slides right inside me.

We both groan. He lowers his head and rests his forehead against mine, and I close my eyes.

I can feel him, all the way up. His hips are flush with the back of my thighs. I'd forgotten what Gaby told me about him being generously endowed, and I feel stretched to my limits, completely full.

He kisses my nose. "You okay?"

I open my eyes. "Oh my God, you're so big."

He gives a short laugh, then kisses my mouth. "But I'm in." He gives me a smug smile. Then it softens. "I love you," he says.

I look into his beautiful eyes. "I love you too."

He kisses me once more. Then he begins to move.

I know I'm tight, but I'm well lubricated, and he's very gentle. He continues to kiss me while he gives long, slow thrusts, moving his hips back until he almost pulls out, then sliding in, until I get used to the sensation of him being inside me.

All the while, he whispers to me, telling me he loves me, that I'm beautiful, that I'm doing great, that I'm amazing. "You're so sexy," he murmurs, kissing up my jaw to my ear again and nibbling the lobe. "I love being inside you. Being one with you."

"Me too," I whisper as his lips return to mine. "It feels so good."

Before long, I can't stop my hips moving with his. Mmm, there's no friction at all, and every time he thrusts and brushes against my clit, I feel an answering ripple of pleasure. I close my eyes, concentrating on the feeling, my teeth tugging at my bottom lip. Ooh, I think I might be able to come like this. That'll be a first. I don't know how it's going to feel... I don't want it to hurt, or to hurt him if I squeeze too tight...

But he says, "Yeah, baby, just relax, and let go if you can," and I realize he knows what's happening inside me, and he wants me to try. So I concentrate on releasing the tension in my body, and just let it happen. I don't have to reach for it—he takes me there with each thrust, each kiss, each brush of his hand over my breast. He wants to give me pleasure, and he's willing to wait as long as it takes for me to get there. He's so patient and gentle, I couldn't have done this with anyone but him. The thought makes tears prick my eyes, and I can't hold them back as my orgasm begins.

My muscles tighten, and strong pulses engulf me, so pleasurable I have to cry out, "Oh God, oh fuck," with each blissful clench as tears leak through my lashes.

James mutters something, but I don't hear him because I'm too busy concentrating on myself and the heavenly sensations inside me. I'm conscious of his thrusts becoming a little more forceful though—he can't help himself; his body is taking over from his desire to be gentle, and I find that so hot that I force my eyes open so I can watch him in those precious few moments before his climax. A fierce frown furrows his forehead, his lips part with a soundless groan, and then his hips jerk and he shudders as he comes. I stroke his damp back as he spills inside me, and I relax back into the pillows, thrilled that we made it, and full of love for this caring, patient, sexy guy.

When he finally opens his eyes, he blinks a few times, then focuses on me. "Owwww..." he groans.

I stifle a laugh, even though I'm half-crying. "Did I crush you?"

"I nearly passed out. Dear God." He withdraws with a sigh, then falls onto the mattress beside me. "Holy shit. Girl, you have a fucking amazing pelvic floor."

I roll onto my side to face him. His arm is over his face, and his skin is covered with a sheen of sweat. He smells amazing. This is my man. My husband. We're married. Wow. I really have died and gone to heaven.

"Sorry," I say.

He lifts his arm and looks at me, disposes of the condom, then rolls onto his side to face me. He cups my cheek with concern and wipes away the tears beneath my eyes with a thumb. "Don't apologize. Did I hurt you?"

"No, not at all."

"Your ribs are okay?"

"I forgot about them, actually. I'm crying because of you." I kiss him. "You were so patient. Thank you so much."

He pulls the duvet up over us, then slides his arms around me, and we cuddle up close, wrapped around one another.

"I am sorry if I squeezed you to death," I tell him.

"No apology needed. It was extremely erotic. We're definitely doing that again."

I giggle and snuggle closer. "I'm so glad."

He yawns and sighs. "Sounds like Leia's asleep."

"She's a good girl." I sigh. "She'll be our daughter soon."

"Yeah. It's funny, isn't it? Neither of us wanted children, but here we are…"

"Mmm. Strange how the world works."

"I love you," he says.

"I love you too."

And even though it's not particularly late, we both fall asleep, content in each other's arms.

*

Over the next few weeks, we have sex a lot.

It's not a linear thing. It's not as if it slowly gets better. Sometimes, we get carried away—one of us gets frisky in the middle of the day when Leia's snoozing, and we close the curtains and just get down to it on the sofa, making the most of the moment, and everything's fine. At other times, maybe when I have too much time to think, my anxiety gets the better of me, and my body tenses up. But when that happens, James just announces it's time for a mega kissing session, making me laugh, and then we make out for ages. Sometimes it ends with us making love, at other times Leia wakes and the moment's gone, but James doesn't seem bothered by it, and gradually I learn not to worry, because we have all the time in the world.

Leia's now twenty-three weeks old, and flourishing. Part of me feels sad that she's too young to miss her birth mother, but mostly I'm pleased that she's doing so well. It'll take a while before it doesn't feel strange to think of myself as her mother, but Leia seems to feel happy with me, and James and I are both looking forward to witnessing her firsts—first word, first solid food, first steps.

James seems happy, too, especially after the coroner's report comes through which states the cause of Maddie's death as accidental. At last he seems to be able to put behind him the fear that she took her own life. Then, the day after, we hear that the court has finally granted him the Parenting Order for Leia, so at last we're on track to adopt her.

Gone is some of the intensity and seriousness that always seemed to surround him in the past. He still misses his sister, but he laughs a lot now, and he's always ready for a kiss or cuddle. We see the guys he works with a lot, and they tease him that he's become domesticated, and that they're going to buy him slippers and a pipe. He bears it good-naturedly, saying they're just jealous.

I don't think he's right where Gaby and Tyson are concerned, and Alex and Missie are obviously happy together. He could be close with Henry, though. I don't know what's happening with him and Juliette. He's been like a bear with a sore head, so something's obviously bothering him.

I hope he'll sort it out, whatever it is. I want everyone to be as happy as I am.

On Valentine's Day, James and I are eating breakfast in the kitchen, with Leia in her highchair, when he says, "Alex is proposing to Missie today."

"Oh?" I stare at him, delighted. I know the two of them are attending some sci-fi conference in Queenstown with Finn and Zelda.

James finishes off his cereal, then says, "I'll be back in a sec." He goes off, then returns a minute later and puts a pretty bag in front of me. "Happy Valentine's Day," he murmurs, bending to kiss me.

"Aw. Thank you!" Touched, I open the bag. There's a card, a large, flattish parcel, and a small square bag. I open the card, read the poem inside, and kiss him. Then I open the large, flat parcel.

I give him a wry look.

He chuckles. "I did promise." The pearl necklace, together with its matching earrings, gleams in the early morning sunshine.

I brush them with my fingers. They're obviously real. "It's lovely, James, thank you so much."

"And I got you this, too." He passes me another velvet box. "It struck me that you didn't have an engagement ring, so…"

I open the box, and my jaw drops. It's an enormous diamond, sitting on a gold band, with two small diamonds on either side.

"I hope you like it," he says hopefully.

"Oh James…" I take it out. The diamonds glitter in the sunlight. "It's absolutely stunning."

"Just like you."

"Smooth talker."

"Come here." He slides it onto my ring finger. It sits above my wedding ring perfectly. "I had them matched," he says. "I hope it's comfortable."

I've never seen a stone as big as this in real life. "Oh God," I say, "I love being married to a billionaire."

He laughs and rises as I get up to kiss him. I lift my arms around his neck and slide my hands into his hair, tilting my head to the side, my tongue teasing his. Fireworks go off all the way through me, and I have to fight not to push him back into the bedroom and make love to him there and then.

Leia bangs on her tray with her toy, annoyed at not being the center of attention, and we both laugh.

"I'm going to cook you dinner tonight," I tell him as he sits back down. "But I made you something, too." I give him my present—a bookmark I've cross-stitched for him. It has my and Leia's names on it, and it's surrounded by hearts. He stares at it.

"It seems a bit silly now, next to your expensive gift," I tell him shyly.

"No." He brushes it with his thumb. "It's lovely. Nobody's ever made me anything like this before. It must have taken you ages." He seems genuinely touched. He has so much money that buying clothing or a tiepin didn't seem personal, and I wanted to make something for him.

I loop my arms around his neck from behind and kiss his ear, then whisper. "I'll give you your final present tonight, in bed."

His eyebrows rise. "Oh?"

I nip his earlobe. "I have a special garment."

"Ow. Oh? Is lace involved?"

"Kinda. Let's just say I couldn't wear it out of the house."

He grins. "Sounds amazing." He catches hold of my waist and pulls me onto his lap, and we exchange a long, luscious kiss.

"I love you, Mrs. Rutherford," he murmurs against my lips.

"And I love you, Mr. Rutherford."

And we continue to kiss, while Leia chews her rattle, and the morning sun fills the room with light.

Newsletter

If you'd like to be informed when my next book is available, you can sign up for my mailing list on my website, http://www.serenitywoodsromance.com

About the Author

USA Today bestselling author Serenity Woods writes sexy contemporary romances, most of which are set in the sub-tropical Northland of New Zealand, where she lives with her wonderful husband.

Website: http://www.serenitywoodsromance.com
Facebook: http://www.facebook.com/serenitywoodsromance

Printed in Great Britain
by Amazon